to Brol
Tim and Mark

DUPLICITY

Conservatives
Forever

your friends

Callista Gingrich

2016

DUPLICITY

⌒ A NOVEL ⌒

NEWT GINGRICH

AND PETE EARLEY

**CENTER
STREET**

NEW YORK BOSTON NASHVILLE

Copyright © 2015 by Newt Gingrich and Pete Earley
Cover design by Jody Waldrup
Cover photography by Dreamstime
Cover copyright © 2015 by Hachette Book Group, Inc.

Center Street
Hachette Book Group
1290 Avenue of the Americas
New York, NY 10104
centerstreet.com
twitter.com/centerstreet

Originally published in hardcover and ebook by Center Street in October 2015
First Trade Paperback Edition: June 2016

Center Street is a division of Hachette Book Group, Inc.
The Center Street name and logo are trademarks of Hachette Book Group, Inc.

The publisher is not responsible for websites (or their content) that are not owned by the publisher.

Library of Congress Cataloging-in-Publication Data

Gingrich, Newt.
    Duplicity : a novel / Newt Gingrich and Pete Earley. — First edition.
        pages cm
    ISBN 978-1-4555-3042-7 (hardback) — ISBN 978-1-4555-8954-8 (hardcover large print) — ISBN 978-1-4555-3846-1 (autographed hardcover); ISBN 978-1-4555-3847-8 (B&N autographed hardcover); ISBN 978-1-4555-9065-0 (international trade paperback) — ISBN 978-1-4789-0360-4 (audio cd)   1. Political fiction.   2. Suspense fiction.   I. Earley, Pete. II. Title.
    PS3557.I4945D87 2015
    813'.54—dc23
                                                        2015023767

ISBNs: 978-1-4555-3043-4 (pbk.), 978-1-4555-3041-0 (ebook)

Printed in the United States of America

RRD-C

10 9 8 7 6 5 4 3 2 1

We dedicate this book to the brave men and women who risk their lives to defend freedom, defeat our enemies, and protect our country.

CONTENTS

AUTHORS' NOTE

Although this is a work of fiction, all religious quotes attributed to radical Islamist terrorists in this novel were taken from actual verbal and written statements.

CAST OF CHARACTERS

Nuruddin Ayaanie "Rudy" Adeogo, Somali American congressional candidate

Sally Allworth, president of the United States

Timothy Coldridge, presidential challenger

Gunter Conner, CIA station chief, Somalia

Mary Margaret Delaney, political strategist, Coldridge campaign

John Duggard, military contractor

Payton Grainger, CIA director

Captain Brooke Grant, military attaché

Abdul Hafeez, Al-Shabaab terrorist

Mallory Harper, White House chief of staff

Ebio Kattan, Al Arabic correspondent

Decker Lake, former U.S. attorney general

Sergeant Walks Many Miles, embassy guard force, Somalia

General Abdullah Osman Saeed, Somali general

Thomas Edgar Stanton, chair, House Intelligence Committee

DUPLICITY

PROLOGUE

Early summer
The city of Dera Ismail Khan
Khyber-Pakhtunkhwa province, Pakistan

Y ou're here, aren't you, to tell us everything we do wrong?"
Prison Superintendent Shaukat Abbas posed his words as a question but the irritated tone of his voice made it clear they were an accusation. Abbas leaned back in a shabby office chair behind a worn, gunmetal-gray desk inside the drab, institutional walls of the warden's office at the provincial prison and lit a Morven Gold cigarette. He did not offer one to the guest seated before him.

Christopher King was not offended. An avid jogger, King didn't smoke. He considered it a nasty, dangerous habit and tended to worry about damage from secondhand smoke. Abbas noticed King fidget and began amusing himself by blowing a series of perfectly formed smoke rings toward his visitor. King already wasn't feeling well, having recently contracted a bout of bacterial diarrhea while touring the prison in Bannu, a town north of Dera Ismail Khan that bordered the so-called lawless area of Pakistan. The strong smell of tobacco mixed with the stench of human sweat and unrecognizable odors that seemed to ooze from the walls of the ancient prison did little to calm his churning stomach or improve his darkening mood.

"Tell me again about this organization of yours," Abbas said.

King had already gone through his spiel, but he robotically repeated the explanation that he had told to every superintendent whose jail or prison he had visited in Pakistan during the past two weeks.

"The International Equal Justice Project is a nongovernmental, non-political, nonprofit, international organization that monitors living conditions in jails and prisons worldwide. We were invited to Pakistan by your nation's new internal security director."

"I'm correct, then," Abbas hissed, flashing a smug half grin that revealed crooked and cigarette-stained teeth. "You've come here to tell me everything I'm doing wrong."

Abbas was correct, but King was not about to admit it. If he did, Abbas might turn him away without letting him inspect the compound. "I've come to observe what you are doing correctly and also suggest possible ways to do things better."

"I thought you said your group was nonpolitical," Abbas replied dryly. "Yet you've given me a very cagey political answer."

King thought to himself, *This superintendent is not as stupid as he looks.*

For a moment, the two men exchanged forced smiles. King was rail thin, tall, and in his early thirties. His shaggy blondish-brown hair needed a trim. He wore a light-blue short-sleeved shirt, black denim jeans, and black loafers. Abbas was in his late fifties, rotund, bald. A thick black moustache served as a bridge between his hound-like jowls. He wore a uniform: khaki pants with a dark green shirt. A Pakistani governmental seal was embroidered on his shirt pocket, topped with a brass nametag.

They were seated in a sweltering office on the second floor of the prison's administration building. It was as if the room had trapped the afternoon heat when temperatures outside had peaked at 107 degrees. A single window air-conditioning unit rattled as it spewed out air only a few degrees cooler. King, who'd arrived in Pakistan six weeks earlier from his group's headquarters in Helsinki, was still trying to adjust to the heat. Tiny beads of perspiration dotted his forehead. Abbas seemed completely unaffected by the temperature.

With his stomach rumbling, King wondered if he had made a mistake leaving his cushy job in Helsinki for fieldwork, which had sounded exciting when he'd volunteered but was proving to be both difficult and unpleasant. The International Equal Justice Project had sent him to Pakistan after receiving hundreds of complaints from prisoners and their families alleging abuse. So far, King's personal observations had confirmed those claims. Corruption, torture, sexual abuse, and diseases were the norm. There was no pretense of safeguarding even the most basic human rights. The seriousness of a prisoner's crime seemed insignificant. What did matter was money. If a prisoner had it, he could survive and even live well behind bars. Those who didn't faced physical abuse and starvation. Guards routinely demanded bribes—either money or sex—from visitors. Even after someone made it past the guards into a facility, if they brought food or some creature comfort to a prisoner, that inmate would have to fight for it. King had seen as many as fifty men in a group cell surge toward the bars with outstretched hands like a swarm of flesh-eating piranha whenever a visitor appeared. Weaker prisoners were immediately stripped of any items handed them while guards watched amused, sometimes placing bets on who would end up with goods shoved through the bars. King suspected his tour at Superintendent Abbas's prison would not be any different from the others, with one exception: This facility was reputed to be the most secure in the region, having originally been built by the British during the colonial period. From the outside, it looked impenetrable.

The prison was surrounded by fifteen-foot-high mud-brick walls topped with razor wire and shards of broken glass. Its main entrance was a thick steel door, only large enough for one person to enter at a time. On either side stood an armed guard. The prison's two-story administration building had been built just inside that doorway. Beyond it were five buildings that resembled army barracks, each holding three hundred men in six large group cells. Guards paid more attention to separating prisoners based on their religious beliefs than on whether they were first-timers or hardened criminals.

Because this was the region's most secure prison, it was where captured radical Islamists were kept. King was especially keen on observing if they were being treated differently from other prisoners. His organization classified them as political prisoners.

Before he could begin his tour, however, he needed to get by Superintendent Abbas.

"If you come into a man's house, especially to cast stones," Abbas said, "you should bring him a gift or token of your appreciation."

So this was why Abbas was stalling. He expected a bribe. King couldn't believe the gall. Part of his task was to identify corrupt superintendents, and Abbas was so corrupt he didn't seem to understand that his thinly veiled demand was against the law. Either that or he simply didn't care.

Glancing to his right, King noticed an eight-by-ten-inch color photograph hanging on the office wall. It showed Abbas arm in arm with several men wearing numbered athletic jerseys. Nodding to the picture, King asked, "You play football?"

Abbas followed King's glance to the snapshot. "No. Kabaddi. Do you know the game?"

"Anything like rugby?" King asked.

The chair underneath Abbas squeaked as he leaned forward to smash out his cigarette in an already butt-filled black plastic ashtray on his desk.

"You're an American, aren't you?" he asked.

"Canadian, actually, but I get mistaken for an American all the time."

"Let me ask you this, Mr. Canadian: How do you expect to tell me how I should manage a Pakistani prison when you don't even know about kabaddi?"

Without waiting for an answer, Abbas barked an order into his desk phone and then told his guest, "One of my wardens will give you a tour now."

King was about to thank Abbas when the wall behind the superintendent exploded. Chunks of mud bricks and plaster flew toward the Canadian, who was blown off his chair by the blast. King flew backward into the wall behind him, slamming into it hard before falling face-first onto the dirty tile floor. Struggling to remain conscious, he felt a jarring pain in his thigh and saw bone poking through his right pant leg. The ringing in his ears temporarily deafened him. Obviously, someone had detonated a bomb outside the building.

Superintendent Abbas had fared worse than King. The Pakistani was buried under rubble and wasn't moving. King crawled toward him and pushed two chunks of fallen wall off the prison official's body. Abbas was dead. There was an opening where the back wall had been. King pulled himself to the gap so he could see into the prison yard.

The explosion had blown a hole in the prison's outer wall that men armed with AK-47 rifles and rocket-propelled grenade launchers were now scrambling through. The gap was so large that several of the attackers were able to ride motorcycles through it. One drove the bike while the second rider fired his weapon. The intruders quickly killed the guards standing watch in the prison's corner towers. They were the only employees who had guns. The prison officials inside the cell-blocks were armed only with clubs—a precaution meant to keep prisoners from obtaining firearms if they rioted and overpowered guards. The cell-house guards quickly realized they were no match for the intruders. They tossed down their clubs and dropped to their knees, voluntarily locking their fingers together behind their heads in hopeful submission. Within minutes, prisoners were being freed from their cells and escaping into the prison yard.

By now, King's hearing was returning, and he spotted a slender black man with a megaphone in the prison yard calling names. The prisoners he was summoning were gathering around him in the yard.

King heard voices outside the superintendent's office and realized the intruders were about to enter the room. He thought about crawling to Abbas's corpse to retrieve the pistol strapped to his belt but quickly rejected that idea.

It would be impossible for him to shoot his way out of the prison, especially with a compound fracture. If the attackers saw him armed, they would shoot first. King's best chance of surviving was to surrender and seek mercy. After all, he wasn't a prison official. He was a guest, a foreigner, someone who had come to Pakistan to help its people.

King removed his shirt and formed a tourniquet above the break in his right leg. A part of him simply wished he could play dead and let whatever was going to unfold happen.

Someone kicked on the office's door, which was blocked by rubble. Another strong kick opened the door wide enough for the barrel of an AK-47 to poke through it. A man's voice yelled in Urdu, Pakistan's most common language.

"Foreigner!" King hollered back in English. "No guns!"

The owner of the AK-47 peeked through the crack. King raised both hands.

The gunman yelled again.

"I don't understand," King replied. "Canadian."

With a final shove, the door opened wide enough for the gunman to enter. Two more fighters followed him. All were dressed in police uniforms—the same khaki pants with dark green shirts that

Superintendent Abbas was wearing, although King doubted any of the men were actual guards.

The first intruder jerked the barrel of his rifle up and down, which King took as a signal for him to stand. King lowered his hands from above his head and pressed both palms against the floor, trying to lift himself, but he couldn't. One of the other attackers shouldered his rifle and grabbed King by his right arm, pulling him up onto his good left leg. The third gunman quickly frisked King. Satisfied, he took King's left arm and the two of them half-carried King from the office down into the prison yard.

It was well after seven o'clock by now and the afternoon sun had set. There were no lights—a sign the attackers had destroyed the prison's generators. The motorcycle riders had formed a circle and were using their bikes' headlights to illuminate their leader. He was still using his megaphone to call prisoners' names.

King was carried into the circle and dumped at the leader's feet. Another man was already kneeling there. Apparently he was a prisoner, because he was not dressed like a guard.

The leader handed his megaphone to an underling and took a long knife from one of his men. Stepping forward, he raised it above his head and yelled something about Allah. He then swung it hard against the kneeling man's neck, partially decapitating him. After the man's body struck the ground, several more chops severed his head completely.

King vomited.

Before arriving in Pakistan, King had read that Taliban fighters were carrying out raids to free radical Islamists from jails and prisons. During some of those attacks the Taliban had executed Shia Muslims by publicly beheading them. He could feel his body shaking. It wasn't shock. It was fear. King was keenly aware of how ISIS had beheaded an aid worker and foreign journalists. No one was safe from the radicals' brutality.

King had been dropped face-first onto the ground. He tried to push himself up, but he couldn't. Instead, he rolled onto his back as the knife-wielding leader stepped toward him. King immediately lowered his eyes, thinking it was best not to challenge the attacker by staring at his face.

The leader was dressed in a *shalwar kameez*—a traditional Pakistani outfit composed of a long shirt that could reach to the knees over pants sewn from the same material. Even so, King suspected the figure now towering above him was not a Pakistani. He looked as if he was from Africa, and the cadence of his voice didn't match what King had become accustomed to hearing since his arrival.

"Canadian," King said. "N-G-O. International Equal Justice Project. Prison inspection. Not military. Not fighter. Observer. Pacifist. Not a soldier. An attorney. A lawyer. Not a soldier."

"A lawyer?" the man repeated in English and then chuckled loudly. He began addressing those around him in Farsi. He spoke slowly, as if Farsi was not his first language, and because he was speaking slowly, King was able to understand several key words. *Injured, prisoner, ransom.*

King was going from someone who inspected prisons to being a prisoner himself. The two men who had brought him down into the courtyard stepped forward and lifted him onto his left leg while the leader started to walk away.

"You're not a Pakistani!" King blurted out. "And you're not an Arab."

His words seemed to come from his mouth on their own, surprising even him.

The leader spun around and stared at King's face.

For reasons that he could not explain, King said, "My God, you're an American."

The man handed his knife to a subordinate and returned to where King was now standing, stopping inches from the terrified captive's face.

"What makes you think I'm American?" he demanded.

"Something about your voice. The way you carry yourself."

The man drew a pistol from his belt and pressed it under King's chin.

"You are very insightful," the leader said. "Too much so for your own good."

He squeezed the trigger, sending a round through King's brain and out his skull into the evening sky.

The two men holding King released their grips and the Canadian aid worker fell lifeless onto the ground.

"You were wrong," the man said, looking down at King's corpse. "I *was* an American."

PART ONE

THE CURTAIN RISES

You have attributed conditions to villainy that simply
result from stupidity.

—Robert A. Heinlein, *Logic of Empire*

CHAPTER ONE

Counterterrorism Center
Central Intelligence Agency
Langley, Virginia

Gunter Conner was not used to seeing fresh fruit, doughnuts, silver-ware, and plates when he arrived at the regular Monday-morning briefing inside the CIA's Counterterrorism Center. Employees usually sauntered in carrying their own snacks. Today was different because Payton Grainger, the CIA's director, was expected. As a rule, the director never attended mundane meetings, especially at this low step on the bureaucratic ladder, but Grainger had recently launched an effort to revitalize poor morale inside the agency by mingling with the rank and file. Conner correctly assumed that Charles Casterline, who ran the Monday briefings, had ordered the refreshments. Casterline was the ultimate schmoozer. In a bureaucracy that loved acronyms, Casterline was the chief of the OA (Office of Operations and Analysis) at the CTC (Counterterrorism Center) inside the NCS (National Clandestine Service), the covert branch of the CIA.

Conner went directly for the coffee, taking it black. His head was split-ting. Reaching into his pocket, he palmed a Xanax, discreetly raising it to his lips. It was his substitute treatment for anxiety when mind-numbing alcohol wasn't available. He slumped into a seat along the con-ference room wall.

"I'd like to start by welcoming Director Grainger," Casterline said, rising from a conference table in the center of the room where all of his managers and other brass were seated.

Conner tuned him out. His eyes wandered and he noticed several of his younger colleagues along the wall were fidgeting in their chairs, trying to juggle a fruit plate and plastic fork on their knees while holding a hot cup of coffee. A few were licking white powdered sugar from their fingers. It was only when Casterline was nearing the end of his briefing that Conner reconnected.

"Oh, we've had a report of a prison in Dera Ismail Khan being overrun by Taliban fighters," Casterline explained as if this news was an afterthought. "Some eight hundred prisoners escaped, including a few dozen militant jihadists."

When no one at the conference table reacted, Conner interrupted. "Excuse me."

Washington bureaucracies follow certain protocols, some written and others not, and one of them inside the CIA was that employees who were sitting along the conference room wall had the status of children in the early 1800s. They could be seen but not heard unless called upon.

An irritated look washed across Casterline's face, while Director Grainger gazed over his reading half-glasses much like a proctor monitoring a final exam.

"That prison break is the eleventh escape during the past two months in the region," Conner volunteered.

"And your point is what?" Casterline asked curtly.

"It's part of a pattern."

"We've been through this before," Casterline replied in a clearly exasperated voice. "This prison break and other escapes in the region are happening because they are allowed to happen. Either guards are bribed or they don't know squat about security."

"I disagree," Conner replied.

"Well, you're wrong," Casterline retorted, his irritation turning to an only slightly veiled anger. "The last time you brought this up," Casterline continued, "I told you to write down your theory in a paper for peer review, or to be more precise, the last time you announced that all of us have been dealing with terrorists in a profoundly wrong manner, I had you explain why in writing."

Removing his reading glasses, Director Grainger said, "This is the first time I've heard any of this."

"That's because no one in the CTC or NCS accepts Mr. Conner's thesis," Casterline said.

"Just because you and my peers don't agree doesn't mean I am wrong," Conner replied. "It simply means none of you has figured it out yet."

Casterline's eyes narrowed at the insult, but before he could respond Conner added, "Any analysis which starts out with a geographic focus on radical Islamists is by definition profoundly wrong. As I explained in my paper, radical Islamism is not a geographic issue even though we keep trying to resolve it through geographical solutions."

"This is not the time to have this discussion," Casterline snapped.

Grainger, however, was intrigued. "You've just insulted your direct supervisor and, actually, everyone in the CIA's top management, including me, as well as your peers, by telling us we're fighting our nation's war on terror incorrectly."

"With all due respect, I was simply pointing out the obvious," Conner answered.

Now Grainger joined the others in frowning as Conner continued. "We went after Al-Qaeda and killed Osama bin Laden. We celebrated, but then the Taliban reemerged. We went after it and then came ISIS and tomorrow it will be some other radical group. Hezbollah, the Muslim Brotherhood, Boko Haram, the Army of Islam. We'll hunt and kill the leaders without ever ripping out the roots. We need to begin fighting these radical Islamists as if they were a virus, rather than waging war on regional factions."

"A virus?" Grainger asked.

"We're looking at Islamic terrorism through traditional military and diplomatic eyes, when we should be looking at it as if we were epidemiologists facing a worldwide epidemic. We need to view Islamic terrorism much like the Ebola outbreak in Africa several years ago."

"Seriously?" Casterline said in a voice laced with sarcasm. "Did I just hear you lump Ebola and terrorism together?"

"If our military approach is too myopic for you," Grainger said, "tell me what your epidemiologic approach would be."

"We should do what every scientist does when a virus first appears,"

Conner replied. "Identify the threat—how many new cases are appearing and how rapidly they are spreading. Then move into an analytical phase. Are there discernible patterns in why and how this disease spreads? Finally, we need to develop intervention strategies to isolate and eradicate the disease, not try to *manage* it. We need to recognize that we will never win an ongoing campaign against terrorism by fighting a war against each separate group. We should be fighting a radical Islamic epidemic."

"There are currently more than a hundred identifiable terrorist groups in the world," Casterline said, challenging him. "Each has its own agenda. Each has its own leader. These prison breaks, for example. We have been told the Taliban was responsible for the Pakistan attack. In Yemen, the jailbreak was led by Al-Qaeda. In Nigeria, it was Boko Haram. In Afghanistan, it was the Followers of Allah. There is absolutely no evidence that these divergent groups communicated between themselves or that these breaks were coordinated. The only thing that unites these factions is their hatred of our country. If they didn't hate us, they would be killing each other. So looking at the whole, rather than the parts, accomplishes nothing useful."

Conner shook his head in disagreement. "I believe these prison attacks are being coordinated, but even if they aren't, you are missing my points, and your inability to understand and accept them is why our current approach is failing. First, we must recognize that radical Islamism is our enemy; it is the virus that gives birth to these divergent groups. If we want to eradicate it, we must first understand why radical Islamism is flourishing. Islam is hardly a new religion. Why are the numbers of radical Islamists rising, even in our own country? My second point is directly related to the first. Since radical Islamism is the common ideology of all these terrorist groups, that means they can be united. Just because we refuse to look at the bigger picture, doesn't mean our enemies are blind. Which brings me to my third point. I believe there is a new Osama bin Laden–like figure currently consolidating power among radical jihadists and yes, we need to identify and stop him before he unifies Islamic terrorists."

"So there's a Super-Osama lurking in the shadows," Casterline said mockingly, "an Islamic boogeyman breaking terrorists out of prisons and forming a coalition of extremists—is that what you're telling us?"

Several of Casterline's fellow managers at the table chuckled. Buoyed by their laughter, Casterline continued, "Tell me, Mr. Conner. If there were a dozen prison breaks in the U.S., would you conclude that a mastermind drug dealer was behind those escapes simply because the inmates who were freed were convicted drug dealers? Or would you conclude that convicted drug dealers escaped because more than half of all inmates in federal prisons are there on drug charges? You're connecting imaginary dots that only you can see. There is no rising Super–Osama bin Laden in the shadows, no modern-day jihadist messiah about to crush us through unification."

Director Grainger had heard enough. Returning his reading glasses to his nose, he glanced at the next item on the agenda and said, "Until you have evidence that backs up your theories, Mr. Conner, they're nothing but theories and, as entertaining as they may be, our agency acts on facts, not speculation. Let's move on."

When the briefing ended ten minutes later, everyone stood while Grainger shook hands and exited. Casterline glared at Conner and barked, "In my office. Now!"

As soon as they were alone, Casterline let loose with a profanity-laced reprimand that ended with him saying, "If I could, I'd fire you."

"I felt an obligation to speak."

"Why?" Casterline asked rhetorically. "Because you didn't say anything new this morning. You and I both know our exchange was window-dressing. It might have been the first time Director Grainger heard it, but you've been trying to sell that prattle about a Super–Osama bin Laden for the past three years, and no one here is buying it."

Conner kept still. The quicker he took his licks, the quicker he could leave.

"Listen," Casterline said. "You and I both know why you're obsessed with your theories. Everyone in the agency is aware of what happened to you and your family in Cairo and everyone regrets that, but you can't let a personal tragedy that happened three years ago skewer your professional judgment. And after three years, all of us are ready to move on."

Conner felt his face becoming flush. "What happened to my family is why I know my so-called obsession is true."

In a voice that was now more exasperated than angry, Casterline replied, "Conner, you were once a good operative, but ever since Cairo you've alienated every one of your coworkers with your conspiracy theories and combativeness. What makes you think you're the only person in this agency who knows what he's doing? What makes you think you're so much smarter than all the rest of us?"

"Being the smartest in the CTC may not be as huge of a challenge as you suggest," Conner replied.

The blue veins in Casterline's neck looked as if they might pop. "Get the hell out of my office."

Conner's anxiety was worse when he reached his desk. Opening a drawer, he removed a bottle of Xanax and swallowed another pill without bothering with water. He glanced at a metal bookshelf next to his desk. The bottom two shelves were crammed with red, blue, and black note binders that held unclassified studies that Conner had once felt were significant but now couldn't recall why. The third and top shelves held a half-dozen autobiographies that Conner had felt obligated to buy because they had been written by former colleagues but hadn't bothered to read. Next to them were books that he had read: the *Historical Dictionary of Terrorism* by Sean Anderson and Stephen Sloan; *Inside the Criminal Mind* by Stanton E. Samenow; *Washington Station* by Yuri B. Shvets; *The World Almanac of Islamism* edited by Ilan Berman and Jeff M. Smith.

Tucked on the top shelf near its left corner was a worn copy of a more sentimental book, a novel that Conner had discovered at age thirteen. He had carried it with him to undergraduate school at Rutgers University, where he'd majored in mathematics because nothing else seemed challenging; to graduate school at American University, where he'd earned an advanced degree in public anthropology; and eventually to his Langley office.

Conner rolled his desk chair over to the bookcase, its wheels squeaking on the tile floor. The racket was a reminder of how he'd let his physical appearance slip. He often forgot to shave. He often wore the same suit. He often forgot to shower. A diet of fast food had pushed his weight to 250 pounds and given him a watermelon-shaped belly that hung unattractively over his belt on his six-foot frame.

Conner plucked his copy of W. Somerset Maugham's *Of Human Bondage* from the shelf. It didn't take him long to find the passage that he was seeking.

> *Suddenly the answer occurred to him: he chuckled: now that he had it, it was like one of the puzzles which you worry over till you are shown the solution and then cannot imagine how it could ever have escaped you. The answer was obvious.*

The answer *was* obvious, so why didn't anyone else see it?

Conner continued reading. It was as if the book were an old friend offering him solace. Like the novel's protagonist, Conner had been trying to decide if there was a meaning to life when he first came across Maugham's classic as a teen in his father's library. By the time he'd read it, he'd reached the same conclusion as the central character. There was no meaning, no master plan, no choreographed destiny designed by an omnipotent being who rewarded those who worshipped him and condemned those who didn't. There was no god. The good and bad in life were caused by great and evil men, not a supernatural being.

Conner replaced the volume on its shelf and wheeled back to his desk. Being an atheist had been easier when he'd not lost what he treasured most in life.

He stared at a framed photograph on his desk. The snapshot showed him with his wife, Sara, and their two children, Benjamin and Jennifer. They were standing outside Dulles Airport with packed bags ready to begin what Sara had called "their great Cairo adventure."

He leaned forward, reaching for the photograph, but his hand began trembling so he pulled it back.

He needed proof and he owed it to himself to find it.

CHAPTER TWO

U.S. Embassy
London Chancery Building
Grosvenor Square, Westminster
London, England

Captain Brooke Grant watched the seconds ticking by on her Luminox F-117 Nighthawk watch while feigning interest in the monotonous chatter coming from the lips of Robert Gumman, the U.S. State Department's regional security officer (RSO). Unless he stopped talking soon, Brooke would be late for a dinner date. She already was pushing her luck. The restaurant was less than a ten-minute cab ride away, but Friday rush hour could be deadly and she couldn't keep a general waiting. She'd give Gumman two more minutes before heading to the exit.

As a deputy military defense attaché, Brooke didn't report to Gumman, nor did she respect him. He was a former Denver police captain who'd gotten his job in the Bureau of Diplomatic Security (DS) by pulling political strings. A Colorado senator happened to be one of Gumman's former fraternity brothers. Behind his back, everyone called the RSO "Dumbman."

On most Friday afternoons, Gumman would have been found perched on a bar stool in a Mayfair pub trying to pick up a lonely woman on an early summer vacation. But he'd received a call from a stateside crony who'd warned that the assistant secretary of state for European and Eurasian affairs was going to pay a "surprise" visit to the embassy on Monday. That had prompted this afternoon's hastily called security briefing.

Brooke checked her watch for a second time and quietly cursed her boss for sending her to Gumman's briefing. She worked for the Defense

Attaché Office (DAO) but she had the least seniority of any attaché stationed in London. The senior attachés conferred with their foreign counterparts and were responsible for warning the U.S. ambassador of "any potential threat against the embassy," primarily from spies or terrorists. As a deputy attaché, Brooke was stuck monitoring endless meetings and attending mindless diplomatic social gatherings. She was the only female Marine attaché in London, was twenty-nine years old, single, and attractive—attributes that her boss suggested were helpful when it came to establishing relationships with attachés from other countries. But Brooke knew she was being shown off at diplomatic affairs and sidelined from more meaty assignments for another reason besides sexism. Her uncle, General Frank Grant, was chairman of the Joint Chiefs of Staff and had a well-earned reputation for being overly protective of her. No one in the military wanted to put her in harm's way or give her a task that she might fail to complete.

A third glance at her watch convinced Brooke she'd had enough. As she rose from her chair, Gumman stopped mid-sentence. "I'm not done yet, Captain."

"Yes," she replied. "That's obvious."

As she left the room, she couldn't help but notice envious smiles from those left behind.

Brooke exited the embassy's entrance and walked quickly across a narrow courtyard to the front gate, where security officers in a glass booth kept track of all comings and goings. The embassy she was leaving was supposed to have been relocated to a more modern one, but endless construction problems, cost overruns, and bureaucratic squabbling had delayed that move. Brooke turned to her right on the crowded sidewalk that edged picturesque Grosvenor Square Garden and headed toward a side street to hail a cab, but as she neared the ten-foot-tall bronze statue of former president Ronald Reagan at the corner of the embassy complex, she nearly collided with a man walking from the opposite direction.

"Oh, I'm sorry," she exclaimed, stepping to her right, but he didn't react. He continued toward the embassy's main entrance. Surprised by his rudeness, she turned to watch him and suddenly sensed that something wasn't right about the stranger.

At first glance, Brooke assumed the man was homeless. Destitute men often panhandled in the garden park across from the embassy. He certainly looked the part, dressed in dirty khaki pants, unlaced worn sneakers, a wrinkled topcoat over a black hoodie, and large sunglasses. He was also carrying a pair of old-fashioned, hard-sided suitcases with brass clasps and cheap brown plastic handles.

Brooke wasn't certain what it was about him that seemed out of place, but she felt suspicious enough that she decided to alert a bobby standing less than ten feet away near the Reagan statue. The Metropolitan Police were responsible for security outside the embassy grounds.

"Officer, I think you should talk to that man carrying those suitcases," she volunteered.

The bobby, who seemed in his fifties, glanced at her Marine Corps uniform and then at the homeless man walking away from them.

"Lots of quirky lads round here, miss," he replied nonchalantly. "Tourists make easy marks for begging."

"I don't think he's really homeless," Brooke replied. "And he's carrying two large suitcases."

"Who exactly are you?" the policeman asked.

"Why's that matter?"

"Okay, luv," he said, shrugging. "I'll go have a chitchat with him after I finish up here." The bobby had just finished having his photograph taken with one female tourist, and her friend was waiting for her turn.

"Listen," Brooke said, lowering her voice. "There could be something in those suitcases."

"Besides his dirty unmentionables?" The officer smirked. "These homeless bums are always carting their worldly belongings with them either in trash bags or old suitcases."

In that moment, Brooke recognized what it was that seemed out of place.

"He's not homeless!" she exclaimed.

Spinning away from the bobby, she broke into a run toward the stranger and the embassy's front entrance.

Her target was only a few steps away from the security booth when she tackled him from behind, striking him with such force that both suitcases flew forward from his hands, hitting the pavement in front of them.

Two security guards from the embassy's glass booth rushed outside. The bobby also had chased after her, drawing a truncheon from his belt as he ran.

Brooke was now lying on the man's back, holding his arms with her outstretched hands to keep them away from his body. As the shock of being tackled passed, he began to move.

"Help!" Brooke shouted. "He's got a bomb."

Bystanders, who had paused to watch the ruckus, panicked. Snatching up her toddler, a mother shrieked, "Run!" A man nearby hollered, "Bomb! He's got a bomb."

Dropping to his knees, the bobby pressed the man's neck against the ground with his baton while the embassy security guards helped Brooke pin his arms to the ground.

"You'd better be bloody right!" the policeman snapped.

"There's wires here," one of the security guards yelled, nodding at the suspect's wrists.

A strand of black wire was dangling from each cuff. They'd been attached to the suitcases but had snapped when Brooke tackled the suspect from behind and he'd lost his grip on the heavy cases.

Another bobby hurried over from the park and used his radio to call for backup while more security officers emerged from the embassy.

"Lock the building down," one of them called over his shoulder. "No one gets in or out. Warn the ambassador."

By now, there were so many men pinning the suspect to the pavement that Brooke could release her hold. She stood and noticed that she'd torn her sleeve and was bleeding from a nasty scrape she'd gotten when she'd taken down the stranger.

"The bomb squad's coming," a bobby said.

The sound of approaching sirens was followed by the arrival of the squad's commander and six other officers, all wearing heavy padding. "We'll take over from here," the commander declared. One took hold of the man's head, another placed his knee on the prone man's spine, while the other four each took charge of a leg or arm, keeping the suspect immobilized.

"You folks need to move away now," the commander said.

Brooke reluctantly retreated but stopped about fifty feet away and watched as the bomb disposal commander cautiously ran his fingers over the man's outer clothing. "I can feel a vest," he announced. "Let's roll him over."

The suspect started to resist but stopped when an officer pressed a forearm against his throat. "Bloke, we can search you alive or dead. You bloody choose."

The suspect turned limp and the commander cautiously opened the man's topcoat, exposing a vest with bricks of plastic explosives duct-taped to it.

"Here it is!" he said when he spotted a detonator. The bomb's maker hadn't tried to disguise it, nor was it complicated. Within seconds, the commander had disconnected it, rendering the device harmless.

A Scotland Yard detective stepped in to take charge of the suspect. After removing the man's sunglasses, the detective photographed the would-be bomber's face. Within seconds, a facial recognition program linked to Scotland Yard's computer network had identified him based on his passport, which had been scanned when he arrived at Heathrow Airport.

Askar al-Seema was a Somali American who'd been born in Minneapolis, Minnesota, and had arrived twenty-four hours earlier on a flight that had originated in Somalia. His name had not been on any No Fly lists.

The detective summoned Brooke as his underlings were handcuffing al-Seema and pulling him up on his feet.

"What made you suspicious?" he asked.

Looking into al-Seema's face, Brooke said, "We bumped into each other on the sidewalk and I sensed something wasn't right, but it took a few moments for me to figure out why. The first tip-off was his sunglasses. What homeless man can afford Dolce and Gabbanas?"

"He could have stole them," the detective countered.

"They weren't the only tip-off."

Al-Seema's eyes were filled with contempt as he listened.

"He's wearing cologne."

"Cologne?" the detective repeated. He stepped forward and sniffed al-Seema's neck.

"Why would someone who is homeless and dirty be wearing cologne?" Brooke asked. "Especially Burberry Brit Rhythm for men. It retails for about fifty pounds in London stores for three ounces."

The detective chuckled and instructed the officers guarding al-Seema to put him in a waiting police van.

"You a cologne expert?" the detective asked.

"Hardly. I recognized the scent because my boyfriend wears the same cologne. I bought him a bottle last week for his birthday."

"Bloody lucky for us you did. My guess is al-Seema didn't think about it this morning when he got up. He probably went about his normal routine and that clearly involved splashing on cologne—either that or he wanted to smell good when he met those celestial virgins he'd been promised." The detective laughed at his own joke, but Brooke wasn't paying attention. She was texting a note to her dinner date, telling him that she was going to be late.

CHAPTER THREE

Brian Coyle Community Center
Cedar-Riverside neighborhood
Minneapolis, Minnesota

With the rhymes of Somali Canadian rapper K'Naan playing in the background, community activist Nuruddin Ayaanie "Rudy" Adeogo spoke in a fatherly tone to an eleven-year-old boy named Yusuf seated in front of him.

"You must stay away from the gangs," Adeogo warned.

"They saying, 'cause of my brother, I gots to join 'em," Yusuf replied.

"I knew your brother. He wouldn't want this. I remember the night he was murdered. Joining Outlawz will only get you killed too."

"No, Outlawz gonna protect me. Them blacks in school don't like us. Whites neither."

"Not everyone is prejudiced, Yusuf. You need to make friends with boys and girls who aren't. Stay in school. Go to the mosque and pray. Don't join a gang."

Adeogo paused. He wasn't certain he was convincing. "Yusuf, I know from inside my own family how it feels to lose a brother to a gang."

"You gots a brother who's a banger?"

"I had a brother who got caught up in a gang."

"What he be? Outlawz?"

"It doesn't matter, Yusuf. It was a terrible thing."

"He dead?"

"Let's not talk about my family, let's talk about you."

Yusuf rose from the cheap molded plastic chair and retrieved his backpack from the tile floor. "I'll be trying," he said.

Adeogo watched him leave the bare-bones conference room. Yusuf was one of a half-dozen Somali teens whom Adeogo met with weekly in a group called Ka Joog, which means "stay away" in Somali.

Life in the city's Cedar-Riverside neighborhood hadn't gotten any easier for Somali Americans from when Adeogo had been born there thirty-nine years earlier. His parents had been part of the first wave of Somalis who had fled their native land in the 1970s to avoid a war. Major General Mohamed Siad Barre, the country's self-proclaimed president for life, had attacked Ethiopia over a border area called the Ogaden region. At first, Barre's troops had won several decisive battles, but the Soviet Union, which had been supporting him, inexplicably switched sides, sending fifteen thousand Cuban soldiers to fight with the Ethiopians. Barre's troops had been driven back and Adeogo's father had fled with hundreds of other Somalis rather than die in Barre's ego-driven, losing campaign to defeat both the Ethiopians and the Cubans.

His parents had settled in Minnesota because Hubert Humphrey, one of the state's favorite sons, had visited the African Horn as vice president, becoming the first and only sitting White House official at the time to show any interest in it. Somalis lionized him. With help from Minnesota's strong contingent of Lutheran churches, Minneapolis had become a beacon of hope for Somali refugees.

In the early 1990s, however, the city's welcoming attitude began to change because of a tsunami of refugees. They fled Somalia in waves after rebel troops forced President Barre into exile, igniting two decades of civil war as power-hungry warlords wrestled for control of their bleeding country. One in every three Somalis who'd sought political asylum in the United States headed to Minnesota. The majority settled in Cedar-Riverside, a poorer section of Minneapolis that had been a haven for immigrant waves beginning with Scandinavians in the mid-1800s. But while earlier immigrant groups had been assimilated and moved to other parts of the city, Somalis had remained entrenched, turning Cedar-Riverside into an isolated neighborhood of Somali American immigrants in a triangle between highways 35 and 94 on the west side of the Mississippi River. The census put the Somali American population at 100,000, but everyone agreed it was a low estimate.

Adeogo had watched his community decline economically and spiritually over the years. Expectations of living the American dream had been crippled by high unemployment, poverty, and prejudice. Somali clans, the backbone of the Somali family system back home, had mutated into vicious street gangs.

Determined to help his community, Adeogo had first run for public office at the age of eighteen. It had been the first in a series of losses. He'd campaigned for the school board, the city council, even the library commission. When he wasn't seeking some public office, he was working for the Greater Somali Association, a nonprofit community group. Over the years, politicians had sought his help and he'd faithfully knocked on doors in get-out-the-vote drives. But he'd grown weary of getting others elected, mostly African Americans who claimed all of the seats controlled by minorities. In 2012, Adeogo helped get the city's election lines redrawn, creating a new ward composed almost exclusively of Somali Americans. Not only had this guaranteed a city council spot for a Somali American, it also had gerrymandered the community inside a single congressional district. The redrawing of lines had set the stage for a Somali American candidate but none had stepped forward until now. Adeogo was seeking election to Minnesota's Fifth Congressional District seat.

As soon as Yusuf exited, Bess Dixon hurried into the conference room where Adeogo was packing up his briefcase. She was one of the volunteer political advisors helping his cash-poor but enthusiastic campaign and one of the few who knew that Adeogo secretly understood that he didn't have a chance of actually getting elected.

Despite the gerrymandering, polls showed Adeogo would finish behind the popular incumbent, Representative Clyde Buckner, a ten-term congressman and staunch member of the Minnesota Democratic-Farmer-Labor Party, known as the DFL. (Hubert Humphrey had helped form the DFL in the 1940s by convincing the state's Democratic Party to merge with the populist Farmer-Labor Party, giving the DFL an edge over their Republican rivals.) If anyone was going to unseat Buckner, it would be his Republican challenger, Buddy Pollard, a former state legislator. Adeogo's campaign as an independent would capture 5 percent of the popular vote at best, placing him last in a three-candidate race.

None of that mattered to Adeogo, because he hadn't entered to win. Both of the other candidates supported passage of a federal immigration bill that was unpopular in Cedar-Riverside. Adeogo was hoping to lock in enough support from the Somali American community to broker a deal. He would throw his voting bloc behind whichever candidate would flip-flop on the immigration bill. So far, neither had taken him or his campaign seriously.

"You've got to read this!" Dixon exclaimed, holding up the front page of the Minneapolis *Gazette* like a shield in front of her.

CONGRESSMAN PUTS MOM-IN-LAW ON FEDERAL PAYROLL, the banner headline read.

"Congressman Buckner has been caught paying his elderly mother-in-law a five-figure salary with public funds," Dixon explained. "He's got her on his congressional payroll, and she doesn't even live in Washington. And that's just the tip of it. His mother-in-law has dementia and is in a locked unit in a Florida retirement home. He's using her as a ghost employee!"

"How did the newspaper find out?" Adeogo asked, as Dixon lowered the paper to her waist.

"Someone tipped off the *Gazette*, and its reporters dug into his financial records."

"He'll need my support now," Adeogo said excitedly. "He'll have to cut a deal on immigration."

"Forget making a deal," Dixon replied. "The newspaper is running a series on all three of you candidates, and a friend of mine has told me the *Gazette* has dug up dirt on your Republican rival too. Scandalous stuff as bad as the congressman's. Has the paper interviewed you yet?"

"I'm scheduled to talk to a *Gazette* reporter tomorrow morning."

"These stories could be game changers," Dixon gushed. "If voters turn against your opponents, you might actually have a shot at winning."

She paused and then added, "Assuming you don't have anything hiding in your past—no skeletons in your closet."

When Adeogo didn't immediately reply, Dixon looked concerned. "Rudy, you don't have any skeletons in your closet—do you? Nothing that is going to embarrass us, right?"

Adeogo smiled. "Of course not. I have nothing to hide."

Rudy Adeogo was not a good liar, but he was good enough to fool Dixon. Without missing a beat, she began blabbering about his upcoming interview with the *Gazette* reporter. But his mind was elsewhere.

CHAPTER FOUR

The sword-wielding American, who had freed his fellow jihadists during the prison break at Dera Ismail Khan and in the process decapitated a Shia prisoner and fired a fatal bullet into the skull of Canadian do-gooder Christopher King, slipped unnoticed into an Internet café in Mogadishu, the capital of Somalia.

In an impoverished country where the average yearly income was less than $500 U.S., Somalis had access to some of the most technologically advanced telecommunications and Internet services in eastern Africa. This was because of telecommunications companies based in the northern tip of Somalia in a region known as Somaliland. The residents there had declared themselves an independent country in 1991, but Somaliland still was not recognized as a sovereign nation by many foreign governments.

According to his Facebook profile, the man was a twenty-year-old Egyptian male studying to become a medical doctor, but none of that was true. Only one descriptive fact in the American's social media profile was accurate. It described his religion as Islam.

Abdul Hafeez couldn't lie about his faith, even if it might help conceal his actual identity from U.S. intelligence agencies. It would have been an insult to Allah.

Typing quickly on a worn Samsung keyboard, Hafeez sent a message to Nancy Rutherford, whose Facebook profile identified her as a Somali American, age forty, employed as an assistant professor at St. Cloud State University, located about an hour outside of Minneapolis, Minnesota. Rutherford was her married name and her profile was factual.

"Please tell mother happy birthday for me," Hafeez wrote.

Within seconds, a return message arrived.

"If you cared about our mother, you would stop what you are doing and come home."

Controlling his temper, Hafeez typed: "Do not ask me to turn away from Allah. Mother understands."

The all-caps response was instantaneous. "NO ONE UNDERSTANDS THE CRIMES YOU COMMIT. YOU BRING SHAME ON OUR PARENTS, OUR BROTHERS AND ME."

"My only brothers are my fellow jihadists. The others are dead to me. You are also a kafir, an unbeliever."

"Little brother, it is you who is perverting our faith. You have taken something beautiful and made it ugly. Your fanatical brothers and sisters kill innocent children with their suicide bombs."

Hafeez could no longer control his anger. "You dare lecture me about Islam? Suicide bomber is a derogatory term created by jews in the western media. It is true that our teachings forbid suicide but martyrdom is rewarded. To quote the Holy Qur'an 4:74 'Let those fight in the way of Allah who sell the life of this world for the other. Whoso fighteth in the way of Allah, be he slain or be he victorious, on him We shall bestow a vast reward.'"

"Little brother. I may not quote scripture, but I know in my heart that Islam is not a violent religion."

His response came lightning quick. "You know nothing. Your heart knows nothing. Listen to the words of the Ayatollah Khomeini: 'The purest joy in Islam is to kill and be killed for Allah.' Hear the words of the prophet Muhammad from the Hadith, al-Bukhari (52:54), 'I would love to be martyred in Allah's Cause and then get resurrected and then get martyred, and then get resurrected again and then get martyred and then get resurrected again and then get martyred.' To be a jihadist is to love death, to welcome it."

"Do not write me again. Reading your blasphemy is too

painful. I will not tell mother about our conversation. Unless you end your fight and return to your senses, it is better for her and our family that you be dead."

Hafeez logged off. Staying connected to the Internet for longer than a few minutes was risky, given the U.S. government's ability to intercept messages. Besides, there was no point in arguing with his sister. She was a woman, and religious matters were beyond her comprehension. He blamed his father for not beating her into submission. Instead, his parents had given her an American first name at birth and encouraged her to assimilate. No one was surprised when she'd married a white American. She was the opposite of him. Hafeez had rejected U.S. culture and changed his name for one more pleasing to him. Abdul. In Arabic, it meant "Servant of God."

Exiting the café, Hafeez turned down a side street into a neighborhood of former homes whose whitewashed exterior walls were pockmarked by bullet holes, creating a polka-dot mural of black splatters across their sunbaked paint. Squatters lived inside these shells now, behind boarded-up windows and patched roofs. A familiar smell came to him: incense being burned in a soapstone *dabqaad* to perfume the strong odors of cheap spices after a morning meal. He could hear a baby crying and another child softly singing. He walked deliberately, as if he were on an errand, and did not make eye contact with anyone he encountered.

In 2006, he had first entered this ravaged city as a triumphant, eighteen-year-old Al-Shabaab jihadist. Not far from where he was now walking was a street corner where he had fired an RPG during the worst of the battle for control of the city. A flying piece of concrete ricocheting from a soldier's .50-caliber round had sliced across his shoulder, leaving a jagged scar as a proud memento of that day's back-and-forth carnage. Allah had protected him and Al-Shabaab had been victorious.

During the next year, Islamic rule had been established in Mogadishu under the Islamic Courts, an Al-Shabaab-backed regime. Hafeez had helped enforce its rulings by overseeing public stonings, including that of a fourteen-year-old girl found guilty of adultery. While flinging softball-size stones at her body, he and his fellow fighters had sung *nasheeds* praising Allah. Justice had been administered as it had been written in the Holy Book.

The Islamic Courts had maintained control of the city for less than a year. Ethiopian soldiers, backed by the West, primarily the CIA, had routed the jihadists and retaken control of Mogadishu.

Al-Shabaab still stubbornly occupied several major southern Somali cities, and someday it would reclaim Mogadishu, of that Hafeez was certain.

Under its Western puppet government, Mogadishu was being revived—at least by Western standards. Somali families who'd fled abroad during the never-ending decades of fighting were gradually returning with suitcases crammed with U.S. and European dollars. Shops were reopening. Local schools where girls could learn to read and write were being established. Cargo ships could be seen at the Mogadishu port, unloading electronics and household goods. Coca-Cola had reopened its long-closed plant. As many as thirty commercial flights were now arriving and departing at Mogadishu's Aden Adde International Airport every day.

A Toyota truck and a taxicab sped by Hafeez, and he smiled. Yes, the city was now under capitalist hands, but Westerners still were terrified of Al-Shabaab. Why else was all travel done in two or more vehicles, the first always being a pickup truck carrying hired guards armed with AK-47s, the second a taxi or private car with Somali gunmen seated next to the windows, paid to be the first to die. Westerners didn't venture outside at night, and during the day they wore protective vests and surrounded themselves with bodyguards to avoid being kidnapped or murdered. It was true that Abdul Hafeez had been driven from the city, but he was not afraid to walk alone on its streets.

Hafeez paused to rest under the shade of a fruitless mango tree. Inserting a wad of khat between his teeth and gums, he slowly chewed the amphetamine-like stimulant. He closed his eyes and thought about how different his life was from those of his American siblings.

He was the youngest son of Somali immigrants. As a child in Minneapolis, he'd whittled wooden blocks into cars for the Cub Scouts' annual pinewood derby, eaten kids' meals at McDonald's, watched *Teenage Mutant Ninja Turtles* cartoons, and played with Transformers. Even so, he'd felt detached. White children didn't want to play with him and black ones made fun of him for being too black. Both told him to go back to Africa, a continent he'd never seen. School work came easy, but he hated class. An anger had begun building in him and it soon burst out. He was a natural fighter, a skill noted by a neighborhood gang. By middle school, his life was a steadily escalating pattern of violence. After his third arrest, his father asked leaders from the neighborhood mosque to intervene. At first it appeared the teachers there had succeeded. In Islam, Hafeez found peace and a purpose. He rejected violence and returned to school filled with religious fervor. He chastised his Muslim classmates for being too relaxed when they would not join him by the school's flagpole for daily prayers. He refused to say the Pledge of Allegiance.

Hafeez was drawn to *salaf*, which in Arabic means "ancestors." Salafi Muslims believed the purest form of Islam was practiced by the Prophet Muhammad's earliest followers—those who knew him and those who followed him immediately after his death in AD 632. By his sophomore year in high school, he had exchanged his denim jeans and Nikes for a long white robe and sandals similar to those worn in seventh-century Arabia. He began avoiding contact with females, refused to listen to music, would not be photographed, never slept with his backside facing Mecca, and began eating with only his bare right hand, as the Prophet had. He dropped out of high school his senior year, devoting himself to *da'wah*, the practice of spreading the Islamic faith. He spent his days wandering through Minneapolis malls armed with the Quran, hoping to attract questions but mostly greeted with angry stares and obscene gestures.

At this early stage in his religious life, he'd viewed politics as *dunya*— a worldly distraction from practicing his faith—until one night when he saw a news broadcast that showed U.S. Marines invading an Iraqi city. The bodies of enemy soldiers on the screen were dressed exactly as he was.

Hafeez began visiting Internet chat rooms, arguing with other Muslims about whether a militant jihad was permissible. After studying the scriptures, he decided violence was justified, but only if an Islamic country came under direct attack by Christian forces. That conflict would then be not about oil, or land, or man-made politics but about defending the one true religion.

His rejection of pacifism happened quickly. Hafeez found himself drawn back to violence, and soon Islam became his reason to delve into the darkness, rather than being his salvation from it. On the Internet, he found a Holy Crusade.

Somalia, a Muslim country, was bordered by Ethiopia, a Christian nation, and on YouTube Hafeez watched recruitment videos posted by Al-Shabaab, which means "youth," explaining how its fighters were dying to create a purely Islamic state free from all Christian influence.

Hafeez was still a teen when he arrived in Somalia with a close friend whom he'd met two years earlier at a Minnesota mosque. His name was Askar al-Seema. The two Somali Americans had moved up the ranks during their years in Al-Shabaab, but because they were Americans, they'd never been fully trusted. Being assigned to lead the early summer attack at Dera Ismail Khan had been Hafeez's biggest test and he had performed perfectly. His bona fides were no longer doubted after he executed Christopher King. The fact that King was a Canadian citizen hadn't mattered. He was a Westerner, and in the eyes of Al-Shabaab's leaders, Hafeez had taken the blood of one of his own.

His Minneapolis friend, Askar al-Seema, had been dispatched to London to complete an even more daunting task—sacrificing himself to destroy the U.S. Embassy there.

A dust-caked Land Rover arrived, and Hafeez uttered the traditional Islamic greeting to its driver when he climbed into its passenger seat: *Assalamu alaykum*, which meant "May peace be upon you."

Hafeez tucked another plug of khat into his mouth in preparation for the two-hour ride to an Al-Shabaab stronghold. As they pulled away, he wondered if Askar al-Seema had accomplished his mission and now was with Allah in paradise.

CHAPTER FIVE

London Hilton on Park Lane
London, England

Genearl Frank Grant, the chairman of the Joint Chiefs of Staff, was not a man who took kindly to being stood up for dinner, even if his guest was his only niece. Nor did he appreciate Captain Brooke Grant sending a rather cryptic text message to his private cell phone only minutes before their scheduled rendezvous. He'd been waiting in the hotel lobby with his military driver outside to deliver them to one of London's finest restaurants when she'd texted: "Sorry. Unavoidable delay. Eat without me. Will stop by later for dessert."

Brooke had not responded to his text or answered when he'd rung her, further spoiling his appetite. Instead of enjoying a leisurely meal, the general had retreated to his hotel suite and tackled a stack of paperwork. His relationship with his niece had always been awkward. He'd felt more comfortable with her older brothers and his own three sons. Based on his military training, he believed that he understood men. Women, especially independent women such as his niece, were both a mystery and an irritant. Grant added tonight's shenanigans to a mental list that he'd compiled.

When he'd not heard from Brooke by twenty-two hundred, the general rode the elevator to the Galvin at Windows restaurant on the hotel's top floor. Dressed in civilian clothes, he ordered the two-man security team that always traveled abroad with him to find an inconspicuous table away from his so he could enjoy the restaurant's highly praised cuisine and sweeping twenty-eighth-floor panoramic views alone without attracting attention.

Grant ordered a scotch and was studying the elaborate menu when he heard a male voice call out loudly, "General Grant, what a surprise!"

Out of the corner of his eye, he saw his security team starting to rise to intercept the approaching man, but Grant recognized him and quietly signaled his bodyguards to stand down.

John Duggard had been a West Point classmate and had risen to the rank of Brigadier General responsible for Army logistics before recently retiring from the Pentagon to work for ProTech, the U.S. military's largest private security contractor.

"What are the chances of us bumping into each other in a London restaurant?" Duggard asked, pulling out the chair across from Grant without waiting for an invitation to join him.

Grant was not a man who believed in coincidences, especially when it came to his "bumping into" a prominent defense contractor.

"You didn't plan this?" he replied.

Forcing a grin, Duggard said, "Frank, you always were the suspicious one." Waving to a waiter, he said, "Bring me whatever General Grant is drinking and bring him another one too."

"No thanks, John," Grant replied politely. "I'm actually a bit uncomfortable about us being seen together, given our positions."

"As pure as Caesar's wife, huh," Duggard said. "C'mon Frank, ease up. We've known each other a hell of a long time. Can't two former classmates have a drink without Congress launching an investigation? Besides, you owe me. There was a time at the academy when I was your only white pal."

Grant bristled. It was true that he'd encountered racial prejudice when he'd arrived at West Point in 1970, even though the academy had admitted its first black cadet in 1870. But Grant had always avoided using his race either as an excuse or as a ticket, and he resented Duggard using it now as a chit.

"Actually, I came over to talk to you, Frank, because I want to do you another favor," Duggard declared.

"I'm not in need of any favors," Grant replied. "Especially ones that come with strings."

"Just hear me out, Frank," Duggard said. "You've got to admit that

I did a hell of a good job for the Army when I r̶ stan years ago. The billions of pounds of good̶ Kazakhstan to keep our people supplied was ̶ given it was a former ward of the Soviet Union̶. can troops at the height of the conflict, and I saw to it ̶ had enough toilet paper to wipe their asses."

Glancing at the diamond-encrusted Rolex on Duggard's wrist, Grant replied, "It appears that you have used your experiences in the Army to reward yourself nicely since leaving it."

"I'll admit it, Frank. Life's pretty sweet," Duggard said. "And Pro-Tech is a very profitable cushion to land on—something you might wish to keep in mind with your own retirement looming. Old soldiers don't need to fade into the sunset, and I'll be happy to pull strings at ProTech, although with you being the chairman of the Joint Chiefs, you certainly can write your own ticket."

"When that time comes, I'm planning on doing some teaching and possibly some writing," Grant replied, "not double-dipping in the private sector."

"Your choice, but is that lovely bride of yours—Miss Geraldine—really going to be happy with you bringing home thirty grand a year when you could be banking a multimillion-dollar salary with stock bonuses?"

Already uncomfortable, Grant said, "Did you ambush me to offer me retirement advice?"

"No. I came to offer you a chance to save the American taxpayers a half-billion dollars. I've got buyers ready to purchase a half-billion dollars of military white goods left over from our ongoing conflicts in various Middle Eastern countries. I'm talking about washing machines, dryers, office furniture, even some brand-new trucks. No weaponry. It's a sweet deal for the buyers, the military, and the U.S. taxpayers—"

"And ProTech," Grant said, interrupting.

"Of course, Frank, everyone is entitled to earn a profit. But a certain Pentagon general overseeing the disposal of those goods has issued a DIP order. He's going to have the military destroy in place a half-billion dollars of salable white goods."

"John," Grant said sternly, "I'm sure the general who issued the DIP

s good reason, and this is not something that we really should be
ssing. The next time you want to bring up a business-related mat-
you need to go through the proper channels. Now, if you don't mind,
m meeting someone."

Grant had actually given up on his niece arriving, but he'd wanted an
excuse to rid himself of Duggard.

Duggard glanced around the crowded restaurant.

"She's late," Grant said and immediately regretted his choice of words.

"Ah, Frank old boy, does Miss Geraldine know?"

"It's my niece."

"Okay, if you say so."

As if on cue, both men heard a woman's voice say "There you are!"

It was Brooke. "You must have forgotten your cell phone," she chided
her uncle when she reached the table. "I've been trying to text you. Luckily your aide told me you were up here getting dinner. I'm famished."

"What happened to your wrist?" Grant said, eyeing the obvious white
gauze bandage.

"An incident outside our embassy. A suicide bomber. Obviously I'm
here, so he failed," she replied, grinning. She extended her hand to Duggard. "I'm Brooke Grant, captain, U.S. Marine Corps."

"I'm Brigadier General John Duggard, Army retired," he answered.
"Your uncle and I went through West Point together. Always a pleasure
to meet a Marine." He paused and then said, "Oorah."

"I didn't mean to interrupt," Brooke said.

"A suicide bomber?" Grant asked, responding to her earlier comment.

"Yes, he's under arrest. I'll tell you all about it over dinner. Like I said,
I'm hungry."

"Was anyone injured?"

"No, Uncle Frank, the only damage was to my wrist, and a torn
uniform, which I've changed, knowing what a stickler you are about
regulations."

"Sounds like a hell of a story," Duggard interjected. "I'd love to hear
more."

"As I mentioned," Grant said, "my niece is joining me for a private
dinner."

"That's your uncle's polite way of telling me to get lost so he can have you all to himself," Duggard explained in a mocking voice. "I'll look forward to hearing your story some other time, but before I go, I want to extend my condolences about your parents."

Brooke lowered her eyes and in a quiet voice said, "Thank you for remembering them."

"Who could forget them, especially after the *New York Times* Sunday magazine published their photographs on its cover? If I remember correctly, they were having coffee with a friend in the Windows on the World restaurant when the first plane hit."

"My father was a preacher, and his congregation had given him and my mother a trip to Manhattan as a wedding present. Their anniversary happened to be September eleventh."

"And you were what— How old?" Duggard asked.

Grant interrupted. "This is not a subject we like to dwell on."

"Your uncle was almost killed too," Duggard recalled, "when the 9/11 terrorists crashed a jet into the Pentagon."

Glancing affectionately at Grant, Brooke said, "Fortunately for me, he wasn't."

"Fortunately for all of us," Duggard said.

"But especially for me," Brooke replied, "since he and my auntie took me in and raised me."

"Semper fi, Captain," Duggard said, rising from the table to leave. Speaking to Grant, he added, "A half-billion dollars of taxpayers' money being wasted, Frank. Think about it. That's a story that *60 Minutes* might like but the Pentagon certainly wouldn't."

A waiter brought Brooke a menu. "What did he mean about a half-billion dollars being wasted?" she asked after Duggard had gone.

"Nothing important. Tell me about this suicide bomber."

She gave him a detailed account, and when she finished, he didn't comment but instead changed subjects. "Your auntie and I miss you terribly. How would you feel about returning to Washington and working at the Pentagon?"

Eyeing him suspiciously, she replied, "I'd rather be deployed to somewhere a little closer to the action."

"Oh, there's plenty of action in Washington."

"Uncle Frank, my first assignment was Paris then you had me sent here to London, and don't try to deny that you were responsible for my deployments."

"Guilty as charged. I thought you'd enjoy seeing Paris and spending time in London. What good is being chairman if I can't help out my favorite niece?"

"Your only niece. But I didn't join the Marines to tour Europe. I joined for the same reason you enlisted. Because I love my country and want to defend it from its enemies."

"I signed up because I had a chance to attend West Point and I assumed I was going to get drafted anyway because of Vietnam."

"Auntie says my daddy tried to talk you out of going to West Point. She says you were offered a football scholarship to Oklahoma University. That's what my daddy wanted you to do, but you were determined to go fight."

"Your daddy tried to talk me out of lots of things when we were growing up."

"And you didn't listen to him—just like I'm not listening to you. I am my daddy's daughter, but I've got my uncle's stubbornness."

"Don't remind me."

"How do you think your own sons feel when their daddy refuses to help them get ahead in the Army but gets me sent to Paris and London?"

The smile on Grant's face vanished. "My sons are soldiers. They've got to prove themselves, make it on their own."

"And your niece doesn't?"

"You're a woman."

"I'm a Marine. Do you know how much trouble you'd be in if I told the media how you really feel about women being in the military?"

"Your mommy and daddy chose me to take care of you if anything happened to them. I made them a promise the day you were born that I'd keep you safe until you got married."

"Until I got married? That's just as insulting. I don't need you or some other man to keep me safe."

Grant wiped his massive left hand across his chin, an unconscious habit he'd developed when frustrated. Brooke had seen him do it before, many times, when she was living under his roof. His male chauvinism and her feminism were neither a new topic nor a pleasant one.

"Brooke," Grant said forcefully, "I'm glad this incident at the embassy was resolved without anyone getting hurt. But you should have let that London bobby take charge rather than impulsively tackling that man."

"If I'd waited, I wouldn't be here. I thought you'd be proud of me, not scolding me."

Neither spoke for a moment, until she decided to break the silence. "I'm not a little girl anymore," she said quietly.

"But you always will be to me."

She looked at his sad face and realized he seemed older and more tired than she'd remembered. He was a bear of a man who stood over six feet tall and tipped the scales at 235 pounds. She'd always thought of him as being omnipotent. Tonight, he looked like a weary soldier well past retirement age.

When Brooke was a child and her family drove from Tulsa to Washington for a visit, she would climb onto her uncle's lap with a tattered copy of *Winnie-the-Pooh* and demand that he read it to her. Now, as they were eating their dinner, she used her childhood nickname to address him. "Oh, Pooh Bear, when will you learn you can't protect me from all the threats we face in life? What happened outside the embassy demonstrates that. Please let me be just another Marine."

It was well after midnight by the time Brooke returned to her London flat, and as she was inserting her key into the bolt lock she heard her phone ring inside. Dashing in, she grabbed it moments before her answering machine took over.

"Finally," a familiar male voice declared. "I've been calling your cell."

"I turned off the ringer while I was with my uncle at dinner. He considers it rude to answer."

"So that's where you've been," the man replied. "Out with another man. Do you realize you're all over the BBC and you're blowing up the Internet? I'm surprised you didn't have reporters camped outside your flat."

"Oh God, did they identify me by name?"

"Yes. A half-dozen tourists got pictures of you sitting on top of that bomber, holding him down. Very erotic, tackling a man and forcing him under you!"

"You're demented, Jean-Paul," Brooke replied, falling into an oversize chair in her tiny living room, the only seat in the cramped loft.

"Maybe you will wear your uniform the next time we make love," Jean-Paul Dufour said.

"Did the BBC mention I suspected he was a suicide bomber because he was wearing your brand of cologne?" she asked, quickly explaining how she had known the bomber wasn't a vagrant.

"Then it should be my handsome face on the BBC instead of yours," he said.

"Oh God, I wish it would be. I don't want to talk to any reporters."

"When they figure out who your parents were and how they were killed, it will be an even more sensational story—especially across the pond."

Brooke suddenly felt ill. "Take me away this weekend, Jean-Paul," she begged. "Somewhere no one will recognize us."

"Unfortunately, I must be in Paris for the weekend."

"That's perfect."

"Ah, it would be perfect but you can't accompany me. As the French *conseiller des affaires étrangères*, I will be traveling with Ambassador Marentette to an international conference, and you know we must be discreet."

"What if I promise to wear my uniform to bed?"

He laughed.

"Which begs the question," she said.

"Ah yes, the question: When will I make you an honest woman?"

"No, that's condescending and rude. It's also impertinent. What makes you think I would accept a proposal from the French *conseiller des affaires étrangères* in London?"

"Your accent is getting much better. You sound less American."

"My accent is perfect. I spent my first tour of duty in Paris and everyone told me I spoke like a local."

"They were being overly polite because you are a beautiful, exotic woman."

"No they weren't," she replied. "They were French. The French are never polite to foreigners. But my question is: How are we going to handle things when our relationship eventually becomes public?"

"Who says it ever will?"

"Don't be naïve. You're a senior French diplomat, and your ambassador and the U.S. Marine Corps are not going to look approvingly on us falling in love. I assume there are rules in your service about fraternizing with foreigners."

"Fraternizing? Such an antiseptic word. That's not how I would describe our lovemaking," Jean-Paul said. "But don't despair. I'm a very capable *conseiller des affaires étrangères*, so I will find a diplomatic way for us to be together. Let me handle it. Enjoy the moment. You Americans worry too much about tomorrow."

"And you French never do."

"In ten minutes, I can be at your door. We'll take a hot bath together and drink some wine. I've never made love to an American Marine hero."

"I've already started the bathwater."

"And the uniform?"

"Just get over here before I fall asleep. It's been a long day."

CHAPTER SIX

Somewhere in the Somali desert

The Al-Shabaab compound several miles outside Jaakumow was so remote that it had neither cell phone nor Internet service, a rarity in Somalia. Because of its isolation, the first word that something had gone awry in London arrived in the form of a flash drive delivered from Mogadishu in the dead of night by a courier.

Abdul Hafeez inserted the drive into a portable computer, and a graphic photograph of a couple engaged in a sexual act flashed onto the screen. For all appearances, the photo had been downloaded from a popular British website where sexually adventurous English couples seeking like-minded couples could meet. Even under close inspection, the image appeared no different from hundreds of other uploaded pornographic snapshots. But when Hafeez transferred the image into a decoding program on his computer, the sweating flesh vanished and written text appeared.

Computer images assign every pixel three numeric values that correspond to the amount of red, green, or blue in an image. By altering those values ever so slightly, radical jihadists were able to hide the 1's and 0's that created computer text, effectively concealing a message inside a photograph, making their communications impossible for anyone to detect and read.

The message from London reported that Askar al-Seema had failed to detonate his suicide vest and suitcases outside the U.S. Embassy and he was now a Scotland Yard prisoner. The writer, a member of an Al-Qaeda cell in London, was angry that al-Seema had failed and concerned that he might talk during interrogation, especially if the British turned al-Seema over to the CIA.

Once Hafeez finished reading the message, he looked at several other items that had been downloaded from the Internet onto the flash drive for him. There were no hidden texts in these files. They were YouTube videos that had been uploaded by spectators outside the London embassy who'd taken footage on their cell phones during al-Seema's capture. One showed a female Marine lying on the Somali American, preventing him from triggering his explosive vest. Another showed a BBC news broadcast, during which a photograph of Captain Brooke Grant was displayed. She was identified as the American hero who had thwarted the suicide attack.

Satisfied that he understood what had happened in London, Hafeez wrote a reply, in which he assured the Al-Qaeda cell leader in London that Askar al-Seema was a devout Al-Shabaab fighter who would die before revealing any information that could jeopardize their group's London operations. He reversed his decoding program and his text disappeared into a new pornographic image.

The courier from Mogadishu was having tea in the compound's kitchen when Hafeez found him. "Upload this new photo as soon as you return to the capital."

Although it was three a.m., Hafeez awakened the Al-Shabaab fighter who had driven him from Mogadishu to this remote Al-Shabaab hideout. The two of them climbed into a pickup and drove into Jaaku-mow, where Hafeez knocked on the door of a nondescript house. He was welcomed inside by a kindly-appearing grandfather. In a whispered voice, Hafeez told the elderly man what had happened in London. Afterward, he returned to the pickup and was driven back to the Al-Shabaab compound.

The older man, in turn, awakened his son and explained that they needed to drive to a house in an even more distant location.

Hafeez knew the grandfather was a courier who was able to memorize messages verbatim. What Hafeez didn't know was whether the elderly courier delivered those messages to another courier or to Al-Shabaab's secretive head.

After he returned to the hideout, Hafeez couldn't sleep. It would be important for morale inside Al-Shabaab to have an immediate victory after the failed London operation.

And by dawn, Hafeez had a fresh bombing target in mind.

Minneapolis, Minnesota

Rudy Adeogo was anxious when an investigative reporter from the Minneapolis *Gazette* arrived at his apartment Saturday morning in Riverside Plaza, the tallest structure in Minneapolis outside the city's downtown business area, to interview him about his dark horse candidacy.

"I've never been in this building before," the young reporter volunteered when Adeogo and his wife, Dheeh, directed her into their living room. "Although I've driven by it many times. My mom is a huge fan of the old Mary Tyler Moore television show, and she told me this is where the show's main character, Mary Richards, was supposed to live."

"I'm not familiar with that program," Adeogo responded, "but I doubt anyone in Hollywood would have a character living in our building now, unless it was a film about Somali Americans and unemployment."

For the next hour, the reporter grilled him about his campaign's finances and his own spending habits before she turned off the iPad that she'd been using to take notes. "I'm sure you know my paper has been publishing a lot of troubling information about your opponents," she said. "I'd just like to say, completely off the record, it's refreshing to find at least one candidate running for public office who seems to be squeaky clean."

"But you missed something," Adeogo said.

The reporter and Dheeh both looked surprised.

"I found a library book in my campaign headquarters yesterday," he said. "It's overdue and I owe at least three dollars in fines. I want to assure you, I'll be paying the fines today."

The reporter laughed and Dheeh looked relieved.

As the reporter was about to leave, she said, "Oh, I almost forgot. Have you seen the news stories out of London about that suicide bomber last night?"

"Yes," Adeogo replied. "It's been all over the news."

"Scotland Yard says the bomber is a Somali American from here named Askar al-Seema. My newspaper has another reporter writing about him, but my editor asked me to see if you knew anything about Askar al-Seema or his family."

Adeogo hesitated, but for only a moment. "I knew of him and his family. I believe his parents both died a few years ago. I've been told he was a troubled young man."

"Oh, you knew him then, but not well?"

"He lived in our building, but as you can see, this is a large building with more than thirteen hundred apartments, so there are people you see but don't really know."

"I'll pass that along to my editor. He might suggest the reporter who's writing about the bomber contact you."

"I'm always happy to help, but I'm not eager to talk about this man. What he attempted to do violates everything we believe as Muslims, and the fact he's Somali American brings shame on our community."

"It would be embarrassing for us," Dheeh added.

"Oh, I understand," the reporter said sympathetically. "Since you didn't really know him, I guess there's no need for me to pass along your name."

"Thank you," Adeogo said. "There's already a tremendous amount of stigma against Somali Americans, and I'm certain his actions are only going to add to those prejudices."

Adeogo and Dheeh rode down the building's elevator with the reporter and watched her exit through the lobby into the parking lot. By the time they'd returned to their apartment, their smiles had disappeared.

"Someone will discover Askar's true name," Dheeh said in a nervous voice. "Then it will be only a matter of time."

"What would you have me do?" Adeogo replied. "We can't go backward. Not now!"

Langley, Virginia

Gunter Conner read the classified cable from the CIA's London station about the failed Friday bombing when he got to work on Monday morning and then reviewed it again before he put in a call to the FBI's field office in Minneapolis. The CIA was prohibited by law from spying on Americans at home or operating on U.S. soil, but after the 9/11 World Trade Center attacks the lines that separated the agency from local, state, and federal law enforcement agencies had become blurred. Within a few minutes, Conner had learned from a helpful FBI station chief that Askar al-Seema was not the jihadist's birth name. His deceased Somali immigrant parents, whose last name was Galal, had broken with their native tradition and named him Phillip, thinking it would help him assimilate as a child into the American mainstream. But on his sixteenth birthday, Phillip Galal had legally changed his name to Askar al-Seema.

Conner wondered if Askar al-Seema aka Phillip Galal could have been the Somali American who had led the Taliban attack at the prison in Dera Ismail Khan. Several escaped prisoners who had been recaptured after the break had told authorities that the leader of the Taliban attack had been a Somali American. But Conner rejected that theory because photos of al-Seema didn't match the descriptions that recaptured prisoners had given of the Somali American in charge of the Pakistani prison break.

Clearly, there were two Somali American jihadists involved in two separate actions. Conner next noted that the attempted London bombing was thought to be the handiwork of an Al-Qaeda cell operating in London, while the Taliban had spearheaded the Pakistani prison break. Conner knew that his boss and his peers would not believe the two events were linked, because different terrorist groups were claiming responsibility. But he suspected they were.

While talking to the FBI station chief in Minneapolis, Conner asked if the bureau had any records that mentioned the names of Askar al-Seema's friends or known associates but there was nothing useful in the files. Conner next tried the Minneapolis police department, but it appeared that Askar al-Seema aka Phillip Galal had never been arrested. At that point, many investigators would have given up, but not Conner. He decided to begin calling principals of public schools in Minneapolis where al-Seema might have been a student. Conner identified himself as a federal investigator with the government's Counterterrorism Center, which impressed the principals. All of them had seen news reports about al-Seema over the weekend and they were eager to help, but a check of school records didn't turn up anything. It appeared as if he had hit another dead end, when one of the principals said offhandedly, "I think there was an incident our school counselor handled, but it wasn't related directly to our school so there's no report in our files."

The principal explained that the counselor had retired, but he offered Conner the man's home number.

The raspy voice of a smoker answered when Conner called. "Yeah, I got a complaint about Askar and one of his buddies," the counselor recalled. "They were handing out religious literature at a strip mall a few blocks from our high school campus during their lunch breaks. One of the store owners was going to have them arrested for trespassing."

"There's no police record of Askar ever being arrested," Conner replied.

"That's because the store owner changed his mind. He thought the Somali American community might boycott his store if he called the police, so he called me instead and asked me if the school could do something about Askar and his buddy hanging around the mall. Of course, we couldn't. There's nothing illegal about a couple of Somali American kids handing out religious materials during their breaks."

"Do you remember what this other kid's name was?"

"Now that's a problem. You see, this other kid had dropped out before I transferred in from another school in our district, so I didn't really know him. Just the same, I bumped into this kid once because he and Askar were inseparable. I remember thinking he was a bad influence on Askar."

"Do you remember his name?"

"His real name or his Muslim one? He and Askar both changed their names after they got religion."

"Either."

"Maybe it was John or maybe George, but everyone called him something else. I'm trying to remember but I only met him once or twice. Maybe if I looked through some old records, but— Oh, wait a minute, I just remembered. He went by 'Abdul.' That was it: Askar and Abdul, our Islamic religious radicals."

"Radicals?"

"Yes, I wasn't surprised at all when I heard on the news that Askar had tried to blow himself up in London. He was a nice kid but he got so you couldn't talk to him about anything but his religion."

"What about Abdul? Was he just as radical?"

"Are you kidding me? He was worse than Askar. If he hasn't blown himself up already, you'd better be on the lookout for him, because he's a ticking clock."

After Conner finished the call, he pulled a clean sheet from the legal pad that he had been using to take notes. Conner knew al-Seema had attempted the London bombing. On one side of the paper, he wrote: LONDON BOMBING. He drew a line down from it and wrote: ASKAR AL-SEEMA AKA PHILLIP GALAL. He knew from recaptured prisoners that a Somali American had led Taliban fighters in breaking jihadists from the Dera Ismail Khan prison. On the opposite side of the paper, he wrote: PAKISTAN PRISON BREAK. He drew a line down from it and wrote: ABDUL?

If these two events were coordinated, then Askar al-Seema and Abdul were obeying orders issued to them by a third party. He drew a circle between the two men's names and put a question mark inside it. What Islamic leader was powerful enough that he could persuade an Al-Qaeda cell in London to cooperate with Askar al-Seema and the Taliban in Pakistan to assist a Somali American named Abdul in breaking jihadists from the Dera Ismail Khan prison?

Who was this leader in the circle? He was the target whose identity Conner needed to reveal. But first he had to prove that a mystery man actually existed.

The attempted suicide bombing in London was soon eclipsed by new headline-grabbing stories, but the ripples caused by that failed attack were only beginning to form and, rather than dissipating, they were about to grow much stronger.

Fate was not done with Gunter Conner in Langley, Rudy Adeogo in Minneapolis, and Abdul Hafeez in Somalia. Along with Captain Brooke Grant in London, their lives were about to intersect because of the actions of a United States president who would choose to put her nation's security at risk for her own polictical gain.

PART TWO

SOMALIA:
A POLITICAL DECISION

Political language ... is designed to make lies sound
truthful and murder respectable, and to give an
appearance of solidity to pure wind.

—George Orwell

CHAPTER SEVEN

Coldridge! Coldridge! Coldridge!"
Presidential candidate Timothy Coldridge wasn't scheduled to appear before the chanting crowd for another half hour, but the momentum inside the Orange County Convention Center already was nearing a fever pitch. Almost from the moment the two-time, popular Florida governor had announced his candidacy, everyone had expected him to win his party's nomination. Crushing victories in the Iowa, New Hampshire, South Carolina, and Florida primaries had cinched it.

The fact that his nomination had been preordained did not keep the fourteen thousand supporters in the great hall from going wild the moment all the major television networks officially confirmed it.

"Coldridge! Coldridge! Coldridge!"

From his complimentary luxury suite in a nearby hotel, Coldridge watched the throng calling his name via a network news channel whose reporter could barely be heard as she described the revelry. Surrounded by his wife, their three children, and his top campaign advisors, the fifty-five-year-old Coldridge looked every bit like the carefully groomed politician that he was. He'd spent decades crafting his image. Confident. Welcoming smile. Handsome. Strong chin. Year-round Florida tan and teeth so well made it was nearly impossible to tell they were caps.

"You've made history!" one of his aides declared. "You're the first-ever nonincumbent to win every delegate's vote in the first round! Congratulations, Governor."

Smiling, his wife, Shirley, chided, "You mean 'Congratulations, Mr. President!'" and gave Coldridge a quick peck on his cheek.

"Not yet, dear," he said. "But soon."

Coldridge felt a sense of satisfaction he seldom allowed himself. His entire life had been one of drive, determination, courage, and relentless ambition. There was no finish line in his future. His was an endless race.

It'd started after he'd received a small inheritance from his parents. Within a decade, he'd turned that cash into $1 billion. One of the start-ups that he'd launched had changed how Americans spent their hard-earned money. They no longer needed to carry cash, swipe credit cards, or use phone apps: He'd funded a tech company that equipped stores with fingertip readers. Press a thumb to a scanner. Payment made. Royalty to Coldridge.

It was only one of the innovative companies that he had helped get off the ground. But the millions he'd earned hadn't been enough. Many business executives toy with the idea of entering politics, but few are skilled enough to make the transition, and when Coldridge announced he was entering the gubernatorial race in the third-largest state, critics had a field day.

They'd badly underestimated him. A relative unknown, candidate Coldridge had pumped $200 million of his billion-dollar-plus fortune into the race, prompting pundits to agree that he'd literally bought the Florida governor's office. He'd always had money and was confident he could always earn more of it. It was a tool, and he had found something that tool could get him. When interviewed, he was fond of quoting fellow billionaire Steve Jobs. "Being the richest man in the cemetery doesn't matter to me."

Once he was in office, something surprising happened. Coldridge had turned out to be as good at running the state as he had been with business. He did it in a way that made people enjoy and like him. Some political pundits wondered how much of Coldridge's success was due to his top-notch staff and the bevy of advisors who he literally bought and brought with him. He was so popular that other politicians had begged him to campaign for them and he had, all the while pocketing IOUs from candidates, with an eyebrow-raising high number in the early primary states.

Coldridge's personal wealth enabled him to build a seemingly unstoppable political machine. He had a bigger staff, more resources, and more IOUs than anyone else in his party by the time he announced he was running for president.

Coldridge knew his business background would appeal to American voters, who tended to cast ballots that favored their pocketbooks, especially when compared to President Sally Allworth. She'd first ridden into public office on the coattails of her popular senator husband after he'd died unexpectedly in office. During her presidency, the economy had been dismal.

Still, ousting an incumbent was always an uphill challenge, and that made Coldridge even more determined. He'd never lost at anything. Plus, he genuinely believed he could do a lot better job than President Allworth, and deep down in a secret place that he never made public Coldridge was convinced that it was his destiny to become president and save the country.

Even before he'd officially declared himself a candidate, Governor Coldridge had challenged his very expensive, very large, world-class team to come up with a strategy that would maximize his chances of beating Allworth. After months of computerized analysis of previous elections, they'd concluded that the key to a Coldridge victory would be winning so big and so early in the primary process that he could spend most of the year focused on defining and attacking Allworth. There could be no bloody, in-party preliminary battles that would open wounds for Allworth to exploit later.

Having developed a campaign plan, Coldridge's team had implemented it with relentless discipline and a lavish expenditure of money, unmatched in previous primary races. Every step had metrics and every metric was met.

While governor, Coldridge had earned back the $200 million he had spent buying the governorship and had discovered during his second term that he could raise an astounding amount of money from companies that did business with his state. When it became obvious he was going to be the front-runner, Super PACs added to his financial arsenal.

Unprepared weaker candidates found themselves crushed in the first four primaries. They were outspent, outmessaged, and also outcampaigned. Coldridge loved meeting people, loved giving speeches, and loved just about everything involved in winning power from the American people.

His nomination tonight was the pièce de résistance.

"We'll send out your children, then your wife, and you'll come out when the cheering becomes so loud you can't hear yourself think," an aide told him while they waited in the hotel suite.

"No," Coldridge said. "Shirley and I will be going out together with our children, projecting the image of a family."

"But we need the spotlight on you," the aide countered.

Coldridge shot him an irked look.

"It will be," Shirley Coldridge chirped. "It always is."

His advisors had been working on tonight's victory speech for nearly a year. They'd decided to target President Allworth's foreign policy. Her busybody meddling was one of the reasons why the U.S. economy was hurting.

"I'm ready," Coldridge declared, rising from his seat.

His appearance onstage ignited five minutes of nonstop cheers, blasts from air horns, and continuous applause, all encouraged by several hundred paid campaign workers moving as cheerleaders through the assembly hall.

Waving his hands for the crowd to quiet, Coldridge finally began.

"Thank you for tonight's honor. I accept your nomination and I will be the next United States president!" The crowd took to its feet, roaring again.

"While we have been focused on American jobs, health care, and education, this president has been wasting American money and risking American lives in futile overseas misadventures. We need a president who is dedicated to solving America's problems for Americans!"

Another standing ovation faithfully recorded by live coverage on the news networks. More chants of "Coldridge! Coldridge! Coldridge!"

"For too many decades, Americans have sent their young men and women—and their money—across the globe. For far too long, the White House has spent more time on the Middle East than the American Midwest. For far too long, the White House has emphasized South Asia at the expense of the American South. For far too long, the presidency has looked to Beijing rather than Boston, to Moscow rather than Miami, to Seoul rather than Sacramento."

He hesitated, feeding off the electricity in the room.

"In a long line of internationalist presidents, the current president has been the worst. She has never met a foreign meeting she did not want to attend, a foreign trip she did not want to go on, or a foreign head of state she did not want to host in the White House!"

The crowd burst into spontaneous laughter.

"I will focus on American meetings to solve American problems. I will visit American mayors and governors working together to create jobs, build roads and bridges, expand mass transit, revitalize schools, and grow the economy. President Allworth worries about the safety and health of the world. I worry about the safety and health of our American people. President Allworth wants to expand our AIDS outreach in Africa, our commitment to fight epidemics such as Ebola, our concern for economic growth in South Asia."

He paused for emphasis, but not long enough to be interrupted.

"I want to expand Medicaid for the American poor. I want to eliminate AIDS here in America. I want to ensure that poor children in the Rio Grande Valley and poor adults in the West Virginia mountains get better health care. President Allworth wants to campaign for reelection as the president for world affairs. I am offering you a sharp contrast. My campaign theme is: 'It's time for America!'"

As Coldridge loudly enunciated those words, huge banners dropped at strategic spots inside the massive hall, proclaiming IT'S TIME FOR AMERICA in large letters, prompting another long interruption of cheers.

"It's time for American troops to come home to America!" he declared.

Another roar from the crowd.

"It's time for foreign aid to become American aid!"

Another roar.

"It's time for an American president who cares about America!"

The loudest roar yet.

"Let me ask you," Coldridge proclaimed, a sly grin appearing on his face as he glanced sideways at the large slogan on the banner behind him. "What time is it?"

The ecstatic crowd yelled back, "It's time for America!"

Coldridge broke into a huge grin. "My governorship has been different because I went right to work confronting Florida's problems and worked with leaders from every party and every constituency to get things done. My campaign for the nomination was different because I went out early and outlined a clear platform of specifics that people could rally around, and they did. My campaign for the general election will be different too.

"Others have relied on attack ads and huge secret funds of money to smear their opponents. I want a straightforward, honest choice between two very different approaches for America's future. I want a direct, honest dialogue with President Allworth that will give the American people a clear choice between her internationalist record and my clear commitment to focusing on America."

With his voice rising, he continued, "I have won my party's nomination the earliest of any candidate in modern times. This gives us an opportunity to start a general election dialogue earlier than ever before. So tonight I am challenging President Allworth to agree now to an unprecedented series of debates. Let's not wait until October. Let's not wait for the last minute. Let's give the American people a chance to see how really different our views are. Let's have a fact-based, adult conversation about her record and my alternative to that record and let's do that first debate during the first week of August. It's time for an American debate for the American people!"

Prompted by his paid campaign workers, the crowd began chanting, "What do we want? We want a debate. When do we want it? August! What do we want? We want a debate," and then seamlessly moved into the now-familiar "Coldridge! Coldridge! Coldridge!"

Joined by Shirley and their children, Coldridge basked in the adulation and energy. When he finally stepped from the stage, his campaign manager rushed toward him. "That worked beautifully, Governor. You've put the president in a box. She won't have a choice now."

"It's time for America!" Coldridge said.

And it was time for him to fulfill his destiny.

CHAPTER EIGHT

July 10
The White House
1600 Pennsylvania Avenue
Washington, D.C.

Armed with her ever-present mug of coffee, Mallory Harper, chief of staff to President Sally Allworth, walked briskly into the Oval Office. Harper walked briskly everywhere. It was one of her techniques for demonstrating how busy and powerful she was. No one intimidated her, not even the president. It was one of the reasons why President Allworth had wooed her to the White House from running the nation's most successful Internet software company. Allworth valued Harper's intelligence, ambition, and unfiltered candor. The forty-something Harper didn't have time to be bothered with either a personal life or a social life. Her entire focus at this moment was on only one thing: getting her boss reelected in November.

She had just come directly from a meeting with the president's top campaign staff and political pollsters. Thirtysomethings. Tech savvy. Eager to prove themselves. Their party's best and brightest. Harper got right to the point when she and the president were alone.

"We've known Coldridge was our opponent for a long time," she noted in a matter-of-fact voice, "so our people have done an immense amount of opposition research and they are confident we can put him on the defensive about several questionable aspects of his business career, along with how he bought the Florida governorship and mistakes he made as governor. No one gets to be a billionaire or a governor without leaving targets for us."

"Good," President Allworth said. "But let's talk about last night. It's clear Coldridge is on a roll. Big crowds, big primary victories, and big pockets. And now this August debate challenge."

"Our people had focus groups in six states watching last night and responding to it. We already know line by line what worked and what didn't—"

"And?" Allworth said impatiently.

"We have three big problems," Harper replied. "People love his slogan—'It's time for America.' It works. Number two: attack ads he's about to unleash. Our people have discovered they're being done by one of Los Angeles's slickest agencies and they're effective. Images of war and chaos overseas superimposed with shuttered businesses and long lines at the unemployment office. Then a few carefully edited clips of you, Madam President, to make it appear that you're more concerned with what's happening overseas than here at home. Every ad ends with Coldridge rolling up his sleeves and declaring he'll put America first. Like he's some sort of modern-day John Wayne. Each ad has an underbelly whiff of sexism. Check that—an overpowering stench of sexism. Strong governor, weak female president."

"How'd your people get an advance screening of his political ads?" Allworth asked.

"The ad agency leaked it. They suggested we hire one of their partners to counter them. Trying to cover all bases."

"Not a chance!" Allworth snapped. "What's our third problem?"

"Coldridge's debate gauntlet," Harper said. "Overnight polling shows Americans want you to accept Coldridge's August debate challenge. If you don't, you'll play into his campaign ads by looking as if you're not interested in what's happening here at home—either that or you'll look weak and afraid of him."

The president frowned. "Don't voters understand I have a country to run and a world to deal with? If I start debating in August, it will tie up my time and, more importantly, give him lots of opportunities to force me into making a mistake."

"I don't think you have to be afraid of this billionaire blowhard causing you to make a mistake," Harper replied. "His bank account is clearly bigger than his brain, but I do think you have to be very worried about his willingness to spend millions and millions of his own fortune as well as the millions that he'll attract. This election is going to go way beyond the billion-dollar mark, and he's pulled together a dynamic campaign. His potential media buy will be critical."

"We can't do much about his deep pockets except raise more money ourselves," the president replied. "But why are you worried about his silly theme, 'It's time for America?' It's sophomoric."

"Sophomoric and, according to our pollsters, effective. Coldridge's team has been working for more than a year to find an approach that would put you strategically on the defensive and drive a wedge between you and a substantial majority of the American voters. We can't underestimate the methodical nature of his campaign. They wouldn't be pushing his 'putting America first' campaign and dumping millions of dollars into attack ads that portray your focus on international affairs as the reason for the weak economy unless they know they will work."

"How can you be so sure this theme is effective? He only unveiled it last night," Allworth asked, leaning forward, totally focused.

Harper took a deep breath before plunging forward. "In all six states last night, our focus groups reacted very positively to his theme. Even your strongest supporters in those groups were attracted to the idea. It's going to resonate with voters. Polls before last night's speech gave you a fifteen-point advantage when voters were asked who was a 'stronger leader.'"

"And I deserve that title," Allworth declared.

"Yes, you do," Harper said. "But we are facing not so much a war-weariness as a world-weariness. A lot of Americans simply want to be able to focus on solving our own problems here at home."

Harper passed a sheet of paper across the president's desk. "I had our people do snap polling last night. As you can see, it was a large enough sample size to compare results between the total sample population and those who watched the speech. Among the entire population, your advantage as the stronger leader is still high—twelve points. But among those who watched the speech, it was nearly inverted—a ten-point deficit. The American people are not satisfied with the state of affairs here at home, and his argument gives them a plausible reason to blame you."

"Isn't it possible that it's a momentary blip, an overnight reaction to his Florida victory and speech?"

"I wish it were, but research about public attitudes says differently. We've not seen this depth of withdrawal from world affairs since the American people forced Congress to pass the Neutrality Act in 1935. Popular support was so great back then that FDR was forced to sign it. Remember, Franklin Roosevelt was a Wilsonian internationalist and he thought the act was a disaster. But he also knew he couldn't get reelected in 1936 if he vetoed it and argued for an American role in an increasingly dangerous world—even with World War Two looming."

"Are you suggesting that I should abandon everything I believe about America's pivotal role in the world in order to get reelected? Because that's not going to happen. I didn't get elected president to let some ignorant blowhard cripple American leadership with a catchphrase and turn our world into a far more dangerous place for our children and grandchildren."

Shifting into her commander-in-chief tone, President Allworth said, "Mallory, you're my right arm because you're smart, tough, and one of the shrewdest political analysts I know. I need you to get our people to figure out how we beat Coldridge and his high-priced team's strategy— not let him intimidate them into asking me to abandon my principles."

Harper drew three straight lines on her ever-present iPad with her stylus and showed it to the president. "We have three strategic choices," she explained. "Over here on this line, we simply co-opt Coldridge. You're the incumbent president. You can set out to show through your speeches and presidential actions that you are even more focused on improving America at home than he is. Simply put, you out-Americanize him. Steal his thunder. The danger is exactly what you mentioned earlier. Coldridge can say and promise anything, establishing benchmarks that will be impossible for you to challenge. He can propose really bold actions to refocus resources here at home because the only audience he cares about is the American people who are going to vote this fall. He isn't responsible for global commitments and a global coalition. He doesn't have to answer calls from foreign heads of state who will begin to tremble if you start mouthing isolationist platitudes."

Harper moved the stylus to the middle line. "Another choice would be to modify your policies without giving them up completely. Adopt some of Coldridge's language. Adopt a few of his proposals. Clearly, we aren't going to throw away three generations of alliances around the world. We aren't going to radically return to an America-only policy. But taking the middle ground would slow down Coldridge's momentum and blur the issues. The danger with the middle ground is that Coldridge can simply keep raising the bar, promising more, and people will believe that he really means it, while it will appear you are only agreeing because you want to be reelected. You will look insincere and, more importantly, you will look weak, as if you are following his lead, letting him set the agenda."

Allworth asked, "What's the third line?"

"It's the riskiest, but I think it's doable," Harper said in a deliberate voice. "I've actually put the most thought into this option because it fits your values, your personality, and your strengths. I also know you. I didn't think you would go for line one, because I knew you wouldn't let Coldridge panic you into reversing your policies. I didn't think you'd like line two, because it would be a halfhearted compromise. Why play on his turf? Why let him set the agenda? Besides, I believe only this third option—the third line, I call it—offers you a chance to beat him decisively."

"So what's the third line?" Allworth asked.

"We challenge his anti-internationalist argument head-on and we beat it."

"And how do I do that? You just told me polls show the American people are weary of America being the world's cop."

"Yes, that's true," Harper replied, "but those same polls reveal there is one area of foreign policy—one subject—that defies that. Americans understand that Islamist terrorists pose a threat to their lives. They might not care about trade barriers or whether some Napoleonic Russian despot is trying to rebuild the former Soviet empire, but they damn well care about the threat of Islamist terrorists."

Without waiting for the president to respond, Harper continued. "Americans may be weary of the world, but they also know the world generates real threats that can kill them and their loved ones. I believe we need to take Coldridge's argument head-on. The public intuitively realizes that Boston can be bombed and New York can be attacked because it has happened in their lifetime. The way we deflate 'It's time for America' is by focusing on how vulnerable America would be with someone such as Coldridge in the White House. You can't create jobs for Main Street if we have suicide bombers killing hundreds in our markets. We prove to the American people that Coldridge has a shallow, uninformed view of the world and he cannot be trusted with the safety of the American people. Voters might be tired of being mired in world conflicts, but they want to be safe and you have kept them safe. Let's convince people that Coldridge's 'It's time for America' actually means, 'It's time for America to be attacked.' Let's force the choice by building on the strength of your policies."

"I like it," Allworth said. "You're right. It suits me. After all, I unshackled our intelligence services more than any of my predecessors. My God, before I took office, five hundred lawyers had to sign off every time the CIA wanted to fire a Hellcat from a Predator. My administration has killed more than a hundred terrorists while Coldridge was doing what? Working on his suntan, urging Florida legislators to give tax breaks to orange growers."

"Exactly," Harper said. "This approach will negate his ads by emphasizing your experience fighting terrorists as a strong female president."

Allworth smiled. "It would be fascinating to let the American people choose between a woman who is a strong, determined commander in chief and a wimpy billionaire who knows nothing about the world and wants to run and hide. I think we can contrast my experience in the Senate and in the White House with his inexperience."

With a note of caution in her voice, Harper said, "Remember, Madam President, a bold, aggressive campaign like this means you have to accept his August debate challenge. You can't claim to be the stronger leader and hide from him until October." Tapping her stylus on the third line, she said, "If we accept his challenge, we should demand that the first debate be on national security and foreign policy, to showcase what you've done. He'll bite because he'll see the forum as a way to attack you and pitch a need to return to isolationism. We can use the debate to show his downright ignorance and lack of experience. Make him seem incompetent. And we would be doing it at the very beginning of the general election campaign. If done correctly, we could break the momentum that his campaign has developed and bring him down to earth."

Allworth smacked her desk with her right palm and exclaimed, "Why don't we steal his theme? Rather than 'It's time for America,' we turn it into 'It's time for America to remain safe.' That would drive him nuts."

Harper laughed and said, "To truly guarantee the type of dominating win we need in the debate, we will need to force a foreign policy issue he will be totally unprepared for."

"Do you have something in mind?"

"Africa."

"Africa?" the president repeated, clearly skeptical.

"I realize what I'm about to suggest sounds strange," Harper said, "but hear me out. During the debate, you announce your administration is taking the fight against radical Islamist terrorists into Africa."

A sour look appeared on the president's face. "Americans don't care about Africa, and voters don't want us getting into another war."

"No one is talking about boots on the ground," Harper quickly replied. "We're talking about continuing our ongoing collaborative fight against Islamist extremists. I'm talking about forging partnerships with African governments, just as we've done in the Middle East, providing training and intelligence to target terrorist camps."

"Mallory, is going after terrorists in Africa really a big or compelling story?"

"It is if you make it one," Harper replied. "You're correct, Madam President. Americans don't give a damn about Africa. That's why we don't make it about Africa. We make it the first step in your aggressive ongoing policy to protect America. I'm talking about hunting down and killing every one of those suicide-vest-wearing, 9/11, deranged SOBs who make everyone think twice before they board an airplane, keep people from traveling overseas, and make people wonder if it's safe for them to drink a beer while sitting in the stands watching an NFL football game. During the debate, you announce you're taking the fight against terrorism into Africa because that's where the terrorists are regrouping, where they're growing stronger. You announce you're going to reopen an embassy in Mogadishu, in one of the most dangerous countries in Africa, and use it as a base, because your administration isn't afraid and is determined to kill every one of those Quran-thumping mongrels."

"That's a huge risk," the president said. "Somalia is a hotbed of jihadist activity. The entire nation is an unstable war zone. Our embassy would be a huge target. I can't risk an ambassador's life for a political stunt. I'm also not yet convinced that Americans will care. At best, they only know two things about Somalia—pirates and Black Hawk Down, and neither of those are pluses."

"Yes, but I'm guessing Governor Coldridge doesn't know a damn thing about Somalia either. We need to throw him off his script and make him say something stupid. If you announce you are reopening an embassy there, he'll immediately denounce the plan as being another risky waste of American resources. And at that moment, we've got him."

"How? How will I possibly have him?"

"Because you will be taking a bold step to defeat terrorism and Coldridge will be perceived as being timid. When he questions the move during the debate, you can show your expertise by explaining the Brits already have been operating an embassy in Somalia for several years without incident. You can make Coldridge seem out of his depth and cowardly. Is he really afraid for Americans to go where the Brits already have gone?"

"Let's say I do what you are suggesting. Would there really be time for us to open an embassy in Somalia before the election? In sixteen weeks. That's not enough time to build an embassy and staff it."

"You're right," Harper said, "but it is adequate time to open a temporary embassy that will serve our purposes until after the November elections. The Brits don't keep their diplomats in Mogadishu. Their ambassador and his staff live and operate out of Nairobi. The British embassy in Mogadishu consists of prefab offices that were flown into Somalia. They're staffed by locals. The only time the British ambassador sets foot in the capital is for a day trip to get his photograph taken."

"You're suggesting we operate what—an embassy-lite?"

Harper laughed. "We don't have to construct an embassy building from the ground up to make good on your announcement. Instead, we find a suitable structure in Mogadishu, send in teams of contractors to work nonstop if necessary to get it ready enough for an ambassador. We open it just before the November election, fly in the ambassador for a largely ceremonial event and photo op before sending him to Kenya, where he will be housed until a more suitable permanent site in Mogadishu can be built after the election."

"Coldridge and the media will see right through that."

"Not if we explain the embassy is temporary until we can find a permanent location. Not if you appoint a respected diplomat. Not if you send in private security guards and the Marines. Not if our ambassador begins serious talks with African leaders about combating terrorism. What I am suggesting is a hell of a lot more legitimate than what the Brits are doing there."

"It's a lot of risk and for what?" Allworth asked.

"A political advantage," Harper replied. "If we plan this ambush correctly, we can steal the debate spotlight. Our post-debate spin team will be standing by with all the experts on eastern Africa, including Muslim professors and leaders who will explain how your actions will help stabilize Africa and make America safer from Islamist terrorists. You will come out as a strong, competent leader and Coldridge will be exposed as the bumbling imbecile he is."

"It could easily blow up in my face."

"Madam President," Harper said. "Great gains demand great risks. We've got to think outside the box. We can't use the same old political playbook. We can't let your poll numbers drop. We can't let Coldridge set the agenda. We can't stay on the defensive."

The president ran the tip of her tongue across her top lip—a nervous habit she'd developed as a child. "All right," she said. "We need to do something dramatic, but let's not do this blindly. I want the intelligence community to do an assessment, and I want it done completely off the radar before the August debate. I want to be able to tell the media that the CIA and State Department are both behind this."

"I can get both agencies to deliver reports to you before the first debate in August," Harper said. "I'll also tell State that its people need to find a suitable building that we can repurpose quickly before November third. It's amazing how fast private contractors can move if given the right incentives. Trust me, Madam President, we're going to catch Governor Coldridge with his pants down."

"Mallory, that's hardly a picture I want to imagine."

As soon as Harper left her alone, President Allworth put in a call to Decker Lake.

"Madam President," Lake said in a voice that sounded coarse and strained. "You've just brightened my day."

"How are you feeling, my friend?" she asked.

"For a man with no eyebrows, I'm doing okay. The odds of me beating this cancer are two-to-one in my favor, and that's better than what they were saying when we launched your first senatorial campaign."

"You've always thrived on difficult challenges, Decker," Allworth said. "And I certainly was one when we started. I think you were the only powerful official in Washington who believed I had gravitas."

"And you have certainly proved me right. You've come a long way."

He was right. Although she'd been through several campaigns with her husband, a popular Pennsylvania senator, it wasn't until after he'd dropped dead from a heart attack that she'd stepped into the political spotlight. She'd been a novice. Decker Lake, her husband's best friend and confidant, had been the first whom she'd confided in. Lake was a former Pennsylvania governor who was then serving as the U.S. attorney general, and he'd pulled the necessary strings needed for her to finish the remainder of her husband's term. After that, he'd mentored her, helping her become twice the politician that her husband had been—and her husband had been very good.

When she'd decided to make a bid for the White House, Lake had been her campaign's strategist. By then, he'd left the Justice Department. Everyone dismissed her candidacy until she shocked the pundits by placing second in the New Hampshire primary. No candidate had worked harder, and Lake had been demanding. Allworth had started each morning with a five a.m. three-mile run, telling reporters assigned to tag along that it was a great way to see whatever city she was appearing in but also to remind the public that she was vibrant and strong. There'd been no photos of her eating triple-decker cheeseburgers or chili-smothered hot dogs. Lake had made certain that photos of her running before daybreak made the front pages of local papers and news websites while her opponents were still sleeping. Allworth appeared ten years younger than her age (she was fifty-six four years ago), and while she didn't overly emphasize her sexuality, she made certain her designer dresses were current, stylish, and showed off her athletic figure—but always in appropriate ways. She'd been marketed as a trendsetter, not a frumpy politico. She epitomized the woman who could have it all, having raised three sons— all overachievers—and been successful in her own right after her husband's death.

When she'd surprised all the experts by winning the election, Lake had been at her side. He'd escorted her to her inaugural ball, and even though she'd quickly killed rumors that they were romantically involved, she had been fully aware of his romantic interest in her. She had kept him away, in part, because he was fourteen years older and she worried how young voters would react to her becoming entangled with such a grandfatherly figure.

Allworth had offered to appoint Lake to any job in her administration that he desired. But he'd demurred, preferring to operate behind the scenes in the shadow of the White House. He had been the president's go-to guy until three months ago, when he'd been diagnosed with colon cancer. His doctors had warned him to cut back on his eighty-hour-plus workweeks. Allworth had known the cause of Lake's cancer.

Washington, D.C.

Years of eating too-rich expense-account lunches, of chain-smoking to calm his nerves, and a too-sedentary lifestyle that tied him to a desk or found him sitting for hours on a cross-country flight.

Since the diagnosis, Lake had sequestered himself in his Watergate penthouse, vomiting each morning from chemotherapy. Allworth had visited him several times late at night as discreetly as possible since he'd become ill. She'd arrived with special meals prepared by the White House chef, but he'd taken only a few bites, preferring instead to listen to her and sip a frowned-upon whiskey. She'd felt torn whenever she left him. Because of his illness, she knew that sex wasn't on his mind, but his eyes told her that he longed for the simple companionship of them sharing a bed, hers being the last face he'd see before falling asleep and the first in the mornings. That was not a gift that she dared give him.

"You picked a hell of a time to get sidelined on me," Allworth complained.

"Damn inconsiderate of me to get cancer. Why'd you call?"

"I need advice."

"You got Mallory Harper for that now."

"I trust you more."

In the next few minutes, the president told Lake about Harper's Africa gambit.

"What do you think, Decker?"

Lake was quiet for a moment, so quiet that the president thought maybe their call had been disconnected. He finally said, "Be careful, Sally. This decision could come back to bite you."

CHAPTER NINE

July 12
A brick building enclosed by a fence
Fairfax County, Virginia

Gunter Conner tapped a four-digit code into the electronic pad, causing the solid metal door to unlock so he could dart inside while the alarm was on pause. He waited for the door to close automatically behind him and the alarm to reset before he moved.

Conner now found himself facing a mural where the word s*m*i*l*e had been painted in bold red letters. A rainbow rose from the top of the *S* and ended on the tip of the letter *E*. A bright yellow sun in the corner of the mural was wearing a happy face.

A teenage boy came walking toward him. Conner immediately stepped out of the youth's path. This was not Conner's first visit to Soft Wind Meadows, and he knew that if he hadn't moved aside, the boy would have walked into him or simply stopped, become frustrated, and started to scream.

As soon as the boy passed, Conner began walking to his right down a hallway. He was inside a one-story, square-shaped building. At each corner of this square was an arched doorway that led to a residential wing. Each wing held twenty-four rooms—two rows of twelve one-bedroom units that faced one another. At the end of each wing was a small dining room and television viewing area. These four residential wings had been named after U.S. cities, to make it easier for residents to identify them— New York, Los Angeles, Miami, and Seattle—although there was some question in most employees' minds about whether the residents understood what those words actually meant.

Conner turned, entering a hallway that made up the square's eastern edge. The building's designers believed that having a "town square" that was linked to the four residential wings made the facility feel more like a community than a locked institution. The hallway that Conner was now passing through featured a mural of a post office manned by three clerks—one black, one Asian, and one white—all smiling and eager to wait on customers.

Each morning after breakfast, residents would emerge from their bedrooms and make their way from their wings to the square that Conner was now walking along. For some unexplained reason, the residents always walked clockwise. Only visitors walked counterclockwise. Some residents would spend their entire day walking around the town square, as if they were commuters looking for their place of employment. Others appeared to be searching for the exit, which was not marked. It was covered with wallpaper and only popped open when a code was entered into an electronic lock located on the wall directly across from the doorway.

When Conner reached the end of the Post Office hallway, he turned left and entered the Beach hallway. The mural here was of sand, waves, and a clear blue sky. Speakers in the ceiling played the sound of waves crashing and seagulls squawking.

This would be where he'd find Jennifer, his thirteen-year-old daughter. About midway along the hallway was a room decorated like a boardwalk arcade, and Conner knew she would be inside it playing the Dance Dance Revolution game. To win, a player had to replicate the dance steps that appeared on a large monitor, stepping forward, backward, or sideways on a thin pad of red and blue arrows to the sound of music. If the player followed directions and finished the song without making any mistakes, a new tune would begin. It would be played faster, and the dance steps would be more demanding. No matter how skilled players were, they would eventually reach a point where it would be impossible for them to keep up with the computer's frantic pace.

Jennifer's auburn hair was already damp with sweat when he spotted her. Her legs were moving at lightning speed as the machine spit out commands: *Left foot right, jump, right foot forward, now back.* Conner had hired a private companion to provide extra care for his daughter, even though Soft Wind offered its residents round-the-clock nursing. Miriam Okpara was from Ghana, and she greeted Conner with a welcoming grin. "She's been playing thirty minutes now, Mr. Conner, sir," she said. "Fortunately, no one else ever wants to play this machine. I'm telling you, this girl is getting better. I don't care what them doctors say."

Jennifer was Soft Wind's youngest resident. Most of the others were much older, including a large number who had Alzheimer's. Despite the age difference, Jennifer's doctors had recommended Soft Wind because of the excellent care that it provided longtime patients and because Jennifer seemed much more at ease living with the elderly than with her own age group. She seemed especially fond of residents with dementia, for reasons her doctors couldn't explain.

Brain scans revealed that Jennifer had suffered a traumatic brain injury. Much of her frontal lobe had been impacted. In addition, doctors believed she was experiencing post-traumatic stress. That combination had turned her mute and often unresponsive. The doctors had no idea how to help her. Their prognosis was bleak, but Okpara insisted that she was seeing subtle signs that Jennifer was slowly recovering.

The arcade machine suddenly sounded an alarm and the music stopped. Jennifer had missed a step. She stamped her right foot and seemed confused when the game didn't begin again.

"Honey child," Okpara said calmly. "Your papa has come to visit."

Jennifer continued to stare at the frozen game screen. She stamped her foot again.

"Jennifer," Conner said, "I need you and Okpara to come outside with me. I want to tell you some important news."

Ignoring him, Jennifer stamped both feet now. She had her mother's Egyptian features—chocolate-colored skin, a delicate nose, and dark eyes. There was a time when her eyes sparkled. Now they were like peering into an abyss. Okpara took Jennifer's hand and said, "Come along, child, your papa has something to tell us."

Together, they led Jennifer outside into the facility's garden, where they found a concrete bench that was large enough for all of them to sit side by side. A jet flew over them en route to Dulles International Airport and Jennifer stared up at it.

Conner took his daughter's free hand. Okpara was still holding the other. "Honey," he said tenderly, "I have to go away for a while on one of those big planes that you just saw fly over. I just won't be able to come by every day like usual."

Jennifer didn't react. There was no way for Conner to know if she understood what he was telling her.

"When will you be leaving, Mr. Conner?" Okpara asked.

"Later tonight."

"Can you tell us where you're going?"

"As you know, I work for the State Department," he said, referring to the standard cover story that he and most other CIA employees used when being sent abroad. "I can't get specific, because my bosses are going to have me on the road traveling most of the time, but I'll leave instructions about who to call if there's an emergency. I can tell you that I'll be mainly in Africa."

The mention of Africa caused Jennifer to tighten her grip on her father's hand.

"It's okay," he said, startled. "I'm not going back to that bad place. I won't be anywhere near Cairo."

He'd meant to calm her, but the word *Cairo* caused her to dig her fingernails into his flesh. "Ouch!" he said, reaching over with his left hand to remove her grip. "I swear, Daddy will be okay."

So she was listening to me, he thought. She did understand.

"Don't be getting yourself upset," Okpara told her. "Me and you will be just fine together, and your papa has to go because it's his work and he's a very important State Department diplomat."

Conner didn't have the nerve to tell either of them that he might be away for a while. His boss, Charles Casterline, had approached him about a discreet operation. Casterline had gotten a call directly from CIA Director Payton Grainger, who'd been contacted directly by White House Chief of Staff Mallory Harper. The president wanted to know if it was safe to open an embassy in Mogadishu and that on-the-ground risk assessment had to be concluded before the first week of August. The agency was giving him two weeks to fly to Africa, familiarize himself with Mogadishu, and submit his report. Conner's name had come up because he had been stationed in Egypt three years ago and was now assigned at Langley to track the activities of radical Islamic groups in Africa. But there were other reasons why the agency was happy to offer him the job—the first being that no one else had wanted to go to a hell-hole the likes of Mogadishu. Plus, his peers and immediate supervisor all wanted to be rid of him.

In her private conversation with Director Grainger, Harper had strongly hinted that she expected the agency to recommend that the White House move forward with its diplomatic agenda. Those "strong hints" had been communicated to Casterline, who in turn had simply told Conner that if he accepted the assignment, the agency expected him to write a favorable report giving the White House an all-clear sign.

Writing toothless reports was not something Conner was known for; in fact, his reputation was for just the opposite. But he had a motive of his own for wanting to go to Somalia, and if it took rubber-stamping an agency report, he was okay with that.

Conner was convinced that he'd done everything he could in Langley when it came to identifying his mystery Osama bin Laden jihadist. He'd also decided that the best way to find that faceless leader was to track down the Somali American known only as Abdul, and since Abdul's longtime Somali American buddy Askar al-Seema had flown to London from Mogadishu, Conner suspected there was a high probability that Abdul was now hiding somewhere in Somalia. If the president decided to open an embassy there, which seemed likely, the CIA would need a station chief, and since Conner already would be in Mogadishu and would be familiar with the terrain, he would be the most likely choice. As a station chief, he would be able to hunt for Abdul and his jihadist leader without Casterline constantly looking over his shoulder. The only downside to the assignment was leaving Jennifer.

"It's almost time for dinner," Okpara announced. "We need to go inside and rejoin the others, and you need to tell your daddy good-bye."

Conner followed his daughter and Okpara into the "town square," where he put his arms around Jennifer. She remained limp as he was hugging her and then she pointed toward the Dance Dance Revolution machine.

"No," Okpara said firmly. "If you get started, we'll never get to dinner. You can play afterwards, baby."

"I doubt she will miss me or even know I'm gone," Conner said.

"Mr. Conner, you don't know that for sure, do you? She hears more than anyone thinks. She knows who you are and she knows you love her."

Okpara's words were supposed to comfort him. But they didn't. If his daughter didn't remember him or know who he was, it would have been easier for him to leave her.

CHAPTER TEN

Mid- to late July
The Rubens at the Palace
London, England

Captain Brooke Grant had been told that the Rubens hotel near Buckingham Palace was one of the most prestigous in all of London, and when her French diplomat boyfriend revealed that he had booked them a suite there to celebrate their four-month anniversary as a couple, she'd hurriedly packed an overnight bag.

Since 1912, the magnificent hotel had been the gathering spot of aristocrats and debutantes before World War Two, and it remained one of the city's most esquisite establishments. Brooke didn't have expensive tastes. She'd been born into a middle-class Oklahoma family but she enjoyed the thought of being pampered in such a grand hotel and appreciated Jean-Paul Dufour's eagerness to treat her, as he put it, "to the best London offers."

They'd arrived at the suite around seven o'clock and immediately stripped and made love. Afterward, they ordered room service before again enjoying each other's bodies. It was now nearly ten o'clock and they were lounging naked on a king-size bed with 100-percent-Egyptian light-gray cotton bedsheets in one of the Rubens's royal-themed suites with red velvet wallpaper, striped red-and-white carpet, and a gunmetal-gray fabric-covered headboard. Anywhere else, the decor might have looked bordello tacky, but at the Rubens it appeared elegant and decadent.

Dufour was resting on his back, she was next to him on her stomach, raised on her elbows admiring his lean, muscular body. When he closed his eyes, she gently placed her hand on his chest.

"Not again," he moaned, keeping his eyes shut. "At least not yet."

"You're ruining my view of lusty Frenchmen," she teased. "But I wasn't touching you for any other reason than to feel your heartbeat."

He grinned and said, "American women are hopeless romantics."

"Tell me, Jean-Paul, since you're older than me and not an American," she said, "why it—"

He interrupted her mid-sentence, "Not to mention that I speak five languages fluently and am a *conseiller des affaires étrangères*."

"Yes, yes, all of that. Tell me why it is that you're always exhausted, while I'm invigorated and can't sleep after we make love."

"Because I do all of the work."

She slapped her hand against his chest.

"Ouch!" he complained.

"You deserve it, calling our love work!"

He chuckled.

"C'mon," she said. "It's early and I don't want to waste the evening. Let's go dancing somewhere or for a romantic ride along the Thames or on the London Eye so we can see the city's lights."

Without opening his eyes, he replied, "The curse of dating a woman who's ten years younger than me. They always want to do something next."

"Did you just say 'they'?"

"In addition to being hopeless romantics, you American women are jealous ones, aren't you? You're upset if there have been others before you."

"Others? Plural, not singular?"

Dufour pretended to snore.

Brooke removed her hand and rolled onto her back.

They'd met four months earlier during a stodgy diplomatic reception hosted by the French ambassador. She had been wearing a jet-black Violetta Couture dress that she'd found when she was rummaging through an upscale London secondhand shop. The silk jersey asymmetric number had been handsewn for someone who could afford designer prices but significantly marked down because few women could have worn it well. It hugged Brooke's athletic, five-foot-seven-inch, 118-pound frame perfectly. She'd looked stunning, and the unattached men at the reception—and several married ones—had found an excuse to speak to her. She'd been pretending to listen to a Swedish cultural affairs officer when she'd noticed Dufour engaged in a conversation with the German ambassador and his wife. Brooke, who was bored and had just finished her second Merlot, gave him a half smile. Ten minutes later, Jean-Paul worked his way across the room. He looked very French to her. Tall, fit, immaculately dressed, with carefully coiffed hair, manicured fingernails, and skin that looked as soft as a woman's even though he had the perfect amount of scruff on his chin, somehow making a five o'clock shadow sexy.

Without introducing himself, he announced, "I would like to propose a contest between us to make this party a bit less tedious."

"What sort of contest?" she replied, adding, "And what makes you presume I'm finding the evening tedious?"

"Your eyes. As the poet said, they are the windows to the soul, but let's discuss our wager. I will identify every Russian here tonight who is posing as a diplomat but is actually an SVR officer," he said, referring to the Russian foreign intelligence service, which had replaced the infamous KGB.

"And if you do, what must I give you?"

"The pleasure of going to dinner with me tomorrow night."

"What if you fail? What do I win?"

"It's pointless to discuss because I will not fail, but if you insist, I will have a case of the Merlot sent to your embassy, as well as flowers."

"This sounds as if it's a win-win situation for me."

"And for me as well, but let us play the game now."

She glanced unhurriedly around the room and said, "That Russian, standing near the bar."

"He is Petr Orlov, an assistant press attaché," Dufour replied. "And yes, his diplomatic credentials are a cover. He's actually a major in the SVR."

"That was too easy," she said. "Remember you claimed you could pick out every Russian agent."

"I must confess," he replied, "that our contest is rigged. I am taking advantage of you." He leaned close and whispered into her ear, "Every Russian here tonight is SVR except the Russian ambassador."

"And how do you know this?"

"Because the Russians have so many of their intelligence officers working under diplomatic cover that their real diplomats have to do three times as much work and they don't have time to come to silly receptions such as this one."

She'd laughed, and they'd spent the rest of the evening talking, or more accurately, she'd spent the rest of the night listening to him. Dufour loved to hear the sound of his own voice and was a self-declared expert when discussing politics, food, wine, and anything about his homeland. He believed France was superior to every other nation, but especially the United States, and he thought everyone should speak French but became disgusted if they did it poorly. They argued for a half hour when she said that California grapes used for Pinot Noir were equal to French ones.

The next night, she'd met him for dinner and, unlike her American suitors, who had waited a day or two before calling, Dufour had sent roses the following morning and called her cell faithfully every day afterward. When they were together, he was focused exclusively on her—when he wasn't talking about himself.

Without warning, Dufour sprang from the Rubens hotel bed to his feet and announced, "If Captain Brooke Grant, USMC, wishes to go dancing, then dancing it will be. If she wishes to board the world's tallest Ferris wheel, then board it she will."

"Finally," Brooke said approvingly. "Take me to the Ferris wheel."

As he was reaching for his silk boxers, she began laughing and said, "Just for the record, Jean-Paul, the London Eye is no longer the world's tallest Ferris wheel—even though Europeans keep saying it is. They've built bigger ones in several cities, even in Las Vegas."

He shook his head in disgust and said, "This is why America is hated by the rest of the world. First you insult my country by building a fake Eiffel Tower along your tacky Las Vegas Strip and then you insult the Italians by turning Venice's Grand Canal into a casino ride and now it's the Brits with their giant London Eye Ferris wheel. Is nothing sacred to you Americans?"

Brooke joined him in getting dressed, and a half hour later they rode the elevator to the lobby. As they were crossing it, Brooke spotted two men emerging from the hotel bar. She immediately released Dufour's hand, which she'd been holding.

"Captain Grant," Robert Gumman slurred, forcing her and Dufour to stop by the hotel's front desk. Gumman's drinking buddy was John Duggard, the retired general from ProTech whom Brooke had met when having dinner with her uncle.

"Good evening, Captain Grant," Duggard said, extending his hand. He appeared completely sober, but Gumman's eyes were glassed over and he was unsteady on his feet.

Looking past Brooke at Dufour, Gumman said, "General Duggard, the gentleman with Captain Grant is Jean-Paul Dufour." And then, in butchered French, he added, "He's the *conseiller des affaires étrangères*."

John Duggard introduced himself.

"I'm afraid," Dufour said, speaking to Gumman, "that I don't remember us meeting before."

"Name is Robert Gumman. We've never met but I'm the regional security officer at our embassy so it's my job to know who you are." Flashing a gotcha grin at Brooke, he added, "Pretty interesting place to be bumping into you, Captain Grant."

Without flinching, she replied, "And an equally interesting place to find you. I thought you preferred the closest pub to our embassy."

"The general here—" Gumman began.

"Retired general," Duggard interjected.

"Okay, retired general," Gumman said dismissively, "has been treating me to some very fine and expensive whiskey while we've been discussing Somalia."

Duggard shot Gumman a nervous glance. It was apparent that he didn't want Gumman to be discussing their conversations with Brooke and Dufour, but the inebriated security officer either didn't notice or didn't care.

"Somalia? That must have been a short discussion," Dufour quipped, "since neither of our countries have embassies in that godforsaken hellhole."

"That could change soon," Gumman declared, slurring his words. "General John Duggard's company—excuse me, retired general John Duggard's company—has a nice, fat hefty contract to do some very important work in Mogadishu." He gave Brooke a hateful look and said, "And I may soon be leaving you behind, Captain Grant, and I must say in all candor, 'Good riddance!'"

Taking hold of Gumman's arm to steady him, Duggard said, "I think we need to be moving along."

But Brooke wasn't going to let Gumman's slight pass without comment. "I'll look forward to your going-away party. Are you retiring and going back to a desk job in the Denver police department?"

Gumman smirked and said in a triumphant voice, "I'm being promoted. The State Department is sending me to Mogadishu to assess the political and diplomatic climate there, and by 'climate,' I don't mean the weather." He laughed at his attempt at humor and added, "And General Duggard, retired, is going along too, isn't that right, Mr. Retired General?"

"Africa is a new frontier," Duggard said in a hurried voice. He started to nudge Gumman to the side so that Brooke and Dufour could pass.

"Are you suggesting your country might be opening an embassy in Mogadishu?" Dufour asked.

Even though Brooke had no interest in protecting Gumman, she realized his drunken bragging was not information that he should be sharing with a French diplomat.

So did Duggard.

"Okay," Duggard said in a commanding voice, tightening his grip on Gumman's arm. "Time for us to be moving on. Nice meeting you, Mr. Dufour, and always a pleasure seeing you, Captain Grant."

Gumman was about to speak, but Duggard literally jerked him out of the couple's path.

As soon as they were outside, Dufour chuckled. "Imagine your State Department sending that drunken ass to assess the situation in Mogadishu."

Brooke was thinking the same thought, but she didn't find anything humorous about it, nor did she like that Gumman aka Dumbman had discovered them together inside the Rubens.

CHAPTER ELEVEN

Mid- to late July
Al-Shabaab compound
A remote area outside Jaakumow, Somalia

The elderly courier arrived unannounced and stayed inside the walled compound only long enough to whisper a message into the ear of Abdul Hafeez. Upon hearing it, he immediately called together the dozen fighters under his command. All of them sat in the courtyard on the ground in the rising morning heat while he addressed them.

"Brothers, it is time for one of you to act as the hand of Allah," he said, searching each of their faces. He stopped when he reached Dilawar Bahar and asked, "My brother Bahar, are you ready to serve our Lord?"

"With his help I will serve him faithfully," the twenty-two-year-old son of a Saudi Arabian family immediately replied.

Bahar was one of the radical Islamic fighters whom Hafeez and his Taliban cohorts had rescued from the Pakistani prison in Dera Ismail Khan. He had followed Hafeez to Somalia to fight alongside Al-Shabaab.

"Your task is an important one," Hafeez explained. "You will bring justice onto the head of Moalim Mohammed Musab, the puppet Somali president living in the presidential palace in Mogadishu."

"But how?" one of the other fighters asked. "Villa Somalia is impenetrable."

Immediately after the Dera Ismail Khan prison escape, no one would have questioned Hafeez, regardless of how reckless a mission. But Askar al-Seema's failed suicide bombing in London had raised fresh doubts about his leadership.

"Allah has shown me a way," Hafeez said confidently, "and He will not fail us. Do any of you doubt our Lord?"

The fighter who'd questioned Hafeez lowered his eyes.

Continuing, Hafeez said, "It's true the presidential palace is heavily guarded. It's impossible for anyone to get close enough to Musab to kill him, even with a powerful bomb. But with Allah, everything is possible if we are faithful and follow His commands."

He hesitated for a moment to ensure that everyone was listening intently to him and then continued. "For the past month, one of our brothers in Mogadishu has watched Villa Somalia, and Allah has revealed a weakness. He's reported the president's wife and daughter leave the palace once a week with only a few guards and drive to a café owned by the sister of the president's wife. Musab sometimes joins them at these family outings for dinner."

"Isn't he well guarded when he attends?" a fighter asked.

"He is always protected by his bodyguards, but the location of the café makes it vulnerable. A car can be crashed into the building, and with the right explosives we can kill everyone inside. Our brother in Mogadishu believes Musab will be going to the café tomorrow."

By nightfall, Hafeez and his men had refined a plan, and the next morning they left at different times and in different vehicles for Mogadishu, which they entered through different routes. When they reassembled in a warehouse near the Mogadishu port, Hafeez showed Dilawar Bahar photographs of the café. It was located in the center of a one-block-long concrete building that was two stories tall. In addition to the café, the structure housed six other shops. There were no windows on the ground level, only seven doors, one for each business. The second floor contained apartments, one above each shop, which is where the store owners lived. Each apartment had a balcony. At night, the apartment owners left the double doors of their balconies open so breezes could sweep through their units.

Spreading out a map in front of them, Hafeez explained, "The café faces east, with the street that it faces running north and south." Pointing his index finger onto the map, he said, "Here is the path that Allah has shown us."

Most of the streets that surrounded the café were crooked and appeared to have been laid out by a drunk surveyor. They looked on the map like a bowl of spaghetti. But if a motorist found his way through this maze, he would eventually reach a short east–west street. It was only about fifty meters long but it emptied directly in front of the café, giving a driver a short but straight shot at its front doorway.

"No one will know you are coming toward the café until you leave the maze," Hafeez explained. "You will accelerate and ram your car into its door."

To make certain the car bomb exploded, Hafeez had a dead man's switch installed on the front floorboard. Bahar would need to keep his foot pressed down on the switch once he began driving the car, otherwise the explosives would be detonated. This precaution would guarantee that the vehicle's deadly contents would explode even if Bahar was fatally shot by the president's bodyguards before he crashed into the café. It also would deter Bahar from aborting the mission if he lost his nerve. There would be no way for him to deactivate the switch from the driver's seat. Nails and other sharp objects would augment the explosives in the car for maximum collateral damage. They would cut a deadly swath, killing or wounding anyone in the street and café.

After Bahar had familiarized himself with the street map and photos of the café, he went with Hafeez for a test drive through the area. Hafeez wanted to be sure that this suicide bombing was a foolproof plan, unlike the London embassy bombing failure.

Satisfied, Hafeez dropped off Bahar at the warehouse, where he spent the afternoon reading the Holy Quran.

Bahar had just said his Maghrib prayer, which was offered after sundown when devout Muslims remembered Allah's presence and asked for His guidance, when he received a text message from Hafeez, who was near the café watching for the presidential party to arrive.

The president's wife and daughter had just entered the café and—praise be to Allah—President Musab was with them. Bahar said goodbye to his fellow Al-Shabaab fighters and slipped into the driver's seat of a Toyota Corolla sedan, placing his left foot on the dead man's switch, which a mechanic working under the hood activated.

When the mechanic closed the car hood and waved at him, Bahar tucked a large wad of khat into his mouth and began to chew as he started the vehicle. He was sweating as he pulled away, and by the time he entered the maze of streets that would eventually lead to his target, Bahar was covered with perspiration. He began chanting out loud, "Allah is Great, Allah is Great" as he turned onto the final leg—the east–west bound street.

The café was now directly in front of him. Four Land Rovers were parked in front of the building but the president's bodyguards were allowing pedestrians to walk unmolested along the avenue and in front of the doorway.

Bahar spotted at least a dozen men, each armed with a Russian-made AK-47, standing watch on the street outside the restaurant's front. Additional guards were stationed on the second-floor balcony, and three more were watching from the building's flat rooftop.

Bahar aimed the Toyota Corolla directly at the café's front door and jammed his right foot down on the gas pedal. Within seconds, the president's security detail noticed the racing car speeding toward them. As Bahar watched, the guards raised their automatic rifles and fired. The Corolla was instantly peppered with rounds. Its windshield became a spiderweb and then imploded. Bahar's face was torn by shards of glass. He cried in pain and felt a jolt on the side of his head.

Bahar slumped forward against the steering wheel.

CHAPTER TWELVE

National Public Radio station FM 90.0
Minneapolis, Minnesota

Thanks to the Minneapolis *Gazette*'s continuing investigation of his political rivals, long-shot congressional candidate Rudy Adeogo saw an uptick in the polls. Enough that he was invited to appear on the *Pamela Saint-James Hour*, the highest-rated talk radio show in the Minneapolis metropolitan area.

"I'm so happy you could join us," Pamela Saint-James said, the moment Adeogo entered her National Public Radio studio. She smiled cordially from behind a console of computer screens and radio dials.

Before Adeogo could respond, Saint-James raised her hand and began counting down the seconds as intro music played through the headset that he'd been handed. He quickly ducked into a seat across from her.

"Joining me now in our studio is Nuruddin Ayaanie Adeogo, better known as 'Rudy' to most of us Minnesotans," the sixty-eight-year-old Saint-James explained as her show went live. "Rudy is currently a candidate for the Fifth Congressional Seat held by Representative Clyde Buckner, but before we talk about the upcoming election and the political scandals rocking this city, let me ask you: Were you named after Nuruddin Farah?"

"Yes," he replied, somewhat surprised. "My parents were great admirers so they broke with traditions and named me after him rather than a family member."

"I'm sure most NPR listeners know that Nuruddin Farah is one of Somalia's most celebrated writers," Saint-James proudly announced.

In the next few minutes, Saint-James asked Adeogo several general questions to put him at ease and then she turned to meatier topics. "You are a Muslim, are you not? More to the point, you are a Muslim running for a public office. And while you have the solid backing of the Muslim community here in Minneapolis, you are going to need more support to be elected."

"That's very true, but I don't think my personal religious views should matter to voters. It is my political views that are important."

"One could argue that your religious views matter a great deal. Although it has been several years since the 9/11 attacks, Americans have long memories, and despite our country's successes against Al-Qaeda, we are still at war with Muslim extremists."

"Did this country condemn all of Christianity because Jim Jones's misguided followers drank poisoned Kool-Aid in Guyana? What about the self-proclaimed Waco messiah David Koresh? Unfortunately, fanatics can be found in every religion."

"As a Muslim, will you be reluctant to support our nation's efforts to hunt down and kill Islamist terrorists if you are elected to Congress?"

"No one is as angry at these radicals as are devout Muslims, because these extremists have corrupted our faith and they spew teachings of hatred and intolerance."

"Do you think Minnesota voters will elect a Muslim?"

"I certainly hope so. Historians tell us that in the 1940s Minneapolis was labeled the 'anti-Semitic capital of our nation.' Today, many Jewish leaders hold office here. This tells me that Minneapolis voters are open to all people. They understand that I will keep my personal faith and public responsibilities separate—just as our elected leaders who are Christians, Catholics, Mormons, and Jews do."

"Rudy," Saint-James said, "how do you explain the fact that it was a Somali American who was reared in Minneapolis who attempted to explode a bomb outside the U.S. Embassy in London earlier this year? Why are American Muslims going to Somalia and other Muslim countries to fight alongside these terrorists?"

Adeogo paused for a moment, as if he were pondering her question. "It's true that a handful of misguided youths in our city have chosen to participate in religious violence. I have talked to the parents of some of these troubled teens, and all of them mentioned their sons' feelings of alienation growing up in our city and, in many cases, of the prejudice against them that they felt here. These were boys who could not find decent jobs after graduating from high school and who felt they were social outcasts because of their religious beliefs. This is why we must work together and fight prejudice and discrimination."

"What kind of prejudice exists here in Minneapolis? Religious, race, ethnicity?"

"Does it matter? All prejudice is demeaning, but Somali American young people face all of the forms you just cited. Recent clashes in our high schools between teenage Somali Americans and black young people poignantly illustrate the need for us to have open and frank discussions about ways to break down and eliminate the ethnic and cultural barriers that divide us."

"You grew up here. Did you face racial prejudice?"

"Yes, of course. But I came from a supportive family and a neighborhood filled with Somali women who kept their eyes on me as if they were my mothers. These were the people who supported me, so when I heard racial slurs, I didn't pay any attention, because the people saying them didn't matter to me."

"Is that true for today's Somali Americans?"

"Sadly, those community supports are not as evident as they once were, which is why many troubled youths are turning to gangs or joining radical Islamic groups."

"You just said your family was a key part of your bedrock, but most of us don't know much about your family, and none of them is campaigning alongside you."

"My beautiful wife, Dheeh, certainly is," Adeogo replied, correcting her.

"Yes, but tell us about your parents and siblings."

"I'm very proud of my parents and my brothers and sisters, but they are not running for office, I am, and I feel obligated to protect their privacy. They support me but wish to remain in the background, living quietly, which is how I believe most Somali Americans prefer to live. We are a proud but modest and humble people who tend to avoid the public spotlight."

"Will you at least tell us how many brothers and sisters you have?"

"I have a large family, so I can count on at least a dozen votes from my relatives who live here."

"You're avoiding my question but I think it's safe to say that you can count on more votes than the ones cast by your immediate family. Let's talk about the congressional race," Saint-James said. "Everyone said you didn't have a chance of being elected."

"My grandmother used to tell me a Somali proverb: 'A baby on its mother's back does not know the way is long.' I am that baby on a journey."

"Well, your chances of winning certainly changed after the Minneapolis *Gazette* began publishing rather damning exposés about the other two candidates."

"All I know is what I read in the papers," Adeogo deadpanned.

Saint-James chuckled and said, "For any listeners who may have missed those stories, the newspaper has reported that Representative Buckner has been paying his mother-in-law eighty thousand dollars annually to work on his Washington congressional staff even though she's in her late eighties and resides in a Florida home for persons with memory loss problems. What say you about that?"

"I'm upset that Representative Buckner has not apologized nor removed his mother-in-law from his congressional payroll. I have called for him to repay her salary to the federal treasury. It's the only way he can regain public trust."

"The newspaper also dug up dirt about Republican Buddy Pollard. According to the *Gazette*, a twenty-year-old aspiring model claims Pollard seduced her when she was only seventeen years old and working for him as a summer intern. At the time, Pollard was a Minnesota state legislator. He's currently fifty-five, the father of four children, and has been married twenty-two years. Recently, photos of this woman have surfaced on the Internet showing her in various stages of undress. Pollard claims she is seeking publicity to help her modeling career. This is pretty salacious stuff—especially here in Minneapolis."

"Yes, and it's unfortunate, because it sends the wrong message to our young people about our elected state and federal officials."

"Well, it certainly hasn't been unfortunate for you. Those newspaper reports have opened a door for you to become the first Somali American in the U.S. Congress—assuming you're scandal-free."

"As you know, the Minneapolis *Gazette* also investigated my background, and the only scandal the reporter found was that I had an overdue library book."

"And the reporter acknowledged in her story that you confessed to that oversight!"

In a somber voice, Adeogo said, "Polls do show me gaining against the incumbent and my Republican opponent, but my campaign is still far behind and we have a long way to go on that journey to Washington."

"Well, I for one," Saint-James gushed, "wish you luck."

Adeogo's cell phone rang as he was exiting the studio. It was his wife, Dheeh.

"You were quite clever," she said, "especially when asked how many brothers you have."

"But?" he replied. "I know there is a 'but' coming. You always are my harshest critic."

"A wife's job is to warn her husband, and while you were avoiding that woman's question a different Somali proverb came to me: '*Runi rag kama nixiso.*' Do you remember it?"

"Yes, the truth does not make honest men squirm."

CHAPTER THIRTEEN

A former meatpacking plant
Outskirts of Mogadishu, Somalia

The terrorist Dilawar Bahar opened his eyes. It was difficult because they were encrusted by dried blood that had sealed his black lashes to his skin while he'd been unconscious. Bahar fought an immediate sense of panic. He was alone in what appeared to be a room where animals once had been slaughtered. Meat hooks dangled from the ceiling. A drain ringed with bloodstains was at his feet. He was strapped with gray duct tape to a wooden chair bolted to the concrete floor. The walls of the room were lined with stainless steel, and the light came from an ancient fluorescent tube that buzzed slightly above him. No one would hear him if he hollered. The fact that he was alive meant that something had gone terribly wrong with the simple plan that Abdul Hafeez had choreographed. The Toyota sedan filled with explosives that Bahar had driven into a Mogadishu café in an attempt to assassinate Somali president Musab obviously had not exploded.

Bahar heard the sound of rusty door hinges. Two men walked from behind him into his view. One was dressed in a laundered blue shirt, tailored dark trousers, and a black beret with the emblem of the Somali Police Force sewn onto it. The other was wearing a threadbare khaki shirt, short pants, and no beret.

The man in the better uniform said, "As you can see, I am not a young virgin welcoming you to paradise."

His companion laughed.

"You were not afraid of dying," the man continued. "At least by your own hand. But you are in my hands now and, if I choose, I can make certain that your dying does not come quickly nor without tremendous pain."

Bahar stared straight ahead, ignoring him.

"Would you like to know why your plan to kill our president failed?"

Bahar remained mute.

"When a bullet struck your head, you passed out and your body froze in position. Your foot did not come off the dead man's switch mounted on the car's floor. My men disabled it. You failed to kill yourself and explode a car bomb that would have murdered our president and killed dozens of others, including women and children."

Without warning, the man in the threadbare shirt and shorts slugged Bahar in his abdomen, causing him to gasp in pain.

His inquisitor said, "You are Al-Qaeda. Your name is Dilawar Bahar and you are Saudi. I know the names of your father and your mother. I know the names of your brothers and sisters. The only reason why you are still alive is because an American has intervened. He wants you to answer some questions for him. Perhaps if you answer them, this American will arrange for you to go to Guantanamo Bay. Otherwise you will be executed tomorrow for attempting to kill our president."

Bahar eyeballed his tormentor for the first time. He was stocky, not thin like so many of his gaunt Somali countrymen. The splotches of white that dotted his carefully groomed black beard and moustache suggested he was in his late fifties. His demeanor suggested he was a man comfortable with inflicting pain. Continuing, the inquisitor said, "I have heard stories about Al-Qaeda training, so I know that you have been told that if you are taken prisoner, you can refuse to speak to anyone. Because of Abu Ghraib and the criticism that the American CIA received for its interrogation techniques after 9/11, the Americans now cannot physically harm you. You have been told the Americans and their allies will give you a copy of the Holy Book if you request one. They will feed you three times a day and allow you to say your daily prayers. You have been told that the African Union troops sent to Somalia by the United Nations as peacekeepers will not physically abuse you. They will abide by the Geneva Convention and international agreements that prohibit torture, even of terrorists. You have been told that if you demand it, they will give you soft toilet paper to wipe your ass."

The man turned his head, and for the first time, Bahar noticed that the man's left ear was missing. Everyone had heard stories about General Abdullah Osman Saeed, the Somali general and police commander with only one ear. Everyone had heard of his sadism and cruelty.

"Ah," General Saeed said. "From your scared look, you have recognized me and you have just realized that I don't care about international treaties or what you wipe your ass with."

Once again, the officer assisting Saeed slugged Bahar, this time in his jaw, nearly knocking him unconscious.

Bahar coughed and began spitting to keep himself from choking on the blood pooling inside his mouth.

"Allah is my strength," he uttered.

The officer struck him again.

"You expected a beating," Saeed said in a calm voice.

The officer struck Bahar in his abdomen.

"Let me assure you, a beating is nothing compared to what is about to happen."

Bahar repeated, "Allah is my strength. Allah is my strength."

"Do you remember the infamous Khalid Sheikh Mohammed?" Saeed asked. "Of course you do. He told the Americans everything, and he was stronger than you. It wasn't the one hundred and eighty-three times that he was waterboarded, as most people think. He talked after being kept awake for seven days straight."

Saeed laughed at the absurdity of it, saying, "He survived having water poured over his face through a towel, knowing it would stop after ten attempts and he'd be allowed to rest. But when they refused to allow him to sleep, when they forced him to stand and squat and stand and squat to keep him awake hour after hour, day after day, after seven days he broke. Seven days. A week. Such a simple thing. Do you think you are stronger than Khalid?"

"Piss on you," Bahar hissed.

In an incredulous voice, Saeed repeated, "Piss on me?" Unzipping his trousers, Saeed sprayed his urine on Bahar, who struggled in the chair. "I decide who gets pissed on here."

Zipping up his pants, he said, "The Americans have decided that torture doesn't work. They have declared that you must befriend your enemy if you wish for them to tell their secrets. But this has not been my experience and it will not be yours."

He paused to allow Bahar to think about what he'd just heard.

Continuing, Saeed said, "It is easy to torture another human being. I have become a student of torture. Amputation. We could begin with your toes. Cut, cut, cut. There is a surgeon under my command who can remove every limb, even your manhood, without killing you. What will you do, Dilawar Bahar, when I dump you on the street with no eyes, no legs, no arms, no tongue, and no penis? Your Al-Qaeda comrades will think, 'No man could endure such torture without talking.' They will call you a traitor and you will pray for your own death."

Saeed's subordinate grabbed Bahar's skull with both hands and pressed his thumbs against his eyeballs. Bahar began screaming.

"Enough," Saeed said. He leaned closer to Bahar and whispered, "Have you not noticed? I've not asked you a single question. This is because I am simply enjoying this experience."

Saeed stepped back from Bahar and said, "It is a paradox. Assuming you understand the meaning of that word. Americans don't permit torture, yet in their movies they glorify it. They even have a movie genre named for it: Western torture porn. In their films, they imagine the most horrible acts. Lighting someone's genitals on fire, jolts of electricity, filleting their skin, hammering nails into a head. Their films are filled with such nightmares. Here in this room, nothing is imaginary."

"Allah is my strength," Bahar declared.

Saeed's assistant grabbed Bahar's hair and for a moment it appeared that he was going to gouge Bahar's eyes again. Instead, he spit in Bahar's face and laughed at him.

"Do you know I once crushed crackers into tiny pieces and placed them inside a plastic bag that I put over a prisoner's head—a man who was sitting right where you are now sitting?" Saeed said. "He had no choice but to breathe, and after he did, I removed the bag. With each breath, those bits of crackers cut into his lungs' lining, inflicting incredible pain. He was coughing up blood for hours. That was genius on my part. I was so pleased I considered writing a letter to those Hollywood filmmakers telling them what I'd invented."

Despite his bravado, Bahar wet himself.

Saeed noticed and said, "This will do for now."

His underling released his grip on Bahar's hair, and General Saeed patted Bahar's head as if he were a dog.

"When I return, we will explore some new creative ideas that I have—something that will truly impress Hollywood. Or perhaps we will see how a pious man such as you reacts when he is abused like a woman. Rape. Can you imagine being violated, not by one man but dozens? Picture a long line of them standing outside this room, each using you as his whore."

Bahar said, "What kind of creature are you?"

"What kind of creature am I?" Saeed asked rhetorically. "You tried to murder our president and maim dozens of my countrymen. What kind of creature are you?" Speaking to his aide, Saeed said, "I will need a sharp knife when I return."

Saeed exited but walked only a few steps across a hallway outside the torture chamber. He entered another room, where Gunter Conner was sitting on a metal folding chair, smoking a cigarette.

"Has he told you anything?" Conner asked.

"I haven't asked him any questions yet," Saeed replied.

"What the hell have you been doing all this time?"

"Getting to know one another."

"I don't need his life story."

"Tell me, Mr. Conner. Have you ever interrogated a prisoner?"

"Not like you're doing."

"Yes, I can see you, sitting across the table from this man in America, offering him and his lawyers tea and tiny finger sandwiches."

"Just find out what Bahar knows about the Somali American who led the Dera Ismail Khan prison break. I believe his first name was Abdul."

Saeed chuckled. "Do you know how many Abduls there are in the Arab world?"

"Bahar was one of the prisoners who was freed during that prison break. He has to know something about its leader. A last name. A description. I want to know how Bahar got to Somalia. When did he get here? And most important of all, find out if he knows anything about

Al-Shabaab's chain of command. Is this Abdul calling the shots or is there someone higher up, as I suspect, pulling Abdul's strings? Find out if Bahar knows about London and the Somali American Askar al-Seema. Find out if they were linked."

"So, so many questions," General Saeed said dismissively.

"I'll make certain it's worth your time to get me answers."

"Yes, you will. But let me ask you a question, Mr. Conner. You said that Askar al-Seema was captured in London. Haven't your people already interrogated him?"

"They tried, but he's an American and he's in London. He has certain rights and he doesn't want to talk."

"Which is why he has told you nothing. Shall I assume this is one reason why you have asked me to keep the attempt on President Musab's life and Bahar's capture a secret from your own government?"

"If my government were to learn about Bahar, it would pressure your government to hand him over and yes, I'd rather that doesn't happen. At least, not at this moment. I'd rather you take this opportunity to question him and get the answers I need."

"So you are deceiving your own CIA, your own people."

"The answers I need will lead to a greater good. I'm doing what I need to do to prevent more attacks and murders."

"Yes, of course, that is what every American says when they wish to justify my special interrogation skills. But tell me, is there another reason why you have asked me to keep this man's assassination attempt on President Musab and his capture secret?"

"You already know the answer," Conner grumbled. "The delegation from the State Department arrives tomorrow. What do you think the State Department delegation will report back if its members are told an Al-Shabaab suicide bomber came close to blowing up your president and failed only because his foot didn't fall off a dead man's switch?"

Conner paused to take a final draw on his cigarette before dropping it onto the concrete floor and using his shoe to crush it. "General Saeed," he continued, "you and I both want our countries to open an embassy here. It serves my aims and also serves yours. If you want access to U.S. military aid, then you will handle this entire matter discreetly for me."

Saeed said, "I am happy to keep your secrets and also interrogate this man. You should join me in the other room. You can't fully appreciate life unless you are responsible for causing a death. Sending a drone to kill a man or even pulling a trigger—what do you feel afterwards? It's impersonal. But with a knife, you feel it in your fingers, slicing through the skin and muscles, hitting the soft tissue of an organ or striking a hard bone. You see the response, the pain in the eyes. It is how a life should be taken. It is respectful."

"Just get my questions answered."

"And afterwards?"

"He's your prisoner. I don't want to know. I don't ever want to hear another word about him. It would be best if he simply disappeared after you torture him."

Saeed returned to the chamber where Bahar was being held. His subordinate was waiting for him with a stainless steel paring knife. Before Saeed took the blade, he slipped a thin Sony digital recorder from his shirt pocket, hit the rewind button, and then hit play.

Conner's voice could be heard clearly. *"I don't want to know. I don't ever want to hear another word about him. It would be best if he simply disappeared after you torture him."*

Saeed hit the record button on the device. He wanted to have a record of Bahar's screams immediately after Conner's orders.

General Saeed had learned from his past encounters with Westerners that it was useful, as Americans liked to say, to have an "ace in the hole."

CHAPTER FOURTEEN

Mid- to late July
Aden Adde International Airport
Mogadishu, Somalia

Gunter Conner popped a Xanax while waiting on the airport tarmac and watched a Gulfstream G550 executive jet make its final approach. The numbers on the aircraft's tail identified it as being owned by a management company based in Reno, Nevada, but that was a CIA front.

Four armed men in black jumpsuits and body armor were the first to step from the plane's belly into the noonday heat, their eyes concealed behind sunglasses, each wearing a flesh-colored earpiece and carrying a Heckler & Koch MP7 submachine gun with a suppressor. Once they were stationed at strategic points around the aircraft, its passengers began to disembark. The State Department's Robert Gumman was the first, followed by retired general John Duggard, who had just been named ProTech's director of African affairs. The last was Charles "Cash" Kelley, a retired Navy SEAL and Afghanistan combat veteran employed by ProTech. If the White House decided to reopen an embassy in Somalia, Cash Kelley would be the private contractor in charge of security. All three were wearing bullet-resistant vests. Conner welcomed them in khaki pants, a flowered Tommy Bahama short-sleeved shirt decorated with blue and yellow flowers, and an L.L. Bean "Bugsaway" floppy hat that had been treated with odorless insect repellant that supposedly stayed good for up to seventy washings.

"Doesn't the CIA have a dress code?" Gumman grunted after everyone was introduced.

"I'm sure it does," Conner replied, "but if an Al-Shabaab sniper is trying to decide who to shoot right now, it's not going to be the man dressed like a tourist."

Gumman nervously scanned the tarmac.

Nodding at a battered Toyota truck parked nearby with six armed Somalis sitting in its bed, Kelley asked, "Who are those guys?"

"My bodyguards," Conner replied.

Frowning, Kelley said, "Make sure they stay away from our security team. I don't want a bunch of amateurs getting in our way."

"Did I mention my guys are probably high on khat?" Conner added, enjoying the disgusted look that appeared on Kelley's face.

Conner waved to his ragtag Somali entourage to follow as he and the others boarded two black SUVs.

"Why aren't we staying at your facility?" Duggard asked, a reference to a walled residential and training compound that the CIA operated inside the airport's grounds. The agency first opened it after helping drive Al-Shabaab from the city and installing Somalia's pro-Western regime. The airport was the most secure facility in all of Somalia, even more heavily fortified than the presidential palace.

"We can't very well report that Mogadishu is safe," Conner replied, "if you're hiding inside the agency's compound. I've booked you a room at the Serenity Hotel just outside the airport."

"The 'best hotel in hell,'" Duggard said.

The retired general had done his homework. "The best hotel in hell" was how U.S. magazines frequently described the Serenity. It was the only hotel in the world where the nightly room rate included your own team of AK-47-wielding bodyguards.

Ten minutes after leaving the airport, the convoy reached a twelve-foot-high wall topped with broken glass that glittered like a rainbow in the African sun. Two armed hotel guards opened solid steel gates, allowing the SUVs to enter the courtyard, but the truck carrying Conner's bodyguards was diverted to park outside along the badly rutted street.

The three-story Serenity Hotel had fewer bullet holes than its neighbors. Its owner and his wife, as well as their four personal bodyguards, were waiting to greet the Americans. Conner stayed in the red-tiled lobby where the ceiling fans turned lazily while his guests checked their rooms.

"What's the chance there's a bar here?" Cash Kelley asked when he and Gumman reappeared.

"Count me in," Gumman said.

"You're in an Islamic country," Conner replied. "No booze, even in hotels catering to Westerners."

"How about whores?" Kelley asked.

"Death by stoning tends to keep thighs shut tight."

Gumman said, "Don't the Brits have an embassy here? Maybe they'll have some booze hidden away and some females eager for male company."

"Their so-called embassy," Conner replied, "consists of six shipping containers jerry-rigged as offices. The British ambassador and white English staff actually live in Kenya. Local Somalis here do the grunt work—visas, passports, et cetera. Whites tend to stand out, and no one wants to risk kidnapping."

"I'm going to demand triple hardship pay," Gumman quipped, "especially if we can't even get a drink."

"Since we're waiting for the general, it might be helpful," Conner said, "if I told you both a bit of Somali history."

"Knock yourself out," Kelley said, falling into a wicker lobby chair, "but all I need to know is who to shoot and who not to shoot."

"The Brits, Italians, and French all staked claims on this area," Conner said, "and in the 1800s, they divided Somalia into different sections. The Brits claimed the north and called it Somaliland. It's still the richest area. The Italians took the south and the French scooped up the coastline. The rest was mostly worthless desert and no one cared what happened. Everyone was happy; at least the Brits, Italians, and French were, until a local tribesman, who the Brits nicknamed the 'Mad Mullah,' returned from visiting Mecca one day with a vision—kicking the white devils out of his country. He raised an army called the Dervishes, and went to war."

"Let me speed this up," Kelley said, interrupting. "As soon as the Africans drove the white devils into the ocean, they began fighting each other and everything went to hell."

DUPLICITY

Conner shook his head and said, "Somalia actually did pretty well
by itself until the Cold War got hot. In 1969, the president's own bodyguards killed him, and a military coup d'état led to the reign of Major
General Mohamed Siad Barre. He got cozy with the Russians until they
betrayed him and began siding with Somalia's longtime enemy, Ethiopia,
at which point Barre turned to the U.S. and began a dangerous game of
playing the Russians and U.S. against one another. He was pretty good
at it until the Cold War ended and both sides lost interest in Somalia."

Kelley yawned and Gumman's eyelids were drooping, but Conner
continued his history lesson. "Barre was finally driven from office during
a bloody civil war that led to the country being carved up by warlords.
People were starving and the country was collapsing because of ongoing
fighting—so the United Nations sent in peacekeepers, including U.S.
troops who tried to arrest one warlord and ended up getting defeated in
what became known as the Black Hawk Down battle."

"Now that's something I remember," Kelley said. "Those bastards
dragged our boys' bodies through the streets."

"After that stinging defeat, we pulled out and gladly forgot about
Somalia for two decades until Al-Shabaab and the Islamic Courts seized
control of Mogadishu. Since then we have been working through inter-
mediaries to install a democratic government."

"By 'we' you mean the CIA," Gumman said.

"Enough history," Kelley snapped. "Let's cut to the chase. How stable
is Mogadishu?"

"As stable as quicksand," Conner replied. "Al-Shabaab terrorists still
control most of the cities outside the capital. Before they were driven out
of Mogadishu, anyone on the streets after five p.m. was shot and any
woman seen without a male escort risked being raped in public. Now
that the African Union troops and President Musab are in power, things
have improved. There's a six-p.m. curfew."

"What about women seen on the streets without a man?" Gumman
asked.

"Still not safe," Conner replied. "Oh, there's something else you need
to know.

"Most young men are unemployed and high on khat by noon, and eighty percent of Somali men own a firearm. An AK-47 costs about thirty dollars U.S. in the Bakaara market."

"So if it's still unstable, why are we opening an embassy here?" Kelley asked.

Gumman exchanged a knowing glace with Conner. "Because the White House wants us here," Gumman said.

John Duggard joined them in the lobby. "The rooms are more comfortable than I thought," he declared. "Now let's get down to business. When do we meet General Abdullah Saeed? Based on all of the intelligence reports that I've read, he's really running things around here."

"Tomorrow," Conner replied.

"General who?" Kelley asked. "I've not been briefed about any general, and your little history review skipped over him."

"The general is a rather unique man. He joined the Somali army at sixteen," Conner said, "and rose quickly as a leader. But he got into trouble for being a bit too bloodthirsty during one of his country's many wars with Ethiopia."

"How does one get a reputation for being too bloodthirsty in this godforsaken hole?" Kelley asked.

"What'd he do?" Gumman added. "Kill a few civilians?"

"Whole villages, including women and children. We're talking babies. And he did it all in public. Burning people in old tires. Awful stuff. In an interview with a French magazine, Saeed said women could fire guns and kids would grow up and become fighters."

"He had a point," Kelley said.

"The government actually put him in prison for his actions but he broke out, escaped into the desert, raised an army loyal only to him, and seized a section of land for himself. He was a warlord, but what set him apart from the others was he was smarter. He actually paid Western scholars to come tutor him and, as unbelievable as it sounds, he became fascinated with the Internet and began taking correspondence courses. He actually is a very well educated man."

"An Internet genius who likes to butcher women and children," Gumman remarked.

"When the radical jihadists seized the capital, everyone in the West panicked, so our intelligence services recruited General Saeed and he helped drive Al-Shabaab out of the city."

"Recruited?"

"Paid him millions under the table," Conner replied.

"So if he's so powerful and in charge, why isn't he president or a self-proclaimed dictator?" Kelley asked.

"Because the African Union and the U.S. government don't want him to be president," Conner replied. "And he's smart enough to know that he doesn't have the firepower or the political allies to take on the African Union or us. At least not yet."

"Sounds like a disaster waiting to happen," Gumman replied.

"Saeed is sort of like keeping a cobra as a pet," Conner said. "But so far, he's kept this city under control and Al-Shabaab from returning."

"When did he lose his ear?" Duggard asked. "Unlike Mr. Gumman and Mr. Kelley, I actually read intelligence reports before coming here and they said he lost one ear but failed to say how."

"No one seems to know, or if they do, they don't want to risk making him angry by talking about it," Conner replied.

Gumman said, "None of this really matters—does it? We all know our fact-finding trip is a ruse. I'm going to send back a favorable State Department report before August first and, I suspect, you already have."

"I have filed my assessment and yes, I believe it's safe to open an embassy here." Looking at Duggard, Conner added, "The White House is not the only one who wants a base of operations in Mogadishu, is it? Congratulations on being named ProTech's new head of African affairs."

"It's no secret that Africa is emerging as the next global hotspot," Duggard acknowledged.

"Which means there's money to be made here," Conner replied.

"Let's not get sanctimonious," Duggard said, with a flash of anger in his voice. "The president has her reasons for opening an embassy here, ProTech has its reasons for wanting this to happen, and I assume that the CIA and even you, Mr. Conner, have a reason for wanting that to happen."

"Enough chatter," Kelley said. "What's our dinner plan? I need to feed my men and tell them there's no booze or women in this emerging global hotspot."

"I've arranged for us to have dinner at the Lido Seafood Restaurant," Conner replied, "which looks out on its own private section of beach and has the best security guards in the city."

"You've selected a restaurant not by its menu," Gumman said, "but the quality of its security?"

"You can't enjoy an entrée if you're shot eating appetizers."

"What about my men?" Kelley said. "When I eat, they eat."

"The restaurant is expecting them too," Conner said. "Not a lot of people go out to eat at night around here."

"What about your Somali bodyguards?" Kelley asked. "I'm not keen on them eating with us."

"Don't worry. Mine are happy sitting outside chewing khat."

CHAPTER FIFTEEN

August 3
Commonwealth Auditorium
College of William and Mary
Williamsburg, Virginia

President Allworth strolled confidently across the red-carpeted stage and extended her hand to former Florida governor Timothy Coldridge. In the three weeks since he'd issued his July 9 debate challenge, aides for both sides had met repeatedly to work out tonight's logistics, arguing about such seemingly inconsqential matters as whether the two podiums onstage would be made of glass or wood, and if wood, what shade: light or dark.

"Good evening, Madam President," Coldridge said, as photographers and television cameras chronicled their pre-debate greeting.

"Good evening, Governor."

Just as they were about to move to their respective podiums, Coldridge whispered—but loud enough for his lapel microphone to pick up—"May the best man win." He broke into a smug grin.

"Don't worry," the president coolly replied. "She will."

A body language guru hired by the president's campaign staff had advised Allworth to avoid making eye contact with Coldridge once the debate began and had warned her against nodding, which might make it appear that she was agreeing with Coldridge and that he was in charge. The president could gesture dismissively toward him. Otherwise, she was to keep her hands apart, subtly letting viewers know that she had no need to protect her chest—it had to do with mutual trust, the body expert had explained. A stylist had put Allworth in the highest possible heels she could wear without attracting undue attention, to make it appear that she was nearly as tall as her challenger. The heels also showed off her toned legs, which were one of her physical assets.

The president's campaign staff had staged three mock debates to ready her for tonight's showdown. A staff member had played the role of moderator, constantly interrupting and badgering her. The actual debate moderator was CNN's international affairs correspondent Bridget Spencer, a no-nonsense veteran reporter who'd interviewed dozens of foreign heads of state and spent time in Iraq, Afghanistan, Iran, and the Palestinian territories. She'd also reported from Somalia, which had given the president pre-debate jitters.

"Spencer knows Somalia," Allworth had complained.

"But your opponent won't," Chief of Staff Harper had assured her, "and he's who you're running against."

Harper had also reminded the president that 90 percent of what was said during a debate was political rhetoric taken from campaign speeches and position papers. Content was not nearly as important as image and what the media told voters afterward. Viewers often picked one candidate as a debate's winner but changed their minds if the television pundits declared the other as the victor. An unexpected question from the moderator or a misstatement could prove disastrous—not because the actual content of a debate mattered, but because of how the media would exploit that flub later.

"I can't afford a Dukakis moment," Allworth said, a reference to 1988 when moderator Bernard Shaw had asked Michael Dukakis: "Governor, if Kitty Dukakis were raped and murdered, would you favor an irrevocable death penalty for the killer?" The candidate had hesitated and then, without the slightest show of emotion, replied, "No." His answer was all the media had talked about for weeks. Dukakis had come across as impersonal, cold, uncaring, and had spent the rest of the campaign trying to break free of his frostbite image. That was before today's twenty-four-hour news cycle and Internet parodies that could get millions of hits within minutes and were nearly impossible to counter.

The 10 percent of the debate that neither side could control was when mistakes were made. Gerald Ford's misstep in 1976 when he said there was "no Soviet dominance of Eastern Europe." George Bush glancing impatiently at his watch in 1992 as if he was bored.

While those blunders had proven problematic, a quick-thinking candidate could gain an edge during an unscripted moment. Lloyd Bentsen's knockout admonition that Dan Quayle was "no Jack Kennedy." When primary candidate Ronald Reagan was being cut off by the moderator in 1980, he snapped, "I am paying for this microphone"—a reference to how his campaign had helped foot the bill for the Republican televised debates. Americans loved how Reagan had put that reporter in his place.

At tonight's debate, Allworth wanted to have a Reagan moment, or at least for Coldridge to have a Dukakis moment. That is where Somalia came in. Too late to back out now.

Once the president and Coldridge had taken their respective positions, CNN moderator Spencer welcomed the 463 individuals in the audience, warned them to save their applause until the final moments of the debate, and began. "Madam President, you have won a coin toss, so you will have two minutes to answer my first question. The governor will then answer that same question."

The next hour and a half held no surprises. Each answered Spencer's predictable questions with sound bites they'd perfected for the campaign trail. Mallory Harper had suggested that the president wait until the final ten minutes to drop her Somalia bombshell. Harper wanted to limit the amount of time Moderator Spencer could ask specifics and Coldridge could take to formulate a clever response.

Twenty minutes before the debate was due to end, the president discovered that she wasn't the only candidate who had a bushwhack planned.

"My opponent's campaign has accused me of being sexist," Coldridge declared, looking directly into the camera. "Yet, as governor, I have appointed a higher percentage of women to top jobs as governor than my opponent has as president."

Moderator Spencer took the bait. "Madam President, isn't it hypocritical to accuse your opponent of sexism if you have appointed fewer women to your cabinet than the governor has in his Florida administration?"

Allworth felt the anger rising in her. Spencer had blindly assumed

Coldridge was telling the truth. By repeating it, she had put the president on the defensive, making it appear as if Allworth had done something wrong.

Coldridge had caught the president cold. Neither she nor her campaign staff had anticipated this attack, and she had no idea how to respond. She couldn't question his numbers because the media would rally around him if he actually had appointed more women.

Think, think.

The image of Michael Dukakis hesitating decades ago swept into her thoughts. She had to say something and she had to say it now or she'd look befuddled.

"I'm pleased the governor has so many women advising him," Allworth said, "because if his answers tonight during our debate on foreign policy are any indication of what kind of president he would be, he certainly will need someone to tell him what to do."

The audience burst into laughter and Allworth relaxed. But Spencer wasn't about to let her off the hook. "Madam President, the American public deserves a straight answer. How can you call your opponent sexist if he's appointed a higher percentage of women to his cabinet than you have to your administration?"

Coldridge chirped, "I have the actual numbers with me." He held up a spreadsheet.

All eyes were on the president. "Unlike the governor," she said, "I haven't prepared a spreadsheet, but we know numbers can be manipulated and I question that any governor could appoint more women than a sitting president who is responsible for appointing not only cabinet members but federal judges, ambassadors, and dozens of others to key federal positions."

Coldridge started to respond but was cut short by Moderator Spencer.

"Madam President, he's talking percentages here, not individual appointments. I don't think you have answered his question. Do you not know what percentage of women you have appointed?"

"I don't have an exact figure on the tip of my tongue."

The president hesitated, and for a moment it appeared that Allworth was floundering.

But she had intentionally paused so she could emphasize her next comment. "The reason why I don't know a percentage is because, as president, I didn't make those appointments based on a person's sex. I made them based on the caliber, abilities, character, and talents of each person I appointed. I chose women—and men—I knew would be the best for the job, because that is what Americans expect and what the American people deserve."

It was a solid answer, but Moderator Spencer still wasn't letting go. "What if there were a man and woman and both were equally qualified—would you give the woman preferential treatment?"

Moments earlier, the image of a failed Dukakis had flashed through Allworth's brain. Now an irked Reagan appeared.

"I didn't realize I was debating you, Ms. Spencer," Allworth said sternly while feigning a smile. "But I can tell you this. Every woman I have appointed would be deeply offended if she suspected the reason why I selected her was because of her gender. Just as I am certain, Ms. Spencer, you would be offended if I suggested that the only reason why you have your job is because of your gender."

Ignoring her campaign staff's instructions, Allworth turned, looked Coldridge in the eye, and raised a finger to lecture him. "I am certain the women whom the governor appointed would also be offended if they believed for one second that he was simply pandering to them and other women by appointing some predetermined percentage of females to office, instead of recognizing them as the best qualified for their jobs."

Coldridge fired back. "You're dodging my question. I have appointed more women than you have; yet you accuse me of being sexist. The truth is, I've always been good friends with women."

"Governor, that's commendable," Allworth replied, once again violating her campaign staff's instructions by agreeing with her opponent. "But I *am* a woman. And I have encountered plenty of sexism during my career from elected officials who claimed to be good friends with women. Actions do speak louder than words and, as governor, you cut programs that helped pregnant women get prenatal care. You cut programs that would have increased time for maternity leave and made day care more affordable. You fought against equal pay for women."

Sensing she was losing control of the debate, Moderator Spencer interrupted. "Let's return to our discussion about tonight's topic: foreign affairs."

Allworth felt she had defended herself well but she was worried the media would focus on Coldridge's charge. If that happened, she would be perceived as losing the debate. Another thought frightened her. She had been unprepared for Coldridge's attack. What if he already knew about her Somali announcement? What if someone at the State Department or CIA had tipped him off? What if her trap for him was actually going to turn into an ambush for her?

She was only half-listening when Spencer asked her next question. If she was going to reveal her Somali plan, now was the moment. Allworth expertly spun Spencer's question into an excuse to mention Islamic terrorism.

"Our great nation will always be at risk," she said, "as long as radical Islamist terrorists exist. My administration has defeated Al-Qaeda. That's a huge achievement, but we are not done. New threats have arisen. ISIS, Boko Haram, the Taliban. This is why I've decided to go after terrorists wherever they are becoming strong, and this includes Africa."

Allworth quickly explained how Africa was becoming a hotbed for extremists. If the United States didn't act now, our nation could suffer another 9/11 or attack. "Tonight, I will be authorizing our military to begin sharing its expertise and our intelligence resources with our African neighbors to help their governments destroy those who intend to attack and harm us." Raising her voice to give her final words more punch, she said, "I will also take the bold step of instructing the State Department to reopen our embassy in Somalia. This will enable us to directly advise and support that war-torn nation as it continues to fight Islamic extremists. My actions are intended to send a clear message to the terrorists. We will take this fight wherever it leads us. You are not safe but we will be. We are coming for you. We will not stop. We will not be satisfied until you are dead and every terrorist organization that seeks to harm the United States is decimated."

For a second, it appeared that Spencer had forgotten she was running a debate. Her CNN news reporter instincts kicked in. "Madam

President, what exactly do you mean when you say you're going to open an embassy in Somalia? Will it be fully staffed? Will an ambassador be based there?"

"I will be spelling out details tomorrow at a media briefing," Allworth replied.

Unsatisfied, Spencer said, "I've been to Somalia many times. It is a country that has been at war with itself for decades. It is commonly called the most dangerous country on the entire planet. Is it really prudent for you to be opening an embassy there—putting U.S. personnel at risk?"

Challenger Coldridge couldn't stand being overlooked. "Ms. Spencer," he complained, "I'd like to respond to the president's announcement. This is a debate between us."

President Allworth held her breath. Had he been tipped off?

"Yes, of course, Governor Coldridge," Spencer said.

"First, I want to say that I deeply resent the president trying to turn this debate into a press conference. This was not the appropriate place for her to announce a major foreign policy decision."

Sounding increasingly irritated, he continued, "This president should have consulted members of Congress before making such a rash announcement during a debate."

Allworth relaxed. Coldridge was clearly grasping. It was Politics 101. If you don't know the facts, attack the process or attack your opponent. Start throwing mud. Some might stick.

Moderator Spencer said, "Excuse me, Governor, but the president doesn't have to consult Congress about reestablishing diplomatic ties or the opening of an embassy. That's a president's constitutional right. And it seems appropriate to bring up Somalia during a debate about foreign policy."

"Well, that's your opinion," Coldridge said, "but if I were president, I certainly would not do something so risky without first talking to Congress. I mean—you just pointed out yourself how unsafe it is there. She should have consulted with Congress regardless of what the Constitution says."

President Allworth went for his jugular. "A president is elected to lead, not run to Congress each time a decision has to be made, and I for one believe that what the Constitution says about the division of powers is not something a president should ignore."

Recognizing he was losing ground, Coldridge said, "I don't see how opening an embassy in a third-world country that's unstable is going to accomplish anything. This is a publicity stunt."

"Fighting terrorism is no stunt," Allworth retorted. "If you're serious about protecting our nation, and I am, then you don't hide on the sidelines or run to Congress. Presidents are elected to act."

"But what you're suggesting is not worth the risk," Coldridge replied.

"Not going after terrorists will simply increase the risks. Since when has America run away?" Allworth replied. "The United Kingdom restored diplomatic contact with Somalia and opened an embassy there years ago. If the Brits can do it, I certainly believe the greatest nation on our planet can too."

"The Brits can open an embassy anywhere they want," Coldridge stammered. "I'm worried about American lives, and I don't see any justification for opening an embassy in Nairobi."

Spencer interrupted. "Governor, don't you mean Mogadishu? Nairobi is the capital of Kenya. Somalia is part of the African Horn."

A surprised look appeared on Coldridge's face. "Yes, you're correct, I meant Mogadishu, but it doesn't really matter. Our president shouldn't be getting us involved in a potential conflict in the Dark Continent without first consulting Congress."

The moment Coldridge uttered the words "Dark Continent," Allworth knew she had a knockout. The media might forgive him for mistakenly thinking Nairobi was the capital of Somalia, but he was sure to be chastised for using such an antiquated and pejorative term.

Coldridge had just had a Dukakis moment.

Time had run out, and when the president shook Coldridge's hand for the after-debate photos, she gleefully whispered in his ear, "Got ya, you bastard."

Mallory Harper was frantically checking websites on her iPad when the president exited the stage.

"Coldridge is toast," she reported. "Everyone has zeroed in on his Dark Continent blunder."

Within minutes, Coldridge's campaign was attempting to minimize the damage. They arranged for an African American university English professor to defend Coldridge. "That phrase has nothing at all to do with race," he declared on the Internet and on television post-debate news shows. "It was coined by explorer Henry Morton Stanley in his 1878 book, *Through the Dark Continent*. Stanley was referring to how Africa was largely unknown and mysterious to Europeans."

But Allworth's campaign dispatched its own team of experts. A Columbia University linguist acknowledged the term was not initially racist but argued that it had become so over time. "A speaker, especially someone who is seeking the presidency, should consider the impact of words before he utters them. Coldridge's use of that term causes me to question his sensitivity to minorities."

Only National Public Radio focused on President Allworth's decision to open an embassy in Somalia, and all of the Islamic and Middle Eastern experts whom NPR invited as guests agreed the White House was taking a long-overdue step.

Twenty-four hours after the debate, Mallory Harper opened a bottle of Dom Pérignon in the Oval Office and raised her glass in salute to the president.

"You've sent Coldridge's campaign into a tailspin," she happily declared.

CHAPTER SIXTEEN

August 4
U.S. Capitol
Washington, D.C.

CIA Director Payton Grainger had been awakened by an early-morning phone call from White House Chief of Staff Mallory Harper informing him that Representative Thomas Stanton was demanding an immediate private briefing about Somalia.

Grainger hated being called to the Capitol, and it wasn't because of the "smell of the tourists," as an ex-senator had once complained about the vacationers who flocked to the magnificent building to witness democracy at work.

Grainger hated being summoned because it meant he was on *their* turf—Congress's—not his. And the fact that it was necessary to go on their turf probably meant he was going there to apologize for something.

As a citizen and patriot, Grainger held the appropriate and expected reverence for the genius of the founding fathers and, if asked, he would have acknowledged the necessary and vital role that congressional oversight played in ensuring the legitimacy of the republic. But as a creature of the executive branch, tasked with the responsibility of keeping America safe from foreign threats, he chafed at the fact that he had to answer both to the president—the woman who received a mandate from the American people to be commander in chief and who had appointed him to serve—and to Congress, the churlish schoolmarm who looked over his shoulder criticizing everything that he did, threatening to withhold funding for vital intelligence programs unless she got her way.

Grainger also didn't fully trust everyone who served on the much-coveted House and Senate intelligence committees. Despite their oaths, they were politicians, and Grainger bore a natural suspicion of their motives, even when it came to a vital issue such as national defense.

By training, Grainger was a lawyer. Harvard Law. But he'd never set foot inside a courtroom. He'd become a lawyer because Washington was a city swimming in them and he discovered early on that lawyers preferred to talk to other lawyers and arrogantly dismissed those who weren't. Grainger had enlisted in the Navy after graduating magna cum laude from Penn State, and it had paid for his legal degree and management schooling. He'd spent most of his career as a military advisor to Mideast peace talks and handling high-profile internal Pentagon investigations before leaving to join a prominent New York law firm. He'd returned to Washington as under secretary of the Navy and been tapped three years ago by President Allworth as CIA director.

She trusted him.

Grainger was now en route to one of Washington's most secure offices, which ironically was hidden in plain sight—just a few hundred yards from the east front of the U.S. Capitol in the basement of the Visitor Center. Each day, thousands of tourists and school groups passed by an unmarked curved staircase in the welcome center without realizing that down those steps behind guarded doors were the offices of the House Permanent Select Committee on Intelligence.

It was Thomas Stanton's lair.

House rules imposed an eight-year limit on how long a member of Congress could serve on the committee, but Stanton had been granted a permanent exemption and had served as its chairman or ranking minority member for the past two decades. There were forty-five committee chairmen in the House and Senate, and even more subcommittee chairs but there was never any confusion in Washington when someone referred to "the Chairman."

The good people of the Third District of South Carolina were poised to reelect him to his nineteenth term in a few months—a record of success cynics might have attributed to his particular skill in arranging a steady stream of federal dollars back to his home district. And it was true that through careful and deliberate favor trading Stanton had become a master at bringing home the bacon.

But there was much more to the sixty-eight-year-old power broker with snow-white hair and a Southern-grandfatherly face. He had a razor-sharp mind and, when necessary, a razor-sharp tongue. His colleagues on both sides of the aisle respected him, and voters reelected him because Stanton had never sought public office for the comfortable trappings of power that came with it. He ran for one reason alone: His life mission was to do what he could to keep America safe.

The Chairman had summoned the CIA director for a face-to-face 7:00 a.m. meeting in the committee's windowless basement hearing room, with its burgundy carpet, fluorescent ceiling lights, and walls designed to prevent electronic eavesdropping, because of the president's Somalia bombshell during last night's debate.

Rather than seeing Grainger in his private office, the Chairman had him escorted into the committee's large hearing room, where he waited for a good ten minutes before Stanton appeared through a separate door and took his seat on the committee's raised platform with the Great Seal of the United States looming above him. Because this was a private meeting, there was no one else present and their conversation was off the record, but the Chairman wanted Grainger to feel uncomfortable, as if he were a witness actually testifying.

The committee's witness chair suited Stanton's plan. It seemed innocent enough. Wide, armless, its fake green leather well stuffed. But when he sat on it, the occupant discovered two steel bars just below the cushion, serving as lateral supports. They jutted into Grainger's tailbone every time he shifted position. The bars were not as painful as the chair's back. Its severe arch forced him to stick his chest out and hips back in order to gain any sort of lumbar support. Sitting there, Grainger suspected Stanton had specially ordered the chair to put witnesses under duress.

He had.

"Thanks for coming in so early morning," Stanton began. "Now tell me about Somalia."

Grainger quickly explained the president's rationale for taking the war against terrorism into Africa, and when he finished, he waited for the Chairman to ask a question. Instead, Stanton stared at him, making Grainger even more uncomfortable.

"Ummmm...Mr. Chairman, do you have any questions for me?" Grainger finally asked.

"I have one simple question," Stanton replied, pausing to let his next sentence sink in. "Do you actually believe any of the crap you just told me?"

Not waiting for the CIA director to respond, Stanton continued, "It strikes me that this is an imbecilic election stunt. So why are you trying to convince me that it is anything more than an imbecilic election stunt?"

"Mr. Chairman, I can assure you this plan has been fully vetted by the State Department and our recently named station chief on the ground in Mogadishu. He assures us it is safe to open an embassy there."

"That's hardly reassuring. I can only imagine what sort of colossal screwup your agency punished by posting him in Somalia," Stanton retorted.

"Actually, Station Chief Gunter Conner personally requested the assignment," Grainger said, conveniently omitting the fact that most of the agency considered Conner a crackpot and malcontent and had cheered when he'd asked to be assigned half a world away.

"This entire plan makes zero sense as a national security strategy," Stanton continued. "During the debate, the president suggested we needed an embassy to establish a foothold in Africa. But the fact is that Somali president Moalim Mohammed Musab already is our close ally. Opening an embassy will do exactly nothing to help military and intelligence coordination with Somalia or in Africa. You know it and I know it."

Stanton hesitated, giving Grainger an opening to respond, but the director didn't.

"This cockamamy plan," Stanton continued, "only makes sense as an election ploy. You wanted to throw Governor Coldridge a curve during the debate. So the president picked a scenario you knew Coldridge would have only the most cursory knowledge about. And he took the bait. End of story."

Grainger was now ready to reply, but Stanton didn't give him the chance.

"Except it's not the end of the story," the Chairman continued, his voice rising and his forefinger now pointed at Grainger, punctuating each word. "Now you've got to live with the consequences of the policy you set. The president of the United States can't make an announcement like that in the middle of a nationally televised news event and then fail to follow through. And despite your genius-on-the-ground's assessment, your so-called plan doesn't pass the smell test."

It was finally Grainger's turn.

"Mr. Chairman," he said. "As you know, the election is only a few months away. It would be a huge blow to the president if you were to criticize her in public for reestablishing diplomatic ties with Somalia."

Stanton scowled and snarled. "Perhaps my eyes are failing me in my senior years, but I thought I was talking to the director of the Central Intelligence Agency. Why the hell are you mentioning an election?"

"Mr. Chairman…"

"I asked to meet you informally, just you and me," Stanton snapped, "but your assuming you could bring partisanship into this chamber was a grave mistake. Yes, I'm a member of the president's party, but national security is not a partisan subject. Why don't we invite the ranking minority member over here right now so you can repeat what you just said?"

Stanton reached for a phone next to his seat.

"Tom, calm down," Grainger said.

"That's 'Chairman,'" Stanton icily replied. "My wife can call me Tom. My constituents can call me Tom. You can call me Chairman Stanton or Mr. Chairman. The national security of the United States is serious business, and I will not be casual when discussing it with you or anyone else in this committee room."

Grainger could feel his face turning flush, something he prided himself on not doing under pressure. Yes, *the Chairman* clearly had a stick up his ass, but he was also a thirty-six-year veteran of Congress. Regardless of Stanton's bluster and seeming outrage, Grainger knew no one survived that long by ignoring political concerns.

"Mr. Chairman," Grainger said apologetically, hoping to ease the alpha-male posturing, "you are right, of course. But with all due respect, you know that as soon as I leave this office I'm going to receive a phone call from Mallory Harper wanting to know how our meeting went. And she's not going to want to know your analysis of our African plan. She's going to want to know if a senior member of the president's party— no less the chairman of the House Permanent Select Committee on Intelligence—is going to say anything publicly that will embarrass the president this close to an election. I'm just saving everyone time by asking for her."

Stanton pulled his hand back from the phone. Grainger was right. While Stanton was dead set against the president's Mogadishu plans, he believed that President Sally Allworth had been an extremely effective commander in chief and the nation would be less safe if Governor Timothy Coldridge became president. Stanton found Coldridge to be shallow, and his neo-isolationism would spell disaster for the country.

Rising from his seat, Stanton said, "Director Grainger, thank you for the operational briefing on your plans to safely open the embassy in Mogadishu. As a courtesy, I am going to let the ranking minority member know we met, relay my concerns, and encourage him to get a similar briefing. Rest assured that my committee will be keeping a watchful eye on this situation."

That was his formal declaration, but there was more that he felt compelled to say. Lowering his voice as if he were afraid the ghosts of previous chairmen could hear, he added, "You can tell Mallory Harper that I will not go public with my misgivings. My concerns stay within these walls. That's as far as I am willing to go."

Satisfied, Grainger rose from the torture chair and turned to leave, but stopped when he realized Stanton was coming down from behind his desk.

"As a Navy man," Stanton said, "I'm sure you are aware of America's greatest military failure of the twentieth century. It was called the Vietnam conflict. Tens of thousands dead, billions lost, and a defeat which provided a template for America's enemies in the decades since: Wage a guerrilla war, force a stalemate, and wait out America's political leadership until they can't take the heat at home anymore from a public weary of conflict."

"I'm aware but am not sure I understand the nexus," Grainger said.

"Vietnam was a failure because America's leaders let politics get in the way of sound national security strategy and reasoning."

Stanton stuck out his hand, a smooth motion that was the result of endless campaigning. Grainger reciprocated, but after a firm pump he found that he couldn't extricate himself. The Chairman kept a tight grasp, and in that second, Grainger thought how an action normally associated with friendship could suddenly become so menacing.

"Mark my words," Stanton said, his voice turning to a whisper. "This is going to blow up in the president's face. Every time this country has let election concerns supersede national security concerns, we have paid for it in American lives."

He released Grainger from his vice-like grip and said in an intentional Southern accent, "Now you all have a nice day."

The Chairman returned to his office, where he sat alone pondering what had just happened. He sought to reassure himself. This wasn't politics guiding his preference. It was an objective assessment of the capabilities of the two candidates. It was his duty to not do his duty. At least, that is what he told himself.

But he couldn't silence a nagging voice in his head, and he wondered if this was the same line of reasoning so many failed leaders had made before him.

CHAPTER SEVENTEEN

August 7
The Pentagon
Washington, D.C.

Y ou've put on a few pounds, Marine," the chairman of the Joint
Chiefs of Staff teased when his niece entered his Pentagon office
suite.

"Not as many as you have, Pooh Bear," Captain Brooke Grant replied,
laughing.

General Frank Grant gave Brooke a hug and a peck on her cheek
before returning to his desk, where he'd been studying a CIA assessment
of Somalia. His welcoming smile instantly turned somber.

"I'm not happy about you being deployed to Africa," he grumbled. "I
don't care what the CIA and State Department say, Mogadishu is not a
safe place for a woman."

"We've been over this before, Uncle Frank. I can take care of myself
and I'm glad you didn't intervene this time."

"Oh, you bet I tried."

"You did?" a startled Brooke said.

"Absolutely! Does that really surprise you?"

"No, what's surprising is that someone kept you from doing it."

"That someone was the president of the United States."

"You're joking. The president doesn't even know I exist."

"Stopping that suicide bomber in London earlier this year made you
an American hero, and presidents love aligning themselves with heroes,
especially during a heated presidential reelection campaign. But I'm
afraid there might be something else going on here behind the scenes."

Grant's frown was replaced by a pained look. "I suspect," he said, "that ProTech put the idea of sending you to Mogadishu into the president's head to punish me."

"The defense contracting firm? Why in the world would ProTech do that?"

"Because I made one of its top executives angry."

"Who?" Brooke asked.

"John Duggard, the retired Army general who just happened to run into us when I was in London. I introduced him to you at dinner that night, remember?"

"I certainly do. I bumped into him after that and there was some mention about him going to Africa, but he didn't say anything about me being sent there too."

"Duggard had a long meeting with the president's chief of staff recently about Somalia. ProTech is pumping a lot of money into the president's campaign, and I suspect he mentioned to Mallory Harper that it would be a good stunt to have you sent there."

"Why would he do that?"

"In London, Duggard asked me to help ProTech get its hands on a half-billion dollars' worth of military goods earmarked for disposal, and I refused. Getting the White House to send you to Somalia is a way for him to get back at me. He knows you're my Achilles' heel."

"Your what?" Brooke snapped. "Is that how you see me? As a weakness?"

"Don't be naïve, Brooke. He knows I love you. This is how the game is played. You scratch my back, I scratch yours, and if you don't, I put a knife in your back by hurting someone you love."

"Isn't it possible Duggard was simply doing me a favor and the White House agreed because the president thinks I can do a good job? Maybe none of this is about you. Maybe it's about me!"

"They're using you," Grant said, sliding a paper across his desk for her to read. "They're using both of us. Just look at your schedule for today."

Brooke had come directly from landing at Dulles International Airport on an overnight flight from London to her uncle's Pentagon office and hadn't yet reported to her commanding officer for orders, so she was unaware of what had been planned for her.

"Yikes," she said while scanning the sheet. "We're supposed to appear together at a Pentagon press conference at sixteen hundred hours today."

"When was the last time you heard of the chairman of the Joint Chiefs appearing at a Pentagon press conference to announce the deployment of a military attaché to some African backwater?" he asked.

Without waiting for Brooke's reply, he continued, "The White House is putting us on display because you're a black female Marine whose parents were murdered during 9/11 and I'm the chairman of the Joint Chiefs who took you in. You stopped a suicide bomber and now you're being sent to Somalia to fight terrorism. That's a hell of a news story and one that will get the president more positive attention for her decision to open an embassy in Mogadishu."

"Oh my God!" Brooke said, still studying the schedule. "Me and you are supposed to attend a state dinner tonight with the president!"

"It's not 'me and you,'" Grant lectured, "despite your younger generation's best efforts to butcher our language. It's either 'we' or 'you and I.' That's the sort of verbal flub-up that will be noticed during a press conference or at the White House."

"And the word 'flub-up' won't be noticed?" she replied, challenging him. "Who talks like that anymore?"

"Just look at the guest list and tell me if you see anything odd."

"I don't see anything. The dinner is being held in honor of the prime minister from England's visit, which probably explains why I was invited, since I was stationed in London."

"The guest list is heavy with prominent women, including several well-known feminists. President Allworth is showcasing women because her presidential rival accused her during their first debate of appointing fewer women percentage-wise to positions of power than he had. This is pure politics."

"Why do you have to be such a grouch about this?" Brooke asked. "I'm happy that I'm being deployed to Mogadishu and I'm happy I'm being invited to a White House state dinner, and you should be happy for me too, not all paranoid and gloomy."

"I'm upset, Brooke," he replied in a serious tone, "because all of this attention is going to paint a bright red target on your back. All of the major networks, plus the Al Arabic channel in the Mideast, will be covering the press conference this afternoon and the White House dinner. By midnight every radical jihadist terrorist in Africa will have seen your face. They will know about your parents and that your uncle is the chairman of the Joint Chiefs of Staff. Do you have any idea about the danger you'll be walking into?"

He was genuinely frightened for her.

"I promise to be extra careful."

Suddenly, a look of horror crossed her face. "I didn't bring anything I can wear to the White House."

Grant released a sigh and nodded his head disapprovingly in frustration. "The White House will expect us in our dress uniforms," he said. "This is about showing you off, not haute couture."

She smiled, but General Frank Grant did not.

After she left his office, the afternoon rushed by. The two of them appeared at the Pentagon news conference without any embarrassing "flub-ups," and by dusk they were being driven to the White House in Grant's government-provided chauffeured Town Car.

"Remember, Brooke," he warned, "there's no such thing as a casual conversation during this dinner. You're onstage and you're representing the U.S. Marine Corps, women, and especially African American women, as well as your auntie and me."

"Thanks for amping up the pressure."

"A less-than-enthusiastic smile during a photo op, a yawn while listening to some self-important congressional blowhard, an inappropriate comment about world affairs—any possible misstep will be posted on the Internet before dessert is served."

"I'll try to remember to use the correct fork," she deadpanned. "Stop worrying. I attended diplomatic dinners in London."

"I doubt those guests were as scheming as tonight's will be. Don't let your guard down. You're not going to the White House to make friends. You're going to be seen and used."

"No matter what you say, I'm not going to let you spoil this evening," she replied.

The Secret Service quickly cleared them through the White House gates, and within minutes they were being escorted to the Yellow Oval Room on the presidential residence floor to await the arrival of the president and her British guests. Brooke stayed by her uncle's side as they mingled with a select group of ambassadors, members of Congress, and cabinet members, plus two Hollywood movie stars who had been invited to have hors d'oeuvres with the president before the state dinner.

Grant was introducing Brooke to CIA director Payton Grainger when a White House aide announced that the prime minister and his wife had just arrived at the North Portico entrance, where they were being greeted by the president. Moments later, President Allworth and Prime Minister Harris Preston entered the room. The president had officially welcomed Prime Minister Preston and his wife, Stephanie, with much pomp and circumstance at a state arrival ceremony on the South Lawn earlier that day. President Allworth had been unaccompanied during that ceremonial event held in front of the press corps and various dignitaries, but for tonight's private reception and state dinner, she was being escorted by her longtime friend and political mentor Decker Lake, who'd welcomed a reprieve from his chemotherapy regime and self-imposed seclusion. As the president and her guests made their way through the handpicked notables in the room, General Grant whispered, "Brooke. Best behavior. That's an order."

"Relax, I won't call you Pooh Bear in front of the president," she teased.

"Madam President and Mr. Prime Minister," Grant said when they reached him, "may I present my niece, Captain Brooke Grant, United States Marine Corps."

"The captain needs no introduction," Prime Minister Preston cheerfully replied. "She's been quite a star on the BBC after preventing the bombing outside your embassy."

"I was assisted by two London police officers, sir," Brooke said. "I couldn't have stopped him without their assistance."

In an approving voice, Decker Lake said, "So, Captain, what you're saying is that it was a good example of U.S. and British cooperation."

"That's correct, sir." Brooke beamed.

Speaking to General Grant, Lake said, "Your niece not only knows how to tackle a suicide bomber but also charm dignitaries."

"We're expecting great things from you in Somalia, Captain Grant," President Allworth said.

"I'll try not to disappoint, Madam President."

After the president and her guests had moved on, Grant whispered, "Well done."

"Oh, I've only just begun," Brooke replied. "I can be very charming, especially after I have a few glasses of wine and start dancing on the tables. Is Frank Sinatra's 'My Way' still one of your favorite songs? I might sing it."

Moments later, everyone but the president, Lake, and the Prestons were escorted downstairs to the White House Entrance Hall, where the United States Marine Band, called "The President's Own," was waiting. As soon as everyone was in place, the band played four ruffles and flourishes before striking up "Hail to the Chief," as the president and her guests appeared at the top of the grand staircase. "God Save the Queen" came next, followed by "The Star-Spangled Banner" as the president and her entourage descended and the hundred guests formed a receiving line so President Allworth could present them to Preston while White House photographers snapped souvenir photographs for the guests.

All of the night's activities had been carefully scripted according to long-standing diplomatic protocol, and after the last guest was welcomed, Allworth led everyone into the State Dining Room.

"No wine and definitely no singing," Grant said, as he and Brooke were escorted to seats at different tables covered with blue tablecloths with red napkins and white china—the colors of the Union Jack.

Brooke was seated between Louise Renée Jugnot, the wife of the French ambassador to the United States, and Thomas Edgar Stanton, whom she immediately recognized as the formidable chairman of the House Permanent Select Committee on Intelligence.

"You must sign my menu," Jugnot said as soon as she and Brooke were introduced. "It's a custom at these state dinners for everyone at the table to exchange and sign the menus, given the importance of the guests."

Brooke handed hers over and noticed when signing Jugnot's that each menu had been personalized by White House calligraphers. She then turned and exchanged her menu with Stanton, who scribbled quickly across it.

"Your first state dinner, Captain Grant?" Stanton asked.

"Yes, sir, but I've been to the White House before."

"And what was that occasion?" he asked.

Brooke suddenly wished she'd not mentioned it. She didn't like to name-drop but she was caught. "My uncle was getting an award from the president."

"You mean your uncle General Frank Grant was getting his fourth star from the president," Stanton said, elaborating for her. "I remember it, because I attended the ceremony."

"You did?"

"Captain Grant, I've been around in this town for a long time. I try not to let anything slip by me, especially when it comes to our armed forces."

The guest seated next to Stanton interrupted them, leaving Brooke to study the now-autographed ten-page menu.

"It's customary for the White House chef to serve courses that honor the foreign head of state's native land," Jugnot said. She was examining her menu too. "Let's see what the cook has prepared for us tonight."

She skipped over the first four pages of the menu, which contained a formal welcome by Allworth to Preston and a short discourse about how thrilled the United States was to have Britain as its ally.

Jugnot read: " 'First course: Halibut with Potato Crust.' Do you like halibut, Captain Grant?"

"I'm sure I will tonight."

According to the description, the fish was being served on a bed of braised baby kale, shaved Brussels sprouts, and micro cabbage sprouts, with a hint of applewood-smoked bacon from a local smokehouse to tie the dish together. The salad course was spring garden lettuces with shallot dressing and shaved radish, cucumbers, and avocados. The main course was Bison Wellington, the classic English Wellington dish given an American touch with the use of buffalo tenderloin. The dessert was

Steamed Lemon Pudding, which was a nod to the traditional British treat but with an American twist: The pudding was prepared with Idaho huckleberry sauce to unite the British and American flavors. At the bottom of the pudding were Newtown Pippin apples, which, according to an explanation in the menu, were believed to have been developed in Queens, New York, in the early eighteenth century and were favorites of Thomas Jefferson and George Washington on their Virginia farms.

Reading from the menu, Jugnot said, " 'Newtown Pippin apples serve as a symbol of the American-British partnership—the apple was so favored by Queen Victoria that she had the customs duty on them eliminated.' "

"Had the English eliminated their tax on tea instead of apples," Brooke quipped, "we might never have declared our independence."

Jugnot didn't laugh, but Stanton, who'd overheard her comment, chuckled and said, "Captain Grant, I understand you're going to be the military attaché at our new embassy in Mogadishu. We've established that you've been to the White House, but have you ever been to Somalia?"

"No, sir, I've never been to Africa, but I've been briefed about Somalia's history and our mission there."

"And what exactly is our mission there?" he asked.

"I believe the president outlined our government's goals during the presidential debate, sir. At this stage, I've been instructed to establish working relationships with Somali military and intelligence officials while our new embassy is under construction."

"And are you looking forward to being deployed to Somalia?" he asked.

"I am, sir. My earlier postings have been Paris and London, so Mogadishu will be quite different for me."

"And tell me, Captain Grant," Stanton said, "do you believe Governor Coldridge will keep our new embassy open if he defeats President Allworth and becomes our next president?"

"With all due respect, sir, I'm only a soldier. I go where I am told and do what I am ordered. I will let our elected officials, such as you, handle the politics."

Stanton took a sip of water and then said, "Unfortunately, the president didn't consult Congress about her decision to open an embassy in Mogadishu, so you may know more about her plans than we do."

Once again, Stanton turned to speak to another guest, leaving Brooke to chat with the French ambassador's wife.

"Did I just hear you say you were stationed in Paris before being sent to dreary old London?" Jugnot asked. "You must tell me what you thought of our marvelous city."

"I found it to be utterly marvelous," Brooke answered, intentionally repeating Jugnot's description.

"Yes, I must say that there is no city like it anywhere else," Jugnot boasted. "The only cities that you can compare to it are London and New York City, and even they don't measure up to Paris."

"How long have you been living here in Washington?" Brooke asked.

"Too long," she said, laughing. "But please don't take offense. Washington may be the most powerful city in the world, but it has little to offer except politics. No grand parties. It's more of a sports town than an opera town. Actually, I find it to be a rather provincial place, more like a shoe you wear every day but certainly not a jeweled slipper like Paris. Did you grow up here?"

"I was born and lived in Tulsa, Oklahoma, but moved here as a teenager."

A pained look appeared on Jugnot's face. "Isn't that mostly inhabited by American Indians?"

"Yes, there is a high population of Native Americans in the state."

"I've never made it to the American middle states. They are so far away. This is something I miss most about Paris. It is so centrally located in Europe," Jugnot explained. "I used to board the Eurostar with my younger sister on a Saturday morning in Paris and arrive for lunch in London in less than three hours. Have you ever made that rail trip?"

"You're referring to the high-speed train that connects Great Britain to Continental Europe via the Channel Tunnel," Brooke said. "Actually, I've always wanted to, but haven't."

"Oh, you must. The Eurostar is much more comfortable than Amtrak, which I've ridden to Manhattan. My sister and I love the Eurostar."

"Does your sister live in London?"

"No, her husband works at our embassy there, but she has her own career in Paris, plus she has two little boys who attend private school in Paris. Hers is a commuter marriage, with him taking the train home whenever he gets away. My sister and I both married into the diplomatic service. We must have gypsy in our blood."

"How interesting. Perhaps I know your sister's husband in London," Brooke said, "since I was stationed there."

"Yes, you may indeed," Jugnot replied enthusiastically. "He is the *conseiller des affaires étrangères*. Jean-Paul Dufour. Do you know him?"

"Jean-Paul Dufour is married to your sister?"

"Yes, yes, then you do know him! My sister's name is Amandine Dufour and she and Jean-Paul are quite a handsome and adorable couple."

PART THREE

A TANGLED WEB

God hath given you one face, and you make
yourselves another.

—William Shakespeare, *Hamlet*, act 3, scene 1

CHAPTER EIGHTEEN

August 11
Mogadishu, Somalia

The digital clock next to Gunter Conner's bed showed 4:12 a.m. in glowing red numbers. He'd been asleep for less than three hours, having washed down two Xanax shortly after midnight with the remains of a smuggled fifth of vodka.

Conner made his way to the toilet without bothering to switch on a light. Overactive bladder. That's what the drug companies called it. Conner called it getting older. He had recently turned forty-six. Alone. Happy Birthday to me. He urinated without lifting the seat, judging the center of the bowl by the sound of splashing. For some reason, he felt more alone tonight than he usually did. The six-bedroom dormitory inside the CIA's airport compound was vacant except for him. He needed a smoke, so he walked outside and climbed the exterior steps that snaked up to the one-story building's flat roof. From his perch, he could peer over the secure compound's walls and across the airport's runway. Mogadishu's heart was dark except for a few lights left burning by those who could afford to waste electricity and shop owners hoping to discourage burglars. In the distance, he could see the glow of campfires at the refugee camps edging Mogadishu, a sea of cast-off trash repurposed into shelters. The first time he'd driven through a camp shortly after arriving in mid-July, the odors had been so pungent that he'd become nauseated even with his vehicle's windows closed. He'd refused to open them for air until the bile rising in his throat forced him to throw open the SUV's door and vomit. Children running beside his Land Rover had dodged his spew and tried to reach inside and snatch anything they could. Conner flipped the spent cigarette over the ledge and returned to his bedroom,

Xanax, and vodka, even though he knew the ghosts haunting him could not be silenced by either.

It was his recurring nightmare that had awakened him. It was always the same one. Why wouldn't it be? It was a haunting memory, a grim reality. Like the Ghost of Christmas Past whisking Scrooge back through time, his nightmare always transported him to the exact same time—some three years ago—and the exact same place: his apartment in Cairo, where he lived with Sara and their children Benjamin, age fourteen, and Jennifer, only ten.

The nightmare always began with his being awakened by his bedside alarm clock, trying to silence it quickly as to not disturb Sara but always waking her.

"Don't forget today is a holiday," Sara said. "We have to leave here for my parents' house by ten o'clock. Please don't be late coming home."

"I won't be late and yes, I know today is an Egyptian holiday."

"*Wafaa El-Nil*," she replied, half-asleep. "It means 'the flooding of the Nile.'"

As he left their bedroom, he thought about how thrilled Sara had been when he'd told her that the agency wanted to send him to Cairo. She had been working as an assistant professor at American University but she'd gladly submitted her resignation to begin their "great Cairo adventure." Egypt was her homeland, and although she'd become an American citizen shortly after they'd fallen in love during graduate school and married, she missed her family and her native land terribly.

Sara wanted their children to know her heritage. "Were it not for the Nile," she'd explained, sounding very much like the professor that she was, "Egyptian civilization would not have developed, because the river is the only significant source of water in the region. The Nile flows south to north and empties into the Mediterranean Sea. In the ancient days, it would flood each year, and when the water receded, it would leave life-sustaining silt behind, which made it possible for farming. My ancestors came from the Nile."

She'd paused and then added, "The ancients believed the Nile flooded every year because the goddess Isis was crying tears of sorrow for her dead husband, Osiris." It was typical of Sara. Facts intermingled with her love for Egypt and its history.

At the time of their move from Washington, D.C., to Cairo, Conner had been on a fast track, rising steadily up the agency's hierarchy. He could have applied for a more promising post than Egypt—such as Moscow, Vienna, or Berlin—but he adored his wife, considered her the most beautiful and talented woman he'd ever met, and wanted her to be happy.

After they'd settled into an apartment, Sara had played tour guide to their children while Conner had gone to work developing sources inside Islamic religious groups. It was frustrating. The CIA's primary targets had always been Soviets, and even after the end of the Cold War, most of the instructors at the legendary CIA "Farm" training facility near Williamsburg, Virginia, had instructed their students about traditional ways to recruit disgruntled Muscovites, not radical jihadists. After months of failures, Conner had recruited one informant, whom he identified in his cables to Langley by the code name RA, the Egyptian god of the sun.

From the start, Conner's superiors had been suspicious of RA. If he wasn't a double agent, then he was an opportunist fabricating stories to suckle off of Lady Liberty's generous teats. But Conner thought him reliable, and over time RA had told him an incredible tale.

In 1997, six gunmen from two radical organizations—the Islamic Group and Vanguards of Conquest—attacked sixty-two people at Deir el-Bahri, a popular tourist attraction near Luxor. Their cruelty stunned Egypt. Armed with automatic weapons and knives, they trapped tourists inside the Temple of Hatshepsut and slaughtered them during a forty-five-minute rampage. Women were mutilated with machetes. A note praising Allah was found tucked inside a disemboweled body. Among the dead were a five-year-old British boy and Japanese honeymooners.

The Luxor massacre had happened long before Conner arrived as station chief in Cairo, but several of the extremists who'd plotted that carnage had never been identified or punished.

Conner's source claimed he knew one of those responsible.

"This man appeared from the desert," RA told him. "Some say

Yemen, others Somalia. A few said Egypt. He came from nowhere but soon he was everywhere."

At each of their clandestine meetings, RA had dangled more and more bits about the faceless religious zealot. His stories about this radical were so extraordinary that finally Langley had sent word that Conner was to cut RA loose. His claims were just too fantastic.

"My superiors do not believe you're telling me the truth," Conner told him one afternoon during a secret rendezvous.

"That's because they are blind," RA replied. "As we speak, the jihadist is calling a parley of the leaders from the Abdullah Azzam Brigades, the Mujahideen of Egypt, and Hezbollah. He is urging them to unite under one banner."

Each of those organizations, Conner knew, had been responsible for brutal attacks and bombings in Egypt.

"Is he plotting another Luxor massacre?" Conner asked. "Do you know when this meeting might happen? Have you discovered this leader's name?"

"When we meet again, I will have more information, but you must promise you will arrange for my family and me to move to the United States, because it will not be safe for me to remain here."

Instead of cutting RA loose, as ordered, Conner had immediately agreed to resettle him and his family in the States, but only if the agency could verify his claims.

"I need to know this jihadist's identity," Conner warned.

"He communicates through messengers," RA replied. "He is like a falcon who flies high above us. He sees and acts but is not seen. But I will try."

Conner had intentionally set the date for their next meeting on August 15, the beginning of two weeks of celebration over the flooding of the Nile, knowing that it was easier to evade surveillance on holidays, because potential watchers would want to be at home with their families.

In his recurring nightmare, Conner saw everything exactly as it had happened, experienced everything just as it had unfolded. His dream always began with the sound of the bedside alarm. He would recall the scent of his wife as he leaned down and kissed her forehead and feel the oppressive heat of the August morning as he exited their apartment and walked down their residential street to a main thoroughfare to hail a cab.

"Khan al-Khalili," he told the driver, instructing him to drive him to one of the largest markets in the world. "Will there be fewer people there because it's a holiday?"

"No, more crowded," the cabbie grunted. "People have to eat, even during holidays. And there are many tourists this year."

Exiting the cab at the market, Conner took his time meandering through the shops and passageways checking for possible tails. When he was satisfied he wasn't being followed, he ducked into a tiny coffee shop, taking a seat in the back where the aroma of Arabic coffee was the thickest. An hour passed. Conner grew impatient. His source was often late but never this late. Still, it was a holiday.

At nine thirty, Conner paid his bill. He didn't want to disappoint Sara and the kids, and they were expecting him in a half hour to leave for his in-laws.

Or so he thought.

Conner had removed the battery from his cell phone, a precaution taken to ensure no one in the Egyptian secret police could track him through it, and he'd forgotten to turn it back on. If he had, he would have heard a message from Sara.

I've decided the kids and I will go ahead to my parents'. We're going to leave before ten because all of us are ready and excited about going. And I know how you are about being late. Don't be angry with me, but I can't trust you to get home on time and we simply can't be late again to my parents, not today. Take a cab and join us as soon as you can. Love you!

Because he had not heard that message, Conner was surprised when his taxi turned onto the long one-way street leading to their apartment and he saw his wife and two children exiting the building. Sara was opening the driver's door of the family Land Rover and slipping behind the wheel while Benjamin was joining her in the front seat, leaving Jennifer to climb in behind them.

"That's my wife and kids," he told the cabdriver. "Can you honk your horn and catch them?"

The driver tapped his horn once, but neither Sara nor the children noticed.

"Please hurry!" Conner urged. "I'd like to go with them."

The taxi was about thirty yards away and closing on the Land Rover, near enough that Conner could see Sara through the vehicle's rear window as she reached for her seat belt and leaned forward to key the ignition.

That's when there was a deafening sound. The explosion from under the Land Rover's hood lifted the front wheels of the car off the pavement. For Conner, time slowed. Bits of metal and shards of glass burst from the explosion. The front of the Land Rover compressed as the crumpled vehicle came crashing down.

Bolting from the rear of the cab, Conner dashed toward the wreckage but he couldn't force open the vehicle's bent front doors. Through a gap in the twisted metal and shattered glass he could see his beloved Sara and son Benjamin inside. Both were unconscious and bloody. Cursing and panicked, Conner ripped open the back door of the Land Rover and pulled Jennifer from the wreckage. An ugly gash across her forehead was bleeding. He bound it with his shirt and left her unconscious on the sidewalk so he could return to the SUV to rescue Sara and Benjamin. But when he forced his way into the vehicle's rear seat and reached forward toward them, he realized both were dead.

Stop. Rewind. Different night. Same nightmare. He awakes to the sound of the alarm and Sara tells him not to be late. It was madness and he was incapable of stopping the nightly looping.

Conner had buried Sara in Egypt with Benjamin beside her. After doctors had stabilized Jennifer, the two of them had returned to the United States, where she'd eventually moved into Soft Wind Meadows for rehabilitation. Conner suspected the bomb that killed Sara and Benjamin had been intended for him. He presumed RA had been murdered because he had never surfaced again. Conner was getting too close to the mysterious jihadist who was attempting to unite Egypt's terrorists.

No one in Langley had agreed with Conner's theory. Car bombs had been exploded at the CIA stations in Yemen and Libya on that same August 15. Conner's loved ones had simply been in the wrong place at the wrong time. That was how Langley saw it.

Conner reached for another Xanax and cursed when he found the pill bottle empty. Luckily, he had a fresh bottle of vodka that he'd smuggled into the country. He had a shot and then another. He needed to rest, so he put his head against the pillow but he didn't close his eyes. Instead, he reviewed what had happened since he'd arrived in Somalia.

He'd told Langley exactly what it had wanted to hear: that Mogadishu was safe enough for the United States to open an embassy. Robert Gumman had sent an equally positive report to the State Department within twenty-four hours of first setting foot in Somalia.

And now it was happening.

A former hotel was being remodeled for use as a U.S. Embassy, and Captain Brooke Grant, the hero of the London bombing and niece of the chairman of the Joint Chiefs of Staff, would be arriving in Somalia in a few hours. Conner had watched her on the Al Arabic network being interviewed at the Pentagon news conference with her uncle. He'd seen photos on Internet news sites of them at the state dinner hosted at the White House.

Did she have any idea what she was walking into?

No matter. Conner focused his analytical mind on the real reason why he had volunteered to come to Mogadishu and why he had agreed to write a threat assessment that was politically—not factually—motivated.

General Saeed's torture of the Saudi terrorist Dilawar Bahar had uncovered additional clues about the identity of the Somali American known as Abdul. His full name was Abdul Hafeez and, just as Conner had suspected, Hafeez was the leader who had commanded the Taliban fighters during the Pakistani prison break at Dera Ismail Khan. Hafeez had murdered the Canadian prison inspector Christopher King.

Saeed's interrogation of Bahar had confirmed other useful information. Abdul Hafeez had grown up in Minneapolis and had been friends with Askar al-Seema, the failed London bomber currently under arrest in England. This is what Conner had first suspected. Hafeez and al-Seema had been childhood friends.

General Saeed had also verified that Hafeez was not in charge of Al-Shabaab. Someone above Hafeez was calling the shots, but General Saeed's skills as a torturer had failed to pry the identity of Al-Shabaab's commander from Bahar.

Nevertheless, Conner suspected he knew who was leading Al-Shabaab. It was the same mysterious jihadist who had played a role in the 1997 Luxor massacre. It was the same mysterious jihadist whom RA had told him about in Cairo. In his gut, Conner knew he was on the trail of a ghost from his past. It was the same mysterious jihadist who had murdered Sara and Benjamin and critically wounded Jennifer.

It was the radical extremist responsible for Conner's endless nightmares and abiding sadness.

This mysterious jihadist needed a name.

Conner remembered his last meeting in Cairo with RA, who had compared the extremist to a falcon circling high above, silently observing his prey and contemplating the carnage he would cause, gracefully soaring, seeing all but rarely being seen by his victims until it is much too late.

The Falcon would do as an identifier until his real name was revealed.

A line from a movie, one of Conner's favorites, unexpectedly came to him. His subconscious, no doubt, was sending him a message. Kevin Spacey. *The Usual Suspects*.

"The greatest trick the Devil ever pulled was convincing the world he didn't exist."

"But *I* know," Conner said out loud. "And I am going to find and kill you."

CHAPTER NINETEEN

While flying into Mogadishu on a CIA-arranged private jet, Captain Brooke Grant read backgrounders on the key embassy employees whom she'd be working with in Somalia. It was a thin and troubling file.

First up was Robert Gumman, the RSO and her irritant from London. Rumors were that his superiors at the State Department in Washington had recognized that "Dumbman" was lazy and incompetent. But rather than going through the multiple steps required to fire him, they'd decided to reassign him to Somalia on the assumption he'd refuse and resign—only he hadn't. So now she was stuck with him again.

There wasn't much in her file about CIA Station Chief Gunter Conner except that he'd once run covert operations in Cairo but for the past three years had been relegated to an analytical paper-pushing job in Langley for what were hinted to be mental-health reasons.

Charles "Cash" Kelley's military record portrayed him as a highly competent Navy SEAL and decorated combat veteran. But his dossier also contained several black marks, including a note about a troubling incident when he had been disciplined for brutalizing several hostages during an interrogation.

The Marine embassy guards assigned to Mogadishu were under the command of Sergeant Walks Many Miles, a pure-blood member of the Crow Nation. A military psychiatrist had noted in Miles's file that Crow were known for being a warrior tribe. "Young males proved their bravery by 'counting coup.' This was often done by riding into an enemy's camp unarmed and taunting an opponent by touching him." The psychiatrist had warned that Sergeant Miles showed great pride in his native ancestry during an initial interview when joining the Marines and therefore might be prone to "take excessive risks" as a leader. Apparently that doctor's warning had dogged Sergeant Miles for much of his thirteen-year career, keeping him from advancing to a higher rank even though there was nothing in his service record that suggested he had acted foolishly.

Brooke spotted Miles as soon as she stepped from the private plane onto the tarmac at the Mogadishu airport. The thirty-three-year-old Marine stood out. He was just under six feet and had a muscular build, a broken nose, and the confident look of a fighter who instinctively knew he could beat you in a bar fight if for no other reason than he would refuse to tap out no matter how bloody he became. He was wearing his Marine Corps uniform and nonregulation mirrored sunglasses and snakeskin cowboy boots.

He saluted when she approached.

"Where's our ride, Sergeant?"

"Got a driver waiting, ma'am."

"That's 'Captain,'" Brooke said in a stern voice. "Not ma'am."

"Yes, ma— ur, Captain. It's a hired car."

"No embassy vehicle available?"

"We've got three Land Rovers at the embassy but I was informed this morning that ProTech is using all of them."

Brooke followed his glance to what had to be the oldest Mercedes-Benz in Mogadishu, probably all of Somalia and possibly Africa. It had come off the assembly line in 1961, but the sedan had been cobbled together with so many replacement parts that it could have passed for any year in that entire decade. The driver standing beside his car was as poorly put together as his vehicle. He was wearing badly scuffed black dress shoes without socks, a black suit at least two sizes too small, a wrinkled red shirt, and an emerald-green bow tie. When he saw Brooke, he reached inside the front seat of the Mercedes and retrieved a tattered English chauffeur's cap.

"Hello, hello, welcome, welcome," he announced with enthusiasm. "I'll be Mosi, your driver."

"I see that," Brooke replied.

While Mosi fetched her gear, Miles asked for permission to smoke.

"Nasty habit," Brooke said, "but go ahead, Sergeant."

"Didn't smoke until my last post in Moscow. Russians might hate us, but they love our Camels and Marlboros."

He took a long drag, blew the smoke through his teeth, and said, "Permission to speak freely, Captain. And I do mean freely as one Marine to another."

"Go ahead."

"I don't think those three Land Rovers are really busy. Cash Kelley has pretty much taken over. We've been here five days setting up internal security measures and he's been strutting around barking orders like he's still one of us and not a private contractor."

"You think Kelley's sending me a message this morning?"

He shrugged. "I'm just giving you a heads-up, Captain. Wanted you to know you might be entering hostile territory, and I'm not talking about the locals."

"Is Robert Gumman at the embassy now?"

"No. He flew out of here yesterday for Kenya."

Brooke felt a sense of relief.

"Any idea what Gumman is doing in Kenya?"

"Truthfully? Probably hiding."

"Sergeant, you are being frank," she replied.

"I don't think the RSO is fond of the Wild West atmosphere here," Miles said. "And I'm frank, Captain, because not being frank could put all of us in harm's way. The truth is, this place is a tinderbox."

"That's not what the CIA and Gumman told the White House."

"So I heard, Captain," Miles replied. "But if it's so safe, then why is Gumman hiding out in Kenya?"

Ignoring his question, Brooke asked, "What about the CIA station chief?"

"Isn't his identity supposed to be secret?" Miles said, grinning. "Frankly, he's strange, but aren't all those CIA spooks? Dresses like a tourist but he hasn't given any of us trouble. Mostly, he stays at the CIA compound at the airport."

The trunk slammed shut and Mosi hurried forward.

"Ready to go?" he asked.

Brooke and Miles got into the rear seat while Mosi cranked the Mercedes's diesel engine, sending a blast of gray exhaust into the air. The air-conditioning rattled loudly as it blew warm air on them.

"The Serenity Hotel is close," Miles said.

Their driver answered his cell phone and began speaking so loudly that Brooke and Miles would have needed to scream to talk over him and the clanging air conditioner.

"Sorry, we must go a different way," he announced after ending the call.

"Why?" Brooke asked suspiciously.

"A police checkpoint. We'll go around it."

"Who warned you?" Sergeant Miles asked.

"My cousin," Mosi said.

"Everyone here is a cousin," Miles told Brooke. "There's a hundred eyes watching these streets. The only thing the Somalis got more of than AK-47s are cell phones. See someone talking on a cell phone, he's probably telling someone about you."

Brooke leaned forward from the backseat and said, "Don't change routes. I want to see the police checkpoint."

Mosi glanced in the Mercedes's rearview mirror at her and Miles. "A new route is better. Only a bit longer." He nodded toward Miles, seeking an ally, and continued driving without changing directions.

"Captain Grant wants to drive through the police checkpoint," Miles said. "So that's what you need to do."

Mosi scowled and turned down a side street.

"Sergeant, I don't need you approving or disapproving my decisions," Brooke said.

"No offense, Captain, but Somali men don't like taking orders from women. Around here, women come in second after camels and cattle, maybe third after a really good camel."

Despite its age, the Mercedes moved nimbly around the ruts and holes in the street. Brooke watched as they drove by whitewashed concrete and mud buildings pockmarked with bullet holes.

Mosi began to slow. A Soviet-made Bronetransporter armored personnel carrier was blocking the road about a hundred feet ahead. A gaggle of Somali policemen were positioned around it, armed with automatic rifles.

The policeman who appeared to be in charge was questioning the driver of the first stopped car at the checkpoint. Their taxi became the third waiting to pass. As they watched, the officer began yelling, and his men jerked the driver from his vehicle out onto the street, forcing him to his knees.

The armored personnel carrier beeped a warning horn and moved aside to allow a pair of black Chevy Silverado SUVs to pass. The two vehicles were traveling in the opposite direction of Mosi's Mercedes and their drivers slowed and then stopped when they neared the kneeling man in the street.

Mosi whispered, "Not good. Not good."

An older uniformed Somali stepped from the first Silverado, and the policemen in the street immediately stood at attention and saluted. Without warning, the officer drew his sidearm and shot the kneeling man several times, killing him.

Brooke gasped.

Mosi said, "I told you not to come this way."

The uniformed officer waved his still-drawn pistol, signaling the others to bring the passenger out of the first car and force him on his knees. The cowering man began pleading for his life as soon as he was brought before the gunman. Reaching inside his shirt, he removed a wad of bills, which he handed to the policemen towering over him.

"Shakedown," Sergeant Miles said. "He killed the driver because he refused to pay a bribe."

"I thought the police were on our side," Brooke said.

Now that the officer had been paid, the motorist was permitted to drag his dead companion back to their car and leave. Satisfied, the Somali officer holstered his pistol and returned to the lead Silverado. Both vehicles continued along the road, passing by the taxi, but the Chevys' windows were heavily tinted, preventing Brooke from looking into them.

The driver in the next car waiting in line already had his hand out of his car's window with money for the police to take.

"Our turn now," Sergeant Miles said.

"I talk, you keep silent," Mosi replied.

"*Assalamu alaykum*," Mosi called as the officer in charge neared, but he ignored that traditional greeting and demanded to see Mosi's papers.

"Americans," Mosi said, nodding at the backseat.

The officer bent down and looked inside the car. A snakelike smile crossed his lips when he saw Brooke. Stepping back, he signaled the personnel carrier to move out of the Mercedes's path.

"*Ma' al-salama*," Mosi said, driving forward.

"Americans must get a free pass," Brooke said.

"Like you said, Captain, they're on our team."

Mosi immediately began speaking into his cell phone. When he finished, he said, "You need to listen next time. I'm not getting shot for you."

The Serenity Hotel's private security guards allowed the Mercedes to enter the courtyard so Mosi could unload Brooke's bags.

"You're due for a briefing with Cash Kelley and Gunter Conner at thirteen hundred in the embassy," Miles explained. "That gives you about a half hour before we need to leave. Mosi will drive us. He knows the way. It's not that far from us or the airport."

"No police checkpoints," Mosi repeated with a sour look on his face.

As soon as Brooke and Miles entered the Serenity's lobby, the hotel's security guards walked out into the courtyard where Mosi was parked and ordered him to move his Mercedes out of the walled compound.

He found a place to park about twenty yards from the hotel's front gates and immediately dialed a number on his cell phone. "I just dropped off Captain Brooke Grant, the woman Marine who was on television," he reported. "I'll be taking her and Sergeant Miles to a security briefing at the embassy in about a half hour."

"Excellent," Abdul Hafeez replied. "She's finally here."

CHAPTER TWENTY

The new U.S. Embassy in Mogadishu was actually an old four-story hotel that was hastily being remodeled. Sergeant Miles gave Brooke a whirlwind tour before her scheduled briefing.

The ground floor was being turned into offices where passports and visas would be issued and would contain a large meeting room with a kitchen. The second floor was reached via a new staircase that had been constructed inside the building. When it had been a hotel, guests had walked to their rooms along an open balcony that ringed each floor's exterior. But those walkways had been closed in with cinder blocks filled with concrete and iron rebar for additional security.

The new stairway ended on the second floor. There was no way to reach the third and fourth levels, which were not being remodeled. No one knew if those floors ever would be used, and contractors decided it was cheaper to simply seal them off, since the goal was to get the embassy opened before the presidential election.

The second floor was being converted into office suites of differing sizes and was where the American diplomats would work. Walking clockwise from the staircase, a visitor on the second floor would first reach the embassy's communications center, manned by ProTech. Television monitors would allow security guards to view the grounds through outside cameras. The embassy's briefing room was being constructed next door. A passageway would connect it to the ambassador's suite, which was designed to have an outer office and spacious inner office with an attached bedroom with bath. Also tucked inside that suite would be a safe room with reinforced walls, where the ambassador could hide during an attack.

The next suite of offices was being readied for the Marine embassy guards. A door from the main second-floor hallway would open into a small lobby area. Inside it were two doorways. One would lead to a secured room protected by an electronic lock that would house crypto-graphic machines and safes containing classified materials. The other door would open to Brooke's office.

Brooke was the first to arrive for the meeting in the nearly finished briefing room. She took a seat at a conference table and waited. Ten minutes after the meeting was scheduled to begin, Gunter Conner and Charles "Cash" Kelley sauntered in together, taking seats directly across from her—a not too subtle reminder in her eyes that she was not part of their male team.

Kelley used a secure satellite connection to call RSO Robert Gumman, who was joining them via a speakerphone from Nairobi. Brooke pictured him sitting poolside with a cocktail, talking while ogling sunbathers. When he came on the phone, his voice sounded just as irritating as it had in London.

"Captain Grant, who'd of thought we'd be working together in Mogadishu," Gumman chirped. "Will you be leaving this briefing early like you did my last one in London?"

Brooke started to give a smart-ass reply but decided to hold her tongue and didn't respond.

"Now that I've officially welcomed our new military attaché," Gumman continued, "let's have Cash give us a security update."

"What we're doing here is pretty standard stuff," the former SEAL said. "Our first line of defense, as always, will be the locals. General Saeed sent word he'll be a few minutes late today for this briefing, but he'll be joining us to answer questions and meet the attaché. So far, he's been cooperative."

Kelley reported that ProTech was in the midst of repairing the twelve-foot-tall concrete wall around the compound and topping it with concertina wire. As an additional deterrent, Kelley had asked for permission to add an electrified strand six inches above the wall that carried a 60,000-volt wallop. "We're still waiting to hear from the Justice Department and State Department about that request. We can't have some Somali telling his kid to climb the wall and then suing us."

ProTech also planned to install motion detectors at strategic points, as well as floodlights, and replace all of the building's wooden entrance doors with reinforced steel ones. Because the old hotel's balconies had been enclosed, there were no exterior windows on the second, third, or fourth floors. The windows on the ground floor were being fitted with bullet-resistant glass and steel shutters that could be closed from inside and locked.

"We are going to convert this temporary embassy into a bunker," Kelley said. "We're on schedule. Barring any unseen events during September, we should meet our mid-October deadline."

"Clearly ProTech is doing its usual commendable job," Gumman declared. "What about the Marine guards? What's their status?"

"Although I've just arrived," Brooke said, "I've been briefed by Sergeant Miles, and he has assured me that he is in the midst of implementing standard protocols." She explained that the Marines would be busy during September color-coding all file cabinets in the building so they could tell instantly during an emergency which documents needed to be destroyed first. Two high-capacity DOD/NSA-approved shredders were on order. Both were capable of turning sixteen pages into confetti within seconds.

"It's my understanding that we don't have a large amount of classified materials here yet," Brooke said, "but what we do have will be well protected along with the cryptographic machines and communications gear that is being installed."

"I don't want anyone to worry," Cash Kelley said after Brooke finished her report. "I'm going to keep a close eye on Captain Grant and her Marines to make certain during September and early October that they meet their deadlines. None of us wants to disappoint the State Department or the White House."

"While I appreciate your concern," Brooke replied, "let's remember that part of my job will be monitoring you and your company's performance, and you should know that I will be filing regular reports to my superiors about ProTech and your security plans. Rather than watching me, I'd suggest you focus on completing your own tasks on schedule. We have a lot to accomplish during September and October without getting in each other's way."

Gumman could be heard chuckling over the speakerphone. "I warned you privately about Captain Grant," he said without offering any further explanation. "That covers my agenda until General Saeed arrives. Anybody else got anything to say?"

Brooke glanced at Kelley and Conner, who both stared blankly back at her. "I'd like to mention something," she said. "I'm concerned about an incident this morning that I witnessed, and before I report it to Washington, I'd like to know if any of you have encountered anything similar."

A rap on the conference room door interrupted her. A Marine guard stuck his head in and said, "General Saeed has arrived. Shall I escort him up?"

"Bring him up immediately," Gumman declared through the speaker. "Let's wait, Captain Grant, until the general arrives, for you to tell us your little story."

General Abdullah Osman Saeed greeted Gumman, Kelley, and Conner by their first names and then turned his attention to Brooke, examining her with his eyes much like a butcher inspecting a side of beef.

"Captain Grant, you are even more attractive in person than on Al Arabic television," he declared. "It's a pleasure to meet you."

"Actually, this is the second time our paths have crossed today," she replied.

A curious look swept across his face.

"You've met the general before?" Gumman asked over the phone, clearly puzzled.

"Not met, but seen—at a police checkpoint when I was coming from the airport." She hesitated momentarily to see if General Saeed would react, but he seemed neither surprised nor concerned. "It was you in the black Chevy Silverado, wasn't it?" she asked.

"So you witnessed that unfortunate police matter this morning," he replied.

Gumman interrupted: "What matter? What's this about?"

"A local situation that really doesn't concern you or your government," General Saeed explained. "A rather routine incident of no importance."

A voice in her head told Brooke to keep quiet, but the image of the

Somali driver being executed by Saeed stuck in her mind. "I certainly hope what I saw wasn't routine," she said.

"What the devil are you talking about?" Gumman asked impatiently. "Does this have to do with the story that you were about to tell us?"

"Your new military attaché saw me execute a criminal and it seems to have troubled her," Saeed answered.

Conner was the first to respond. "Local police work is not our concern."

"That's right," Gumman added. "This is none of our business."

General Saeed waved his hand as if he were shooing away a pesky fly. In a condescending voice, he said, "Tell me what you saw, young lady, that has given you such a poor impression of me."

"I saw one of your officers pull a driver from his car at a checkpoint. The motorist was unarmed and forced to his knees. I saw you walk up and shoot him while he was pleading for his life and then I saw a second man taken from that same car. Only he was allowed to leave after he handed one of your officers money."

In an alarmed voice, Gumman said, "I apologize, General. As Mr. Conner said, this is a local matter and none of our concern."

But General Saeed appeared more amused than offended. "I asked the captain to tell me what she saw and she did," he replied. "Apparently she has mistaken me for a stickup man."

"I was merely relating the facts, not drawing conclusions."

"Come now, Captain," Saeed replied, coaxing her. "If I had seen what you believe you saw, I would be disturbed too. I might even believe I'd witnessed an execution. There is an old Somali proverb." He spoke in Somali, which no one understood, and then translated: " 'An elephant cannot see the fleas on itself but can always see the one on the other elephant.' "

"I don't see how that proverb is germane," Brooke replied. "I've never executed anyone in the street."

General Saeed glanced at Conner and said, "Your government executes plenty of people but always through surrogates." Returning his eyes to Brooke, he said, "The man I shot was a criminal, a notorious thief who'd stolen money. That was the cash that you saw his son return to us at the checkpoint. That money was not a bribe; it was returned to its rightful owner."

Over the speakerphone, a relieved Gumman said, "I knew the general had a logical explanation."

"You thought you saw brutality," General Saeed continued, "when I was merely implementing our laws. We do not have a viable court system established, so public executions are done as a warning to others who might be tempted to steal."

"Glad that's settled," Gumman declared, hurriedly retaking control of the briefing. "There's one more item for us to discuss now that the general has joined us. Let's get to it. The White House will name the new ambassador in early September. He will be traveling here along with a group of U.S. reporters a month later in October. My schedule will keep me here in Nairobi until the ambassador arrives, so I'm counting on all of you to do the heavy lifting in Mogadishu and make sure we're ready."

Gumman paused for a second to collect his thoughts before continuing. "I'm not expecting any disturbances or protests, but if there is one, I want to reiterate our rules for engagement so everyone is clear on this. Neither ProTech nor the Marines are authorized to use lethal force against Somali residents. Period. Getting into a firefight with locals would only result in high numbers of American casualties and strained relations. There are more of them than there are of us."

"A lesson learned, no doubt," General Saeed said, interrupting, "the last time you Americans attempted a military operation in Mogadishu."

"Yes, General, we're all familiar with Black Hawk Down," Gumman said. "All of us knew before we got here that this is a dangerous environment for Americans. Everyone understands being taken hostage is one of the risks we face as professionals."

Brooke thought about reminding Gumman that he wasn't in Mogadishu to be taken hostage, he was hiding in Nairobi, but that would have only prolonged the briefing. For the next ten minutes, Gumman spewed out meaningless chatter before the briefing mercifully came to an end.

As Brooke was rising from her chair, General Saeed said, "I would like to show you around my city, perhaps dinner first to make you feel most welcome." He handed her a slip of paper that contained his private cell number. "Call me."

"Thank you, General," she said, taking it, "but I'm going to be swamped during the next several weeks getting everything up to speed by October." She had no intention of ever having dinner with him.

"Perhaps after you get more settled," he said. "Meanwhile, I've left a welcome gift for you with the Marine guards."

"But I can't accept a gift from you. It's against the rules."

"You are in Mogadishu, not America, and it's a custom in Somalia to present gifts to important guests," Saeed replied, "especially beautiful women."

"You'll be insulting the general if you don't accept both his dinner invitation and his gift," Cash Kelley chimed in.

"I don't wish to insult you. I will accept your gift and turn it over to the U.S. government." She was about to exit the briefing room when she had a parting thought. "General Saeed, that criminal you executed today, you did say he was a thief?"

"Yes. A rather well-known one in Mogadishu, which is why I chose to make a public spectacle of him."

"What did he steal?"

"He robbed a bank."

Brooke walked down the hall to the Marine Guard suite, where Sergeant Miles was waiting with a wrapped package.

"The general left you this at the front desk."

"I heard. Tell me, Sergeant," Brooke said. "Since you've been here, have you heard anything about banks being robbed?"

Miles laughed. "Someone's messing with you, Captain. There aren't any banks in Mogadishu. Haven't been for years."

"That's what I suspected."

Brooke removed the box's lid.

"What is that?" Miles asked.

Brooke pulled a bulky black garment from the package.

"A burqa."

CHAPTER TWENTY-ONE

August 12
Mogadishu, Somalia

I miss you," Jean-Paul Dufour said the instant Brooke answered her cell phone.

"I imagine your wife in Paris doesn't," she replied.

The last time they had spoken was when Dufour had driven her to London Heathrow airport for her flight to Washington, D.C. Theirs had been a tearful good-bye that had ended with them promising to talk daily. But Brooke had ignored his telephone calls and e-mails after discovering by accident five days ago that he was married.

"I should have told you," he said quietly.

"But you didn't, did you? Instead you pursued me and told me you loved me. We talked about sharing a life together and that entire time you were just using me. You were just having a little fling at my expense."

"Yes. I will not lie—"

"As you have been doing?" she asked, interrupting him.

"Please, let me explain. At first it was my intention to simply have an affair. Some harmless fun. You can't deny we were attracted to one another. It was mutual animal magnetism. But my heart belongs to you and now I'm trapped in a living hell."

"Are you kidding me?" Brooke said. "You're in a living hell? Do you expect me to feel sorry for you? You have a wife in Paris!"

"It's true. She lives there."

"Call your wife by her name: Amandine. She's not some casual acquaintance who you bumped into on the street."

"Yes, yes, Amandine is her name. But Brooke, I love you more."

"That's funny, since you're married to her more!"

"You make me sound cruel when I am simply following my heart. My marriage is complicated."

"That's what all men say when they're caught cheating. Will you tell me next that she doesn't understand you?"

"Actually, she understands me too well. We've known each other a long, long time."

"If she knows you so well, does she know you've been cheating on her?" Brooke asked, but before he answered, it struck her that this was not his first affair. "Oh my God! You've done this before to her, haven't you?"

"I'm a man with an appetite for life and I've been unhappy for a long time," he said. "I've felt empty. But it's not only me. She is unhappy. We have grown apart. Me going to London was a way for us to see if what we once had was something we could make fresh again."

"So you had an affair with me as a test?"

"No. Because of our affair I will never know the answer."

"The fact you had an affair—and I'm assuming that I'm not the first—doesn't *that* tell you anything about your marriage?"

"Oh, Brooke, please. I'm French. You Americans make sex so much more than it is."

"And your casualness cheapens it."

"You must believe I never meant to hurt you."

"Do you realize how sad and lame that line is, regardless of whether you're French or American? You knew what you were doing and that meant you knew it ultimately was going to hurt me. How else could it end? I never would have given you a second look if I'd known you were married."

"Brooke, I will divorce her if you promise to come back to London to be with me. How long will you punish me?"

"I'm not a homewrecker, Jean-Paul. I'll not have you blame me for destroying your marriage. That's too easy. You should have decided to either end or stay in your marriage before you invited me to dinner that first night. And what makes you think I'd marry a cheater and a liar?"

"Because even though you are furious right now, I believe and trust our love. I know you and I know you love me and therefore you will forgive me. Plus, I'm clever, charming, and sexy. Admit it, Brooke, I'm irresistible."

"Oh, I'll admit you *were* all of those things—before I found out you were married. I can't trust you now. What else haven't you told me? Tell me, do you have children?"

Dufour hesitated.

Brooke said, "It was a trick question. Your sister-in-law already told me that you had children, but right now you paused, because you weren't going to admit it, were you?"

"I have two boys," he said. "So it was Louise Jugnot who told you about me. Did you tell her about us?"

"No!" Brooke replied. "We were attending a White House state dinner. I wasn't about to discuss my love life with her. It was hard enough for me to hear it and then have to keep my composure. I don't believe you have any idea how I felt and feel now. I loved you, Jean-Paul. Totally. Completely. I planned on spending the rest of my life with you."

"You still love me."

"I do, but you have ruined it. If I were married and I was cheating on my husband, then we both would be guilty. But I'm not married and I didn't know. You turned me into the other woman without me even knowing I was one. I didn't know that you had children. You have turned me into a homewrecker without giving me a choice. If you divorced and we married, what would your children think? I would be the evil step-mother. Worse, you knowingly broke my heart."

"So you are considering the idea of being a stepmother," he said.

She was so furious she could barely speak.

"Brooke," he said softly. "I'm not a liar. I am not some terrible man you don't know. The truth is, I never lied about being married. Or that I have children. I simply didn't tell you. There is a difference between omission and lying."

"A true diplomat's answer."

"But an accurate one. Do you think you are the first woman to fall in love with a married man or that I am the first man to fall in love with a single woman without telling her the facts? These things happen,

Brooke, because love chooses love. It does not play by society's rules and ordinances. Do you not believe it possible to be in love with more than one person? Why must we limit love? Because religion tells us? Because we have children?"

"Let's ask Amandine," Brooke replied.

"Is it so terrible I found you exciting? Is it so terrible that you opened my eyes to a new world of possibilities where every scent is sweeter, ever color is more brilliant? If you really loved me a few days ago, how can you not love me now? If it is so easy for you to turn off love, then you are the liar for telling me that you love me. How can you walk away now?"

"I don't want to talk to you anymore right now. I need to focus on my work. I've got a lot to get done before October. I need space to think. I don't need to be distracted."

"Am I merely a distraction now? I just told you I will divorce Amandine if you will marry me."

"This is not exactly how I envisioned having you propose."

"I am willing to leave my wife and children for you," Dufour said. "Does that mean nothing? Before you knew I was married, you would have said yes. What's changed?"

"Everything."

CHAPTER TWENTY-TWO

September 5
The White House
1600 Pennsylvania Avenue
Washington, D.C.

President Sally Allworth strolled confidently into the news conference inside the East Room, flanked by Jacob Sacks, the deputy chief of mission at the U.S. Embassy in the Democratic Republic of the Congo.

"I am pleased today to nominate Jacob Sacks as our ambassador in Somalia," Allworth announced. She quickly cited the career diplomat's qualifications and then stepped aside so the ambassador-elect could field questions. Sacks looked every bit like the fifty-eight-year-old blue blood that he was, dressed impeccably in a navy microdot suit that had been hand-tailored on London's Savile Row.

So far, everything was going exactly as Chief of Staff Mallory Harper had planned. She'd called the press conference, rather than announcing the nomination through a press release, because it would give the president free airtime on the networks and remind voters before the approaching election of the White House's determination to fight terrorism.

But Harper grimaced when Marwin al-Suri, a Syrian reporter for the Al Arabic network and the White House's least favorite correspondent, raised his hand.

"Ambassador Sacks," al-Suri said, "you are an evangelical Christian. Do you truthfully believe you can be effective working in an Islamic country?"

"The world knows we respect a total separation of church and state in the United States," Sacks replied dismissively. "My religious beliefs have never been an issue during my eighteen years in the diplomatic service."

"Aren't you a member of the Southern Baptist Christian faith—a religion that is clearly anti-Muslim?" al-Suri asked.

"You're misinformed. Southern Baptists are not anti-Muslim."

"Southern Baptists believe you have to accept Jesus Christ if you wish to go to heaven, do they not?" al-Suri retorted. "Your appointment to Somalia is like naming a Nazi as ambassador to Israel."

Chief of Staff Harper shot an irked look at the White House's press secretary, David Sheese, who immediately stepped toward the podium to intervene. In a moment of arrogance and smugness, Ambassador-elect Sacks refused to yield.

"Your comparison," Sacks said indignantly, "is disrespectful and meant to incite. If we judged diplomats based purely on their religious proclivities, Muslims would not be welcomed in our predominately Christian nation. Thankfully for you, we do not."

"Can you tell me the name of a single U.S. ambassador who is a practicing Muslim?" al-Suri shot back.

"I believe the ambassador-elect has made his position clear," Press Secretary Sheese said, literally stepping between Sacks and the podium microphones. "Unless someone has a legitimate question, this conference is concluded."

Sheese assured the president, Harper, and Sacks that no one took al-Suri seriously as a journalist, but within the hour, the Al Arabic correspondent's news report was igniting a firestorm in the Middle East. The president watched al-Suri's story with Harper and Sacks on a large monitor inside the 5,500-square-foot White House Situation Room located under the West Wing. It began innocently enough with footage of a smiling President Allworth naming Sacks as the new ambassador to Somalia, before cutting to footage of al-Suri questioning him about his religious beliefs. Al-Suri established that Sacks was a Southern Baptist, then the image on the screen switched from the press conference to a distinguished-looking man who was quoting scripture. "In John chapter fourteen, verse six," the minister said, "we read: 'Jesus saith unto him, I am the way, the truth, and the life: no man cometh unto the Father, but by me.'"

The camera returned to al-Suri, who now appeared standing outside the White House. "The preacher you just heard is the president of the

Southern Baptist Convention, the world's largest protestant denomination," al-Suri explained. "So Ambassador-elect Sacks was lying when he said his personal religion is not anti-Muslim. Clearly, Southern Baptists believe only Christians can enter heaven."

The next image to appear on the screen showed the Reverend Anderson Windsor, whom al-Suri identified as a Southern Baptist minister, burning a copy of the Holy Quran outside his rural Mississippi church.

Returning to the screen, al-Suri said, "This is how Ambassador Sacks and his fellow Southern Baptists would create their perfect Christian world"—followed by a clip of Sacks at the news conference uttering these carefully edited words: "Muslims would not be welcomed in our predominately Christian nation."

Inside the Situation Room, Sacks bolted from his seat as if he were about to attack the televised image of al-Suri being shown on the monitor. "This is outrageous! This isn't journalism. It's anti-American propaganda."

"That film of the Quran being burned," Harper said, "was taken years ago, and that self-ordained minister isn't a Southern Baptist or a member of any organized denomination."

"He's edited my remarks to make me appear like I'm a bigot," Sacks angrily continued. "He's defamed me. Madam President, you've got to hold another press conference and set the record straight."

"I disagree," Harper interjected. "I don't think the president should dignify this reporter's propaganda by responding directly to it. That will just call more attention to it. Instead, let's pull al-Suri's White House press credentials. Let's kick him out of the building."

"What good will that do?" Sacks asked indignantly. "My reputation has been impugned."

"Pulling his credentials," Harper replied, "will switch the focus of this story off you and onto al-Suri. The *New York Times* and other respectable organizations will write about al-Suri and how he lost his press pass. The media loves to talk about itself—its responsibilities, objectivity, and morals. Rather than us condemning al-Suri, the media will eat one of its own for us."

"Let's not just pull his credentials," President Allworth said. "Let's get his visa withdrawn too. I want him out of the country."

"We need to make sure the Southern Baptists and the Reverend Windsor don't do anything to exacerbate this situation," Harper said. Looking directly at Sacks, she added without flinching, "We also need to have a frank discussion about whether Ambassador-elect Sacks can now work effectively in Somalia."

"You can't let Al Arabic dictate who's fit to be a U.S. ambassador," Sacks said, defending himself.

"That's true," Harper said coldly. "However, if the president continues to push your nomination in the Senate, she'll be keeping this story on page one. Of course, if she withdraws your name, she'll be accused of bowing to Islamic radicals. This news report has created a no-win situation for the White House."

"My chief concern is whether this story will cause another wave of anti-American violence," President Allworth said.

"The last time Al Arabic showed that footage of the Quran being burned," Harper volunteered, "five United Nations workers were murdered and there were massive demonstrations in four Middle Eastern countries."

"Madam President," Sacks said, "if you think it would be best for me to withdraw my name, I'll do it and make it perfectly clear this was entirely my decision and had nothing to do with you or the White House."

Sacks and Harper waited for the president to reply.

"Ambassador Sacks," she said quietly, "thank you for your loyalty to me personally and to this administration. You would have made a wonderful ambassador to Somalia, but under these circumstances I believe it would be impossible for you to accomplish our goals there. Mallory, have an aide escort Ambassador Sacks upstairs to work out a statement with our press office withdrawing his name."

A stunned look appeared on Sacks's face. Despite his gesture, it became clear he hadn't thought the president would accept it. Mustering his dignity, he replied, "Thank you, Madam President."

"This is for the best, Jacob," Allworth said in a soothing voice.

As soon as Sacks left them, Harper said, "We need to make sure our news release blames Sacks for misspeaking. We don't want anyone to believe you're bowing to Al Arabic."

"That's fair," Allworth said. "He tripped over his own ego and dug his own grave arguing with that reporter. Now I need a replacement."

"I'll go through the list of career diplomats in Africa," Harper said.

"No. Anyone we choose will be attacked just as Jacob Sacks was. It won't matter if he's a Southern Baptist, Catholic, or Jewish. We can't appoint a Muslim, because it will appear as if I am attempting to appease Islamists. We have to find a candidate whose reputation trumps religious affiliation."

For several moments both were quiet as they thought about choices.

"I should appoint someone from Congress from an area with a large Islamic population," the president said.

"That's brilliant," Harper replied.

"Someone with foreign affairs experience who isn't seeking reelection or is likely to be defeated and may want a graceful way out."

"I know a perfect candidate," Harper gushed. "Virginia senator Todd Thomas. He's got foreign affairs experience and, as odd as it may sound, Virginia has the second-highest population of Muslims in America because of its proximity to D.C. He's always polled well with them."

Allworth nodded approvingly as Harper continued: "Thomas is retiring this term because he knows he'll be defeated if he seeks reelection. He's in our party, and the idea of serving as an ambassador will appeal to his ego—even if it's in Somalia. He's perfect."

"Talk to him, and if he agrees, tell him that we'll work out the details and announce his appointment in a few weeks. Only this time we'll do it through a press release, no televised news conference. I'll hold a little ceremony for him later this month at the White House and expect him to be ready to report to Somalia in October."

CHAPTER TWENTY-THREE

Mid-October
Mosi's private residence
A neighborhood on the fringe of Mogadishu, Somalia

"*A*ssalamu alaykum*,*" Mosi said, welcoming his guest. "All praise be to Allah, the Lord of the Worlds, and prayers and peace be upon the highly praised Prophet and his family and companions."

"Praise be to Allah," Abdul Hafeez replied. "Why have you put us both at risk by calling me to your home?"

"I've learned the new American ambassador will be arriving October twenty-fourth, a Saturday," Mosi reported. "But he will only be here overnight, so we must act quickly if we wish to kill him."

"You were right to call me," Hafeez said. "How reliable is your information?"

"The Americans speak openly in front of me. My sources in General Saeed's police force and at Villa Somalia have confirmed the dates. The Americans are afraid we might attack, so the new ambassador will meet with the president on Saturday, attend a presidential dinner that night, and then leave the next day for Nairobi, where the British diplomats hide."

"I must devise a plan to take this American ambassador hostage."

"Hostage?" Mosi replied, clearly surprised. "Are we not going to kill him?"

"I have been given orders to take him hostage, along with the woman Marine whose relative is an important U.S. general. The only American who must be killed is the CIA station chief."

"Gunter Conner, the man who had our brother Dilawar Bahar tortured and killed," Mosi said. "But taking the ambassador and Captain Brooke Grant as hostages will be impossible. They will be heavily guarded. It would be better to kill all three after the ambassador lands at the airport. We could place a car filled with explosives along his route."

"Mosi, why are you questioning my orders?"

"I am not questioning them," Mosi replied. "But everyone is nervous. The arrest of Askar al-Seema in London earlier this year and the failed attempt in July to kill the president. The capture of Dilawar Bahar this summer and his execution. None of us want another embarrassing defeat."

"Are you now the speaker for the men under my command?" Hafeez asked, his eyelids narrowing in anger.

"I am simply telling you the truth about how all of us feel."

"So it is not the order that I have been given to take hostages that you are questioning, but my ability to accomplish it?"

"The men," Mosi said without flinching, "are concerned. Some of your plans are reckless."

"The scriptures tell us," Hafeez replied, "that those who turn their backs on the servants of Allah will dwell forever in the fire, where they will be given boiling water to drink that will be so hot it cuts up their bowels into pieces." Without warning, he drew a 9-millimeter pistol from his belt and pointed it directly at Mosi's face.

"My brother," Mosi said, his voice turning from cocky to fearful. "I would never turn my back on Allah."

"And what of me?"

Lowering his eyes, Mosi said, "I accept you as Allah's humble servant. I accept you as our leader."

"And are you willing to die at my command?"

"If you think otherwise, shoot me now. I am loyal to Allah, to Al-Shabaab, and to you as my commander."

Hafeez knew that Mosi was constantly questioning his leadership behind his back. One way to silence a critic was to shoot him. Another was to raise questions about his loyalty.

"I no longer feel comfortable with you having contact with the Americans or serving as my intermediary with our men," Hafeez declared. "You need to go underground until you hear from me."

"Disappearing now will only make the Americans suspicious. And what will our brothers think? How will you explain my absence?"

"Mosi," Hafeez said in a firm voice. "Are you questioning me once again?"

"No, no, my brother," Mosi replied. "I will do as you have instructed. I will vanish with my family until you call me."

"The scriptures teach us that the Garden which the righteous are promised contains rivers of water, incorruptible; rivers of milk of which the taste never changes; rivers of wine, delicious to those who drink; and rivers of honey, pure and clear. Do you wish to drink and eat in paradise, Mosi?"

"I welcome death in the service of Allah and you," Mosi said obediently.

Hafeez lowered his gun and returned it to his waistband. "General Saeed and the Americans will have the ambassador under heavy protection whenever he travels. Tell me, what they have done to protect their new embassy since arriving here."

"The Americans have installed bulletproof glass, cameras, razor wire, and steel doors in their embassy. But they have missed the most obvious. Five of our brothers are helping with the construction, and the American foreman has entrusted one of our brothers with a master key that unlocks most of the rooms, to expedite their labor."

"Allah is showing us the way," Hafeez said. "When our brothers in Iran seized control of the U.S. Embassy in Tehran, the Americans did not fight. This is because they are under orders not to fight us. They are trusting General Saeed to protect them."

"Then they are not only cowards but fools," Mosi said. "They have put their fate in the hands of a murderer whose loyalty can be bought and sold. Our fate is in the hands of the Almighty Allah."

"We need to keep General Saeed and his troops occupied so he cannot defend the embassy. He is a mad dog and will protect himself first if attacked, not his master."

During the next hour, Hafeez and Mosi devised a plan. When it was time to leave, Hafeez insisted they pray.

"O Allah!" he said. "Foil the plots of our enemies and their crusader allies! O Allah! Expose what they have done in secret to the whole world! O Allah! Cause enmity and hatred to grow between them! O Allah!

Punish them for their crimes against the Muslims in this world, and the next! Open the eyes of the people! Soften their hearts to their Al-Shabaab brothers who have left their homes and their families to defend Muslim women and children! O Allah! Grant victory to the jihadists fighting all over the world! And our final prayer is that all praise by every hand be to Allah, the Lord of the Worlds. *Was salaam alaykum.*"

CHAPTER TWENTY-FOUR

October 24, a Saturday
Aden Adde International Airport
Mogadishu, Somalia

With his chest covered with medals and ribbons that he'd awarded himself, General Saeed waited impatiently at the dilapidated airport terminal for the arrival of Senator Todd Thomas, the newly named ambassador-elect to Somalia.

Waiting with him were Robert Gumman and Waabberi Samatar, vice president of the Federal Government of Somalia, along with two aides. The senator's jet had landed and was taxiing to the terminal when Gunter Conner hurried to join the delegation, dressed in an olive-green polo shirt, khaki shorts, sandals, and a navy blue blazer threadbare at the elbows.

"Don't you own any appropriate clothes?" Gumman asked.

Still trying to catch his breath from rushing, Conner said, "Relax, I won't be posing for any ceremonial photos."

"You're a representative of the United States," Gumman declared. Dropping his voice to a whisper, he added, "You're also working under State Department cover, so I would expect you to show at least a modicum of decorum in your appearance. I'm sure our new ambassador will feel the same."

"Our new ambassador is only going to be here for about twenty-four hours, hardly time to implement a dress code, and the only Somalis who don't know I'm CIA are the ones out wandering in the desert. This isn't exactly a country of refinement." Conner nodded at the aged terminal with its cracked and badly stained floor tiles and white paint peeling from its walls.

Ignoring Conner, General Saeed asked, "Mr. Gumman, do you know this ambassador well?"

"I've never met him in person but I know he's giving up his Virginia Senate seat to become an ambassador here."

"Giving up?" Conner interjected. "Polls showed he wasn't going to be reelected so he decided not to run. He needed a job."

Gumman shot Conner another nasty glance, but that didn't stop him from continuing. "Senator Thomas got Potomac fever, and his conservative Virginia constituents didn't like that."

In a concerned voice, Vice President Samatar asked, "Is he healthy now?"

"Mr. Vice President," Gumman said, "there's nothing physically wrong with Ambassador Thomas. It was a bad joke by Mr. Conner."

"Potomac fever," Conner explained, "is when a politician gets so involved in what's happening in Washington, D.C., that he forgets the voters back home. In Senator Thomas's case, he got a bit too liberal for southern Virginia's voters."

"That explains much," Samatar said. "No American has ever come here unless he wants something from us or he has no choice. Is there some American expression for that too, Mr. Conner?"

"Yes, we call it taking one for the team—taking a bullet so someone else doesn't have to."

Samatar laughed. "Bullets and politicians. Now that is something we understand in Somalia."

Conner joined him in smiling. "With all due respect, Mr. Vice President, perhaps you could call that Somalia fever—bullets and politicians."

A horrified look appeared on Gumman's face, but the Somali vice president continued to grin.

Charles "Cash" Kelley and a team of ProTech security guards had positioned themselves at key locations on the tarmac. When airport workers pushed a metal staircase to the door of the jet so its passengers could disembark, Kelley rushed forward and stood guard at its base. Five men and two women were the first to exit the jet, all wearing blue bulletproof vests with the word PRESS stenciled on the front and back in bright yellow letters. They congregated at the bottom of the steps and craned their necks upward in anticipation of Ambassador Thomas. One of the photographers snapped photos of Cash Kelley standing guard. The fierce-looking sentry was wearing an all-black ProTech uniform and a baseball hat with the company's insignia on it—two automatic rifles being clutched in the claws of a golden eagle. Dark sunglasses shielded his eyes, and the requisite thin microphone headset rested near his right cheek.

Ambassador Thomas paused at the jet's entrance for photographs before briskly stepping down to meet Vice President Samatar, General Saeed, Gumman, and Conner. The ambassador's deputy, Skip LeRue, came tagging behind him.

While the ambassador was busy shaking hands, a final figure emerged from the jet. ProTech's John Duggard had flown from Somalia to the United States a week earlier so he could accompany Thomas to Mogadishu and, of course, ingratiate himself with the new ambassador during the return trip.

"Welcome back to the earth's rectum," Kelley whispered as Duggard descended the metal stairs.

The formalities lasted only a few minutes. Everyone boarded vehicles and, upon exiting the airport, split away from one another in different directions. Somali vice president Samatar returned to Villa Somalia to brief President Musab, General Saeed drove to his police headquarters, and the news reporters were taken to the Serenity Hotel while Ambassador Thomas and his entourage headed to the U.S. Embassy.

Inside the lead Land Rover, Thomas dropped his happy-face façade. "The sooner I'm out of this hellhole, the better," the seventy-year-old Virginia senator grumbled.

Duggard, who was seated next to him, said, "We got you scheduled to be leaving in twenty-four hours. Before you know it, you'll be off to Nairobi, which is a modern city and will be much more to your liking."

Thomas glanced through the vehicle's windows at the ruins of buildings along the road. Sweat glistened from his English-bulldog jowls. "Anyplace would be better than this dump," he snapped. "Now let's go over my itinerary again."

His deputy opened a briefing book, which held Thomas's schedule along with photographs of Somali president Musab and his top cabinet officials. "As soon as we arrive at the embassy," Skip LeRue explained, "you'll be greeted by the Marine embassy guards as well as our military attaché. You'll have about an hour to freshen up in your office suite there before a series of radio interviews with three Somali reporters."

"But not that Al Arabic reporter, right?" Thomas asked.

"That's correct, sir. The Al Arabic reporter is Ebio Kattan, and she'll meet with you after the three Somalis have gone. She's the one who you'll need to be wary of and to handle carefully."

With an unconcerned shrug, Thomas replied, "I've dealt with plenty of reporters. They aren't nearly as smart as they think they are. What's scheduled after her interview?"

"You will attend a dinner in your honor tonight with Somali president Moalim Mohammed Musab at Villa Somalia, the presidential palace. In keeping with Somali customs, dinner will be served around nine p.m. and end after midnight, so you might wish to have a light snack beforehand."

"Is there a chef at our embassy?"

"No," said Gumman, who was sitting in the front seat with the Pro-Tech driver. "But we can have something from the Serenity Hotel sent over. It's pretty good."

"How about the American press corps who's tagging along. Will they be at the dinner tonight?"

"Only long enough to take a few photos of you and President Musab," LeRue said. "Then they'll be transported back to the hotel by ProTech. We've snuck in several bottles of liquor for them to have their own little party, so they should be content at the hotel."

"What about tomorrow?"

"You have a meet and greet with clan leaders in Mogadishu at ten a.m., followed by a luncheon with them at the embassy catered by the hotel, but after it you'll leave for Nairobi, where the British ambassador is hosting a 'Welcome to Africa' party for you tomorrow night."

"Civilization, thankfully!" Thomas declared. "Now, this woman, this Marine, the one the Pentagon put on CNN. The niece of the chairman of the Joint Chiefs. She's the military attaché here, right? I met her briefly at the White House state dinner for the British prime minister. Is she coming to the dinner tonight?"

"She was invited," Gumman said, "but I decided it would be best to have her remain behind and oversee operations at the embassy. The White House and State Department would like to lower her profile a bit for security reasons now that she's actually here, and so would she. Besides, we want to keep the spotlight on you, not her."

"Too bad," Thomas replied. "She's easy on the eyes."

"I'm sure there will be plenty of attractive women at the British ambassador's party for you in Nairobi," Gumman replied. "And while Captain Grant may be easy on the eyes, trust me, her personality is less than appealing."

Brooke and the Marine guards were waiting inside the embassy's walled compound in their dress blues when the motorcade arrived.

"Nice to see you again, Ambassador Thomas," Brooke said.

"Nice to be seen," Thomas replied.

He hurried her along when she introduced Sergeant Miles and his men, and then rushed upstairs in the embassy to relax in his freshly painted office and bedroom suite.

Thomas made the three Somali radio reporters who arrived that afternoon wait for a half hour before he came downstairs. He deftly handled the predictable questions asked by the radio reporters and then girded himself for Al Arabic correspondent Ebio Kattan, who arrived with her cameraman, a sound technician, and an attitude. Predictably for a television correspondent, Kattan was model tall, with a curvaceous figure that even her conservative Islamic clothing couldn't conceal and full lips that caused many a Muslim to engage in sinful thoughts. She'd been hired after winning the World Muslim Woman competition, a pageant exclusively for Islamic women in which they were judged on their piety and religious knowledge as well as their appearance. Much to her employer's surprise, she had proven to be a tougher and more aggressive reporter than most male correspondents.

Kattan began their on-camera interview by throwing Thomas several easy questions to flatter his ego, but after about five minutes of such coddling, she went for his jugular.

"Why does America allow the burning of the Holy Quran?"

"The unfortunate incident you are referring to happened years ago.

Our government had nothing to do with it and we strongly condemn such acts."

"Condemning and punishing someone for burning the Holy Quran are two different matters, are they not? Your government didn't arrest the man responsible, did it?"

"I'm not certain what this has to do with my arrival in Mogadishu. I've already explained the incident happened two years ago."

"Please answer my question. Was this minister arrested or punished?"

"We believe in free speech in America even if we don't agree with what is being said," Thomas answered curtly.

"Then why did your government expel Marwin al-Suri, my Al Arabic network colleague?"

"We didn't expel him. Your correspondent violated acceptable journalistic practices by knowingly broadcasting a news report that was inaccurate and meant to inflame viewers. His press credentials at the White House were revoked because of his egregious conduct. But my government did not expel him."

"Of course it did. Without his White House credentials, his work visa became invalid and he was forced to leave the U.S. He was punished because he broadcast a story that your government didn't approve."

"I'm not going to argue semantics."

"It's not semantics, it's a matter of you and your government censoring him and his reporting."

"Do you have a question or did you come here to attack the U.S.?"

"Tell me, Mr. Ambassador, what does it say about your government when a foreign journalist who broadcasts a story that Al Arabic deemed fair but was unacceptable according to the Western Zionist press is expelled, but an anti-Islamic zealot who burns the Holy Quran in your country is protected by your government and is not punished? What message does that give to Arab viewers?"

"You're mixing apples and oranges. Your correspondent lied. That's got nothing to do with the unfortunate incident years ago involving the Quran."

"As a journalist, I'm concerned about all forms of censorship," Kattan replied. "If your nation really believed in free speech, you wouldn't retaliate when a view other than the Zionist acceptable version is broadcast. You can't have it both ways—punishing al-Suri for speaking freely and then saying the burning of the Holy Quran is acceptable free speech."

"There's a difference between reporting news and creating propaganda," Thomas said. "You're obligated to tell the truth if you're a legitimate journalist broadcasting to millions of viewers."

"Whose truth? The Arab truth or the Zionist truth?"

"The truth's truth," Thomas sputtered. "If you don't have any other questions, we're done."

"I do have one more question and it's specifically about Somalia. Is it true your government relies heavily on the Mossad and the Israeli military intelligence branch, the Aman, for much of the information you use to identify individuals who you consider to be Islamist terrorists?"

"I will not comment about where the United States obtains information, but it is no secret that Israel has been a welcomed partner in helping countries that have come under attack by terrorists. We also receive information from other foreign intelligence services, including those in Arab states."

"Would it be accurate to say the U.S. shares intelligence information with Israel?"

"We share pertinent information with all of our partners waging the global war against terrorism."

"You do understand, Mr. Ambassador," Kattan said, "that many of our viewers, especially those in Gaza, consider Israel a terrorist organization? You do understand that Somalia does not recognize Israel as a legitimate nation? Your arrival here in Mogadishu will be giving the much-hated and illegal nation of Israel, whom many of our viewers consider to be a terrorist state, a set of eyes and ears in Africa that it can use to identify anyone who Israel identifies as an enemy of Zionism."

"My arrival has nothing to do with Zionism. It's about my country building a bridge with Somalia to help us achieve our mutual goals— security, democracy, and prosperity for the Somali people," Thomas said angrily. He whipped the Al Arabic microphone from his lapel and rose from his seat. "I need to prepare for my next event," he snapped, leaving the room.

Kattan smiled. She was happy with the footage and her bosses would be too.

While her crew was packing equipment, Kattan stepped into the embassy's front lobby to call her editors but immediately put her phone aside when she saw Brooke coming down the stairs from the building's second floor.

"Excuse me," she called out. "You're the female Marine I saw on CNN. Captain Grant."

"Yes," Brooke said. She recognized the popular Al Arabic reporter. "I'm sorry, but I'm not authorized to make any official statements to the media."

"I am not asking you to. I simply wanted to tell you how sorry I am that your parents died at the World Trade Center. A majority of us who live in the Arab world were horrified by that violence."

"Really, because that doesn't come across in your reporting."

"You misjudge me. I actually am very fond of America. I earned my master's in international relations in the States."

"All I've ever heard about you was that you won a beauty pageant," Brooke replied, fully expecting Kattan to bristle.

"What do you expect?" the reporter replied nonchalantly. "Isn't that how all women are judged at first, including you? I graduated from Georgetown University with honors before I entered what you are calling a beauty pageant."

"Off the record, may I ask you a personal question?" Brooke asked. "Assuming I can trust you to keep this conversation private, just between the two of us."

"Yes, I will keep it private and I will answer your questions frankly, unlike your ambassador."

"Did you enjoy living in the States?"

"Very much."

"Can I assume you enjoyed the freedoms you had, especially as a young woman?"

"Yes, yes, yes. America was liberating, but I see where this is going and living in the U.S. doesn't change my political viewpoint about your country and what it is doing now in the Arab world."

"I don't understand how you can go to school in the U.S. and enjoy all that it offers you and then go back to how you live and are treated here."

"Our Arab culture is thousands of years old," Kattan replied, "and there are parts of it that are even more beautiful than what I found in the U.S. Let me ask you: Does living in a foreign country make you want to rescind your citizenship? Of course it does not. Then why do you think that everyone who spends time in America suddenly believes your country is number one?"

"It's not a matter of me wanting you to become a U.S. citizen. What I don't understand is how someone can live in a democracy where people are free and then go back to countries where people aren't free. Especially women."

"What makes you believe I want your type of freedom? That's typical U.S. arrogance."

"You prefer tyranny?"

"Tyranny? Do I look oppressed simply because I am not an American? Islam is what guides us, not man-made laws. And you can't speak to an Arab about freedom and tyranny as long as you support Israel, a terrorist nation that would be overrun if you turned your back on it."

"How can you be an objective reporter if you are anti-Israel?"

"Journalists expose wrongs," Kattan replied. "That's what I was taught at Georgetown. If the world decided that your state of Georgia was needed by the Jews and the world told you to turn it over to the Jews, how would you react?"

"No one has ever called Georgia a holy land," Brooke replied.

"So you hide behind wit rather than answering my question."

"I wouldn't be happy about it. But if Jewish people had a direct tie to that land, as they do to Israel, then I would understand why they wanted to live there and I certainly wouldn't go to war against them. I'd live in peace with them."

"If your home was in Georgia, you would fight them," Kattan replied. She removed a business card from her satchel and scribbled a telephone number on its back. "Take this," she said, thrusting it toward Brooke. "It won't bite you. It's my private cell phone. I'll be here in Somalia for several days. Perhaps we can meet for coffee and continue our discussion. I hope to change your mind about us Arabs."

Brooke took it but said, "As I mentioned earlier, I'm not authorized to speak on the record to the media."

"Yes, I forgot, you're a free American who doesn't believe in censorship."

"And you're an objective and fair-minded journalist who happens to hate Israel and the Jewish people."

With that, Kattan called her producer and Brooke continued outside, where a Somali driver named Ridwaan was waiting for her by a dusty Toyota Corolla. He was holding a dozen red roses.

"Some man must love you," Ridwaan said, thrusting the flowers toward her.

"I didn't think there were any florists here," Brooke replied, taking them from him.

"The only flower that blooms in Somalia is khat," he joked, revealing several missing teeth when he smiled. "The roses arrived this morning from Nairobi. A cousin at the airport called me to bring them to you."

"A cousin, just like Mosi is your cousin. Do you know how long Mosi will be gone? I was growing fond of having him drive me. You said he's away on a trip."

Ridwaan shrugged. "Mosi will return when Mosi returns. Until then, I will drive you."

Brooke opened the card accompanying the flowers.

I love you! Signed Jean-Paul Dufour.

"Do you have a wife, Ridwaan?" she asked.

"I have two wives," he said, beaming with pride, "and six children."

Brooke handed him the flowers. "Then divide these roses and give them to your two wives. They're from a man who would like to be in your shoes."

CHAPTER TWENTY-FIVE

CIA station
Mogadishu, Somalia

There was a time when Gunter Conner enjoyed a refined meal and a fine glass of wine on a Saturday night. But ever since his wife's death, meals had become functional necessities in his day, as evidenced by the bowl of *cambuulo* that he was now preparing inside the CIA's airport compound. Cambuulo was one of Somalia's more popular dishes because it was cheap and simple—adzuki beans mixed with butter and sugar and simmered for several hours at a low temperature.

As he sat down to take his first bite, Langley called.

"The NSA has sent us a phone intercept that has us concerned," his boss, Charles Casterline, announced. "It's a conversation between two suspected Al-Shabaab fighters and it sounds like they're discussing a possible attack on the embassy compound tonight."

"It sounds like?" Conner asked. "What does that mean?"

"It means the Somali translator we normally have working at this hour went home sick and the guy who's filling in for him isn't as familiar with the dialect these guys were speaking," Casterline replied, sounding irked. "As a precaution, I want you to get Ambassador Thomas and his entourage out of Mogadishu ASAP."

Conner checked the local time. It was 9:10 p.m. "He's at a dinner in his honor at Villa Somalia with President Musab. No one gets into the presidential palace with a cell phone, so I'll need to drive there and talk to Thomas face-to-face. It's not that far."

"Then that's exactly what I want you to do. Do it in person. We need to handle this discreetly without the media finding out." As an afterthought, Casterline asked, "Why aren't you at the presidential dinner with him?"

"Just lucky, I guess. I don't think Robert Gumman wanted me tagging along."

"It's reassuring to know you are as well liked in Somalia as you were here."

Ignoring the slight, Conner said, "The dinner ends around midnight. That gives me plenty of time to warn him. But how do you expect me to keep his departure secret? He's got press traveling with him, remember? What exactly do you want me to tell him?"

"Tell him that he needs to leave tonight for Nairobi because our ambassador there wants to meet with him first thing in the morning. Tell him it's imperative that he be there for this previously unscheduled meeting. That excuse should work with the reporters traveling with him too."

"He'll want to know what this meeting is about," Conner said, "especially since it will be held on Sunday morning. And he'll also ask why I'm telling him instead of the State Department."

"Damn it, Conner, use your imagination. Come up with some plausible justification. Just make sure you get his ass and his entourage to the airport after the dinner. I'll arrange for the jet that brought him to be standing by."

"And the reporters at the hotel who came with him?"

"Yes, get them out to the jet too. If there is trouble, we don't want them hanging around telling the world."

"What sort of attack were these guys discussing?"

"Like I just said, our interpreter didn't understand every word, but he understood enough to know they were talking about the Al Arabic news report that showed the Holy Quran being burned. We think Al-Shabaab is going to stage a protest tonight outside the embassy and mix its fighters in with demonstrators."

"Copying Tehran way back in 1979," Conner said.

"Benghazi too. Not an original idea but an effective one. Obviously, if that's the plan, they'll be waiting until after the presidential dinner ends for our people to return to the embassy. They'll be after the ambassador. So if you transport him out of Mogadishu first, they won't have a target and the chances of them causing a scene will diminish."

"Have you alerted the embassy?"

"No. I had one of our people call there and ask some generic questions, and the ProTech security guards said the streets around the embassy were clear. Again, we just don't know if this is a genuine threat and I don't want some reporter getting wind of this and writing something if it's all bluster."

"In the entire agency, you don't have an interpreter who can clarify the intercept?"

"Conner, it's a Saturday and interpreting Somali dialects hasn't been a top priority around here. We don't have a dozen people on standby with the right clearances to transcribe messages. Instead of worrying about what we're doing, you need to focus on your assignment."

"How about General Saeed? He's responsible for protecting the embassy. Shouldn't I inform him about the intercept in case all hell breaks loose even if the ambassador leaves town?"

"Yes, go ahead and warn him. Let him handle the demonstration if there is one. But given the attention the White House has put on opening the embassy, urge him to be temperate in his response. We don't need him on the news cracking heads and turning a peaceful protest into a violent international incident, especially if this intercept turns out to be two Al-Shabaab fighters shooting the bull."

Casterline seemed finished, but before he ended the call, he decided to add one more comment.

"Conner, don't forget that it was your name on the security assessment that we sent to the White House assuring the president it was safe to open an embassy in Somalia. If there is an attack on the very first day our ambassador sets foot in Mogadishu, well, you're a smart man, Conner—you figure out who's going to get the blame."

CHAPTER TWENTY-SIX

Ambassador Thomas's three-vehicle motorcade was pulling away from Villa Somalia's secure perimeter gates when ProTech's John Duggard got a cell-phone call from the embassy communications center.

"We've got protesters gathering outside our walls," Charles "Cash" Kelley reported.

"How many?"

"From the monitors, it looks like maybe thirty. They're milling around."

"Have you notified Washington?"

"Haven't been able to get through. Something screwy with the communications satellite. What's Gumman think, since he's the RSO?"

Duggard glanced over his shoulder into the Land Rover's backseat, where Gumman was sound asleep.

"He's no help," Duggard replied. "I'll call General Saeed and get back to you."

He dialed the general's private cell phone. "General, my people at the embassy are telling me there's a crowd gathering outside. Should we divert to the airport rather than continuing to the embassy?"

"It's nothing to be concerned about," General Saeed replied in a calm voice. "They're upset about the burning of the Holy Quran. My men are watching them and will make certain nothing happens."

"I don't want to put Ambassador Thomas at risk," Duggard replied. "Hell, I don't want to put me at risk either."

"Mr. Duggard, this is nothing but a few late-night troublemakers," General Saeed said, "but I will send my men to meet your motorcade and escort you into the embassy compound so you will feel safe. You and the ambassador will get a good night's sleep."

Duggard called Cash Kelley in the embassy communications center.

"General Saeed says it's nothing to worry about. His men have been alerted. Just to be on the safe side, he's sending men to escort us into the compound. Once we're inside the walls, I want you to seal up the building."

"We've turned this place into a fortress," Kelley replied confidently. "If there is going to be trouble, this is the safest spot inside the city for everyone to be. Our people will be ready."

About a mile from the embassy, two military trucks carrying Somali policemen intercepted the ambassador's motorcade. The officers formed a human shield around the Americans riding in the three Land Rovers. Most of General Saeed's men were armed with riot shields and long nightsticks, but six were carrying AK-47s. The motorcade slowed to a crawl to keep pace with the officers now marching around it on foot toward the embassy.

Peering through a tinted window, Ambassador Thomas asked, "Is this really necessary? My God, it looks as if we're about to enter a combat zone."

"I'm sure General Saeed wants to show the protesters that he means business," Duggard replied. "A strong show of force will intimidate them."

"Maybe we should divert to the airport," Thomas said. "I don't want to get stuck here any longer than I have to."

"It's a bit late for that now," Duggard replied. "The general has assured me he has everything under control, and my people believe the safest place for us right now is inside the embassy complex."

Duggard used his cell phone to call Kelley again at the embassy communications center.

"General Saeed's men are bringing us in," Duggard reported.

"There's about twice as many demonstrators now as there were when we last spoke," Kelley replied, "but they appear to be completely unorganized. No one seems to be in charge. There's a lot of women in the crowd. I guess they get to break the rules about being seen alone in public if they're part of a demonstration."

"Weapons?"

"Not any that we can see."

"Are you ready for us?"

"Absolutely," Kelley said. "We'll have the ambassador tucked in bed ten minutes after you pull through the front gates."

"Who's at the embassy besides our security team?"

"Captain Brooke Grant and Sergeant Miles are here in the communications center with me, monitoring things. There's also four Marine guards. We're in good shape."

After he finished his call, Duggard glanced over his shoulder and noticed Robert Gumman was still asleep. "Please wake up the RSO," Duggard told Skip LeRue, who was seated next to Gumman.

"You might want to take a look outside," Duggard told Gumman as soon as he opened his eyes.

"Holy crap!" Gumman exclaimed. "When did this happen?"

"Don't worry. General Saeed and my ProTech team have everything under control."

Like Moses entering the Red Sea, the spear of police officers escorting the motorcade forced the protesters to step clear as the vehicles reached the embassy's gated entrance. The motorcade's arrival was met by an eerie silence as the three SUVs moved forward at a walking pace toward the seven-foot-tall double gates that, when opened inward, would create a space wide enough for only one vehicle to pass through into the compound.

Duggard telephoned Kelley. "Do you see us on the monitors?"

"Yes, I see you on our monitors," Kelley replied. "Stay on the phone."

Covering his cell with his palm, Duggard said, "Everyone can relax. In a few minutes we'll be inside." Looking through the SUV front window at all of the women in black burqas and teenagers gathered on the street, he added, "Just a bunch of angry women and bored young people letting off steam about the Quran being burned years ago."

"Get ready," Kelley said. "We're about to pop the gate."

A camera mounted next to the gate was giving Kelley a sweeping view of the street. Brooke and Sergeant Miles, who were standing behind Kelley's chair at the communication console, had their eyes on the monitors too.

"I'm opening the gates now," Kelley said, pushing a button on the console before him. The two gates began to swing inward.

"Look!" Brooke exclaimed.

Dozens of men suddenly appeared on the monitors, racing from buildings around the embassy into the mob. Several fired AK-47s into the air, causing immediate panic.

"They've got guns!" Kelley exclaimed into the headset that linked him to Duggard's phone. "We've got to get you inside now!"

As soon as the ProTech driver in the lead Land Rover heard gunfire, he pushed the vehicle's horn and pressed on the gas, causing the Somali officers marching between his vehicle and the opening gates to leap sideways. The first SUV shot forward into the compound.

The second vehicle, carrying Ambassador Thomas, was right behind it, leaving only the third SUV still outside the walls. As it started to move through the open gates, a blast from an RPG struck its rear, turning the vehicle into an instant inferno and stopping it a few feet beyond the threshold.

Inside the communications center, Kelley jammed hard on the button that controlled the gates, but neither side could close because of the burning vehicle now blocking them.

As Kelley, Brooke, and Miles watched helplessly, five of the six Somali policemen armed with AK-47s—who were supposed to be protecting the motorcade—turned on their fellow officers. The mutineers began firing at the policemen who'd been escorting the motorcade—the officers armed with riot sticks and shields. Simultaneously, the Al-Shabaab fighters who'd come rushing forward from their hiding spots herded the demonstrators like cattle through the entrance and by the SUV. The mob streamed into the courtyard.

Two loud explosions shook the embassy. Monitors along the back wall showed dozens of Al-Shabaab fighters pouring through two blast holes in the wall.

Kelley yelled into his headset, "We've been breached!"

Brooke and Sergeant Miles ran from the communications center toward the Marine Guard suite. As they entered its tiny lobby, Brooke could hear Al-Shabaab fighters racing up the staircase onto the embassy's second level.

"They're inside!" she hollered. "Destroy the crypto machines!"

"How'd they get inside?" Miles demanded as he slammed shut the reinforced hallway door behind them, sealing off the suite from the rest of the second floor.

"I'll clear my office," Brooke said, hurrying into it.

Miles dashed into the chamber opposite Brooke's office. That room was where the embassy's classified information and code machines were kept.

Within seconds, Brooke heard Al-Shabaab fighters inside the small lobby outside her locked office door. *Impossible!* she thought. *They couldn't have breached the suite's reinforced hallway door so quickly.*

The upper half of Brooke's office door had a one-way mirror in it that enabled her to look into the lobby without being seen. Glancing through it, she saw a dozen intruders now crowded outside her door, including a familiar figure holding a key. He was the foreman of the Somali construction crew helping remodel the building. She immediately understood. He had a master key.

Fortunately, the digital lock protecting the cryptographic room, where Sergeant Miles and the other four Marines on duty had taken cover, was stopping the Al-Shabaab fighters from breaking inside. They were trying to bust the lock and for the moment, none of them was paying attention to her office, which was now behind their backs.

Brooke was trapped. The only way in and out of her office was through the door to the lobby. As she watched through her office door's one-way mirror, she could see women and several young men shove their way into the small lobby, eager to loot anything they could from it.

Within seconds, someone in that outer lobby was sure to notice Brooke's office doorway. She had to act. Her eyes swept around her, looking for a safe hiding place. There was none. No closet, no air vents large enough to climb into, no windows for her to use as an escape. Her sidearm would do her no good. There were too many of them.

She noticed the burqa.

The gift that General Saeed had given her was still in its box near her desk. She quickly removed the heavy black gown and dropped it over her Marine Corps uniform. She fitted its veil over her head. The burqa covered every part of her body except for her hands. She squinted until her eyes adjusted to the mesh screen now covering them.

Brooke walked to her office door and unlocked it.

At that moment, the Al-Shabaab fighters broke through the door directly across the lobby from her and began yelling at the Marines inside the cryptographic room to surrender or be killed.

With all eyes watching that side of the lobby, Brooke drew her office door inward and slipped forward into the crowd. No one noticed.

Weaving slowly through the protesters, Brooke moved into the hallway. She heard more yelling behind her but no gunfire. A hand suddenly grabbed her shoulder and Brooke fought a surge of panic rising inside her.

The hand shoved her to the side of the hallway to allow two Al-Shabaab fighters to pass, clearing a path. Pinned against the wall with demonstrators, Brooke watched helplessly as four captured Marines, wearing blindfolds and with their wrists tied, were brought from the suite. An Al-Shabaab fighter was holding each Marine's right arm, directing him through the onlookers. One Marine appeared to have been wounded in the leg and was limping to keep up. Brooke didn't see Sergeant Miles. After the other four had passed by her, Miles finally emerged. There were two Al-Shabaab fighters holding him. His nose and lips were bloody from fighting. He was hustled down the gauntlet toward the stairs.

CHAPTER TWENTY-SEVEN

I t was as if Brooke were a surfer caught by a crashing wave.

She was swept down the embassy hallway, propelled by a frantic mob of terrorists and looters. The Al-Shabaab fighters began setting fires as the looters stripped everything they could carry from the building. Within moments, she was shoved down the staircase and out the embassy's front doorway. Now outside in the blackness, she was met by a chorus of screams and gunshots, the pandemonium illuminated by the flames coming from the now-burning embassy before her.

Brooke looked at the embassy's front gates and saw police officers firing indiscriminately. Were they General Saeed's men or mutineers loyal to Al-Shabaab? There was no way for her to know. She felt constricted by the heavy burqa—a feeling intensified by her limited vision through the veil's mesh—but she dared not remove it. Instead, she stumbled into a pack of other women running toward the rear wall of the compound.

Despite the clumsiness of her burqa, Brooke was able to climb through one of the gaping blast holes in the compound's wall. A figure, blurred by her veil, jumped from the darkness, striking her in the head with his fist, catching her off guard and sending her onto the dirt.

Brooke struggled to remain conscious as two men grabbed her legs and dragged her some twenty feet between two nearby buildings before releasing their grips. A hand squeezed her left breast, another her crotch.

In the midst of the embassy attack, Brooke was being sexually attacked. One of the men assaulting her took hold of the hem of her burqa and lifted it, revealing her Marine Corps pants. Stunned, he momentarily froze. With the burqa now above her waist, Brooke drew her Beretta M9 sidearm, sweeping it effortlessly from its holster, and fired two rounds—as taught—at the Somali's chest. The impact of the 9-millimeter slugs sent him falling backward. He collapsed on the ground.

His partner, who was standing next to Brooke, swung an AK-47 from his shoulder and chambered a round.

But Brooke fired first. One slug hit the would-be rapist's right shoulder and the second his chest. The rifle fell from his hands as he also dropped to the street. Scrambling to her feet, she kicked his weapon out of reach and peered down at her attacker. The Somali looked to be in his thirties and was panting, gasping for breath. Brooke glanced around. In the confusion, no one was paying attention to her.

She slipped off her veil so he could see her face.

"*Naxariiso!*" her attacker uttered, which roughly translated to "mercy."

But Brooke was not feeling merciful. The rage from watching her fellow Marines being captured and from the attempted rape unleashed a visceral anger inside her. She fired her pistol again, killing the wounded man, guaranteeing that he would not later reveal that she had escaped from the compound.

It was the first time she'd ended human life. Two lives. In Marine Corps basic training, she had thought about a moment such as this and how she might react. She'd assumed she'd be distraught, given her deeply religious upbringing. But she didn't feel any remorse. At least not in this moment. If anything, she was surprised at how little emotion she felt. They had both deserved a bullet.

Still clutching her 9-millimeter, Brooke removed her cell phone from her front pants pocket and discovered its screen was shattered and it didn't work. She placed her pistol on the ground, picked up the veil that she had removed earlier when showing her face, and used her fingertips to rip away the mesh that covered the veil's eye slot so she could see more clearly while still keeping her face concealed. Slipping it over her head, she smoothed the burqa and retrieved her pistol, which she now pressed close against the dress's folds to conceal it. She turned and began to hurry away from the two dead Somalis, the burning embassy, and sounds of shooting still coming from inside the U.S. complex.

Her rushed footsteps turned into a run in the burqa. She'd gone about a half mile from the embassy when the adrenaline racing through her system gave way to a need to catch her breath and collect herself. She had no idea whether General Saeed and his police force had reclaimed control of the embassy or if the general had been murdered by his own men during the mutiny.

She had two options: the Serenity Hotel or the CIA compound at the airport. Of the two, the compound was the closest and made the most sense. She could reach it in less than an hour at a swift pace.

A pickup truck filled with Somalis turned onto the street where she was resting. She'd already been attacked once and didn't want to risk it again. Tightening her grip on her Beretta, she ducked into the shadows of a building and watched. Her anger overcame any fear she felt. She had fired five rounds from her Beretta. The pistol's magazine held fifteen. She readied it but the truck whisked by her without its passengers noticing.

As she continued toward the airport and the CIA compound, a dozen questions raced through her mind. *Had Al-Shabaab captured Ambassador Thomas? What about Cash Kelley and her fellow Marines, especially Sergeant Miles? Was Al-Shabaab in control of the city now, or had the embassy attack been an isolated event?*

Brooke refused to allow herself to be frightened by her own thoughts. Instead, she concentrated on thinking about the individuals who loved her. Who would miss her if she were killed? Her Uncle Frank, aka Pooh Bear, and Aunt Geraldine. Her older brothers who still lived in Tulsa. She thought about Jean-Paul Dufour. Was he in some London bar flirting with a new naïve conquest while she was alone running on a Mogadishu street? Or had he been sincere in making his marriage proposal? In her mind, she saw his handsome face smiling at her, and she longed to have him embrace her and hold her close, protecting her.

She had fallen deeply in love with him and he had broken her heart.

In a city under siege, with the only sound being her labored breathing, Brooke felt abandoned.

PART FOUR

TWO UNLIKELY HEROES

There is no hunting like the hunting of man and those who have hunted armed men long enough and liked it, never really care for anything else thereafter.

—Ernest Hemingway

CHAPTER TWENTY-EIGHT

October 24, Saturday
Rudy Adeogo's Cedar-Riverside apartment
Minneapolis, Minnesota

An exhausted Rudy Adeogo kicked off his shoes and sank into an overstuffed living-room chair. Dheeh placed a plate of *kashaato*, his favorite coconut-based dessert, on a table near him. "I know you've been too busy campaigning today to eat," she said. "Your sister is preparing something for you, but I thought you might like to start with dessert first! You deserve a treat!"

As Adeogo reached for the tray, his sister screamed in the kitchen and came running into the living room. Grabbing a remote, she flipped on the flat-screen television.

"Mogadishu!" she exclaimed.

Adeogo checked the time. It was 4:20 in the afternoon on Saturday in Minneapolis, which meant it was twenty minutes after midnight Sunday in Somalia.

Al Arabic correspondent Ebio Kattan appeared, standing on the street in front of the burning U.S. Embassy. The sounds of automatic gunfire and men hollering could be heard in the compound behind her. The reporter's breathless speech matched the chaotic scene. "General Abdullah Osman Saeed's security forces are still exchanging gunfire with suspected Al-Shabaab terrorists!" Kattan exclaimed.

The camera panned behind her. Flames were flickering from the building.

"Eyewitnesses say Al-Shabaab fighters rushed the compound around midnight during what had been a peaceful protest over the burning of the Holy Quran in the United States. Several of General Saeed's policemen turned their weapons against their fellow officers and assisted Al-Shabaab in this devastating attack."

A loud boom from inside the embassy caused Kattan to instinctively shriek and duck. She quickly regained her composure and continued her report. "It hasn't been confirmed, but it appears the American chosen to be the new ambassador here, former U.S. senator Todd Thomas, has been taken hostage along with several other Americans who were accompanying him inside the embassy. At least three Americans were killed when a Land Rover SUV they were riding in was struck by what reportedly was an RPG. The bulk of the fighting is over now, but as you can hear and see behind me, there is still a sense of confusion and uncertainty."

Kattan touched her earpiece to better hear what her producer was telling her. "I've just been told," she announced, "that a car carrying explosives was driven into General Saeed's police headquarters near the center of this city at roughly the same time the embassy was attacked. More than two dozen officers were killed during that bombing. We've also learned that mortars were fired at the presidential compound and fighters also attacked security forces guarding the Port of Mogadishu. President Musab is urging Somalis to remain in their homes. It's unsafe to be on the streets, as fighting between Al-Shabaab and the government forces is continuing across the city."

Again, Kattan touched her earpiece and nodded as she listened intently to the message she was receiving. "My producer just told me that Al Arabic has received an e-mail message at our Dubai headquarters that contains a video statement from a man who claims he is a member of Al-Shabaab and was in charge of tonight's attacks here."

The image of a man wearing a black hood with only his eyes showing appeared on the television screen.

"Blessed be Allah," he declared. "Al-Shabaab has tonight attacked the U.S. Embassy in Somalia. America, the head of infidelity and the symbol of aggression and tyranny, was punished for poking its head into Africa, bringing behind it an alliance of the crusaders and their apostate agents to fight Islam. We will continue our war against the sons of Zion and worshippers of the cross until they are destroyed."

Kattan reappeared and told viewers, "The reputed spokesman for Al-Shabaab has not been identified."

Dheeh Adeogo took the remote control from her sister-in-law and muted the television.

"Did you recognize him?" she asked.

"Yes, of course I did," Adeogo snapped.

"Do you think we are the only Somali Americans in Minneapolis who will recognize him?" she asked, clearly frightened. "How long can we keep this terrible secret?"

"Let's have our dessert," Adeogo said, trying to calm his wife. "There's nothing we can do but continue to focus on the election."

"And pray for his death," Dheeh said bitterly.

CHAPTER TWENTY-NINE

October 24, early Saturday evening (seven hours behind Somalia)
George Washington Memorial Parkway
Arlington, Virginia

W hat's happening in Mogadishu?" CIA director Payton Grainger growled over a secure phone in the backseat of a Toyota Prius, a government-issued car that he personally abhorred but which had been forced upon him by the eco-friendly White House.

"Nothing new since the initial reports," Charles Casterline replied. "The satellite footage of the attack has been uploaded for your briefing with the president but our best source of information right now is social media emanating from Somalia."

"I'm about to brief the president of the United States at the White House and the best you can give me is information based on tweets and Facebook?"

"Al Arabic is reporting live from the scene," Casterline said, "and their correspondent confirmed moments ago that Ambassador Thomas and other Americans have been taken hostage."

"Information I already know," Grainger grumbled. "Anything new from President Musab or General Saeed?"

"An attempt was made on General Saeed's life, but he survived, and security forces have been sent to protect President Musab. The situation is highly volatile, but Saeed has assured us his men are bringing the city back under the government's control."

"What about our station chief?"

"We haven't been able to reach Gunter Conner. The last contact we had with him was around two p.m. our time, roughly three hours before the embassy was attacked." Casterline hesitated and then added, "There's something more you need to know. Before the attack, the NSA sent us an intercepted telephone conversation between two suspected Al-Shabaab fighters who appeared to be discussing a possible attack on our embassy."

"Are you telling me we had intelligence that indicated an attack was imminent?"

"It wasn't that clear, sir," Casterline replied, choosing his words carefully. "Our regular Somali interpreter was sick, and his replacement didn't understand the dialect being spoken in the telephone call NSA forwarded to us. But in retrospect, I believe if you were to read a written transcript of that call, you would conclude the two men were discussing an attack on our embassy."

"So we were warned!" Grainger let loose with an expletive and then asked, "When did you intercept this call?"

"About four hours before the attack. I called Gunter Conner in Mogadishu and briefed him."

"Let me make certain of what I'm hearing. Our agency learned four hours before the attack that the embassy might be—no, was likely to be a target. You then called our station chief and told him about the intercepted phone conversation."

"Yes, sir. I actually did more than that. I instructed him to take steps to protect Ambassador Thomas."

"What, exactly, did you tell him?"

"At the time of my conversation with Gunter Conner, the ambassador was at a presidential dinner hosted by President Musab at Villa Somalia. I told Conner to drive there and handle this alert discreetly."

"Which meant what, exactly?"

"I told him to inform Ambassador Thomas that there'd been a change in schedule that required him to attend an early-morning meeting in Nairobi. This meeting necessitated the ambassador leaving Somalia immediately after the presidential dinner. I specifically told Conner that Thomas and his entourage were to be driven directly to the airport from the presidential dinner to board a flight to Kenya. They were not to return to the embassy."

"Then why did they return there?"

"Something must have caused Conner to change that plan."

In an angry voice, Grainger asked, "Why am I only hearing about this intercept now?"

"I didn't want to alarm you unnecessarily. I thought the two suspected Al-Shabaab fighters might have been engaging in bluster, sir. As I said, our regular interpreter was sick and—"

Grainger interrupted. "You thought the intercept was legitimate enough to call Gunter Conner in Somalia and warn him. You thought it was legitimate enough to order him to get our diplomats out of Mogadishu. But you didn't think it was legitimate enough to notify me?"

"Clearly, it was an error in judgment."

Grainger wanted to curse again, but he'd already used the most profane word available and he disliked redundancies. One of the directives President Allworth had given him when she appointed him director was to clean up the CIA. It had been rocked by a series of scandals prior to her election, including revelations that the agency had been reading private Capitol Hill e-mails written by elected officials and their top staff members. Since his arrival at Langley, Grainger had worked eighty-hour weeks tightening up controls, building employee morale, and restoring the agency's tarnished reputation. He'd regained the trust of both Congress and the American public. He'd been meticulous, respected, smart, dedicated, and loyal. He'd proudly earned his nickname: Mr. Clean.

Now all of his painstaking work was being threatened.

Congress and the American people would demand to know why the Central Intelligence Agency had issued a report to the White House—under his watch—that had concluded it was safe to open an embassy in Mogadishu when today's attack clearly showed that it wasn't safe.

Director Grainger knew why. Politics.

Grainger had not done his job by allowing that report to move forward. He'd looked away. He'd let it be sent to the White House. He'd told himself at the time that he had chosen not to do his job for a higher purpose: the good of the country. He did not believe in Governor Timothy Coldridge's isolationistic worldview. The White House had wanted to open an embassy for political gain and he'd fed that desire.

Deep down, he knew there was another reason why he had allowed a whitewashed assessment to leave Langley. Payton Grainger liked being CIA director and knew he would be forced out if President Allworth lost her upcoming reelection bid. There would be no place for him in a Coldridge White House.

What was done was done. He couldn't recall Gunter Conner's Somalia assessment. He'd already accepted the fact that he and the agency would be pilloried. Because a U.S. ambassador had been taken hostage, his critics would attack with a vengeance. There were plenty of them in Washington. Congress was eager to cut the agency's budget, disperse its powers, limit its authority, and restrict its ability to operate. Sometimes Grainger didn't think he could use the men's room without having a dozen government lawyers and a congressional oversight committee watching him. The worst of the armchair quarterbacks was the Chairman.

Representative Thomas Stanton had warned him during their private session that permitting politics to seep into foreign policy was always disastrous. But like Grainger, the Chairman had looked the other way. He'd kept quiet, and his silence made him culpable.

From the moment Grainger had heard the embassy was under attack, he'd been doing a political damage assessment in his mind and he'd concluded that despite the heat, the odds were in his favor that he and the agency would weather the criticism. *Is any embassy truly safe from terrorists? Didn't the State Department also conclude Mogadishu was safe?*

But Casterline's revelation—that the agency had intercepted a telephone call warning about the impending attack four hours before it had happened—would tip the balance against him and the CIA. Grainger could visualize himself being grilled by the Chairman during a congressional investigative hearing.

"Your agency was told an attack was imminent and did nothing?"

An even more chilling thought came to him. What would happen if news of the intercepted call leaked out before the presidential election, which was only ten days away?

He needed time to think about how to handle this unfolding disaster.

"I apologize, sir, for putting you in this awkward position," Casterline said, interrupting Grainger's thoughts.

" 'Awkward' is a bit of an understatement," he replied, "and an apology is not going to rectify what's happened. We need to locate Gunter Conner. We need to know if he is alive, a hostage, or in hiding. We need to know why he didn't get everyone to the airport as he was ordered."

"Yes, sir," Casterline said.

"If he is alive, he must have had a good reason to ignore your orders. Until we hear it, we won't have all of the facts, and I'll be damned if I'm going to tell the president this news in bits and pieces."

"I understand, sir," Casterline said.

"Do you understand?" Grainger repeated angrily. "From this point on, you will deal only with me about this matter. Call me as soon as you locate Gunter Conner and hear his explanation. Meanwhile, keep this information compartmentalized."

He paused and then repeated the obvious: "Find Gunter Conner and do it quickly."

CHAPTER THIRTY

Early Sunday morning Somali time
Aden Adde International Airport
Mogadishu, Somalia

Everything had gone as planned except at the airport.

Abdul Hafeez had sent his Al-Shabaab fighters to crash a car loaded with explosives into General Saeed's police headquarters, attack the Port of Mogadishu, launch mortar rounds at Villa Somalia, and assault the Aden Adde International Airport simultaneously while he was overseeing the attack on his primary target: the U.S. Embassy. The blitz was intended to confuse, weaken, and preoccupy General Saeed and his troops.

Hafeez's onslaught had been carried out with precision, with one exception—the assault on the international airport. The Aden Adde airfield was built along the coast of the Indian Ocean, and rather than approaching the airport at its heavily fortified front entrance, Hafeez had instructed his fighters to land on its eastern shoreline, where the only security was a chain-link fence and periodic Humvee patrols. Two dozen jihadists in fishing boats had been given that job. They'd been ordered to beach their boats silently on the rocky shore and immediately split into two groups. One would head southwest to assault the CIA's enclosed compound, while the other would move directly west across the landing strip and engage security guards at the terminal's less protected rear.

It was a clever plan but Hafeez had not considered how rough the Indian Ocean waves were that Saturday night and how challenging it would be for his fighters to arrive on schedule at the shoreline, given that they were rowing their small boats to keep their approach a secret. This miscalculation resulted in the airport assault beginning nearly an hour after the other targets had been hit, including the embassy.

When he first heard gunfire, Gunter Conner was in the CIA compound trying to reach General Saeed by telephone while ignoring a rash of incoming calls from Langley. Grabbing his CIA-issued P229 Sig Sauer semi-automatic pistol, he extinguished the lights in his room and peered through one of the residential building's bullet-resistant windows.

Two intruders were coming over the ten-foot-high concrete walls that protected him.

Conner hurried through an exit out into the courtyard. He wasn't going to be taken prisoner, and the sight of wall jumpers could mean only one thing: The ragtag band of khat-chewing private security guards that he'd hired to protect him either were dead or had fled from their sentry posts outside the compound.

He made his way across the courtyard to a doorway in the perimeter wall behind the mess hall. It was used by cooks for food deliveries. After punching a code into its digital lock, he shoved the heavy door outward with his left hand while clutching his pistol in his right. Behind him he could hear the sound of men hollering as more of the intruders scaled the walls. They were starting fires. Just as he was about to escape through the doorway, a large propane tank near the mess hall used for cooking exploded, blowing him off his feet and through the opening.

Conner smacked the ground face-first and gasped. Lying on his stomach, he took a momentary inventory. *Arms, okay. Legs, okay.* It didn't appear as if he'd broken anything, nor was he bleeding anywhere except for tiny cuts on his chin. But he'd dropped his pistol and it was nowhere to be seen in the blackness. Still prone, he glanced back at the walls. It didn't appear that anyone was following him—yet.

Now unarmed, Conner raised himself from the ground and began running east away from the compound. He could hear the cracking sounds of AK-47s and explosions from RPGs coming from the airport's main terminal. It too was under siege.

When Conner reached the airport's 10,335-foot-long runway, which ran northeast–southwest down the center of the grounds, he took a knee. He would be completely exposed while crossing it. If he was spotted amid the confusion, the airport's private security guards were as likely to shoot him as Al-Shabaab fighters.

Sucking in a deep breath, he bolted onto the runway, his shoes making a flip-flopping, smacking noise on the landing strip concrete. He was running so fast that when he reached the other side, he tripped and toppled forward. Conner thrust out his hands to break his fall and hit hard, tearing the flesh on his palms and knees on the jagged fist-size rocks that edged the landing strip. Hurrying up a small embankment, he found a hiding spot between two small, corrugated-metal storage buildings and caught his breath.

He wasn't certain who was winning the battle for control. His survival instincts told him to keep going and find refuge elsewhere. The airport's perimeter was protected by an eight-foot-tall chain-link fence topped with strands of razor wire. He would have to cross it to escape. Conner removed his shirt and wrapped the cotton fabric around his right palm, forming a thick pad. Glancing to his right and then left, he quietly walked to the fence and began scaling it. When he reached the top, he pressed his shirt onto the razor wire and straddled the barrier. He let gravity pull him over.

Conner hit the ground with a dull thud.

"Conner!" a voice said. "Gunter Conner."

He froze.

"Who's there?" he whispered.

"It's Captain Brooke Grant."

She stepped from behind a large pile of rubbish and rubble along the road. "I thought it was you climbing the fence."

"Are you wearing a burqa?"

Brooke removed her veil. "General Saeed gave it to me as a joke. Remember? I came here from the embassy hidden in it."

"What's happened there? I wasn't able to reach Saeed."

"We were attacked, overrun. Everyone else has been taken hostage— Ambassador Thomas, Cash Kelley, Duggard, Sergeant Miles—all of them. The embassy is burning. I thought the airport would be safe. I thought we could call for help."

"That wasn't supposed to happen!" he exclaimed, clearly alarmed. "General Saeed was supposed to protect the embassy."

"His own men mutinied. Al-Shabaab had its fighters hidden in nearby buildings. They had RPGs. It was a nightmare. Saeed lost control within seconds after the attack started. None of us had a chance."

"Were any of our people killed?"

"Yes, at least three riding in the last Land Rover in the ambassador's motorcade."

Conner leaned against a half-standing wall, bracing himself, clearly distraught. "What have I done?" he asked quietly.

"What have you done? Are you talking about your security assessment? Even if you had written it differently, the White House would have gone ahead and opened the embassy anyway. The president wanted it opened before the election. Everybody here knows that."

"I'm not talking about my assessment for the White House."

"Then what are you talking about?"

Ignoring her question, Conner said, "We need to keep moving. It's not safe here."

"Where? We don't know if Al-Shabaab has taken control of the city or if General Saeed has restored order."

"I have a friend who will hide us until we figure that out. Follow me."

CHAPTER THIRTY-ONE

D irector Grainger was in the president's gunsights as soon as she entered the White House Situation Room trailed by Chief of Staff Mallory Harper.

"How many were at the embassy?" Allworth asked.

"Nineteen," he replied. "I'll start with the Americans who were riding in the motorcade returning from the presidential dinner at Villa Somalia."

The president reached for a pen and a pad embossed with the White House seal that was on the conference table.

"They have Ambassador Thomas; his deputy, Skip LeRue; ProTech's head of African affairs, John Duggard; our RSO, Robert Gumman; and two staff members from the State Department. In addition, three ProTech security guards who were riding with them in the motorcade have been captured. That adds up to nine hostages."

The President tapped nervously on the pad. "Who else?"

"We know there were four ProTech guards on duty at the embassy, plus five Marines, as well as our military attaché, Captain Brooke Grant."

At that moment, the door to the Situation Room opened and General Frank Grant walked in.

"Have a seat, Frank," the president said.

"Thank you, Madam President, for calling me. I apologize for interrupting, but I'd like to know if my niece is a hostage."

"We're not certain but it's highly likely," Grainger answered in a somber voice. "We're going down the list of potential hostages right now. We know your niece was at the embassy when it was attacked."

"How do you know that?" President Allworth asked.

"My people have been in touch with the Americans who were inside the Serenity Hotel," Grainger explained. "There are six embassy guard Marines at the hotel who were off duty, and they were able to give us the names of everyone attending the presidential dinner and identify who was working at the embassy."

Rising from his seat, Grainger picked up a remote and said, "My staff has prepared satellite footage for you that shows a portion of the actual assault."

"You had a satellite monitoring the embassy?" Harper asked, clearly surprised.

"No, but we were able to turn one into position after we heard our embassy was under attack. The footage we have shows us what transpired after Al-Shabaab penetrated the compound's perimeter walls but not what led up to the violence."

Grainger used a laser pointer to clarify the grainy, highly magnified black-and-white images that appeared on the large monitor. "These pictures were taken about ten minutes after the walls were breached."

The footage showed the embassy on fire and ant-size individuals running wildly in all directions near it. Grainger pointed to several figures in the courtyard. Unlike the others, these individuals were marching in a straight line toward holes that had been blown in the compound's rear wall.

"These are our people who were taken hostage," Grainger explained.

Moving frame by frame now, the film showed the Americans exiting through the wall onto the street, where they were placed into eight waiting vehicles.

"Our satellite tracked them to three different locations," Grainger said. The giant television screen split into three separate parts, each showing hostages being escorted into different structures. With another click of the remote, Grainger returned the screen to a single image, this one showing a magnified picture of a man. Although it had been filmed at night, exterior lights of a building had illuminated the snapshot of the lone figure.

"We believe this is Ambassador Thomas."

"How certain are you?" President Allworth asked.

"Sixty-five percent," Grainger replied. "He's being held in a private, heavily guarded residential compound off Jidka Sodonka Road."

"Can you tell if my niece is one of them?" General Grant asked.

"This is the only individual who we've been able to spotlight."

"How large is Mogadishu?" Allworth asked.

"Size-wise about six hundred and forty square miles and close to two million residents, not counting about twenty to forty thousand refugees in squatter camps that ring the city. The house where we believe the ambassador is being held is in a part of the city currently under Al-Shabaab control."

"Where are the other hostages?" Mallory Harper asked.

"One group was taken to what appears to be a Mogadishu warehouse and the other an apartment building. Our analysts believe Thomas, his deputy, the RSO, and John Duggard are being held together in the private residence."

"I counted eighteen hostages being led out of the embassy grounds in that satellite footage," President Allworth said, momentarily glancing down at her scribbled notes. "You told us that nineteen Americans were at the embassy compound when it was overrun. That's one less than your head count."

"Yes, Madam President," Grainger replied. "Our analysts also counted eighteen, which means one American who was at the embassy wasn't in that line of hostages who were being led away."

"How do you account for that?" Mallory Harper asked.

Grainger shot General Grant a nervous look and said, "Our initial assumption was that one American was killed and left in the building to burn. But now that General Saeed has retaken control of the embassy, we've been told no American corpses were found inside."

"One of the Americans at the embassy must have escaped," General Grant said in a hopeful voice.

"It seems unlikely that anyone could do that," Grainger replied.

"You don't know my niece," Grant said. "Let's get real here. She would have been a prime target, along with the ambassador. Based on your analysis, Al-Shabaab is holding all of its prized hostages—Ambassador Thomas, John Duggard, the RSO, and Thomas's deputy in that single residence. It makes sense they would put my niece there too—if she'd been captured."

"That sounds reasonable," Grainger said. "I agree that Captain Grant would be a prime target, but she is a Marine and they could have kept her with the other Marines. We simply don't know who that missing American might be or what happened to that individual."

"I hope Captain Grant did escape," President Allworth said.

"Where was your station chief when the embassy was attacked?" Harper asked, adding in a sarcastic voice, "The one who assured us that Mogadishu was safe."

"We're not sure," Grainger replied. "We've not been able to reach him."

"So we have two Americans unaccounted for," the president said. "Our CIA station chief and whoever managed to get out of that embassy without being captured."

"That's right, Madam President."

"What have you learned about the actual attack?" the president asked Grainger.

"It apparently happened when Al-Shabaab breached the exterior walls during what had been a peaceful protest about the Al Arabic news reports—the burning of the Holy Quran," Grainger explained. "We are seven hours behind Mogadishu. It's still early Sunday morning there. The city is in chaos. Until the situation settles down, we won't be able to collect additional information."

"As soon as I learned of the attack," General Grant interjected, "I notified our Fleet Antiterrorism Security Team in Rota, Spain. As you know, Madam President, our FAST teams have been specifically trained to rescue Americans caught in hostile environments. A team will be landing in a few hours aboard the Navy amphibious assault ship—the USS *Hornet*—which is en route to the Somali coast."

"Sending a rescue team into Mogadishu is going to be problematic," Harper announced while looking at the president.

Allworth said, "Go ahead, Mallory, you can tell them."

"The Somali ambassador met with the president earlier today and told us President Musab has declared martial law in Mogadishu. Apparently there's rumors being spread on Facebook and Twitter that we allowed the embassy to be attacked so we could have an excuse to invade Somalia."

"President Musab," President Allworth added, "is worried Ethiopia might attempt to take advantage of this turmoil to seize contested land along the Somali border. President Musab has told us—through his ambassador—that any military intervention by a foreign power will be viewed as a deliberate act of aggression against his nation and his government. That includes a military rescue operation by us."

"The ambassador told us General Saeed has been put in charge of finding and freeing our people," Harper added.

"I have offered President Musab our help," President Allworth explained, "and he has refused. He's concerned that if U.S. troops enter Somalia, Al-Shabaab will use their presence to cause additional civil unrest, demonstrations, and more violence—setting the stage for the collapse of his already fragile democratic government."

Addressing her remarks to General Grant, the president said, "Frank, the Somali ambassador has assured us that freeing the hostages will be his government's and General Saeed's number one priority after he restores order and reclaims the city. But if we send troops in now on a rescue mission, our people will find themselves fighting not only Al-Shabaab but General Saeed's security forces and the heavily armed Mogadishu population."

"We can't risk another Black Hawk Down fiasco," Harper said.

"The longer we wait, the more likely Al-Shabaab will separate the hostages and move them out of the city," General Grant warned.

"I've got drones watching all three sites where the hostages are being held," Director Grainger replied. "We'll know if Al-Shabaab tries to move them. Our analysts believe Al-Shabaab will try to barter with us for their release."

"That's not what ISIS did," Grant replied in a somber voice.

"Yes, but Al-Shabaab hasn't been as extreme as ISIS," Grainger noted. "We believe Al-Shabaab will copy a playbook from the best-organized terrorist group in Africa—Al-Qaeda in the Islamic Maghreb, a Salafi-jihadist militant organization better known by the acronym AQIM. We haven't paid much attention to AQIM because it originated in Algiers and its main target has been France—given that Algeria used to be a French colony. But its aims are identical to Al-Shabaab. AQIM wants to create a fundamentalist Islamic state and it has generated millions in cash by kidnapping aid workers, tourists, diplomats, and employees of multinational corporations and holding them for ransom, so many that the international community now has an acronym for it: KFRs. Kidnappings for Ransom."

"Is Al-Shabaab affiliated with AQIM?" Harper asked. "Do these folks talk to one another? Share information?"

"More often than not they fight against each other. They've only formed a syndicate episodically in the past. But they do learn from each other."

"What can we expect?" the president asked.

"They will rank hostages by their importance. The more important you are, the safer you are from being harmed, although someone such as Ambassador Thomas might be beaten or forced to issue some scripted Internet denunciation attacking the West. There is one exception," Grainger said. "All of these terrorist groups execute our people. If they can identify someone as being CIA, they kill them."

"What about women hostages?" Harper asked quietly.

"Al-Shabaab tends to be as cruel with women as they are with men or even worse," Grainger quietly replied.

Everyone glanced at General Grant, but he did not physically react.

"Surely, these terrorists know our policy," Harper said. "The United States does not barter with terrorists. We are not France."

"They will assume ProTech will pay for the release of its employees," Grainger replied, "and they'll expect our government to funnel money through ProTech. That's how France has done it when its people have been captured—by working through a shell. Al-Shabaab and other Islamic fundamentalists have been hurting for cash ever since we rid the world of Saddam Hussein. Another important financial faucet was switched off when Libya's Colonel Gaddafi was toppled. Iran has been pulling back its support because it wants to improve its relations with the West. We've always suspected the Saudis are funneling money to radical jihadists for their own protection, but those funds aren't enough alone to pay these extremists' bills. They need cash, and that will work in our favor here. As long as they believe we are willing to pay a ransom, it's to their advantage to keep our people alive."

Speaking specifically to General Grant, President Allworth said, "I want your FAST team ready, but given the uncertainty right now in Mogadishu, as well as President Musab's declaration that we not violate Somalia's borders, I believe the wisest course of action is to wait—until things settle down—at least until we hear what Al-Shabaab has in mind."

"There's something I need to make clear," General Grant said. "It isn't easy for me to say but it needs to be said." His voice began to crack with emotion. "Captain Grant is my niece and I love her, but she is first and foremost a Marine, a soldier, and I can't ask you, Madam President, to do anything for her that you are not willing to do for the other hostages."

"Thank you, Frank," President Allworth said, "but I'm personally responsible for sending her there. You asked me not to do it and I didn't listen and now I feel horrible about that. Captain Grant is different from the other hostages. Al-Shabaab knows it and so do I."

CHAPTER THIRTY-TWO

October 25, predawn Sunday
Somewhere in the streets
Mogadishu, Somalia

How do you know we can trust your friend to take us in?" Brooke asked.

"He's on our payroll as an informant," Conner replied.

"Hold it," Brooke said, stopping mid-step in the darkness. "If he's taking money to betray his own people, how can we be sure he won't tell Al-Shabaab about us for money?"

"He owes me personally and I just told you, we are friends. I helped him with his daughter. But don't say anything when you meet him. He'll be embarrassed."

"Embarrassed about his daughter or being your friend?"

"Cute," Conner said, but he didn't chuckle. He'd barely spoken since she'd told him about the embassy attack.

"So what did you do for his daughter?"

"Does it matter?"

"You're putting my life into his hands. I'd like to know."

"His daughter has schizophrenia. Korfa's relatives think there's a devil living inside her and they threatened to kill her, so he brought her to me and I arranged for her to be flown to the U.S., where she now lives in a facility."

"Nice relatives."

"It happens, and not just in Somalia."

"What kind of facility? A mental hospital where they give people electric shocks, lobotomies, use straitjackets?"

"Soft Wind Meadows isn't like that," Conner snapped. "You shouldn't talk about something you don't know anything about."

Brooke was exhausted and didn't appreciate Conner's ill mood. "My father was a minister," she said, "and he took me into a state mental hospital just north of Tulsa to visit a man, and I wouldn't have put my dog in that place."

"I just told you Soft Wind isn't like that."

"Those places can act all nice when a visitor shows up but—"

He interrupted and said in an impatient voice, "I know it's a good place because my daughter is there."

"You have a daughter with schizophrenia?"

"No, a traumatic brain injury and post-traumatic shock. It's not really something I want to discuss right now or that you really need to know. Let's just keep moving."

Brooke decided to change the subject. "How much farther is it?" she asked.

"We should be at Korfa's apartment in about an hour if you stop asking me questions."

Neither spoke again as they made their way through the vacant streets of Mogadishu, stopping to hide whenever they saw the headlights of an approaching vehicle.

It was nearly daybreak when they reached a three-story apartment building. Conner led her through a broken wrought-iron gate hanging on one hinge into an interior courtyard and up a flight of stairs to the top floor. In one of its earlier incarnations, the building had been a hotel, but that had been when tourists flocked to Mogadishu for its festive markets, pristine beaches, and crystal-clear waters. That was before the seemingly endless civil wars and before a Somali warlord accepted a $3 million bribe from a European-based waste disposal company in return for permission to dump a tanker full of toxic chemicals off the Somali shoreline.

The door to the apartment cracked open when Conner knocked.

"Master Conner," a fortyish-looking woman said, peeking out. She opened the door for them. *Master?* Brooke thought. When was the last time she'd heard a black woman call a white man master?

"This is Caanood," Conner said. "She's Korfa's sister. She's a widow, and his wife died several years ago, so they live together now."

"My brother is still sleeping," Caanood said. "He only returned home less than an hour ago, but I will wake him."

They were standing in the apartment's main room, which also served as a kitchen with a refrigerator and sink along one wall. Brooke could see a bathroom through an open door. She correctly assumed another door, which was closed, led to the apartment's only bedroom, and she noticed a mat on the floor nearby, where Caanood slept, in keeping with gender separation. The room smelled of *unsi*, a combination of sugar, perfume, and spices burned as incense. The windows were covered with three different layers of thick and colorful curtains, a Somali tradition. The only furniture were three knee-high tables. Rectangular mats served as seats on the floor. A muted television was broadcasting CNN in a corner near several eight-by-ten-inch color photographs framed on a wall. Each of the family photographs showed the same smiling couple. There were no pictures of a daughter. The man who emerged from the bedroom was the one shown in the photographs. In his early forties, he looked haggard, with saucers under his eyes. He was wearing a Nike T-shirt and a black-and-white skirt that reached to the top of his bare feet.

"General Saeed believes you're dead," he said.

"Believes or wishes?" Conner replied.

"How do you know General Saeed?" Brooke asked Korfa.

Ignoring her, he continued addressing Conner. "The general believes Al-Shabaab took you hostage at the airport and then killed you."

"He's always been an optimist," Conner said. "Tell me what went wrong at the embassy."

"I asked: How do you know General Saeed?" Brooke interrupted, louder this time.

Conner said, "Korfa knows the general because he's responsible for keeping the general's communication equipment working. He's an electronics genius."

Still ignoring her, Korfa said, "Al-Shabaab attacked our police station with a car bomb. Luckily, I wasn't injured. It fired rockets at Villa Somalia and attacked the port. When the general heard about these attacks, he sent men to respond. He thought he had kept enough soldiers back to protect the embassy, but half of his men mutinied. Only too late did he discover the embassy was always Al-Shabaab's primary target. The terrorists made a fool out of him, and he is not a man who likes being made to look foolish."

"I was inside that embassy," Brooke said, sticking out her hand for him to shake. "I'm—"

"I know who you are," Korfa said, ignoring her hand. "Everyone knows about the black Marine woman who was on CNN. General Saeed thinks you've been taken hostage too. He thinks Al-Shabaab is holding you for ransom."

Brooke said, "No excuse to be rude. I offered you my hand."

Korfa looked directly at her and then shook her hand.

"It's difficult for Korfa to interact with Western women he doesn't know," Conner said.

"I've not met a Somali man yet who knows how to deal with a Western woman," she answered.

"There is an old Arab saying," Korfa said. "'A woman belongs in the home and the grave.' They do not belong where men belong. They should not try to be men."

"Oh, I don't try to be a man. I'm better than that. Do you have a cell phone? Mine doesn't work."

"Why do you need a phone?" Conner asked.

She frowned and said, "Why else? To call Washington. They need to know we're alive. We need to tell them what's happening here and I want my uncle and aunt to know I'm safe."

Korfa glanced at Conner, who approved. The Somali retreated into the bedroom and returned with a first-generation BlackBerry. "It's old, but it was made in Canada," he said, handing the phone to Conner. "It's harder for the U.S. to trace or anyone else, including the general, especially with the modifications I've made to it."

Brooke snatched the phone out of Conner's hand.

"Korfa," Conner said. "Did the general capture anyone from Al-Shabaab?"

"Not the man who you hoped—"

"What man?" Brooke asked, only half-listening as she began dialing the cell phone. "Who was the general trying to catch? What are you talking about?"

"It's not important," Conner said.

"Yes it is, otherwise you wouldn't have asked." She finished dialing the number and hit the connect button but there was no dial tone. "I'm not getting a connection."

Korfa opened his palm and she handed it back to him. He held it to his ear. "Cell phone towers are down in some areas because of the fighting. Maybe later this morning you can get a signal."

"I'd like it back then," she said.

Korfa shrugged and gave it to her. "I have a dozen more."

"May I use your bathroom?" Brooke asked.

He nodded toward the open door.

After using the toilet, Brooke washed her face using a sink that oddly reached only to her knees. When she returned to the living room, Caanood was boiling tea on the stove.

"Excuse me," Brooke said to her, "but there was water all over the floor in the bathroom. You might have a leaky faucet."

Caanood hurried in with a cloth to dry the floor.

"You embarrassed her," Conner said.

"By telling her there's a leaky faucet?"

"It wasn't a leak. It's because of *wudu*. Didn't you notice the sink was lower than what you see in the States?"

"What's *wudu*?"

Korfa said, "It's what a woman must do before praying. She must wash herself according to Islamic tradition. She must wash her arms, face, nostrils, hair, mouth, and feet three times. We do not own a shower or tub, so washing the feet three times in the sink five times a day and cleaning up after it often becomes a burden. That's why the floor was wet."

"I'm sorry. I didn't mean to offend her or you. Do men have to do this ritual too?"

Korfa said, "There are different rules for men."

"Of course there are," she replied. "That never changes whether you're in Somalia or the States."

"Korfa says we can stay here until the situation settles down," Conner explained. "I'm going to have some tea and get some sleep."

"You're what?"

"Going to have tea and rest. I'm tired and I want to clean up too."

"Why don't we have Korfa drive us to General Saeed's headquarters? We can contact Washington from there."

"Everyone thinks I'm dead or being held hostage," Conner said. "It won't hurt for them to keep thinking that for a few more hours while I get some rest and General Saeed continues to drive Al-Shabaab out of Mogadishu."

"You can take a nap," Brooke said, "but I want Korfa to drive me to General Saeed."

"Korfa can't do that," Conner replied in a stern voice. "I told you Korfa is one of my sources. The most important one for our agency here in Mogadishu. How would he explain being with you? We can't put him at any more risk than we already have by coming here."

"If General Saeed discovers I have been helping the CIA, he would kill me and my sister," Korfa said. "No one must know you're staying here. I'm afraid you have no choice but to accept my hospitality at least until order is restored."

CHAPTER THIRTY-THREE

A residential compound off Jidka Sodonka Road
Mogadishu, Somalia

Wearing orange jumpsuits mimicking the garb of jihadists held by Americans at Guantanamo Bay, the four American hostages were paraded blindfolded into a bare room and forced to their knees in a straight line.

Bright lights were aimed at their faces, causing them to blink when their blindfolds were removed. A man wearing all black, including a hood that revealed only his eyes, was filming them. Five other Al-Shabaab fighters, covered head to toe in black garments with only their eyes exposed, were positioned behind the hostages. Each jihadist was armed with an AK-47 except for their leader, who stood in the center holding a sheet of paper. A black flag inscribed with white letters in Arabic was hanging on the wall behind them. Only ProTech's John Duggard was familiar enough with radicals to recognize the so-called "black flag of jihad" with its Shahada inscription: *There is no god but God, Muhammad is the Messenger of God.*"

When the cameraman signaled he was ready, the Al-Shabaab leader began to read his script.

"We thank Almighty God, who said in His Holy Book: '*Ye who believe, take not the Jews and the Christians for your friends and protectors. They are but friends and protectors to each other. And he amongst you who turns to them is of them. Verily God guideth not the unjust.*' May God's peace and blessings be upon our Prophet Muhammad, his companions, and those who followed his course."

Glancing up from his text at the camera, he said, "I address this message to the entire Muslim nation to tell them the crusader war has been launched against its people who have faith in God. We now live under this crusader bombardment. The Islamic nation should know we defend a just cause. The Islamic nation has been groaning in pain for decades under the yoke of the joint Jewish-crusader aggression. Palestine is living under the yoke of the Jewish occupation and its people groan from this repression and persecution while no one lifts a finger. The feet of those who came to occupy these lands, usurp these holy places, and plunder these resources are defiling the Arabian Peninsula. And now infidel crusaders are expanding."

Speaking to the hostages in front of him, he said, "State your name. You first, Ambassador."

Todd Thomas didn't respond.

The cameraman stopped filming while the jihadist leader bent down and whispered into the ambassador's ear.

"What's wrong, Senator? Cat got your tongue?"

"Are you an American?" Thomas asked as soon as he heard that idiom.

"I was born in the United States, but I am no longer an American."

"You should be on our side, not the terrorists'."

"America is the world's biggest terrorist. Is it logical for the United States and its allies to carry out repression, persecution, plundering, and bloodletting over these many years against Islam without their actions being called terrorism, while when the victim tries to seek justice, he is described as the terrorist?"

"I'm not going to debate you," Thomas replied in an indignant voice.

"Speak your name into our camera."

Its operator began recording again.

"No," Thomas stubbornly declared.

Without hesitating, the jihadist slapped the older man with an open hand across the back of his head.

"State your name!" he yelled. "Unless you want one of your friends to die."

"I am Ambassador Todd Thomas, and I'm proud to be an American."

He braced himself for another slap, but the jihadist didn't react.

"Skip LeRue," his deputy, who was positioned next to him, hurriedly announced. "And I'm proud to be an American too."

"My name is John F.U. Duggard," the retired general said with a smirk.

"Robert Gumman," the final hostage replied.

"Let the United States know: Our Islamic nation will not remain silent," the hooded leader said, reading from his script. "Jihad is an obligation on every Muslim in this land if he has no excuse. God Almighty has said: '*Then fight in God's cause—thou art held responsible only for thyself—and rouse the believers. It may be that God will restrain the fury of the unbelievers, for God is the strongest in might and in punishment.*'"

Sweeping his right arm upward as if he were directing a choir, he declared in a louder voice, "Every Muslim should carry out his role to champion his Islamic nation and religion against crusader aggression. Committing terrorism against the crusaders is one of the fundamental tenets of our religion and Sharia, which commands us to strike terror into the hearts of the enemies of God and your enemies."

Thomas couldn't take any more rhetoric. "You're preaching a known perversion of the Holy Quran and Islam," the feisty diplomat declared.

Releasing his script from his hands, the jihadist grabbed Thomas around his neck from behind with both hands and began choking him.

"Don't talk unless I tell you!" he yelled.

Thomas's face turned bloodred.

Duggard yelled, "Stop it! Get control of yourself!"

Releasing Thomas, the infuriated jihadist took an AK-47 from one of his fellow fighters and put its barrel against Duggard's temple.

"You think we're not serious?" he hollered. "You think because I was born in America I won't harm you?"

Duggard closed his eyes as the terrorist cocked the weapon, but just as he was about to pull the trigger, he shifted the barrel sideways.

He fired, and a single round pierced the side of Robert Gumman's head. He collapsed.

Ambassador Thomas, Skip LeRue, and John Duggard stared at Gumman's lifeless body.

Handing the rifle back to its owner, the jihadist said, "Now you understand. The fact I was born in America means nothing to me. I spit on it and you."

The jihadist picked up his script from the floor and began reading again to the camera. "I urge you, my Muslim brothers and sisters, to shoulder your responsibility against these crusaders. It would be a disgrace if the Islamic nation fails to do so. I ask Almighty God to grant us victory over our enemies, make their machinations backfire on them, and defeat them. May God's peace, mercy, and blessings be upon you."

He bent down and exchanged his script for a knife with a slightly curved blade. Raising it for the camera to record, the jihadist declared, "The scriptures tell us to cut off the hands of the crusaders!"

Two Al-Shabaab soldiers grabbed Skip LeRue, forced him chest down on the floor, and pulled his arms out in front of him. They placed his hands on top of a concrete cinder block while the other two fighters in the room pressed the tips of their rifle barrels against the heads of Thomas and Duggard.

The jihadist raised the knife.

"No! Please no!" LeRue screamed as the jihadist swung his blade down. The American screamed in pain. The jihadist swung again and a third time before cutting through the flesh and bone. LeRue stared in shock at his severed limbs.

"Any hand raised against us will be cut off and discarded," the jihadist declared. He swept the severed hands to the side.

Thomas and Duggard were pulled up onto their feet.

"You two will live for now," the jihadist leader declared. Taking one of his comrades' rifles, he fired a burst into Skip LeRue, ending his anguish.

The cameraman stopped filming, and Abdul Hafeez had Thomas and Duggard taken from the room. As soon as they were gone, he removed his hood. He was proud of himself. "Did you get close-ups of the hands?" he asked the cameraman.

"Yes," his subordinate replied, handing him the camera.

Hafeez hurried from the room into a hallway that led to an exit. A courier was waiting outside.

"When you deliver this," he said, giving him the camera, "tell our leader that I am waiting to hear his next instructions. We are ready to strike again against the enemies of Allah."

CHAPTER THIRTY-FOUR

October 25, two thirty a.m. (EDT) Sunday
The White House
Washington, D.C.

Mallory Harper gently rapped on the door of the president's bedroom in the southwest corner of the White House's second-floor residence before slightly opening it.

"Madam President," she said.

The president was already awake. She'd been thinking about her deceased husband and one of the last times they'd been together before he'd suffered a massive coronary. It was after he'd finished giving a campaign speech to a union group and they had been riding in their car back to their Pennsylvania home. "You looked bored during my speech," he'd complained. "I'm just exhausted," she'd replied. He'd been cruel. "If you're not at the top of your game, I don't need you with me, dragging me down."

Politics had strained their marriage. Many of the political families that Allworth knew were in similar states of dysfunction. There had been a time when elected officials moved their families to Washington, D.C., and socialized with one another. Husbands and wives knew each other. Their children went to the same private D.C. prep schools. But that was before constituents expected their public servants to be available for every county fair, Rotary Club luncheon, and neighborhood forum. What did it matter that her husband spent more time in airports than at home with his family? What did it matter that he missed his children's weekend soccer games and high school plays because he was driving across the state listening to voters' endless complaints? Sally Allworth had felt what it was like to be a widow long before her husband had collapsed dead. The first time he'd been elected to the Senate, she missed him terribly at night when he was not in their Pennsylvania home, where she'd remained to raise their three sons, leaving him to spend weeknights sleeping in a one-bedroom Capitol Hill efficiency. But as time passed, his visits home became more of an inconvenience than a reason for celebration. Little irritations had been nurtured by resentment. He'd taken to belittling her, finding fault in her slightest misstep. There could be nothing less than perfection in his public persona. She could hold no opinion other than his, voice no ideas other than his, and never question or even slightly criticize him. The normal give-and-take in a marriage had been replaced with defined roles, and her role had been that of a smiling cheerleader whose most important attributes were her smile, her figure, and her charity work, not her intellect.

"Madam President?" Harper repeated, louder.

"Somalia?" Allworth asked wearily.

"Al-Shabaab just posted a video. They've murdered two hostages."

"Damn it!" Allworth exclaimed.

She rarely swore, which made her outburst even more stinging.

"Who are they?"

"Robert Gumman, the State Department's regional security officer, and Skip LeRue, a career diplomat who was Ambassador Thomas's deputy. It's gruesome, horrible stuff."

Allworth let out a sad sigh as she swung her legs over the side of the bed and sat on its edge. "I should have never, ever pushed for opening that embassy before the election. I'm responsible."

"No, Madam President. I'm the one who believed it would give your campaign a boost. I gave you bad advice and I'm terribly, terribly sorry. I never realized until this moment how different what we do is from the corporate world where I came from. I was used to making tough calls that cost people their jobs, but not their lives."

"This is no time for self-pity," the president replied. "We might have done it for the wrong reason, but I was not wrong in my commitment to hunt down and kill these rabid dogs. Tell me about Gumman and LeRue."

"LeRue was a career diplomat. Age forty-two. Never married. Mormon. They cut off his hands and then shot him."

Allworth winced. Despite her tough façade, she felt sick to her stomach.

"They chopped off his hands?" she repeated, turning the statement into a question.

"Yes," Harper replied softly.

"And Robert Gumman?"

"Divorced. No children. Former Colorado police captain."

"That's not enough information. Get someone to fill in the blanks and also work up backgrounders about the three security guards who were killed during the embassy attack. I want them to be more than names when I talk about them at a press conference."

"Madam President, we need to be careful how you respond—given that Al-Shabaab continues to hold sixteen Americans, including our ambassador," said Harper, who suddenly seemed more cautiously aware of the impact of her counsel.

"I didn't make you chief of staff to tell me the obvious," Allworth snapped. Pushing herself off the bed, she walked into an adjacent dressing room, where she exchanged her pajamas for a navy-blue jogging suit bearing a presidential emblem. She moved to a sink and turned on the faucet. Tears formed in her eyes. She splashed her face with cold water to help cover them and steadied herself. She was no longer the obedient wife of a senator. She was commander in chief and she understood how she needed to present herself, not only to Harper but to the nation and especially to the terrorists. This was no time for tears.

"Did they make any demands?" she asked as she was emerging from her dressing room.

"Not on the Internet. Just a bunch of self-righteous prattle. I've arranged for us to watch the video on the monitor in the Situation Room, assuming you want to see it."

"Yes," she said. "It's something I need to see. And Mallory, you need to find your backbone. You're no good to me if you're going to second-guess yourself."

They left the bedroom and five minutes later were watching the Situation Room's large monitor. Neither spoke while the Internet footage played.

"When did this go online?" Allworth asked.

"Less than an hour ago. It's nine thirty in the morning in Mogadishu. They're seven hours ahead of us."

"Can we get it removed from the Internet?"

"The agency is doing its best to crash the foreign sites that are showing it, but they can't touch the Web server here in the States, and it's already issued a statement defending its right to host it."

Harper read from a printout. "Just as television news programs often show upsetting images of atrocities, people can share upsetting videos on our site to raise awareness of actions or causes. While this video is shocking, our approach is designed to preserve people's rights to describe, depict, and comment on the world in which we live."

"What self-righteous drivel," Allworth said. "I should call the site's founder and ask if he would like for someone he loves to be shown having their hands chopped off."

"The clip already has gotten a hundred thousand hits, but it will be in the millions once everyone wakes up and word spreads." She paused and then said in a thoughtful voice, "Despite the horror of this, I don't think you should rush on to television and react. You talked to the press last night about the embassy attack and hostages. For now, I think we should just issue a statement condemning Al-Shabaab's brutality while we study your options."

"I'm going to take a lot of heat, especially from Governor Coldridge," President Allworth replied. "At a minimum, I should call the victims' parents to express my sympathies."

"Gumman's parents are dead but Skip LeRue's live in Salt Lake."

"Get the switchboard to find them before the media shows up on their front lawn. Also, get me Director Grainger and General Grant."

"They're already on their way here. I've also sent word to Decker Lake. I assumed you would want to speak to him about a campaign strategy."

"You're still my campaign strategist, Mallory, but I want him to help us during this crisis. With the election only nine days away, this crisis could very well end my presidency. Regardless, I'm not leaving hostages behind. I'm not leaving their fate in the hands of my opponent. Regardless of what I do, it will be smarter than any choices Coldridge might make."

"You'll need someone defending you on today's Sunday morning news shows," Harper said. "Decker would be the best. He's not officially part of your administration so anything he says can't be construed as White House policy. He's got credibility and he's a pit bull."

"What about the Hill? Who's going to handle the Chairman? He'll be breathing down my neck."

"Director Grainger and I will keep Representative Stanton off your back. You let us worry about the political fallout while you're focusing on getting our hostages home."

The president returned upstairs to shower and dress. Under the warm water, the image of a terrified Skip LeRue begging for mercy kept replaying in her head no matter how she tried to stop it. Fury replaced the tearful regret that she had felt earlier. By the time she was dressed and entering the Oval Office, where Grainger, General Grant, and Harper were waiting, she was steadfast, calm, and in command.

"General Grant," she said, slipping behind her desk, "are your people ready to rescue our hostages if called on?"

"Yes, Madam President," Grant replied. "My commanders are working on different rescue models but I need to warn you that even our best rescue plan is given less than a ten percent chance at successfully rescuing the hostages alive. In all models, we would sustain heavy American casualties."

An aide quietly entered the room and handed Harper a note. "Excuse me," she said, interrupting, "but I finally have some good news out of Mogadishu. General Saeed has just put the Marines and journalists who were staying in the Serenity Hotel on an African Union helicopter. They're being flown to the USS *Hornet*, which is anchored off the Somali coast. All of them are safe."

"General Saeed and his men," President Allworth said, "are an option that we've not thoroughly discussed. What's his status?"

"The general appears to have regained control of the center of the city," Grainger said. "There are still pockets in Mogadishu that are under Al-Shabaab, but Saeed is slowly reclaiming the capital and restoring order."

"If he's gotten Mogadishu secure, then perhaps it's time for us to share information with him," the president said. "We could tell him where the hostages are being held."

"His own men mutinied," Harper warned. "He's unreliable at best."

"General Saeed knows the city," General Grant countered. "He knows the enemy and he's undoubtedly eager for revenge after being humiliated at the embassy. It was his job, after all, to protect our facility. From a military viewpoint, the odds of him rescuing our people safely are better than if we send in our own people."

"Madam President," Grainger said. "If you choose to tell him, I would suggest that we give him the coordinates of only one of the sites."

"Why hold back?" Allworth asked.

"Given the volatility in Mogadishu, it would be equally as daunting for him to launch three simultaneous rescue attempts in three different areas as it would be for us. Having him focus on only one rescue will improve his odds of success."

"And it would give us a chance to assess his ability to carry out a successful rescue," Harper added.

"Which location would you recommend?" Allworth asked.

"The warehouse where we believe the ProTech security guards are being kept is in an area of Mogadishu where Al-Shabaab is losing ground, and based on our drone surveillance of that warehouse, it's the least well guarded."

For a moment, no one spoke, while the president considered what she'd just heard.

"Madam President," Grainger said, breaking the silence. "We have another option besides General Saeed. A few hours ago, I was informed that our station chief in Cairo has been contacted by Abasi Mubarak, an Egyptian cleric who is known in the Arab world as a conduit to these radical groups. Mubarak told us that he's been in contact with Al-Shabaab. He says its leaders are willing to negotiate the release of the remaining hostages in return for a ransom payment."

"Unbelievable," Harper said. "They murder two of our hostages and post it on the Internet and then send word they want to negotiate."

"Unbelievable but predictable," Grainger said. "They wanted us to see that they have our ambassador and also demonstrate that they will not hesitate to kill him and the other hostages."

"I don't want to pay these murderers a dime," Allworth said. "The United States does not negotiate."

"None of us want to," Grainger replied, "but it would be prudent to keep this backdoor line of communication open—if for no other reason than to buy time." Glancing at General Grant, Grainger added,

"I instructed our station chief to tell Mubarak that we need some credible evidence that he's actually in contact with Al-Shabaab. I also told him that we wanted a sign of the terrorists' good faith. I asked Mubarak to give us a list with the names of every hostage."

"Thank you," General Grant said.

"I not only did it for you, Frank," Grainger said. "I'm also trying to find out if Al-Shabaab has our station chief, Gunter Conner."

"Did this cleric mention how much ransom they want?" Harper asked.

"The cleric did not cite a figure," Grainger replied. "Although he did tell us that his fee would be additional."

"His fee?" President Allworth asked.

"He wants ten percent of whatever ransom is paid."

"That's unbelievable."

"Did he say how quickly the hostages could be freed if a payment was made?" Harper asked.

"Actually, he did. He claimed Al-Shabaab would be willing to release them before the presidential elections if we meet its leaders' demands."

President Allworth reacted instantly. "I'm not keen on having radical extremists in Somalia playing havoc with our electoral process. Clearly, they're dangling a carrot, hoping I'll grab it."

She leaned back in her chair behind her desk, placing her palms together in front of her lips, her thumbs tucked under her chin, while she silently evaluated her options.

Lowering her hands and leaning forward, she said, "They've already killed two of our people and posted it. We'd be derelict to not assist General Saeed. I want you to provide him with intel about the ProTech hostages being held at the warehouse. But only the warehouse. The terrorists are smart enough to know he's hunting for them. They can't hold us responsible for his actions, and if he can rescue some of our people, he'll not only be saving their lives but also putting more pressure on Al-Shabaab to negotiate."

"I'll contact the general immediately," Grainger said. "And the Egyptian cleric?"

"Tell him we're interested in hearing Al-Shabaab's demands but first we want a list of the hostages. We need to find out what's happened to Captain Grant and Gunter Conner."

CHAPTER THIRTY-FIVE

CIA headquarters
Langley, Virginia

Immediately after leaving the White House, Director Grainger called General Saeed in Somalia. He began the call with flattery.

"General Saeed, the president asked me to thank you personally for getting our people at the Serenity Hotel out of your nation safely during a clearly difficult time in Mogadishu."

"Two reporters," Saeed replied, "didn't wish to go, but I informed them they were not safe here. My people are afraid Al-Shabaab will kidnap more Americans and you will react by invading with your military. Like you came into our city during what you people call Black Hawk Down."

"You and President Musab have made it quite clear that you would view any military intervention on our part unfavorably. We certainly have no intention of invading Somalia. Our president is respecting your wishes."

"These weren't wishes," Saeed replied. "I do not need your military's help to defeat Al-Shabaab or to liberate your hostages. President Musab has assigned me both jobs and I will perform both."

"President Allworth and the American people would be grateful," Grainger replied diplomatically. "And we want to help—not by sending in a rescue team but by providing you with helpful intelligence. We have identified where seven of the hostages are being held in your city. We believe they are employees of ProTech International Security."

"How did you find these men?" Saeed demanded.

"That doesn't matter. What matters is that I can supply you with the coordinates you need to find them. I'd also like to put you in contact with several U.S. military advisors who are specialists in hostage rescues."

"You forget you are talking to a general who has been fighting Al-Shabaab much longer than you Americans. I don't need your advisors telling me how to rescue hostages."

"I simply was offering these advisors' expertise."

"I don't need expertise. I need the coordinates and six Apache attack helicopters."

In a surprised voice, Grainger replied, "Are you requesting our help militarily with Apaches?"

"No," Saeed snapped. "Any attempt by your military to enter Somalia will be seen as an act of aggression. The helicopters are payment."

"General Saeed, are you suggesting you and your government will not rescue our people unless we provide you with six Apache helicopters?"

Saeed laughed. "You think I'm blackmailing you? I'm not. I'm only asking you to deliver what I already have been promised by your agency."

"I'm not clear on what you are saying. Someone in my agency promised you six Apache attack helicopters?" Grainger replied. "Who?"

"Your station chief, Gunter Conner."

"I'm sorry, General, but this is the first I've heard of this."

"That fact does not nullify his promise. Was not Conner your representative? Of course he was, and he promised me six helicopters."

"We've not heard from him since the embassy attack. We don't know if he's been captured or escaped, but I can assure you that Gunter Conner was not authorized to promise you helicopters."

"But he did, didn't he? He asked me for help, and in return he told me that I would receive six Apaches."

"What sort of help?"

"This is a question for him, not me—assuming he's still alive. But the obligation carries forward. I will rescue your hostages and I will expect delivery of my helicopters. Now, tell me the coordinates."

After hearing them, Saeed said, "I am still dealing with pockets of strong resistance, but do not worry, I will rescue these Americans as soon as possible."

"And when will that be, General?"

"Monday. As I just told you, I have limited resources and regaining control of the city must be achieved first. But I will be ready tomorrow."

Grainger thanked Saeed and, after ending the call, summoned Charles Casterline to his office.

"General Saeed claims Gunter Conner promised him six Apache helicopters in return for a favor," Grainger explained. "What do you know about this?"

A puzzled look appeared on Casterline's face. "I don't know anything about it. I certainly never told Conner he could promise General Saeed helicopters."

"And you have no idea what favor he asked?"

"None. Is it possible General Saeed is making all of this up?"

"No, I don't think he is. You told Conner about the telephone intercept before the embassy attack and ordered him to get the ambassador and his party out of Somalia, which he didn't do," Grainger said. "Now Conner is nowhere to be found and we've got General Saeed telling us Conner promised him six Apaches in return for a favor. What the hell was Conner doing in Mogadishu?"

"I have no idea, sir," Casterline replied, "but whatever it was, it was not something authorized by me."

CHAPTER THIRTY-SIX

October 25, early Sunday morning
Penthouse, Watergate apartments
Washington, D.C.

The chemotherapy treatments attacking Decker Lake's colon cancer made him violently ill. There was no gradual resistance, but when Mallory Harper telephoned, Lake rallied himself.

"The president needs your help," she said.

That's all she'd needed to say.

Like an aged prizefighter eager to reclaim past knockouts in the ring, Lake was showered, dressed, and departing from his Watergate penthouse within the hour, ready for the first of a grueling schedule of Sunday morning television interviews. Makeup artists camouflaged his ghost-white skin and penciled in his eyebrows. They checked the costly toupee that was good enough to fool a casual viewer but not anyone who knew Lake from Georgetown parties and political fund-raisers. Before going on air, he'd wondered if his failing health would draw sympathy and weaken the attacks that would be lobbed at him by the president's opponents. He doubted it. Had the tables been turned, he would not have shown mercy but instead would have seized the opportunity, seeing the cancer as an opening for a quick kill—much like lions culling an aged and sick zebra from the pack.

Only Lake was no one's zebra.

Every morning show broadcast the grisly Al-Shabaab tape that showed Robert Gumman being shot in his head and Skip LeRue having his hands amputated before he was executed, although the social media footage was edited with blurred pixels for television. News reports describing the U.S. Marines who'd been stranded with reporters at the Serenity Hotel arriving safely on the USS *Hornet* did little to mitigate the public outrage. Those old enough to remember Black Hawk Down felt a frustrating déjà vu.

Instant polls conducted by the president's campaign staff found the public thirsty for blood—if not the terrorists', then the president's. A half-dozen members of Congress already were pandering to that sentiment. They took to the airwaves demanding the United States use its military might to invade Somalia and rescue the hostages.

Lake entered the Sunday news shows' studios following a gaggle of Washington think-tank experts and Arab scholars who had mouthed all-too-familiar polemics. A spokesman for the Islamic Muslim World Center for Peace called the Al-Shabaab jihadists "criminals and murderers who do not represent any community or religion." A spokeswoman for a group called Arabs Telling the Truth declared that "Islam is not just another religion but a totalitarian political cult-like ideology which compels its followers into blind obedience, teaches intolerance and brutality, and locks all Muslims and non-Muslims in a struggle deriving directly from the seventh-century, nomadic, predatory, Bedouin culture." The most liberal network morning talk show unshackled its favorite leftist commentator, who quickly blamed America. "I do not understand how anyone can say the fundamental problem is jihad when you look at how our Western civilization—a civilization of colonialists and oppressors who always operate in the name of liberation and democracy—created the foundation for these acts to occur."

For Decker Lake, these so-called experts were fodder. None could touch him when it came to feeding pabulum to the masses. While many in Washington, including Representative Thomas "the Chairman" Stanton, believed in the inherent wisdom and goodness of the American people, Lake did not. His was a much more arrogant and cynical point of view.

Polls of everyday Americans had revealed a grim truth that Lake had pounced on. Twenty-nine percent of Americans couldn't name the vice president, a quarter didn't know whom the United States had declared its independence from on July 4, 1776, and only 40 percent could name the three branches of government. This appalling ignorance had forever tainted Lake's image of representative democracy. One of his fondest stories was based on the New Testament account of Pontius Pilate washing his hands after giving a mob the choice between freeing Jesus or Barabbas. "The last time anyone asked the public to make an important decision," Lake liked to brag, "it voted to turn loose a murderer and thief and crucify the Son of God." Through his caustic lenses, the electorate was a flock of mindless sheep who required manipulation. It was a view shared by many of his fellow K Street lobbyists and professional spinmeisters who peddled their wares to the highest corporate bidders. Their role was to direct the lemmings and be paid handsomely for it.

In back-to-back appearances, Lake politely ridiculed the president's critics by reminding viewers that the talking heads who'd praised the president when she'd first announced her plans to open an embassy in Mogadishu were now condemning her. *How could anyone take their finger-in-the-wind opinions seriously?*

Sending the U.S. military into Somalia would only alienate a friendly government, he warned. It was not time for the United States to unleash its hounds from hell. Not yet. The president's priority was saving the American hostages, and that was a frightful burden that required leadership, patience, and, most of all, public support. It was time for a circling of the wagons around the president, not nipping at her heels.

In each appearance, Lake subtly shifted the blame away from President Allworth by reminding viewers that the State Department and the entire intelligence community had given the president a green light for opening the Mogadishu embassy. She'd agreed because going into Africa was necessary if our nation wanted to prevent future 9/11 attacks.

"Islamic extremists realize that our great nation is what keeps the world in balance," he declared. "America protects the weak from the dictators, puny thugs, and tyrants ruling countries where innocents are enslaved and good people victimized." Lake made it sound as if the embassy attack, in a perverse way, had been a badge of honor.

President Allworth watched Lake's appearances from the Oval Office with raptured admiration. He was a master of sound bites, an unmatched verbal swordsman who projected the persona of an omnipotent pope capable of forgiving all sin. Little wonder that power seekers agreed to his $4,000-per-hour consulting fee without a whisper of complaint.

"The monstrosity of these cowardly acts is a reminder of why we must never give in to religious fanatics," Lake declared while peering into the camera. "It is why I support our president at a time when all Americans need to put their political differences aside and rally behind our leaders and the brave Americans who are still being held hostage by savages who defile their own religion."

He was so convincing, the president wanted to applaud.

Lake returned to his penthouse suite just as presidential challenger Timothy Coldridge was being interviewed outside a Methodist Church in Emporia, Kansas, where he'd just attended a Sunday service before continuing his whistle-stop campaign through the Midwest.

"Now is not the time to criticize our president," he said in a sober voice and then he did exactly that for ten minutes, ending his soliloquy by declaring: "We need to not put our people at risk overseas, as this president has done. And the best way to achieve that is by paying attention to America's problems at home, not meddling in a third-world country that has been at war with itself for decades."

As soon as Coldridge finished, his political handlers unleashed his party's lapdogs. A handful of senators accused the president of "continued global interference." The party faithful in the House issued statements chastising her for playing the role of "world policeman."

Coldridge and his supporters' declarations didn't alarm Lake. He knew Americans were already beginning to rally behind the White House in support of the remaining hostages. Despite his cynicism, Lake knew that Americans did not abandon their fellow Americans in times of war, and the embassy attack was clearly an act of war by jihadists.

But as he was savoring his television performances, he received a telephone call in his home office that did concern him. It was from a private contractor who provided travel services to federal agencies. Lake had used his influence to help the contractor win a number of lucrative government contracts and, in doing so, Lake had made the businessman indebted to him. Lake had sought help from the travel agent as soon as Timothy Coldridge had locked in his party's nomination. At Lake's urging, the contractor had approached the Coldridge camp and volunteered to arrange travel for the campaign. He offered to delay invoices—a tactic that campaigns used to hide debt. The governor's campaign staff had immediately accepted that seemingly gracious offer without realizing that Lake had instigated it as a way to keep tabs on when and where Coldridge and his people were traveling.

The travel agent was calling Lake at his penthouse office now with a useful tip. After hearing it, Lake telephoned the White House.

"Did you know Coldridge has broken off his schedule to fly to Utah?" he asked Mallory Harper.

"No," she responded. "Should I assume he's flying to Utah for a photo op with Skip LeRue's grieving parents?"

"You should. Now tell me, did either you or the president notice that LeRue was forty-two years old and single?"

"Yes," she replied. "Did you notice he was a Mormon?"

"You don't believe Mormons can be gay? I made some phone calls, and he's got a partner here in D.C."

"His sexual orientation is hardly germane."

"It could be, because Coldridge opposes gay marriage," Lake said. "Get word to the media that LeRue has a fiancé who's willing to be interviewed. I've been told he is devastated that he hasn't been given any say in LeRue's funeral or any claim to his estate. Paint Coldridge into a corner. He's pandering to LeRue's parents in Utah but totally insensitive to his life partner. I shouldn't have to explain to you how this will outrage a huge bloc of voters."

"I like it," Harper replied. "It will give the media something besides Mogadishu to chew on."

"Trust me, we can milk this. The moment Coldridge learns that LeRue was gay and hears his partner has been giving interviews about equal spousal rights, he'll turn his plane around. He's not going to risk being ambushed by reporters in front of a weeping mom and dad about his antigay views. And as soon as he cancels his trip to Utah, we can leak the reason why he's running away. It'll be a new bone."

"Decker," she said admiringly. "Chemo seems to agree with you."

PART FIVE

~

THE COUNTDOWN BEGINS

Men should be either treated generously or destroyed,
because they take revenge for slight injuries—for heavy
ones they cannot.

—Niccolò Machiavelli

MONDAY

Eight days before the presidential election

CHAPTER THIRTY-SEVEN

Korfa's apartment
Mogadishu, Somalia

Brooke felt like a caged animal. Sheer exhaustion had forced her to sleep for a few hours Sunday after she and Gunter Conner took refuge in Korfa's apartment. But she didn't understand why Conner seemed unconcerned about contacting Washington, and when CNN broadcast the video that Al-Shabaab had posted of Robert Gumman and Skip LeRue being murdered, she became even more alarmed. Every few minutes, she tried to use the BlackBerry that Korfa had given her, but without luck.

While she paced the floor, Conner seemed content to drink tea, sleep, and do nothing. She was about to confront him when Korfa burst through his apartment's door and exclaimed, "General Saeed is going to rescue the Americans today!"

"How'd you find out?" Brooke asked.

"I told you," Conner said, "he is in charge of the general's telecommunication equipment. He can listen to all of Saeed's phone calls."

Addressing Korfa, Conner asked, "When's this happening?"

"He's getting his men ready now. The Americans told him where he can find seven of the hostages."

"Which seven?" Brooke asked.

"The security guards who work for ProTech."

"We need to do something to help."

When Conner didn't react, she turned her attention to Korfa. "I've been trying the cell phone you gave me. It still doesn't get a signal."

"Even if it worked," Conner volunteered, "what can you do?"

"I don't know, but I'm not going to just hide here. What's wrong with you? It's like you don't want Washington to know we're alive."

Addressing Korfa, she said, "I've been thinking about this. If I wear my burqa, will you take me to police headquarters?"

"No," Korfa said. "It still would be too dangerous for me and my sister."

"Then how about driving me to the area where the hostages are being held? I'll wait until you've driven away before I go anywhere near the general."

"That would be very dangerous too," Korfa answered.

"How will you explain showing up there?" Conner asked. "You can't just say you were in the neighborhood and thought you'd drop by."

"I'll tell him I escaped from the embassy and followed the hostages to the warehouse."

"That's not believable."

"Okay, I'll tell General Saeed that Washington told me where the hostages were being held and told me to rendezvous with him there. He won't know that I haven't been able to contact Washington."

"The general will believe that," Korfa said.

"I'm not asking for permission from you," Brooke told Conner. "I'll walk if necessary but I'm not just going to sit here any longer."

"You're safe here," Conner said. "We both are."

"Our government doesn't pay us to be safe. I don't get you, Conner. I've been thinking about you and I've decided that you're either a coward or there's a reason why you want everyone to believe you're dead."

"Caanood, do you have any fresh tea?" Conner asked, ignoring her.

"Only enough for a half cup," she replied from across the room in the kitchen. "You drank the rest."

"Caanood, you can ride with us to get more tea," Korfa said. "We'll go to a market near where the general is heading. We can drop you off there. It will explain why we are in that vicinity if I'm seen. But we must hurry."

Brooke ducked into the bathroom to put on her burqa while Caanood retreated to the bedroom to change her dress.

"Conner," Brooke asked when she reappeared, "are you coming with us?"

"No. I'll be fixing myself that half cup of tea."

He handed her the BlackBerry that she'd left by the television.

Taking it from him, Brooke said, "And I guess that answers my question. You really are a coward."

CHAPTER THIRTY-EIGHT

A neighborhood controlled by Al-Shabaab
Mogadishu, Somalia

General Saeed sent an older police officer, who walked with a limp, in street clothes to do reconnaissance near the warehouse where the ProTech hostages were being held. Al-Shabaab fighters intercepted him as soon as he neared, but he explained that he was on his way to visit his ill mother and was convincing enough that they let him pass unharmed.

When he returned, he drew a crude diagram for the general. The warehouse was a two-story mud-colored building whose ground floor was used for storage, while its second served as living quarters. Exterior stairs led to the second-floor apartment. Nearly all of the surrounding buildings had been destroyed during fighting and were vacant. Many didn't have roofs.

The general's spy reported that three Al-Shabaab fighters had been stationed on the warehouse's flat roof as sentries. Two Toyota pickup trucks had been parked at the front of the warehouse with six armed fighters lingering around them. There were no windows on the warehouse's ground floor, a precaution to keep thieves from breaking inside. There were two windows on each side of the rectangular building's second level, but none was big enough for a man to climb through.

General Saeed considered himself a brilliant military tactician, and he realized his best option was to send a tightly knit group of skilled commandos to surgically attack the guards at night and free the hostages.

But the general didn't have any skilled commandos. Most of his men were street thugs. There were no night-vision goggles, no communication headsets, no silenced weapons.

Having nixed that idea, the general considered his other options, beginning with air power. There had been a time when the Somali Air Force was the best equipped in East Africa. Its Soviet allies had provided President Mohamed Siad Barre with a fleet of Russian MiG-17 and Chinese Shenyang F-6 fighters. But those jets had been cannibalized in the civil wars that followed Barre's ouster, and even if General Saeed had access to the former fleet, he would not have pilots capable of flying the jets. Barre had hired mercenary pilots to guarantee they'd be loyal only to him.

The general did, however, own an Italian Agusta A129 Mangusta attack helicopter that he'd recently purchased from Turkey. It was piloted by two South Africans. But for the Agusta to be effective, it would need to hover close to the warehouse, which would make it vulnerable to RPGs.

Saeed decided the American hostages weren't worth risking his most prized armament for.

Next, Saeed considered the three 1950-era Russian-made T-55 tanks that he commanded. The T-55s were the most widely used in third-world countries because they were cheap, easy to operate, and often the only ones available because of Western embargoes. He had modernized his tanks by adding "reactive armor" that enabled them to withstand a hit by an RPG-7 grenade—the most commonly available to terrorists. Still, there was a risk.

A good number of Al-Shabaab fighters had been trained by Al-Qaeda soldiers who had been trained by the Mujahideen who had been trained by the CIA to fight the Soviets in Afghanistan. The CIA had taught the Mujahideen ways to make their RPG-7 rounds effective tank killers. Firing two or three RPG-7 grenades simultaneously during an ambush from a range of 65 to 160 feet could immobilize most tanks, giving Mujahideen fighters time to reposition, reload, and reengage. If a tank had reactive armor, the Mujahideen would fire one RPG, destroying its first level of protection, and then fire a second and third round at the exact same spot.

Again, the general decided it wasn't worth risking his tanks to save Americans. Instead, he would use assets that he could easily replace—his men.

The general hand-selected fifty soldiers and drove with them to a staging area a half mile from the warehouse. He'd chosen the evening Maghrib prayer time to mount the rescue, when the sun dropped beneath the horizon but the sky was still light. He dispatched his two best marksmen to the roof of a four-story building on a slight hill about three hundred yards from the warehouse. From their vantage point, the sharpshooters could see the three Al-Shabaab sentries on the warehouse roof. The marksmen positioned their scoped rifles ten feet behind two basketball-size holes that they had punched through a waist-high wall that ringed the roof. This enabled them to see through the openings but would hide them from the jihadists on the warehouse rooftop below them. They would have a difficult time firing up through the holes and hitting them.

Saeed divided his men into three squads and directed one to approach the warehouse from the west, another from the east, and the last from behind the building. He sent two Toyota pickup trucks with .30-caliber machine guns on tripods welded onto their beds to support them. Machine guns in the back of trucks were a common sight in Somalia but they were effective only when the vehicles stopped. Firing accurately from a truck bouncing down a rut-filled street was nearly impossible.

Saeed waited until his snipers told him that two of the Al-Shabaab sentries on the warehouse roof had put their guns aside and were now on their knees facing Mecca in prayer.

"Kill them!" he ordered.

The snipers fired instantly at the easiest targets—the two kneeling jihadists. But while both snipers were excellent shots, they were untrained, and neither asked the other whom he had targeted. Both fired at the same man, killing him, leaving the other to grab his AK-47 and seek cover behind the knee-high wall that ringed the warehouse roof.

The sound of gunfire caused the jihadists on the street to panic. One leaped into a waiting Toyota truck and sped away with two of his comrades in the pickup bed firing their weapons. They were immediately met by a wave of rounds fired by Saeed's approaching soldiers. The truck careened into a wall, killing the driver and catapulting the truck's two riders into the air. They landed in the street and scrambled for cover in the shell of a nearby building. One lost his weapon but the other kept shooting.

The three fighters still guarding the warehouse's front crowded behind the Toyota truck parked there, firing haphazardly while the remaining two sentries on the roof dealt with Saeed's snipers. Working in tandem, one of the sentries showed himself, intentionally drawing fire while his partner shouldered an RPG. Saeed's snipers killed the sentry when he made himself visible but missed the second man, and with a puff of smoke he fired the RPG grenade.

At three hundred yards, the odds of an RPG-7 hitting its target were only one in five, but the powerful round hit its mark, exploding and killing both of Saeed's snipers.

While praising Allah, the jihadist reloaded and turned the RPG on Saeed's approaching troops. He aimed at one of the pickup trucks speeding toward the warehouse, and with another puff of telltale smoke the RPG ripped across the street, striking the truck. It exploded, killing both men.

Having seen the fate of his fellow machine gunner, the Somali soldier riding in the bed of the remaining truck unleashed the fury of his .30-caliber gun. Shiny brass cartridges spewed from its chamber as the truck sped forward, bouncing over the rutty road. Rounds ripped into the building's second-floor façade. Hiding behind the warehouse's parapet, the jihadist loaded a third RPG round, but just as he was about to stand and fire it, one of the machine gun's rounds penetrated the knee-high wall protecting him and he collapsed.

Five minutes into the rescue, only five jihadists were still alive outside the building. Three remained crouched behind the truck parked at the warehouse entrance, the other two were hiding close to where they'd been thrown from their crashed truck. Yelling praises to Allah, a defiant Al-Shabaab fighter stepped into the open street, where he fired an RPG at the machine gunner. The grenade was poorly aimed but it hardly mattered. It struck a building's wall adjacent to the machine gunner, and that blast peppered him with bits of concrete, killing him.

Now it was Saeed's ground troops who returned fire with their own RPGs. A grenade fired at the Al-Shabaab truck at the warehouse front exploded in a fireball, clouding the air with white dust and black smoke. One of the terrorists hiding behind it began screaming, his body ablaze. His two companions already were dead.

That left only the two fighters who'd been thrown from the pickup and now were hiding in the abandoned house. They were easily overrun. Saeed's soldiers killed the armed fighter and captured the unarmed one.

When General Saeed was informed that the warehouse's exterior was secure, he arrived in a camouflaged Soviet-made BTR-60PA armored troop carrier capable of repelling small arms fire. He strutted triumphantly from it into the street, where his men had brought the captured Al-Shabaab fighter before him.

"How many are inside?" the general demanded.

"Three."

Saeed punched the jihadist in his face and growled, "Liar."

The fighter, a fifteen-year-old Somali, began to cry.

"If you're lying," Saeed threatened, "I'll cut out your tongue and make you eat it."

A bullet smacked against the BTR-60 only inches from where Saeed was interrogating his prisoner, startling the general, who immediately ducked for cover. A second shot downed a nearby soldier and a third killed another.

It was the Al-Shabaab sniper's fourth round that revealed where he was hiding—a crumbling two-story building about two hundred yards west of the warehouse. One of Saeed's soldiers fired an RPG but the grenade missed the building and exploded uselessly in the air.

For several moments, it was quiet while the sniper moved to a new hiding spot in a nearby building. Once safe, he again began drawing blood. His targets were the soldiers who'd climbed the rear of the warehouse and were now on its roof. An officer prying open a rooftop trapdoor was shot in the chest.

Pinned down on the street behind his armored personnel carrier and furious, Saeed barked an order into his cell phone, and within minutes the swooshing sound of an approaching Agusta helicopter could be heard. Its South African pilots began firing their 20-millimeter Gatling-style cannon as soon as the sniper's new lair was within range. At a rate of five hundred rounds per minute, the slugs from the three-barreled gun sounded like hot popcorn exploding against a metal pan. The armor-piercing rounds easily punched through the building's exterior walls.

Worried that the sniper might have somehow survived, the pilots fired two of the helicopter's 70-millimeter rockets, which hit with such explosive force that the entire ramshackle building collapsed. The pilots retreated as Saeed's men hurried to search for the sniper's remains.

Once again, Saeed stepped from behind the armored vehicle and watched as three of his soldiers climbed the exterior stairs to the apartment where the hostages were being held. They burst through its doorway at the same time Saeed's men on the roof forced open the trapdoor and dropped through its opening into the apartment.

General Saeed could hear the sounds of AK-47s firing. Minutes later, two of his men appeared on the second-floor staircase supporting a wounded man whom they carried between them, his arms draped around their shoulders. He'd been shot in the leg.

At first glance, the wounded man appeared to be an Al-Shabaab fighter, because he was dressed like one of them. But as he was carried to the front of the armored personnel carrier, General Saeed looked into the man's grimy face and realized he was one of the ProTech hostages. Al-Shabaab had dressed him as one of its fighters to fool rescuers.

The American looked up at the general.

"Thank you," he said, his voice a hoarse whisper.

Saeed smiled, nodded, and raised his pistol. He shot the American in the forehead. The general's two men released their grips and the former hostage fell on the dirt street.

"Collect our dead and the bodies of the Americans, but leave the others for the dogs to eat," Saeed ordered.

By this point, curious Somalis had gathered around the perimeter, drawn like a pack of hyenas hoping to strip clean the bones of whatever the police left behind.

Saeed entered his armored personnel carrier and ordered his driver to return him to his command post. He didn't pay any attention to the Somali gawkers as they stepped out of his vehicle's path. He did not notice the woman in a burqa who'd watched him murder her fellow American.

CHAPTER THIRTY-NINE

Situation Room
The White House
Washington, D.C.

At first, no one spoke.

President Allworth, Chief of Staff Harper, CIA director Grainger, and chairman of the Joint Chiefs General Grant had gathered inside the White House Situation Room to watch what was supposed to be a rescue. Grainger had notified them as soon as the operators of a drone, which the agency had positioned over the Mogadishu warehouse, reported that General Saeed was moving his troops into position near where the seven ProTech hostages were being held.

"That wasn't a rescue!" Harper exclaimed, her voice a mixture of shock and contempt. "It was a full-blown military attack."

"I'd call it more of a slaughter," President Allworth said. "Based on what we've just witnessed, it doesn't appear that any of the seven American hostages were rescued."

"Sadly, I believe you are correct," Director Grainger replied. "I'm afraid all of the seven ProTech employees, as well as a number of General Saeed's men, perished during that rescue attempt."

"The only person who General Saeed's men brought out of that warehouse alive was that Al-Shabaab fighter at the end who was taken into the street and executed by General Saeed," Harper said. From twenty thousand feet, the drone's camera had not sent them a clear enough photograph for anyone in the White House to realize that Saeed had murdered an American who'd been dressed like an Al-Shabaab fighter.

"I'm fairly certain General Saeed didn't know we were watching," General Grant volunteered. "Not that he would have cared."

"It would appear that General Saeed's recklessness may make him as big of a threat to our hostages as Al-Shabaab is," Harper dryly noted.

"Unfortunately, General Saeed is not much different from other third-world strongmen we deal with," Grainger said. "He's narcissistic, egotistical, ruthless, and has little concern for human life. He's a murderer. But he's our narcissistic, egotistical, ruthless, deadly murderer. That's the grim reality. As reckless and inept as he is, it's still better to have him on our side than working against us."

"Not when it comes to rescuing our people," President Allworth replied. "We certainly can't trust him to rescue Ambassador Thomas and the others after seeing how he bungled this attempt."

Speaking directly to Harper, the president continued. "You'll need to inform the family members of the ProTech security guards of their loss. We need to get a statement ready before word leaks out of Somalia about this failed rescue." The president appeared weary. "This debacle just keeps getting worse and worse."

"This certainly wasn't our fault, Madam President," General Grant said. "Director Grainger urged General Saeed to consult with our military experts and draw up a viable rescue plan but he refused. In fairness, all military operations can result in casualties, but if Saeed had accepted our help, I'm certain there would have been fewer deaths than there were."

"What's happening with your back-channel talks in Cairo?" President Allworth asked Grainger.

"My last communication with Abasi Mubarak was positive," Grainger answered. "Although he still hasn't supplied me with a list of who exactly Al-Shabaab is holding, he did tell me a ransom amount."

Glancing at General Grant, the president said, "I'm sorry, Frank, that we still don't know if your niece is one of the hostages."

General Grant nodded but said nothing.

"Nor have we been able to reach our station chief, Gunter Conner," Grainger added. "Finding both remains a high priority."

"What figure did they tell you for a ransom?" Harper asked.

"Al-Shabaab is willing to release all of the hostages for a lump payment of twenty-five million dollars. Plus, we'd need another two and a half million to pay Mubarak's fee."

"Do you think Al-Shabaab will still be willing to negotiate now that General Saeed has attacked the warehouse?"

"I can't predict how they are going to react," Grainger replied, "but because General Saeed was responsible, I doubt they will blame us."

"Will they demand the same amount of cash?" Harper asked.

"Mallory, I certainly am not going to counteroffer because there are fewer hostages!" the president exclaimed. "This is not about money."

"For ProTech's insurance company it is," Grainger interjected. "Pro-Tech's president told me less than an hour ago that the company's insurance company is willing to pay upward of two million in ransom for John Duggard's release, and it had agreed to pay as much as ten million for the other seven hostages."

"ProTech isn't going to pay that extra ten million now," Harper noted. "From a cost-benefit ratio, a twenty-five-million ransom makes financial sense when compared to the expense and danger of launching a military rescue."

"Your corporate background is showing," General Grant quietly replied. "As the president said, this is hardly a financially based decision. People's lives are at stake."

"If we pay a ransom," Grainger said, "the cleric claims the hostages could be released as early as this coming weekend."

"This weekend! That sounds a bit too good to believe," President All-worth replied.

Although no one in the Situation Room mentioned it, everyone understood the significance of what the CIA director had just said. Al-Shabaab was claiming it would free all of the hostages before Tuesday's presidential election.

"ProTech has offered to help us conceal any additional funds we might want to include with its insurance payment," Grainger said. "Pro-Tech has also offered to handle the negotiations and delivery of the cash. In addition, my people have spoken to the Saudis, and they're willing to pay the entire ransom for us with the understanding that we will reimburse them through foreign and military aid. There would be no link between our government and the ransom to Al-Shabaab."

"This is beginning to smell a bit like the Iran-Contra affair," Harper noted.

"The media isn't stupid," President Allworth said. "If the hostages are suddenly freed, the public will know a ransom was paid, and you can bet that Al-Shabaab will rub our noses in it. You can't sign a no-comment pact with terrorists."

"Al-Shabaab can boast and the media can speculate all it wants," Grainger replied. "But I can assure you there will be no paper trail to the White House if we decide to pursue this course. There will be no proof that we actually negotiated a cash payment with Al-Shabaab."

"Can you guarantee a malcontent isn't going to call the *New York Times*?" Allworth replied. "Let's not be naïve."

"What guarantee is there Al-Shabaab will release the hostages if we pay them?" Harper asked.

"Ransoming hostages has become a common business practice in Somalia," Grainger answered. "It's a multimillion-dollar industry that is a staple for its economy. Pirates have financial backers, including policemen and Somali businessmen, who front them cash to hire crews and rent boats to kidnap ships. It's standard practice for pirates to pay kickbacks—at least twenty percent to Al-Shabaab for protection—after a ship has been seized and is sailed to a safe harbor under the terrorists' control. A piece of the ransom goes to pay the cooks who feed the hostages, the doctors who address their medical needs, and the landlords where the crews are held hostage. The pirates enforce a penalty system too. If a hostage is mistreated, the guilty pirate has five thousand dollars deducted from his cut."

"That's simply unbelievable," President Allworth said, clearly disgusted.

"How does one deliver a twenty-five-million ransom to Al-Shabaab?" Harper asked. "It doesn't have a Swiss bank account, or does it?"

"These transactions are cash-only in Somalia, all hundred-dollar U.S. bills. No matter the source, the cash would be delivered to Cleric Mubarak to take to Al-Shabaab."

"How trustworthy is he?" Harper asked.

"He's not, but he'd be a fool to cheat Al-Shabaab. We would have to send someone we trust along with the cash to make sure he doesn't try to cheat us."

For a moment, no one spoke.

"We have three options," Grainger volunteered, "and I don't see them improving. Waiting is not an option. We can send a military rescue team into Mogadishu, knowing it will harm our ties with Somalia, possibly undermine President Musab's government, and result in heavy casualties and possibly the deaths of the hostages. We can tell General Saeed the coordinates for the other locations where our hostages are being held and pressure him to accept our advice and assistance about how to actually rescue someone. Or we can dispatch an envoy who we trust to Cairo with the ransom payment to meet with Cleric Mubarak and pay the ransom."

"You're overlooking a fourth choice," President Allworth said. "All of the above."

"I'm not sure I understand," Grainger replied.

"I want you to speak to General Saeed and make it clear that we are disappointed in his tactics at the warehouse. See if you can convince him to accept our military's advice and help. But don't tell him where the other hostages are. Just gauge his willingness to accept our help." Switching her glance to General Grant, the president continued. "I want our people to finalize a rescue plan and be ready on my command to execute it."

Speaking to both General Grant and Grainger, she concluded, "I want a twenty-five-million-dollar payment on its way to Cairo within the hour. I don't want the Saudis involved. Let's work through ProTech, but I want someone from our military to be in charge as our negotiator and courier. Someone with a high enough rank and experience that he can speak for me if it becomes necessary. Someone who can deal with both Cleric Mubarak and Al-Shabaab and make a decision on the spot."

"Madam President," General Grant said, "send me."

"Impossible," President Allworth instantly replied. "You would be a bigger kidnapping target than our ambassador."

"Then I will tender my resignation and go as a civilian. My niece is somewhere in Mogadishu—possibly being held hostage—and I promised my brother that I'd always protect her and look after her."

"I appreciate your gallantry," Allworth said, "but—"

For the first time in his life, General Grant rudely interrupted the president of the United States and said in a stern voice, "I asked you personally not to send my niece to Somalia, but you sent her there anyway. With all due respect, Madam President, you owe me this."

CHAPTER FORTY

H e murdered them!" Brooke exclaimed, while removing her veil. "General Saeed murdered the hostages."

"Calm down," Conner replied, "and lower your voice."

"Did you hear what I said?" she demanded. "I saw General Saeed execute an American hostage in cold blood outside that warehouse. I don't believe he ever meant to rescue any of them."

"If he killed them, why are you still alive?"

"Because I didn't let him see me. And thanks for your concern."

"Tell me exactly what you saw."

"After Korfa and Caanood dropped me near the market, I walked in the direction of the warehouse, but before I reached it I heard gunfire, and an attack helicopter flew over me. It began firing its cannons at a building less than twenty yards from where I was standing. I had to jump for cover."

"Where was General Saeed?"

"By the time I reached the warehouse, the fighting was over and I joined a crowd of Somalis who were watching him and his men."

"General Saeed?" Conner said impatiently.

"He was standing in the street and I was about to call out and approach him when I saw two of his soldiers helping a wounded man out of the building's second-floor apartment. He was dressed like an Al-Shabaab terrorist and that's what I thought he was at first, but when he reached General Saeed I got a clear look at his face and I recognized him. It was Charles 'Cash' Kelley. Rather than helping him, General Saeed shot him point-blank in his forehead."

"Are you absolutely certain it wasn't a terrorist? Maybe someone who resembled Kelley?"

"I know what I saw. I wasn't close enough to hear what Kelley said to him, but Kelley said something right before the general shot him. At that point, I just stood there in the crowd. I wasn't going to let General Saeed know I'd just seen him murder Cash Kelley."

"The general would have shot you too," Korfa said. "You are lucky to still be alive."

"He rode right by me in the crowd when he left, but he didn't notice me. Once he was gone, everyone around me rushed forward. It was horrible. They began stripping the bodies of the terrorists. They left them completely naked. But Saeed's soldiers stopped them from touching their people and the Americans. I waited and watched them bring all of the ProTech men out of the building. All of them had been dressed to look like terrorists. I moved close enough to the bodies to confirm that the man who was shot in the street was Cash Kelley. General Saeed killed him in cold blood."

Brooke pulled off her burqa. Her Marine Corps uniform underneath it was drenched in sweat. She felt her hands begin to tremble.

Caanood said, "I'll bring you fresh clothes." She disappeared into the bedroom and returned with two dresses. The first was a *dirac*, a short-sleeved Arabian kaftan dress worn over a *gorgorad*, an underskirt made of silk. It was the finest dress Caanood owned and had gold-stitched borders. The other was a *guntiino*, a simple white-and-black dress with a leopard pattern, made from a long piece of cloth tied over the shoulder and draped around the waist. She offered Brooke both.

The last thing Brooke cared about was fashion. She took the less glitzy guntiino from Caanood, thanked her, and stepped into the bathroom to wash her face, calm her nerves, and change. As she was slipping on the guntiino, the irony of the moment struck her. For one of the first times in her life, being black was going to work to her advantage. She could easily pass for an African in the guntiino. After taking several more deep breaths to steady herself, she returned to the apartment's main room.

"Caanood, I'll pay you for this dress," she said.

"No," Caanood replied, "you're a friend of Master Conner's. It's my gift to you."

"Caanood," Brooke said sternly. "Mr. Conner and I are not friends. We work together. That's all. I'll pay for the dress."

"Enough about dresses," Conner said. "Who else have you told about this?"

"How could I tell anyone?" she replied. "The cell phone Korfa gave me still doesn't work."

Korfa reached out his hand. "Let me see the BlackBerry," he said, taking it from her. He examined it quickly and asked, "What have you done to its battery?"

"What are you talking about? I thought the phone didn't work because I broke it when the helicopter began shooting and I hit the ground really hard."

"This phone has no battery. It had a battery when I gave it to you," Korfa replied. He ducked into the bedroom and returned after inserting a fresh battery. He handed the phone to her. "It works."

Brooke looked momentarily puzzled and then glanced at Conner. "The only time I didn't have that phone with me was this morning when I went into the bathroom to put on the burqa before leaving for the market. When I came out, you handed the phone to me, because I'd left it by the television."

"Caanood," Conner said. "Could you bring us some tea?"

"Tea? I don't give a damn about having a cup of tea. You took that battery out, didn't you?" she said, glaring at Conner. "You didn't want me to call Washington. You haven't wanted me to call since we got here."

Caanood handed Conner a cup and he sipped the tea slowly. "This is delicious," he said. "Very calming. Thank you." He spoke next to Korfa. "Can you and Caanood give us a moment, please?"

After they stepped into the bedroom and shut its door, Conner said, "Let's sit down. There's something I need to explain to you and it's going to take a few minutes."

They sat facing each other on two tiny red carpets.

"Are you certain you don't want some tea?" he asked.

"Get to the point. Why did you take the battery?" she said, making no attempt to hide her building anger.

"I'll tell you, but first I need to explain some background so you'll understand why I've been reluctant to contact Washington or have you contact them. Please hear me out. All I ask is that you keep an open mind."

"Go ahead," she said.

"Let's begin by recalling the bombing that you stopped in London. Did you know that before that attempt, the Taliban broke into a prison in the city of Dera Ismail Khan and freed several hundred prisoners?"

"No. I didn't. But I don't see what either of those events has to do with you sabotaging my phone."

"It has everything to do with it. I asked you to be patient." He took another sip of tea. "I am convinced that the Pakistan prison break and the London bombing were orchestrated by the same man, a radical Islamist who is trying to forge an alliance. A man who is clever and charismatic enough that he can carry out attacks through more than a dozen different organizations—Al-Qaeda, Al-Shabaab, Boko Haram, AQIM, ISIS…"

"Jumping ahead," she said, "you believe this figure is responsible for the attack Saturday night on the embassy, is that right?"

"It is. I do," he replied. "I believe this same man ordered that attack. I further believe that he is using a Somali American to carry out his commands. His lackey goes by the name Abdul Hafeez. I believe Hafeez was in charge of the attack on the embassy and is now in charge of the hostages."

"What do you mean, a Somali American who goes by the name Abdul Hafeez?" she asked. "What's his real name?"

"Hafeez is not the name his parents gave him, but I don't know his real identity—not yet," Conner replied. "I believe that Hafeez was the masked figure who you saw earlier on CNN. He is the terrorist who murdered Robert Gumman and amputated Skip LeRue's hands before killing him and uploading that video on the Internet. As I just explained, I believe Abdul Hafeez is a puppet. He reports to the real leader behind these attacks. I also believe that Abdul Hafeez is the only man alive right now who can lead me to him."

"I was thoroughly briefed before coming to Mogadishu," Brooke replied, "and there was nothing in any of the materials about any jihadist you are describing—nothing about some powerful figure who is aligning different groups."

"That's because Langley doesn't believe this man exists. Our analysts don't think any Arab could bring such divergent groups as ISIS and Boko Haram together. I've tried repeatedly to warn them that this man has that ability and that he poses a major threat to our nation. If he isn't stopped, he'll be capable of attacking us from dozens of different directions with different forces. He'll be capable of slaughtering thousands and thousands of Americans. But no one has listened to me."

"Who is he? What's his name? Do you know anything about him? Where's he from? If you can't answer those questions, how can you prove he really exists?"

"He's real but you're correct. I know virtually nothing about him. That's why I call him the Falcon. I realize it's a bit dramatic, but he was once described to me by an informant as someone who soars above the fray."

Brooke thought for a moment and said, "Is hunting this Falcon why you volunteered to come here to Mogadishu?"

Conner nodded. "I've been tracking him for more than three years. Now let me ask you a question, Captain Grant. Do you believe the end justifies the means—that sometimes to achieve a greater good an individual must engage in a known wrong?"

"It's been a while since I took Philosophy 101 or a course in situational ethics. What's your point? How did taking my cell phone battery serve a greater good?"

"It's not a theoretical question for me or for most of my agency colleagues. At the Farm during training for covert operations we were told that we do not have to follow the laws of any country except for the United States. I could break into a house in Cairo. I could kidnap someone. Professionals such as myself are not the only ones who sometimes elect to do horrible things for a more noble cause. A scientist who gives lifesaving serum to one test group and allows another to die, for example."

"You're doing a lot of posturing and rationalizing here," Brooke said, "without telling me why it's necessary."

Conner put his teacup on the small table next to him. Tea had become his substitute for the Xanax he was missing. For some reason it helped. "Langley called me Saturday night when Ambassador Thomas and the others were still attending the presidential dinner at Villa Somalia and told me a telephone conversation between two suspected Al-Shabaab terrorists had been intercepted. The translation was muddled, but Langley suspected they were discussing a possible attack that night at the embassy."

It took a moment for the enormity of his revelation to sink in. "You knew we were going to be attacked," she said, "and you didn't warn anyone?"

"I was told it was a possibility, not a certainty. Langley didn't want to alarm everyone. I was ordered to handle it discreetly and I *did* tell someone. I explained the situation to General Saeed, and he assured me that he could protect the embassy if there was an attack that night. He assured me there was nothing to worry about."

Her mind was racing now, thinking back to the events before the embassy attack. "General Saeed never warned us," she said. "I was in the communications center when Cash Kelley telephoned John Duggard in the motorcade and told him that protesters were gathering outside the embassy compound. Ambassador Thomas and his party had just left Villa Somalia. There was plenty of time for them to turn around and return to Villa Somalia, where they would be well guarded. There was plenty of time for them to be diverted to the airport. Why didn't General Saeed warn them or us? Why didn't you warn us and not just him?"

She looked suspiciously at Conner and said, "There's something more you haven't told me." And then another thought came to her. "General Saeed sent his officers to escort the motorcade into the embassy compound through the protesters. Why would he do that? If he knew the embassy was going to be attacked, it doesn't make sense. He had to know that he was putting them—and all of us inside the embassy—at risk."

Conner showed no expression, gave no hint.

"Oh my God! You wanted the ambassador there!" she exclaimed.

"You wanted them there because you wanted Al-Shabaab to attack. It was supposed to be a trap. You and General Saeed were using them, using all of us as bait."

All of the disjointed pieces rushed together in her mind.

Without warning, Brooke lunged forward from her seat on the floor at Conner. She hit him in his chest with her left shoulder, knocking him onto his back. Before he could react, she was sitting on his chest, her hands now fists. She punched him hard in the face with her right hand but he grabbed her wrist before she could hit him again and spun sideways out from under her.

Korfa and Caanood came running from the bedroom just as Brooke was about to lunge at Conner again. Korfa grabbed her from behind, his arms wrapped around hers, trapping them at her sides.

"That's why you asked Korfa when we first got here if Saeed and his men had captured anyone," she shrieked. "It was Abdul Hafeez you were after! You were trying to trap him so you could have him identify the Falcon. How could you use us as bait?"

She squirmed to break free, but Korfa tightened his grip. "Let loose of me!" she ordered. "Now."

Korfa glanced at Conner, who was wiping blood from his broken lip. He nodded, and Korfa released her.

For a second, Brooke thought about attacking him again. But didn't.

"I never intended for anyone to be hurt," he said quietly. "It wasn't supposed to happen like it did. General Saeed promised to protect everyone."

"Not hurt. Dead. Killed," she replied. "You're responsible for those seven men's deaths today, not Saeed. You! They're on your conscience. Just like Robert Gumman's death and Skip LeRue."

"I believed General Saeed could control the situation. It was a calculated risk."

"A risk for others, not you. You weren't even at the embassy when it was attacked."

"I gave General Saeed ample warning."

"Does he believe in your jihadist mastermind theory too?" she demanded. "Is that why he went along with your insane plan without telling anyone?"

"No. I promised him six Apache helicopters if he helped me."

She wanted to scream. "Now I understand why you don't want to tell Washington you're alive. Why you're afraid of General Saeed. You're as horrible a monster as he is—no, you're worse. He put us at risk for six helicopters. You did it for your ego, to prove everyone was wrong but Gunter Conner."

"It wasn't for my ego," he replied in a stern voice. "The Falcon is real and he's going to find a way to attack our country unless I stop him— unless *we* stop him."

"You can't prove any of that. You can't even prove he actually exists."

"He's real," Conner said. "I know he is."

"You don't know that!"

"I know it," Conner said with certainty, "because the Falcon murdered my wife and son in Cairo. He's responsible for my daughter's brain injury and for my nightmares. I got too close to him in Cairo three years ago. I had a source who told me what the Falcon was trying to do—how he was trying to unite everyone. He planted a bomb in my car. It was meant for me but it killed the people I love the most."

Conner paused for a second and then he looked directly into Brooke's eyes and said, "I'm sorry General Saeed failed to keep you safe. But I'd do it again tomorrow if it would help me catch Abdul Hafeez and lead me to the Falcon."

Conner bent down and picked up the knee-high table that had been knocked over during their scuffle. He sat down next to it and retrieved the teacup that had fallen from it. Fortunately, it was not broken.

"Caanood," he said. "Is there any more?"

TUESDAY

Seven days before the presidential election

CHAPTER FORTY-ONE

Somewhere in Somalia

The elderly courier woke him.

"He wants you to say *Fajr* with him," the courier said.

Abdul Hafeez immediately dressed, leaving one pant leg pulled up, which was part of the ritual he observed when saying his morning prayer.

After an hour ride, they arrived at a house where Hafeez was escorted into a room so dark that when he first entered it, he believed he was alone. As his eyes adjusted, he recognized the shape of a man seated on the floor wearing a black robe with a hood over his head. Hafeez could not see the face of the leader.

The leader stood and Hafeez stepped beside him so he could face the Kaaba, the most sacred site in Mecca.

"*Allahu Akbar,*" the leader said in a soothing voice.

Hafeez bent his arms at the elbow and raised his hands to the top of his ears. He folded his arms across his chest and performed an act of supplication known as the *dua.*

"*Subhaan-Allah, wal-hamdu Lillaah, wa laa ilaaha ill-Allah, wa Allahu akbar, wa laa hawla wa laa quwwata illa Billaah,*" the hooded figure said, which when translated means "Glory be to Allah, praise be to Allah, there is no god except Allah, Allah is Most Great and there is no power and no strength except with Allah."

During the next ten minutes both prayed to Allah, each bowing in obedience at key points to press their foreheads against the prayer carpets on the floor. When they neared the end, the leader said in Arabic:

I bear witness that none has the right to be worshipped except Allah and I bear witness that Muhammad is His slave and messenger.

I take refuge in You from the punishment of the grave, from the torment of the Fire, from the trials and tribulations of life and death, and from the evil affliction of the false Messiah.

Having finished praying, the leader said, "The Prophet was walking through a market and saw fruit being sold. He stuck his hand inside the fruit and found dampness, but the fruit on top for sale was dry. 'O owner of the food, what is this?' he asked. The merchant said, 'It was damaged by rain, O Messenger of God.' The Prophet said, 'Why did you not put the rain-damaged food on top so that people could see it! Whoever cheats us is not one of us.'"

For a moment, the hooded leader was quiet and then he asked, "How did General Saeed know the location of the warehouse where you were hiding the American security guards? Abdul, is there a deceiver in our midst?"

"I do not believe so," Hafeez said.

"Search your mind. Search their souls."

"There could only be one possibility," Hafeez replied. "Mosi. He was with the Americans, especially the woman Marine and sergeant, for many days as their driver, and he constantly questions my decisions, undermining my leadership."

The leader said nothing. It was as if he were waiting for Hafeez to continue to build a case. Hafeez said, "If Mosi told the Americans about the warehouse, they will know where the other Americans are being kept. We must move them."

"No," the leader replied. "Take the ambassador and John Duggard away from the city but leave the Marines and any others where they are in Mogadishu."

"Then I will double the number of men watching them. We will be ready for the general when he comes to rescue them."

"No," the leader said. "Remove all of our guards except for two."

"Two men cannot fight the general."

"Are you the deceiver in our midst?" the leader asked. "You tell me that Mosi questions you. Then you question me. The Prophet Muhammad said: 'Those who obey me enter paradise, but those who disobey me refuse to do so.'"

"Forgive me," Hafeez said. "It was wrong for me to question you."

"Abdul, you have been a faithful servant but you still have much to learn. We will not fight General Saeed over these other Americans. I will not have more and more of our people killed because of them. Tell me how you are treating the Marines."

"They are tied and gagged and only freed when they eat, drink, or use the toilet."

"There is no need to feed them, no need to give them water or take them to the toilet. Let them feel hunger and thirst. Let them piss on themselves and sit in their own excrement. Let them suffer and be humiliated like our brothers at Abu Ghraib and in Guantanamo. Remove everyone guarding them but two men, and put explosives in the apartment with the Marines, enough to destroy the entire building."

"Praise be to Allah. I will do it immediately."

"Have you found the CIA man—Gunter Conner?"

"He escaped before we could kill him. Our brothers in the police tell us General Saeed is searching for him too."

"Do not underestimate him. Conner escaped from me in Cairo. I do not want him to elude me again. A man who is seeking vengeance will not quit, but his rage can be used to blind him. He will make a mistake. Now, what of the woman Marine?"

"The Americans keep showing her photograph on television. They are telling the world we have taken her hostage."

"Find her too. She can be useful," he said.

The leader did not speak for several moments. "I have one more instruction," he said finally. "Choose Mosi as one of the men you leave to guard the Marines. Tell him to stay inside the apartment guarding the Americans."

"But can he be trusted?" Hafeez asked.

"Give him a cell phone. Tell him that if he calls a number you will give him, he will detonate the explosives in the building, killing himself and the Marines. Tell him to dial it if either General Saeed or the Americans come to rescue the Marines."

"But if Mosi is a traitor," Hafeez replied, "he will not call that number. He will not kill himself or the prisoners. Relying on him is a huge risk."

"This is why the telephone number you tell him will not detonate the explosives. You will give that number to the other sentry, who will be waiting outside the building. He will be responsible for blowing up the building, not Mosi. But I want Mosi there with the Marines."

CHAPTER FORTY-TWO

Korfa's apartment
Mogadishu, Somalia

When Brooke awoke Tuesday morning, Gunter Conner was gone. "He and my brother went somewhere," Canood explained. "I don't know where, but they told me they would be back later today."

Brooke tried the BlackBerry. Still no signal. She switched on CNN and seethed.

She confronted Conner as soon as the two men returned.

"Where'd you go?" she snapped.

"We've just come from the closest cell phone tower," he replied, removing a large pair of sunglasses and a kaffiyeh, a square scarf commonly worn by Arabs as a headdress. It was, at best, a risky disquise given his pale white skin. "Korfa has worked his magic. Where's your BlackBerry?"

"You helped him."

"I figured I owed you. I also need to ask you a favor. Don't mention my name when you call."

"Are you kidding? I am going to tell them everything. I am not going to lie for you."

"I'm not asking you to lie. We both have had some time to think about this. You were understandably upset last night, especially after seeing Cash Kelley being murdered. I understand that. But now you've had time to digest what I explained to you. The reasons why I did what I did. All I'm asking is for you to leave me out of any conversations when you finally get through to Washington. Just don't mention my name."

If anything, Brooke's resentment and anger had grown since their last confrontation, not lessened. "You've got blood on your hands for what you've done," she replied. "I'm not going to overlook that because you helped Korfa fix a cell tower."

"I saved your life. I brought you here from the airport. You didn't have anywhere to go. What if you had been captured?"

"My life was threatened because of you! You can't take credit for saving someone if you're the one responsible for putting their life in danger."

"If you won't keep quiet for my sake, what about Korfa and Caanood? If General Saeed learns I'm alive, he'll hunt them down."

"No one will tell Saeed anything after I explain how I witnessed him murder Cash Kelley."

"You can't be certain of that," Conner said. "All it takes is one slip of the tongue. Do you think the agency will want the White House, Congress, and the American public to know what I've done—that I used the ambassador as bait? My bosses would be relieved if I disappeared permanently."

"You're being overly dramatic and paranoid," she snapped. "But is that what you're going to do—disappear? Go into hiding? Run away from this mess that you've caused?"

"Give me forty-eight hours. I need time to work a few things out and then you can talk about me all you want to Washington."

Korfa, who'd been listening, said, "Conner is telling the truth. If the CIA knows he's alive, they will want to find him. They will notify General Saeed, and if he learns we've been hiding you, the general will come for us."

"All you have to do," Conner continued, "is tell Washington a Somali couple gave you shelter after you escaped from our embassy, but you swore to keep their names confidential because they're afraid of General Saeed. That's believable."

"It's also the truth," Korfa added.

"The fact we both went missing," Conner continued, "is no reason for anyone to assume we've been hiding together in Mogadishu, especially since you were last seen at the embassy and I was at the airport. I doubt they'll even ask you about me. Unless you bring up my name."

Caanood came from the kitchen to join them in the apartment's main room. She was visibly scared. "Please," she said, her voice breaking, "don't tell anyone about us. Please give Master Conner another chance. He's a good man who has helped our family. General Saeed is an evil man."

"Okay, okay," Brooke said reluctantly. "I'll not mention any of you when I call Washington, but I'm not doing this for you, Conner. I'm doing this for Caanood and Korfa. If you decide to vanish or you don't call Washington on your own in forty-eight hours, I'm telling everyone what you did. You're responsible and you need to be held accountable."

Conner didn't reply but Caanood whispered, "Thank you."

Brooke dialed the number of her commanding officer at the Defense Attaché System, part of the Defense Intelligence Agency (DIA) in Washington. Conner, Korfa, and Caanood all watched as she waited for the call to go through.

When a duty officer answered, Brooke identified herself and within minutes her call had been relayed to the DIA's director, a three-star general responsible for reporting intelligence information directly to the secretary of defense and the Joint Chiefs of Staff. Because of the seven-hour time difference, the general had been awakened in his home, but he didn't care.

"How did you escape from the embassy?" the general asked.

"By wearing a burqa. I blended in with the looters and Al-Shabaab fighters and managed to get away. I've been hiding in the home of a family that took me in."

When the director asked her why she hadn't contacted the local police, Brooke said, "Because General Saeed murdered an American hostage. I saw him execute Charles 'Cash' Kelley."

Brooke quickly explained: "Everyone in Somalia is related or seems to be. I'd heard the police headquarters had been attacked. I didn't know how safe it was to go there. But the family that took me in has a relative on the police force who heard that General Saeed was going to rescue hostages at a warehouse. I put on my burqa and went there, thinking I'd join the other Americans after they were rescued. I thought the general would get all of us out of the country. I didn't know he was going to kill Cash Kelley."

After asking several more questions, none about Gunter Conner, the general said, "It's amazing you're not a hostage and even alive. Stay where you are until we develop a plan to extricate you from Mogadishu. And for god sakes, avoid any contact with General Saeed."

"Sir," Brooke replied, "I do not want to be evacuated at this time. I want to help rescue the Americans who are still being held hostage here. Neither the terrorists nor General Saeed know I'm free and alive. There must be a way for me to assist you on the ground."

CHAPTER FORTY-THREE

Morning
Oval Office
The White House
Washington, D.C.

The joy President Sally Allworth felt after she learned Captain Brooke Grant had surfaced alive and in hiding in Mogadishu was short-lived when Decker Lake met with her and Mallory Harper in the Oval Office to discuss campaign strategy.

"If you don't end this hostage crisis before Election Day," Lake warned, "none of us will be sitting in the Oval Office meeting like this come January."

"The deaths of seven more American hostages have driven your polling numbers into the subbasement," Harper added. "That failed rescue played right into Governor Coldridge's 'It's time to put America first' campaign theme. Somalia is just the latest international quagmire shackling our nation. He's not only talking about bringing our troops home from the Middle East but also mothballing our bases in Europe."

"Next he'll be saying we need to withdraw from NATO," President Allworth said sarcastically.

"If he does, his numbers will take another bump upward," Harper retorted. "Like it or not, our polls show his rhetoric is working."

"Let's talk less about how well my opponent's campaign is doing and more about how we are going to turn this election around," the president said.

"If you sent in a rescue team and it successfully rescued the hostages, well, that would be a game changer," Harper replied. "I believe we would win the race. After all, President Obama's popularity went up dramatically years ago when SEAL Team Six killed Osama bin Laden."

"Yes," Decker Lake agreed, "but a military rescue will only help you if it is successful. Look back further at Jimmy Carter. He sent a team to free the

Iranian hostages in 1980 and the result was eight servicemen killed and the team never even made it to Tehran. The public lost faith in his ability to lead."

Lake and Harper waited for President Allworth to speak next.

"How do you think voters would react," she asked after several moments, "if I resolved this crisis before the election in seven days through diplomatic channels?"

"Bring the hostages home alive and you'd be reelected," Lake said, adding, "It wouldn't be a slam dunk but it would be an at-the-final-buzzer shot." Decker Lake had a fondness for sports metaphors.

"And if those diplomatic channels included paying Al-Shabaab a ransom?" the president asked.

"That could be problematic," Harper volunteered. "President Reagan set our policy when he went on television and said the United States does not pay a 'ransom for people who have been kidnapped by barbarians.' He explained that paying a ransom would only encourage more kidnappings, and polls have consistently shown that Americans agree with that no-pay stance."

"What Mallory is saying is true," Lake said. "The entire world knows that we don't negotiate, except we have. President Obama negotiated with the Taliban for the release of one of our soldiers. In return, he freed five terrorists from Guantanamo. The White House spun the story, claiming it was a prisoner-of-war exchange and no money changed hands. Obama's people made it sound noble, saying it was a reminder of our unwavering commitment to leave no man or woman in uniform behind on the battlefield."

"Yes, but polls showed that fifty-six percent of Americans disagreed with what Obama did," Harper interjected.

"That was one poll," Lake countered, "and if you added in the margin for error, then I'd wager the results would have been closer to dead even. If we put the right spin on it, I think the American people could be convinced that paying a ransom made sense."

"I'm not so sure," Harper countered. "President Obama was a lame duck when he cut a deal with the Taliban, and voters reacted negatively to him during the next congressional elections by giving the Republicans control of both houses. I realize there was more to that overwhelming rejection but still, the Taliban deal was part of it."

"What if the hostages were released before the election but the public didn't learn about the ransom until after you were reelected?" Lake asked. "You told me earlier that you dispatched General Grant to Cairo to pursue backdoor negotiations through diplomacy with Al-Shabaab. You have our military readying a military rescue option. You have seven days, counting today, before the election. My advice is that you give yourself another twenty-four hours before making a decision."

"Your sage advice is that I sit on my thumbs?" President Allworth asked.

"No. While you are weighing your options, I want you to take the gloves off and put heat on Governor Coldridge. Our campaign needs to get our people on social media, in chat rooms, and on the radio and talk shows, attacking his simpleminded isolationism. We need to tell the public that the White House hasn't made any missteps in handling this crisis. You didn't cause the deaths of those security guards in Somalia. General Saeed did that. In fact, General Saeed has screwed the pooch from the beginning. It was General Saeed's responsibility to protect our embassy. He blew it. Next, he bungled the rescue and all of our people were killed. He didn't protect the embassy and now he's getting our people killed by his recklessness. We need to remind voters that both the CIA and State Department assured the White House that Mogadishu was safe. You are a victim here of their incompetence. We need to remind voters that your vigilance and ongoing war against terrorists is all that is standing between them and another 9/11 attack. You need to remind them that we now live in an era when it is impossible for a great nation to simply close its borders and ignore what is happening in the rest of the world, which is what Coldridge would have us do."

Lake was on a roll. "Realpolitik, Madam President. There are no Queensberry rules in presidential politics. If you want to keep Coldridge from ruining our country, we need to kick him in the nuts. Gouge eyes or lose. The mother who eats her young doesn't starve."

"That's hardly a comforting image, Decker," the president said.

"We're way past comfortable campaigning," Lake replied. "It's time to collect political chits. Start with Chairman Stanton. We need him to make a public statement defending your decision to open the embassy in Somalia. We need him to get involved in helping you win reelection."

"I can give the Chairman a call," Harper volunteered.

"Don't call him," Lake replied. "Go see him personally and twist his arm."

"I agree with what Decker is saying about Chairman Stanton," the president said. "You need to talk to him face-to-face."

"Meanwhile, I'm going to do a bit of snooping around," Lake declared. "I have a good friend who happens to run the travel agency that the Coldridge campaign is using, and he told me the governor is bringing a Somali American to Washington today to blindside us. He's running for Congress from Minneapolis and he's handsome, clean-cut, charismatic. My guess is that Coldridge is going to have him appear at a press conference when the bodies of our dead hostages are returned from Somalia."

"Using those men's deaths for political gain is in extremely bad taste," Harper said. "I can't believe voters will think otherwise."

"Voters will never know Coldridge is behind that press conference," Lake explained. "That's why they're bringing in a Somali American shill. He'll criticize you for opening an embassy in Mogadishu prematurely, for causing twelve Americans to die and for getting our diplomats taken hostage. He'll tell the media that the millions of tax dollars that were spent opening an embassy could have been better used helping unemployed Somali American kids in Minneapolis get jobs so they wouldn't be seduced by radicals such as Al-Shabaab. He'll say the best way to fight homegrown terrorism is by increased spending on social programs, not global policing. It will be tailored to fit with Coldridge's 'America First' campaign theme."

"How do you know that is what he will say?" Harper asked. "Do you have a spy in Coldridge's upper echelon?"

"I don't need one," Lake replied. "I know that's what the Coldridge campaign will have this shill say because that's what I would have him say if I were advising their campaign."

"How much damage can one press conference and one critic do?" the president asked.

"Oh, it won't just be that press conference," Lake said. "Our opponents will find a way to use clips from that news conference in a last-minute media blitz," Lake replied. "That is why I am going to take care of this shill personally for you. I've already got my people digging into his past."

CHAPTER FORTY-FOUR

Ronald Reagan Washington National Airport
Arlington, Virginia

Mary Margaret Delaney spotted Rudy Adeogo pulling an overnight roller bag as he exited from the secure area of Terminal B, having just arrived on a Delta Air Lines flight from Minneapolis.

Weaving her way through the waiting crowd, Delaney introduced herself. "Governor Timothy Coldridge, our next president, sent me to welcome you to what soon will be your new hometown."

Adeogo took her hand while simultaneously eyeballing her. She was in her late thirties, wasn't wearing a wedding band, and was clearly Irish, given her red hair and freckled face. She was what his father had once described to him as a "perfect woman"—a statuesque female with "enough meat on her bones to not break in the bedroom." His father had been critical of his daughter-in-law, Dheeh, who was petite.

Adeogo followed Delaney out of the terminal and they slipped into the back of a waiting limousine. "You're not scheduled to meet the governor until Wednesday morning," she explained. "I'm here to brief you and introduce you to our fabulous city. I was told this is your first visit."

"Isn't the real reason you're meeting me here is to evaluate me before taking me to meet Mr. Coldridge?" he asked.

She smiled. "I like a man who is direct. Yes, I'm a handler. This is the big league, and an innocent slipup that might be meaningless in Minneapolis could ruin you here. Lesson One: You just said 'Mr. Coldridge.' In Washington, you always address a politician by the highest rank that he held. It should be 'Governor Coldridge.' That's a small thing. The big thing is for me to make certain you know who the major players are in this town—the power brokers who can make or break you."

"First I need to get elected."

"I wouldn't be meeting you at the airport if you weren't going to be," she replied.

"I was told Governor Coldridge is going to guarantee my election. How is that possible?"

"You are direct, aren't you?" she replied. "You haven't been here more than ten minutes and you're asking me that question. My associates were supposed to have explained everything to you when they met you yesterday at your apartment in Minneapolis and invited you here."

"They told me that Governor Coldridge could arrange for my congressional opponent to withdraw from the election and support me—if I would do a favor for the governor and his presidential campaign."

"That's correct," she replied. "You do us a favor and Governor Coldridge will do you a favor by convincing Representative Buckner to withdraw, virtually guaranteeing your victory."

"What is Governor Coldridge holding over Representative Buckner's head?" Adeogo asked.

"While I like a man who is frank, being too blunt is not an admirable trait. Let's talk instead about what you already know. Even though Representative Buckner is taking heat for putting his mother-in-law on his congressional payroll, he's still running ahead of you in the polls. You can't beat him or his Republican challenger, who also has run into image problems. But with Governor Coldridge's help, you've been told you will be elected the Fifth District representative from Minnesota. So here is Lesson Number Two for today: Sometimes in Washington, it's smart to know when to stop asking questions."

Delaney slipped a packet from her saddlebag briefcase. "I've booked you a suite at the Hyatt Regency on Capitol Hill. You'll have a view of the U.S. Capitol. I've included a tourist map and useful information about our city."

Handing him the folder, she added, "You'll find Washington is an easy place to navigate. Do you enjoy history?"

"I'd rather talk more about my campaign and why you have invited me here."

"Patience," she replied. "Now, I was about to tell you a bit of history about Washington. Our founding fathers didn't want one state to be more important than any other, so they decided the federal government would be located in a federal district, not a state. I'm surprised how many people don't know that. They cut a ten-mile-by-ten-mile square out of Maryland and Virginia to create this new federal district. Part of their thinking was that anyone who lived in the District of Columbia should not be represented by a voting member of Congress. They were worried its residents would become a plutocracy."

Glancing at the map that she'd given him, Adeogo said, "This shows D.C. having a jagged edge, not being square."

"That's because in the early 1800s, Congress decided it didn't need a ten-by-ten-mile swath of land. It never thought the federal government would grow as big as it is today, so it gave Virginia back its portion. The airport where you just landed and Arlington Cemetery are built on land that was originally part of the federal district but was surrendered back to Virginia. When D.C. was a square, the U.S. Capitol building was located directly in its center. Now it's not. But it helps with learning directions if you understand that history, because the city is divided into four quadrants, called Northwest, Northeast, Southwest, and Southeast."

Through his passenger window, Adeogo could see the Thomas Jefferson Memorial as they prepared to cross the Potomac River. He appeared to be only half-listening to her.

Continuing her tour-guide spiel, Delaney said, "Washington was laid out by Pierre Charles L'Enfant, who used letters to identify streets that run east and west and numbers to name streets that run north and south, except for a handful that have actual names, such as Pennsylvania and Massachusetts Avenues."

"Tell me, Ms. Delaney," Adeogo said, "where would the corner of Fourteenth and J Streets put me?"

"Mr. Adeogo," she replied, "you've been toying with me. You know there isn't a J Street in Washington, don't you?"

"I read about it during the flight. Yours is not the first tourist map I've seen."

"And did that incredibly important airplane resource explain why the letter *J* was missing from our street alphabet?"

"It said L'Enfant skipped it because he was angry at our country's first chief justice of the Supreme Court—John Jay. Something about him signing a treaty with England that was not popular."

"Ah," Delaney said. "Lesson Number Three: Washington's practice of ignoring facts in favor of a good legend. The truth is, L'Enfant didn't include the letter *J* because that letter and the letter *I* were nearly indistinguishable when handwritten in the eighteenth century and largely interchangeable in England. It had nothing to do with a personal feud with John Jay."

"I prefer the tourist version," he replied. "As you mentioned earlier, sometimes it is better not to ask too many questions in Washington."

She smiled.

As their limo pulled under the hotel portico, she said, "I'll meet you in the lobby at seven thirty for dinner."

"I would prefer you tell me less about history and geography and more about Mr. Coldridge during dinner."

"It's Governor Coldridge," she replied. "Remember?"

CHAPTER FORTY-FIVE

Late afternoon Somali time
Korfa's apartment
Mogadishu, Somalia

"Captain Brooke Grant."

It was an unfamiliar male voice on Brooke's borrowed BlackBerry.

"This is Commander Seth Jackman. I'm in charge of the Navy SEAL teams aboard the USS *Hornet* stationed off the Somali coast. We've replaced the FAST team initially sent here for a possible rescue operation. The White House has ordered us to develop a rescue scenario to implement upon the president's command, and I need your eyes and ears on the ground."

Brooke recognized Jackman's name. He was a legend for his handling of the Naval Special Warfare Development Group or DEVGRU, better known as SEAL Team Six.

"Are you mobile, Captain Grant?" he asked.

"Yes, sir. I've been able to move around the city wearing a burqa, but I think I can pass undetected as a Somali woman in other clothing as well."

"I don't care how you outfit yourself, soldier," Jackman replied. "All I want to know is if I give you map coordinates, can you reach an apartment building in Mogadishu where Marine hostages are being held without encountering Al-Shabaab or General Saeed and his security forces."

"Yes, sir, I can."

"Is the phone you're using capable of taking photographs?"

"No, sir, but I'll get one that will."

During the next several minutes, Commander Jackman described what he wanted Brooke to photograph outside the apartment building.

"Based on telephone intercepts and drone footage," he explained, "we believe there are only one or two Al-Shabaab fighters actively guarding the hostages."

Brooke thought she misheard him. "Did you say Al-Shabaab has only one or two guards watching five Marines?"

"Five Marines plus two State Department hostages. That's a total of seven men who need to be evaced. We have no idea why Al-Shabaab pulled off its other guards. Based on the number of fighters who were killed when General Saeed attacked them earlier at a Mogadishu warehouse, they simply may not want to lose more men. Or the apartment could be rigged with explosives. Terrorists like to pull stunts like that. Just get me the photographs I need without being seen or engaging the enemy."

"Sir," Brooke asked, "what about Ambassador Thomas and John Duggard? Do you need me to recon their location?"

"To the best of our knowledge, they are under heavy guard in a residential compound in an area controlled by Al-Shabaab. You let us worry about developing a plan to rescue them. Now, let me be clear about this, Captain. The White House has not green-lighted any rescue operations. But if it does, we will be coming in fast and hard on foot, so I need recon as quickly as possible. Obviously, you'll need to do it during the day when it is bright enough for you to take footage without using a flash and safe for women to be walking the streets alone."

"I'm not sure I can get to that neighborhood before dusk."

"Go first thing tomorrow."

"I'd like permission to be part of your rescue team when you come in."

"That's a negative. My SEAL teams will deal with the hostiles. You get the recon and stand down until we can get you out too. Are we perfectly clear about that, Captain?"

"Yes, sir," she replied, but she didn't like it.

"What are you carrying?"

"My M9 with ten rounds left, sir."

"Don't use it. We don't need a hero. Avoid contact with Al-Shabaab and General Saeed. Remember, you are eyes and ears, nothing else. Are we clear on this?"

"Yes, sir," she replied.

Almost as soon as Brooke finished speaking to Commander Jackman, her BlackBerry rang again, only this time she recognized the caller's voice.

"Thank God you're okay!" General Frank Grant exclaimed. "Your auntie and I have been worried sick. I can't tell you how relieved we were when we heard you escaped from the embassy. I'm en route to Cairo right now but will be coming to Somalia to get you."

"You're coming here?"

"Yes, the president has sent me to negotiate with Al-Shabaab for release of the hostages. Now that you've finally surfaced, I'll arrange for you to get out of Mogadishu too."

"Uncle Frank, I just got a call from Commander Jackman, who told me SEAL teams might be coming into Mogadishu to rescue the hostages—maybe as early as tomorrow."

"What?" Grant replied, clearly surprised. "I'm not aware of any rescue mission. I'll call Washington as soon as we're done talking. Now you just sit tight until I can get you out of there. And for goodness' sake, don't do anything foolish."

For a moment, Brooke thought about telling him that Jackman had ordered her to conduct reconnaissance, but she decided against it. If she did, she knew he would get that order rescinded.

"Uncle Frank, when will you and auntie realize I'm not that scared little girl who you took in?"

"Those Marines being held hostage were more physically able to defend themselves than you are, and look what's happened to them," he said in a dismissive voice.

"I will never measure up, will I? Haven't you noticed that I wasn't taken hostage? I've managed pretty well so far."

"Don't get on some feminist soapbox, missy. You're damn lucky you weren't taken hostage. You could have been beaten, raped, or even worse. This is exactly why women shouldn't serve in dangerous areas. In Vietnam, we didn't have to worry about our Marines getting gang-raped for the enemy's amusement. Just do as you're told. Lay low and I will rescue you. We don't need any more of our family members murdered by radical jihadists."

Brooke didn't reply. She'd already disconnected their call.

CHAPTER FORTY-SIX

Afternoon (EDT)
1300 Longworth House Office Building
Capitol Hill
Washington, D.C.

The Chairman was bored.

In addition to his Intelligence Committee duties, Representative Stanton was a senior member of the House Committee on Agriculture, and because his native South Carolina ranked first nationally in peach production, he'd called today's hearing to review proposed EPA standards for pesticide residue. It was a subject that he had no real interest in but was of major concern to peach growers in his district.

In the midst of testimony by an EPA expert, an aide whispered in Stanton's ear. "Mallory Harper is here to see you."

"Without an appointment?" Stanton replied in an equally hushed voice.

"She's in your private office," the aide replied, which is how the Chairman referred to the Intelligence Committee's suite of offices hidden in the basement of the Visitor Center.

"Harper should've made an appointment," Stanton said. "It's disrespectful. Tell her I can be over in about twenty minutes, if she cares to wait."

Twenty minutes was enough time to disrupt her busy schedule but not so much that she would leave. The Chairman checked the clock on the hearing room wall, waited for the EPA expert to finish reading his written testimony, and then asked enough questions to convince the peach growers attending the hearing that he had listened to their complaints. After exactly twenty minutes, he excused himself.

Representative Stanton didn't like Mallory Harper. On Capitol Hill, she was regarded as the president's pit bull. Coming from a corporate background, Harper was too pushy and showed little understanding for the necessity of explaining her actions or the need for compromise. She was used to barking orders and to hearing nothing but compliments from her corporate underlings.

The Chairman was no one's underling and he didn't take orders.

He spotted her speaking on her cell phone while pacing across the white marble floor outside the locked doorway to the committee's chambers. Phones were not permitted inside its secure suites. Stanton waved casually as he strolled by her and entered the committee's well-guarded offices. He was not going to stand idly in the hallway waiting for her to finish her phone call.

Moments later, she was escorted into his office, and as a courtesy he invited her to sit on a dark-burgundy leather couch with him rather than in a chair opposite his imposing walnut desk.

Neither mentioned the petty Washington posturing they'd been engaged in, although both understood the dance.

"I assume you read the *New York Times* this morning," she began.

"You're speaking about the editorial criticizing the president's decision to open the embassy in Somalia for what now appears to have been purely political reasons."

"Yes," she replied. "The president wants you to offer the *Times* a counter-view from your perspective as chairman of the congressional committee. She wants you to call a press conference and defend her action and stress our nation's need to fight terrorism in Africa and the rest of the world rather than retreating to isolationism."

"Please thank the president for her suggestions," he replied, smiling, "but I'm not inclined to correct opinion pieces in newspapers, especially when I suspect there's truth in what's been printed. Nor am I inclined to call a news conference to defend her actions."

"It wasn't really a suggestion, and the president is not asking you to justify her decision," Harper snapped. "She's calling on you to reinforce the value of this administration's commitment to fight Islamic extremists abroad."

Her dictatorial tone made him seethe, but he continued to mask his growing anger. "Thank you, Ms. Harper, for clarifying the White

House's intentions, but the president actually has not asked me to do anything. You have asked me. Secondly, as we both know, it would be impossible for me or any member of the House Intelligence Committee to comment about global terrorism without reporters inquiring about our personal opinions about Somalia and this administration's actions there. This is not something the president should risk."

Harper sensed she had offended him, but she didn't feel a need to back down—not yet. She was the White House chief of staff. Despite the Chairman's reputation, he was merely a House member.

"Maybe I need to clarify this for you," she said, sounding much like an elementary school teacher berating a stubborn student. "The president is calling on you to defend her actions. She wants you to become more visible and more vocal. I shouldn't have to remind you that the election is only a week away."

The Chairman didn't reply. He simply continued to smile.

Releasing a sigh, Harper said, "Let me start over. On behalf of our president, I am asking you this morning to do your duty for our party by speaking to the media about the wisdom of our foreign policy."

"Ms. Harper, you may tell the president that I've already supported her. When Director Grainger first briefed me about this administration's decision to open an embassy in Mogadishu—which the president decided to open without consulting my committee or Congress and without informing us beforehand about her decision—I agreed to not question her actions in public. And I have kept quiet. In retrospect, that now appears to have been an error."

Harper decided to soften her approach. "Mr. Chairman, the president is aware of your support and thanks you for it. Perhaps you should tell me what you would suggest we do to counter the criticism being aimed at us in the *Times* and also by Governor Coldridge. The president always appreciates your advice based on your experience and wealth of knowledge."

"Flattery and pandering," he replied in a calm voice, "are even more insulting than having you lecture me. You can tell the president that a growing number of voices on Capitol Hill are questioning the timing of her decision to open an embassy in Somalia. Notice I said 'timing,' not 'validity.' Tell her I am supporting her by ignoring calls from my colleagues for congressional investigative hearings. That chorus has grown louder because of the embassy attack, the murder of two State Department employees—one of whom had his hands chopped off—and the deaths of ten American security guards. So far, the president has benefited from my support in both my silence and my holding her critics at bay. That should be sufficient. And the president should be grateful, not critical or unappreciative."

Harper started to respond, but Stanton wasn't finished. "I suspect our president received bad advice about Somalia. I further suspect that advice came from you. If the president truly would like my advice, as you just said she would, it would be this: that she bring Decker Lake back as her campaign manager to resuscitate her reelection bid before it is too late and let you return to your job of overseeing the White House staff."

Harper's cheeks turned red from both anger and embarrassment. Still, she forced a smile. "Clearly, our talk this morning got off on the wrong foot," she replied. "I apologize for interrupting your hearing. I should have called for an appointment."

"Showing up unannounced was discourteous," he remarked, making no effort to let her off the hook.

"I understand you were reviewing the EPA's new pesticide standards for peaches that apparently have your constituents concerned," she continued.

Stanton had been around long enough on the Hill to suspect what Harper—a relative newcomer to Washington politics—was about to say next, and he sat quietly to see how polished her approach would be.

"As White House chief of staff," she continued, "I'm concerned about every aspect of the executive, including our governance over federal agencies and changes in federal standards and regulations."

His suspicions had been spot-on. Having failed to cajole him, having failed at flattery, she now was poised to offer him a carrot. A thinly veiled bribe that he certainly was not going to accept.

Continuing, she said, "I'm certain the president would not be opposed to having the EPA take a second look at those new EPA pesticide standards as they apply to peach growers, or at least delay them for some period of time if it is important to you."

He rose from the couch and said, "I need to return to my hearing, but please tell the president that I will be calling Director Grainger to request a private briefing about the events in Somalia. Perhaps after receiving that update, I might look more kindly on her request to defend her actions."

"As always," Harper said, extending her hand, "it was a pleasure speaking to you."

CHAPTER FORTY-SEVEN

CIA headquarters
Langley, Virginia

Listening to General Saeed over a secure satellite connection reminded CIA director Payton Grainger of when he was confronted by a bully in the military prep school that he'd attended. He hadn't liked it then and he didn't now. In a threatening voice, Saeed was demanding delivery of six Apache helicopters.

"Had you been successful," Grainger replied to the general's rant in a stern voice, "in rescuing the seven ProTech security guards who were killed at that Mogadishu warehouse, I might have been able to arrange for you to receive those helicopters."

"Have you considered that I could have rescued them alive," the general retorted, "if you'd kept your station chief's promise and assured me that your country was going to deliver my helicopters?"

So that was why Saeed had attacked the warehouse seemingly without regard to the hostages' safety, Grainger thought. *He was punishing the U.S.*

"General Saeed," Grainger replied. "We've been over this before. You claim Gunter Conner promised you helicopters but Conner is still missing. There is no way for me to verify it."

"Are you accusing me of lying?"

"It might be useful if you told me why our station chief would promise you six helicopters."

"Since he cannot tell you himself, I will. On the night of the embassy attack, Gunter Conner came to the presidential palace at Villa Somalia and told me your agency had intercepted a telephone call. You had been warned an attack was being planned for later that night and he'd been told to get your people to the airport. Am I not telling you the truth?"

"It's my understanding that Conner was told to warn you and to get the ambassador and his people to the airport. Unfortunately, that's not what happened."

"The reason it didn't happen is because Conner didn't want it to happen. Your station chief urged me to let the Al-Shabaab attack happen."

"What you're saying doesn't make any sense."

"Gunter Conner asked me to set a trap. He asked me to hold back my men. He asked me to let Al-Shabaab attack and then encircle them. He was trying to capture one of its leaders, a Somali American named Abdul Hafeez. Conner told me that he needed Hafeez to identify a mysterious jihadist leader."

The memory of Conner's outburst during the CTC briefing after the prison break at Dera Ismail Khan flashed through Grainger's mind.

Continuing, General Saeed said, "I agreed to his plan in return for him promising me the six helicopters."

"If what you said is true, then what happened to your ambush?"

In an icy voice, Saeed replied, "Al-Shabaab launched other attacks in the city that drew my men away, and some of my own men proved to be traitors. But that does not negate Conner's promise. Now that you know what happened that night, let me ask you a question. How do you think the Western world would react if I revealed that the CIA station chief allowed the U.S. Embassy in Mogadishu to be attacked and its people to be taken hostage because he wanted to capture Abdul Hafeez?"

Grainger was in no mood to be blackmailed. He reacted to General Saeed's threat with one of his own.

"How do you think the Western world would react if it were told that you executed Charles 'Cash' Kelley, an American hostage, in cold blood during your failed rescue at that Mogadishu warehouse?"

In an eerily calm voice, General Saeed said, "You know about that. And what? Do you think anyone in my country would dare charge me with murder?"

"I'm certain that President Allworth could persuade the International Court of Justice to investigate. We have an eyewitness."

"Is this a game that you wish to play?" Saeed asked. "I threaten you, now you threaten me. So let's play this game—only remember, my friend, that in all games there can be only one winner. I want you to hold on a minute. There is something you need to hear. Something important."

The line was quiet, and then Saeed returned. "Your president sent Gunter Conner to Mogadishu to decide if my city was safe enough to open an embassy here—do you remember this?"

"Of course," Grainger answered.

"Your State Department sent a team too. This you already know. But what you do not know is that before that State diplomatic team arrived, Al-Shabaab attempted to assassinate President Musab. Conner didn't tell you that, did he? He didn't inform your State Department team either, and he didn't warn your president, did he?"

Saeed hesitated but Grainger didn't reply.

The general continued, "Conner didn't tell anyone that a jihadist had driven his vehicle into the entrance of the café where President Musab and his family were eating with relatives. He didn't tell anyone that assassin's car bomb did not explode or that he was captured alive."

Saeed paused again for a bit of unnecessary drama. He was clearly enjoying himself.

"But I will tell you," he continued. "The assassin was a Saudi named Dilawar Bahar. I would have executed him on the spot but Gunter Conner asked me to keep him alive long enough to interrogate him. Conner wanted to know if Bahar knew anything about a Pakistan prison escape at Dera Ismail Khan and an attempt to bomb your London embassy. Shall I continue with my little story?"

"I'm listening," Grainger said.

"Your station chief asked me to torture Dilawar Bahar. Yes, I said torture, and it was while Bahar was being tortured that the name Abdul Hafeez was first mentioned. From that moment on, Conner became obsessed with catching Hafeez. This I have already explained to you. It is why he used your own ambassador as bait."

Grainger remained quiet.

"You see, Mr. Director, I understand everything about Gunter Conner and his need to identify Abdul Hafeez's commander. He is seeking this mysterious jihadist not only because he poses a threat to your nation, but because Conner believes this man planted a bomb in Cairo that murdered his wife and son. See, I know more about your own station chief than you do."

At this point, General Saeed placed his phone against the speaker of a digital recorder and hit play.

Director Grainger heard Gunter Conner's voice over the secure phone line discussing Dilawar Bahar, the captured assassin. It was the recording that Saeed had made secretly prior to torturing him.

"I don't want to know. I don't ever want to hear another word about him. It would be best if he simply disappeared after you torture him."

Conner's words were immediately followed by Dilawar Bahar's screaming.

Flipping off the recorder and returning the phone to his ear, General Saeed asked, "Is it not worth six Apache helicopters for me to keep silent about Mr. Conner's actions?"

"I'll need time to sort this out," Grainger said.

"I'll give you until this weekend—two days before your presidential elections. If you don't confirm delivery of my helicopters, I will make this recording public and tell the West that your station chief asked me to torture a man. I will tell the world that the CIA knew the embassy was going to be attacked but did nothing to stop it."

Back in military school, Payton Grainger had sucker punched the bully who'd threatened him and had lost a tooth during their subsequent fisticuffs. Yet Grainger had retained his pride and the bully had found easier prey.

Dealing with General Saeed would not be so simple.

After their phone call ended, Grainger considered the "should haves" that always come whenever someone is caught in a dilemma. He now realized that he should have told the president about the initial NSA telephone intercept as soon as he'd learned about it from Charles Casterline. Instead, he'd chosen to wait. At the time, he'd thought his actions were prudent. He had wanted to collect all of the facts and hear directly from Gunter Conner about why he'd not followed Casterline's direct order to evacuate the ambassador and his entourage. Now Grainger realized his decision to wait would smell of a cover-up.

And what of the facts that he'd wanted to collect before telling the White House?

As related by General Saeed, those facts only further muddied a crisis that already was threatening to unravel a president—a president whom Grainger had promised to serve with diligence and honesty, a president who had trusted Grainger to rid the CIA of scandal.

The disclosure of a damning audio recording of Gunter Conner condoning—no, requesting—the torture and death of a prisoner would be the end of Grainger's career. It might even lead to criminal indictments. Coming after a wave of other grim news from Mogadishu, it would surely destroy all chances of President Allworth being reelected.

Grainger needed a way out—a way out for himself, the agency, and the president. He needed that voice recording and he needed General Saeed's silence.

His executive assistant interrupted his thoughts.

"Chairman Thomas Stanton is asking for you to come to the Hill tomorrow to brief him about the Somali crisis," his assistant announced. "He wants to be briefed about what happened when the embassy was attacked on Saturday and what we're doing to free the remaining hostages."

The Chairman's request couldn't have come at a worse time, but he had no choice but to agree. "Tell the congressman I will be happy to meet with him but I would like our conversation to be unofficial because we are still sorting out the facts."

Grainger had always thought of himself as being a good and decent man. And he was furious that Gunter Conner, a midlevel bureaucrat far beneath him in the agency hierarchy, had put him into a position that now threatened to destroy his career and his Mr. Clean reputation.

Where was Conner? Grainger wondered.

And did Conner have any idea what his obsession with identifying the phantom jihadist had wrought?

CHAPTER FORTY-EIGHT

Capitol Hill
Washington, D.C.

At seven thirty p.m., Rudy Adeogo was waiting in the hotel lobby wearing what his wife had assured him was the city's unofficial uniform for men his age, according to magazines that she'd studied. Brown dress shoes, khaki pants, a light-blue collared shirt without a tie, and a navy blazer with three brass buttons per sleeve.

Mary Margaret Delaney arrived fashionably late wearing black-and-tan Chanel ballet flats and a dark-blue Donna Karan two-piece pants suit featuring a single-button blazer with notched lapel worn over a sheer white silk camisole.

His clothes had cost less than $300 in a Minneapolis department store. Hers had cost ten times that in a Georgetown boutique.

They walked to the Dubliner, a nearby Irish pub where Delaney breezed by a dozen people waiting at the doorway and was immediately seated by a host at a table for two near a crowded bar.

"It's loud," he said, raising his voice.

"Harder for people to overhear your conversation if they're trying to hear each other," she replied, clearly unconcerned.

The waiter handed him a menu while serving Delaney a Murphy's Irish Stout that he'd brought her without asking.

"People in this town tend to eat later than in many other cities," she explained as he studied the dinner entrées. "It's because we all work late. Hundred-hour workweeks aren't uncommon. They say sex, money, and star power define who you are in LA, how much money you earn defines you in Manhattan, but here it's what you do. You are only as important as your job."

She took a long swig of stout and asked, "Have you decided?"

"I'm not really familiar with Irish cuisine."

"That's because there is no such thing," she said, laughing. "There's a bunch of dishes with cabbage and potatoes and meat ground up together, but identifying it as a culinary art is a stretch. Order the shepherd's pie if you want a bit of the Olde Emerald Isle."

He told the waiter that he'd take the pie along with a glass of water.

"Oh no," Delaney said, interrupting him. "You can't eat shepherd's pie with water. Bring him a Guinness."

"I don't drink alcohol."

"The pie won't taste right without it," she explained, overruling him. "Just take one sip and you'll see why you need a good Irish brew to finish the rest of your meal."

"You don't make shepherd's pie sound appetizing."

"I didn't say it would be. In Ireland, eating was about avoiding starvation, not taste." She paused and said, "That's actually a great segue. You come to Washington with high expectations and lofty goals but much of what you do here is meat and potatoes. I don't want to depress you by sounding cynical, but you'll discover as a member of Congress you'll soon be spending much of that hundred-hour workweek on the phone asking for money. It starts the morning you're elected and never ends. The more money you raise, the longer you stay and the better chance you actually will do something lofty."

"Is that why you brought me to a pub? For a lecture about meat and potatoes and political reality?"

"No, I brought you here because I love Irish stout and I knew if you were boring, I could at least have a few drinks to help make the evening go faster."

She leaned in closer so it was easier for him to hear. "Fortunately, you aren't boring. Not yet. Now, let's talk about you. Tell me about your wife. How did you meet?"

"Let's not talk about her right now. If you don't want to tell me anything more about how Governor Coldridge is going to guarantee my election, at least tell me why you are working for him."

"Besides the fact that he pays my salary?" she replied, smiling. "I believe in him. It's my job to help develop the sound bites and create the image that's so important to getting a candidate elected president. But personally, I don't pay attention to any of that. I cast my vote based on a candidate's character, because issues are fluid. Just look at the issues raised during past presidential campaigns and compare them to what actually happened after a president was elected."

"Give me an example," he said while the waiter delivered a Guinness for him and another stout for her. She immediately reached for her glass but he didn't touch the frosted one in front of him.

"Here's to you," she said, lifting the stout, gentling taunting him. "C'mon, you can at least tap glasses for luck."

He raised the Guinness and tapped it on her glass but returned it to the table without tasting it.

Satisfied, she continued. "I vote for someone I believe will make the right decision when our nation gets caught in a crisis rather than voting for someone who makes a bunch of unattainable campaign promises. Lyndon Johnson got blindsided by the Vietnam War. The Iranian hostage crisis and economic malaise undid Jimmy Carter. George W. Bush had to deal with 9/11. What I'm saying is that the real test for a president comes when there's a crisis."

She took another long draw and then said, "Like our current hostage crisis in Somalia. During the first presidential debate, President Allworth caught our campaign unprepared with her announcement, but now the crisis has come back to bite her, and her handling of this bloody affair ultimately will be what defines her presidency and, hopefully, keeps her from being reelected."

"What don't you like about the president—besides that she's in the other party?"

"Being in the other party is enough. Nearly everything the president supports, I oppose, but there's a personal reason why I want her defeated and it actually has more to do with someone else—a power broker named Decker Lake."

"The former U.S. attorney general and the man who's always seen at her side?" Adeogo asked.

"Yes. He's responsible for her political career and for getting her into the White House. He's reigned as this city's kingmaker for too long.

Every four or eight years, the White House changes hands, but people such as Lake remain entrenched. They're rich puppeteers who operate behind the scenes. In his case, he wields tremendous power over the president and White House."

"And you think that's wrong?"

"Not at all," she replied. "I'm not opposed to our power broker system. I simply want to take his spot."

The waiter brought them their entrées and Adeogo noticed that Delaney was having a hamburger.

"My wife is going to be furious with me," he said, chuckling. "Before I came, she researched the Internet and gave me a list of five-star French restaurants to try. And here I am, eating shepherd's pie while you eat a hamburger."

Delaney pushed her fork into the mound of French fries and transferred them over onto his plate. "Here's some French food for you."

They both laughed.

"So tell me," he said, "as my assigned handler, what makes a good congressman?"

"To begin with, don't say 'congressman.' It's sexist. Say 'representative' or 'member of Congress.' And to answer your question, there are three types. One sticks a finger in the air and mindlessly does whatever the voters back home want. That sort of representative is a megaphone for them—or their puppet, depending on how you look at it. The second type studies the issues, holds investigative hearings, then listens to the folks back home but makes an independent decision."

"Which should I be?"

"You tell me. The ones who simply vote like a majority of the folks back home last longer."

"You said there was a third type."

"That's right," she said, "Representative Thomas Stanton is that third type. Everyone calls him the Chairman and he keeps voters happy using his clout to make sure plenty of federal funds flow into his district. He has a crack administrative staff that addresses his constituents' needs whenever they call. But he also happens to be a true leader."

After pausing to take a bite of her hamburger, she continued. "True leaders lead. They see into the future. Let me give you an example. After the Berlin Wall fell, everyone in Congress was talking about how democracy and capitalism had defeated Communism. And it wasn't just Congress saying that. One popular book described the events that led to the collapse of the wall and later the Kremlin as an 'end of history,' meaning that freedom, the democratic process, and capitalism had triumphed."

"But not Representative Stanton?" Adeogo asked.

"He went against the grain. He warned that globalism and the rise of Islamic radicalism was destined to lead to a conflict between democracy and savagery—a conflict the modern world was ignoring and ill suited to wage. And on September eleventh, 2001, Chairman Stanton was proved painfully right."

"I remember seeing him being interviewed on every television network after the towers fell," Adeogo said.

"That's because, in a time of crisis, the Chairman was someone who the American public trusted to tell them the truth. He did it in a calm, responsible way. That's true leadership. The Chairman believes that if he can speak to the public honestly, voters will understand and trust him to do the right thing. Sadly, people like the Chairman are a dying breed."

"Isn't part of the reason why they're a dying breed," Adeogo asked with a sly smile, "is because of people such as you? Professional handlers and spinmeisters who use their talents and the media to create images, to build and to destroy careers?"

"Even if you put lipstick on a pig, it's still a pig."

Adeogo gave Delaney an admiring look. He felt relaxed talking to her. He was enjoying himself. Reaching for the Guinness, he said, "I think this pie would be better with a small taste of beer. But only one." He lifted his glass, and she immediately tapped his with her own.

He noticed at that moment that she had green eyes.

"Enough politics," she said. "Tell me about your wife. Will she be comfortable moving here?"

"She will love being in such a beautiful and historic city, but she hates politics. It makes her nervous."

"Then she'll be very nervous here," Delaney dryly noted. "Is yours a classic boy-meets-girl American love story?"

"Our marriage was arranged, even though I was born in Minneapolis."

"Now that's an interesting twist. You might be the first member of Congress who had an arranged marriage."

"Marriage is considered a sacred and blessed event in Somalia. It's an important decision generally left up to parents. I respected my parents' wishes."

"My God, if I'd let my parents pick a husband for me, I'd be sitting in a low-rent Boston duplex with four screaming rug rats and a beer guzzler wearing a sweat-stained Boston Red Sox T-shirt."

"My mother took great care in selecting a wife for me."

"My mother married a drunk who beat her," Delaney replied.

"I'm sorry to hear that. You must understand that Somalia is a country of clans, social groups, and traditions. Traditions define a person. Family defines a person. Clans define a person. Jobs do not."

"With my pedigree, I prefer being defined by my work," she said, laughing. "When did your mother choose your wife?"

"I was twenty when they told me I needed to marry. My mother returned to Somalia and chose her. She was sixteen."

"Your wife was sixteen. That's very young."

"Because of the civil wars, many families were eager to arrange marriages for their daughters, some at younger ages than that. Ages that would shock Americans."

"I don't shock easily. How young?"

"Age nine."

"You're right. I'm shocked."

"Even today, in many clans, a girl's suitability for marriage begins when her chest develops, regardless of her age. In those clans, if she reaches the age of fifteen and is not yet married, she is considered to be flawed in some way. She is considered an outcast or bad luck for her family and often punished."

Glancing down at her own ample cleavage, Delaney said, "That's frightening. I would have been one of those nine-year-olds. What does a nine-year-old know about being married?"

"In Somalia there is a name for marriage training. It is called *Guur Kukoris*, which roughly translates into 'she will learn her duties after they are married.'"

"You'd be arrested for child abuse here if you had sex with someone that young." A mischievous smile crossed her face. She was feeling the stout. "Wasn't it a bit intimidating, not to say awkward, consummating your marriage on your wedding night with a sixteen-year-old stranger?"

He'd never been asked that question, especially by a stranger, especially by a woman.

"This is not something I care to discuss."

"You might not have a choice. Once you get elected to Congress, your life becomes an open book." Pushing her plate to the side, she said, "If you have a skeleton, tell me now before it's too late."

He dabbed his napkin to his mouth and looked directly into her penetrating green eyes. "The worst the press will find is an overdue library book."

She didn't flinch. "I read that line in the Minneapolis newspaper. But you need to convince me. Are you as chaste as Caesar's wife?"

"Yes," he said, reaching for his Guinness. "I think I'll have another taste."

"I'll order you another one," she said, motioning their waiter.

Adeogo turned the tables. "What are your secrets?" he asked.

"I'm an open book, as they say. Ask me anything."

"Why are you not married? Have you not met the right man?"

"My problem is, I've met a number of right men," she replied. "But none as interesting as my job."

WEDNESDAY

Six days before the presidential election

CHAPTER FORTY-NINE

Korfa's apartment
Mogadishu, Somalia

Brooke was frustrated. She'd wanted to get an early start, but Korfa had been called out during the night to work and got delayed in the morning. It seemed that everything in Somalia involved waiting, and it frustrated her. Korfa finally appeared just before noon. As she was leaving the apartment, she glanced at Gunter Conner, who was seated on the floor talking quietly to Caanood.

"Remember, Conner," Brooke said bitterly, "the clock is ticking. Yesterday I promised you forty-eight hours. That's it. You call Washington and tell them what you've done. Or I will."

He ignored her.

Korfa was waiting outside to drive Brooke to a neighborhood near the W. 21ka Oktoobar/Warshahada highway, which cut a line across the northwest corner of the city. From there, it would be about a mile to the apartment building where she'd been told the five Marines and two State Department hostages were being held.

At Caanood's suggestion, Brooke was not wearing the heavy and cumbersome burqa but instead was wearing the guntiino. It was lighter and easier to move in. Caanood had added a pale blue *khimar*, which was so long that it dropped well below Brooke's waist, giving her ample room to hide her Beretta M9 in the center of her back. To further conceal her identity, Caanood had insisted Brooke wear a *niqab* as well. That second veil covered Brooke's nose and mouth, leaving only her eyes exposed.

As she walked along deserted dirt streets under the noonday heat, she could feel herself perspiring. She lowered the niqab from her nose, leaving it gathered like a burglar's mask at her chin.

It took her fifteen minutes to reach the intersection where the apartment building was located. The streets around it were empty. The apartment building anchored the southeast corner of a block of former homes and businesses, all destroyed during fighting. Most were missing their roofs and had crumbling walls. The exterior of the apartment building had been painted five different colors, beginning with a rusty red that started at the concrete sidewalk and rose to the height of an average man's shoulders. From that height to the base of the second floor, the walls had been painted turquoise. The second floor was ringed by a narrow balcony of decorative blocks painted white. The exterior walls on the second floor were a bright orange, and there was a yellow trim around the rim of the building's flat roof. The building looked like the base of a rainbow and Brooke silently wondered if its owner had intentionally chosen a sandwich of colors or simply used whatever paint he could salvage.

Brooke counted six solid wooden doors on the building's street level, all former shops now padlocked. The windows on the second-floor apartments were shuttered. To reach the apartments, a visitor had to pass through an archway in the side of the building that was protected by a decorative iron gate. That opening led to a courtyard staircase.

Directly across the intersection to the south of the apartment building was the shell of a destroyed house, and Brooke spotted a single *ghalab* tree outside it. She walked under the scant shade of the evergreen, hoping that anyone who might be watching through slits in the apartment building's second-floor shutters would assume she was simply resting. The aroma of the tree's flowers reminded her of the honeysuckle that her mother used to pick from bushes in the family's backyard in Tulsa.

Brooke slipped a Samsung cell phone that Korfa had loaned her from the front pocket of her dress. Holding it close to the fabric to help conceal it, she pressed the phone's video record button and slowly panned across the apartment building and the surrounding shells of former structures adjacent to it.

Brooke assumed the hostages were being held on the second floor directly across the street from her. During boot camp, she'd been "taken" hostage by "enemy combatants" who'd pushed and screamed at her. She had been uncomfortable, but she had known it was a training exercise that would quickly end. She gazed across the intersection at the second floor and wondered about Sergeant Walks Many Miles. *Had the terrorists vented their anger by torturing him and the other four Marines and two State Department employees being held hostage?* According to the embassy's personnel records, a Marine private named Jasper McDaniels had been a medical student before enlisting. *Had he been allowed to treat his fellow hostages' injuries?*

After carefully capturing images of the front and the side of the apartment building, she focused on the two streets that ran adjacent to it. The street running east to west crossed in front of the rectangular building. A south to north avenue ran along its most eastern side. This is where the gate that opened into the courtyard was located. Brooke stepped from under the shade and began walking north across the intersection and up the avenue toward the gate. She kept the camera phone next to her right side pointed at the apartments, which were on her left. She swung her hand slightly forward, positioning the lens in front of her thigh for an unobstructed view.

Just as she was about to reach the courtyard archway, a Somali man appeared at its gate with an AK-47 slung over his shoulder. Brooke instinctively lowered her eyes while silently wishing she had kept the niqab veil in place across her nose and mouth. She tilted the phone slightly upward as she passed by him, hoping to photograph his face. Without looking directly at him, she took note that he was wearing tan pants, sandals, and a long-sleeved, bright red, collared shirt that was open at the front, exposing a dirty white T-shirt.

He unlocked the iron gate and swung it outward over the sidewalk. It was at this point that Brooke noticed there was another Al-Shabaab fighter standing behind the first. This second man saw her passing in the street in front of them and hollered, "*Joojin!*"

Brooke didn't speak Somali, but she recognized the word *STOP*.

She did.

Brooke was now standing at the east side of the apartment building about four feet north of the gate, with both of the terrorists behind her on her left side. Shifting her head in their direction, Brooke glanced over her shoulder and immediately froze.

The second jihadist was Mosi, the Somali driver who had welcomed her at the airport and had served as her chauffeur until he'd disappeared. Mosi had been friendly then, but now he glared at her and yelled, "She's an American!"

In an effortless move, the first Al-Shabaab fighter slipped the AK-47 from his shoulder and pointed it at Brooke's chest as he rushed from the gate into the street. Mosi was less than a step behind him.

Brooke spun around. Because she was right-handed and still clutching the camera phone, she couldn't reach for the M9 pistol hidden under the heavy veil at the center of her back.

Gripping the Samsung tight in her palm, she waited for the fighter to come nearer. When he was close enough, she threw her right hand upward from her side and smacked the rifle's tip with the phone, slapping the gun to one side while twisting her body.

The gunman fired a burst of rounds that whizzed by her left arm, barely missing her skin.

Having used her right hand to slap the gun barrel, Brooke turned like a prizefighter and swung upward with her left fist, catching her assailant under his chin. Caught completely off guard by the punch, the jihadist lost his footing and stumbled backward into Mosi.

Dropping her cell phone, Brooke reached behind her back under the khimar with her now-empty right hand for her pistol.

But Mosi was faster than she'd anticipated.

Shoving past his Al-Shabaab comrade, Mosi lunged forward, hitting Brooke with his lowered shoulder, knocking her off her feet. She barely had time to free her hand from under the khimar to keep it from being pinned between her body and the street.

Her back hit the dirt with a thud, knocking the wind from her lungs as Mosi scrambled on top of her chest. He wasn't carrying a gun but he was wearing a *billaawe* attached to a belt on his waist. The eighteen-inch-long Somali dagger was no match against an opponent armed with an AK-47, but it was deadly in close combat.

Brooke thrust her hips up like a bucking bull, trying to throw Mosi off her, but he didn't budge. Drawing the billaawe from its sheep-hide sheath, he held its tip directly above her eyes and hollered, "I'll kill you!"

During that panicky moment, Brooke considered grabbing Mosi's wrist, but the other Al-Shabaab fighter had regained his footing and had hurried toward them with his AK-47 cocked and ready to fire.

Brooke was trapped.

CHAPTER FIFTY

Shortly after six a.m. (EDT)
Capitol Hill
Washington, D.C.

Rudy Adeogo's mood matched the stormy weather. He stared out the rain-splattered window of the limousine that was carrying him and Mary Margaret Delaney through Washington's slick streets to Governor Coldridge's campaign headquarters.

When Delaney finished what had to be her tenth phone call, she asked, "What's bothering you? You've barely spoken."

"I'm a religious man. A family man. Unlike you," he snapped.

Delaney's smile vanished. "Let me ask you something," she said in a stern voice. "Are you going to tell your wife about last night?"

"No! I'll never tell her."

"Only two people know what happened. Don't make more of it than what it was. We both were excited and had too much to drink. Just forget about it."

Her cell phone rang, and when she answered, Adeogo again stared out the window at the crawling morning rush-hour traffic. *How could he just forget about something so intimate?* He had never wanted a woman as much as he'd desired Delaney last night. Their lovemaking had been more intense than any relations he'd shared with his wife, his only other intimate partner. Yet this morning, the sight of her disgusted him. He felt ashamed.

Delaney ended her phone call as their limo crossed the Anacostia River into Prince George's County, Maryland. Coldridge's campaign headquarters was located inside a building previously used as an upscale men's clothing shop at the National Harbor, a menagerie of hotels, restaurants, and offices. One of the Harbor's attractions was *The*

Awakening, a seventy-foot-long sculpture of a bearded giant trying to free himself from the ground, with only his head, arms, and legs breaking through the surface. It had been one of the draws for Coldridge, who envisioned himself as a giant rising from the earth to do battle against the political establishment across the Potomac.

Delaney scooted from the limo as soon as it stopped, forcing Adeogo to quicken his pace as they entered the ground floor. Displays of Alexander Amosu and Dormeuil suits had been replaced by rows of rented gray metal desks manned by volunteers of every age crowded together in lines. Hand-stenciled signs perched atop chrome poles identified different geographic regions. Only three states—California, New York, and Governor Coldridge's home state of Florida—had their own individual markers. Yard signs—in red, white, and blue—that proclaimed AMERICA FIRST were stacked upside down near the front doorway, their wire legs jutting out, eager to snag a passing skirt or pant leg. Cardboard boxes crammed with bumper stickers and campaign buttons were next to the welcome desk for easy distribution to precinct captains.

There was a sense of urgency, of too many tasks that needed to be done yesterday. On one wall, campaign workers had hung a large digital clock that was counting down the days, hours, minutes, and seconds before polls opened next Tuesday.

Delaney expertly wove through the desks to an open staircase that rose from the middle of the room. As they climbed its metal steps, Delaney's heels made a clacking sound like drummers in a parade clicking their sticks together to keep marchers in step.

"You need to snap out of this funk," she whispered. "I understand this was the first time you cheated on your wife. But man up and deal with it."

The second floor was configured much like the first, except the callers here were not charged with rallying voters. They were paid fund-raisers, and the digital clock hanging on the wall tracked donated dollars and automatically reset itself every sixty minutes with a new hourly goal.

By the time they reached the third floor, Adeogo had forced off his sullenness. A security guard stationed at the top of the staircase waved Delaney by, and they entered a hallway that led them through temporary walls erected to create dozens of offices, each manned by administrative assistants and Coldridge's bevy of advisors. Governor Coldridge's suite was at the far end of the building.

His personal secretary welcomed them, and moments later Governor Timothy Coldridge stepped through a pair of double doors with an outstretched hand.

"Thrilled you've come to help us," Coldridge said.

"Thrilled to be asked," Adeogo replied.

"I have a rather unique office," Coldridge bragged over his shoulder as they followed him inside. "My campaign staff insisted it be laid out exactly like the Oval Office. They told me I needed to get myself familiar with the White House so I'll feel at home when we move there during January."

He motioned them toward two sofas that faced each other. A pair of leather-covered chairs at the far end created a U-shaped design with a circular carpet bearing the Great Seal of the United States at the U shape's opening.

"The furniture is nearly identical to what's in the Oval Office too," Delaney said. "Except the president's desk. The actual presidential desk is one of a kind."

Coldridge's own ornate desk sat a few feet above the presidential seal in front of a plate-glass window that overlooked the Potomac and, beyond, the Washington skyline.

"Rudy," Coldridge said, "I hope you don't mind me calling you by your first name. I prefer being informal around here. Mary Margaret says you're a man of honor. Can I trust you to keep what's said between us today private?"

"This conversation will stay between the three of us," Adeogo said.

"Good," Coldridge replied approvingly, as he took a seat on one of the sofas. "As we both know, Washington is a city of doublespeak, of innuendo and subtleties. It's a city where people are guarded when they speak. But I don't want there to be any misunderstandings between us, not at this critical point."

"Please, I'd also prefer if we spoke frankly," Adeogo said.

Delaney slipped down on the sofa next to Coldridge, while Adeogo sat opposite them.

"The crisis in Somalia has given my campaign traction right when we need it," Coldridge said. "My pollsters are telling me if the election were held today, we would win. The American people remember Allworth's stunt in the first debate when she announced the embassy opening, and they rightly blame her personally for this crisis. It's to our advantage to make Allworth suffer as much damage as possible. That is why I've invited you here to help me."

Coldridge stood and walked behind his desk, where he looked out his office's large window. "It's an impressive view, isn't it?" He turned and said, "You asked me to be candid so I will be. An Air Force plane bringing home the bodies of the twelve American heroes who were murdered in Somalia will be arriving at Dover Air Force Base shortly. On the day that happens, I'd like you to hold a press conference in Dover criticizing President Allworth for her mishandling of events in Mogadishu."

"You asked me to hold a press conference. Does this mean you will not be there with me?"

"That's right. I have to be careful not to make it appear that I am trying to take advantage politically of these brave men's tragic deaths. You will be the featured speaker at this press conference. This must look like a grassroots effort. I'll be far away from Dover, campaigning, so the media will not accuse me of being ghoulish."

Returning to his seat on the sofa, Coldridge leaned forward and said, "I want to ask you again: What's said here stays here, is that correct?"

"If you're worried, there are two of you and only one of me," Adeogo replied. "But I give you my word."

Coldridge nodded approvingly to Delaney, her signal to take over.

"Some friends of ours," Delaney said smiling, "have created a political action committee—called Citizens for a Sound Foreign Policy. I want you to become its face."

"Isn't it illegal for a presidential candidate to be involved in a PAC that was created to support his campaign?" Adeogo asked.

"Why don't you let our lawyers worry about the formalities and legalities?" Delaney replied. "We need a PAC's help for practical reasons. It will pay for the cost of hosting a press conference and for the expense of bringing in relatives and friends of the deceased Americans, who we'll hand pick. They'll criticize the president too. The PAC will pay your expenses, including the cost of your trip here and a generous honorarium for your time. We already have five-million dollars in the PAC so money is not an issue."

"Trust me," Coldridge said. "There'll be five times that much available through the PAC if we need it."

"In addition to the press conference, the PAC will pay for television campaign ads," Delaney explained. "We'll have our people write a speech for you that will guarantee national news exposure during the press conference. Our media experts will take snippets from that speech and incorporate those clips into a national ad campaign attacking President Allworth."

"How long will all of this take?" Adeogo asked. "I'm scheduled to fly home tonight to attend a fund-raiser."

"Not to worry," Delaney volunteered. "I've already talked to your people in Minneapolis and they're covering for you tonight. I've canceled your flight and told the Hyatt you'll be spending at least one more night here in D.C. I hope you don't mind."

He did, but it seemed pointless to object.

"We can spend today drafting your speech," Delaney said. "Hopefully, the flight with the returning heroes will be arriving Thursday, but if not, the plane will definitely be here by Friday."

"Friday? I can't afford to wait here until then, not during this final week of campaigning."

"Actually, you can," Coldridge replied.

"What we're offering you is better than any Lions Club or Rotary Club luncheon you'd be attending in the Twin Cities," Delaney continued. "The television ads we prepare will air nonstop seventy-two hours before the polls open, and we'll make certain that some are tailored specifically for the Minneapolis market to support your local campaign."

Lowering his voice to a whisper, Coldridge added, "Rudy, those ads are icing on the cake. I believe Mary Margaret told you last night that Representative Buckner is going to withdraw for personal reasons from the Fifth District race this weekend and endorse you. Assuming you help us. You play ball and you've got nothing to worry about on Tuesday."

"She did tell me that my opponent will withdraw," he replied, "but she didn't say why."

Coldridge raised his hands in mock protest. "There are some things in politics it's better for a candidate not to know. That goes for me and for you. You'll just have to trust us on this, Rudy, when we tell you that Representative Buckner is going to take himself out of the race."

"What about voters who've already cast their ballots?" Adeogo said.

"Between the ads that we will deliver for you and Buckner's withdrawal, you will get enough to overcome those preelection day votes," Delaney said. "It's not just me saying that. We had our team of statistical experts do the metrics and run the numbers in Minneapolis. Right now, Buckner is leading you by a wide margin and no matter how many doors you knock on and hands you shake between now and next Tuesday, you'll never catch him without our assistance."

"I'm going to be the next president," Coldridge said confidently. "I'd sure like you to be serving in Congress when I take control of this government. I think we could work well together."

Delaney stood. "The governor is on a tight schedule, so it would be best if we returned to the Hyatt. I'll introduce you to the lawyers helping us with the PAC, and we can begin thinking about some catchy sound bites for your speech."

"Mary Margaret is the one who came up with the idea behind my 'America First' campaign," Coldridge said proudly. He stood and placed his hand on Adeogo's shoulder. "You're going to make a great congressman."

"Don't you mean 'member of Congress'?" Adeogo asked. "Mary Margaret told me I shouldn't risk irritating women voters by referring to someone—even a man—as a congressman."

Coldridge shot Delaney a mischievous smile. "We'd better be careful here, Mary Margaret. If Mr. Adeogo gets as famous as I think he will be, he'll be ready to run against me in four years for the presidency."

"And I'll offer to run his campaign," Delaney quipped.

CHAPTER FIFTY-ONE

Early afternoon Somali time
Outside an apartment building
Mogadishu, Somalia

Mosi scanned the street to see if Brooke was alone.

Embarrassed by Brooke slapping his AK-47 to the side, Mosi's partner stayed out of her reach with his rifle now aimed at her chest. Brooke was still lying flat on her back on the dirt street.

Returning his billaawe to its sheath, Mosi stepped away from her and picked up the Samsung phone that Brooke had dropped.

"Get up!" he ordered.

Brooke sat but didn't stand. "You knocked the wind out of me when you tackled me. Give me a second."

Mosi walked to where his partner was standing guard and lifted up the captured cell phone.

"She's been taking our pictures," Mosi announced.

As soon as they were distracted by the phone's screen, Brooke reached behind her back and grabbed her pistol. She fired two rounds at the chest of Mosi's partner from where she was sitting. Her first missed, but the second hit his right shoulder near his neck. In a split second, she lowered her aim and fired two more rounds at his heart, causing him to collapse.

With the cell phone still in his hand and his knife in its sheath, Mosi was at a disadvantage.

"We've got a saying in the U.S.," Brooke said, standing from the street while keeping her M9 pistol aimed at Mosi's chest. "Never bring a knife to a gunfight."

To her surprise, Mosi didn't appear frightened.

"How about bringing a cell phone to a gunfight?" he asked.

He began punching a telephone number into her Samsung but stopped before hitting the call button.

"When I push this, my phone will detonate explosives in the apartment building and all of the American hostages inside will die," Mosi declared, breaking into a toothy grin. "The blast should kill us too!"

"I don't believe you. Put down the phone."

"There were only two of us left here to guard the hostages, and now I am the only one still alive. You should ask yourself why. I am holding the answer. I was instructed to blow up the building if General Saeed or any American soldiers came to rescue the hostages. All it takes is me touching the call button."

He was holding his finger less than a half inch above the dialing pad.

"I can shoot you before you can press send," Brooke said. "At this range, I won't miss."

"Yes, yes, but will you kill me? We're not in the movies, where one shot always kills a man. Even if you hit my heart, there is sufficient oxygen in my brain to support ten to fifteen seconds of activity and life. Long enough to touch the keypad."

"You a doctor," she asked sarcastically, "as well as a terrorist?"

"I was taught to always shoot for the head. You Marines are taught to shoot two rounds at the chest and then re-aim."

"Thanks for that tip." She raised her aim.

A sudden movement behind Mosi caught Brooke's eye. Fifty feet behind them a boy appeared on the street in front of the apartment building, apparently drawn by the gunfire. Within seconds another appeared, along with a woman wearing a burqa.

In a calm voice, Mosi said, "Put down your gun or I will kill us all."

"Put down the phone or I will kill you."

"Aren't you wondering why my Al-Shabaab brother was not standing watch outside the building? I had called him into the courtyard to tell him the news."

"What news?"

"An Egyptian friend of ours has told us your government has decided to pay a ransom. The money will soon be arriving from Cairo along with your uncle, General Frank Grant."

Brooke looked surprised.

Mosi noticed. "How would I know this if it wasn't the truth? There is no reason for your fellow Marines to die. There is no reason for *you* to die. Let us resolve this peacefully. After the money is delivered, if you'd like, I will drive you to the airport in my Mercedes."

Behind Mosi, Brooke saw another figure join the two boys and woman watching them from down the street. It was a man armed with an AK-47. This neighborhood was still under Al-Shabaab control. She wasn't supposed to engage Al-Shabaab. Another thought flashed into her mind. Even if she killed Mosi, how was she going to get the hostages out of Mogadishu?

"Put your pistol on the ground and kick it away from you and I will put away this phone and no one will die," Mosi said. "We will go have tea in the apartment and wait for news about the ransom payment and your uncle arriving to take you and the Marines home. There is no need for any more killing."

The man with the AK-47 starting walking toward her. She was outnumbered. Reluctantly, she placed her pistol on the ground and kicked it a few feet away.

"A cell phone is not such a bad weapon to bring to a fight," he declared triumphantly, tucking the phone into his breast shirt pocket. "But a knife is even better." He drew his billaawe and twisted its blade in the sunlight. "Have you ever been in a knife fight, Captain Grant?"

"I thought we were going upstairs for tea."

She looked at her pistol, now out of reach, and felt foolish.

"You Americans are naïve." His voice had changed from one of sympathetic reasoning to one of scorn.

"Shouldn't we both have knives if there's going to be a knife fight?" she asked.

"Such a clever girl. A clever American girl."

"And you're a liar."

"There is no sin in lying to an enemy of Allah."

"How convenient for you."

"The Americans who came to teach us how to fight the Soviets told us to hold a knife with the blade pointed up, jabbing it from underneath."

He illustrated, thrusting the blade into the air. "But this is wrong." Turning the blade so its tip was aimed at the ground, he said, "A Somali warrior always stabs downward from above with his billaawe, because he can deliver a more forceful blow and keep his enemy from grabbing his forearm." He jammed the blade downward through the air.

"I'll keep that in mind the next time I meet a liar armed with a badly made knife."

"Do not insult the weapon that will take your life. My great-grandfather made this billaawe and used it to kill a dozen English soldiers. My grandfather and father used it during our civil wars. Many of my Al-Shabaab brothers laugh at me for carrying it. They see it as a useless antique, but my father taught me how to use it and I spent hours practicing as a child. In my hand, this blade becomes part of my body."

He fondled its buffalo-horn handle and three-pronged pommel.

"Murdering people with a knife," she said dryly. "What a lovely family tradition and heirloom to pass down."

Before she could react, Mosi leaped and swung the billaawe across her chest, cutting through the fabric and slicing her skin. But only the tip of the blade touched her, creating more of a paper cut than a serious wound.

Retreating, he said, "How does your sharp tongue compare to my sharp blade? I only wish I could be here when you are sold back to your government for a ransom like the whore you are, along with your ambassador and his friend. As for your Marine friends upstairs, they will die. I will see to that." He patted the cell phone in his shirt pocket. "But now it's time for me to show you more of my skills."

Brooke clenched her fists and readied herself for his attack. A well-trained Marine, she knew how to deflect a knife and disable an attacker.

Mosi saw her stance and chuckled. Once again, he flew forward. Brooke did exactly as she had been trained, but Mosi easily countered her defensive moves and, as he spun around her, he brought down his blade across her back, this time cutting her slightly deeper, causing her to yelp in pain.

Strutting in front of her like a matador toying with an angry bull, he declared, "My next cut will be across your face. No man will ever want you, and when you awake each morning and look into a mirror, you will remember Mosi, the man who cut you and made you an ugly whore."

As Brooke was raising her hands in front of her face, Mosi sprang forward and then seemed to freeze in midair. His right arm fell limp and the billaawe fell from his hand. She'd been so focused on protecting herself that it took her a moment to realize Mosi had been shot. A bullet had shattered his right arm, making it useless. A second round had grazed his temple, causing his head to jerk sideways as if he'd been punched. He fell at her feet and didn't move.

Brooke looked at the spectators who'd been watching. The man with the AK-47 was nowhere to be seen. Only the two boys and the woman were still there.

And it was the woman who was holding a raised pistol.

CHAPTER FIFTY-TWO

The woman in the burqa who'd shot Mosi moved toward Brooke cautiously as the boys standing near her scattered.

Removing the veil, Gunter Conner said, "I thought you might recognize the burqa but I assume they all look alike. Black and shapeless."

"You followed me," she said in a voice that was clearly more surprised than grateful.

"I was tired of drinking tea and watching CNN," he quipped.

"I didn't know you were such a good shot."

"I was just trying to hit him before he stabbed you. Although, for a moment, I did think that if he killed you, it would be easier for me to simply disappear. That's what you thought I was going to do, isn't it?"

"You're still holding a gun," she said.

"Regardless of what you may think about me, I am not a coward and I'm not a traitor. I regret what happened but it hasn't changed my resolve to hunt down and kill the Falcon."

"This doesn't change anything between us," she said. "You're still responsible for the embassy attack and you need to be held accountable for your actions."

Lowering his pistol, he said, "It must be nice to live in a world of white knights and black knights."

"We live in the same world."

"No," Conner said, "we don't. I live in a world where there are no knights at all. I live in a dark world of shadows, a murky world that people like you don't want to admit is even there. A world of lies and deceit. I live in a world where sometimes a man must do evil in order to achieve good."

"Don't confuse your personal vendetta against the killer you are calling the Falcon with honor."

"And don't confuse your certainty with truth. The Falcon is real, and if he is not stopped, more will die. I was trying to achieve a greater good."

Mosi moaned.

"Grab the phone in his shirt pocket!" Brooke yelled. "Don't let him touch the dial pad."

Conner stooped down over him to retrieve the phone at the exact moment Mosi opened his eyes. With his good left hand, Mosi grabbed Conner's pistol and twisted it upward, forcing the gun to discharge. Conner fell sideways, wounded, but managed to keep hold of his pistol.

Mosi pulled the cell phone from his pocket.

Brooke grabbed Mosi's dagger, which was lying on the street near him, but before she could stab him, he hit the call button on the phone with his left thumb. He expected an explosion.

"Hello?" a male voice said, answering the call.

The grin on Mosi's face vanished as he realized that his own people had not trusted him with the actual phone number needed to detonate the explosives.

Brooke slammed the dagger into Mosi's chest.

"That's how you do it, right, Mosi? Swing downward, right? You enjoying your last fifteen seconds of life before your brain shuts off? Do you hear me, Mosi? Go to hell!"

She had plunged the blade with such force that it had passed completely through his body and its tip had become embedded in the dirt.

Conner was gasping for breath.

"Jasper McDaniels," Brooke said to Conner. "He's a hostage. He went to medical school. I'm going to get him."

"Wait," he said, reaching a hand up toward her.

She took it and he squeezed hard. "My daughter," he said. "Jennifer. Promise me you'll take care of her."

"I'm not letting you die here," she replied. "I'm not letting you off the hook that easy."

He tightened his grip. "I saved your life. Promise me you'll take care of Jennifer."

"I will," she promised.

Prying her hand loose, she darted through the apartment building archway into the courtyard, where she hurried up its interior staircase. All of the doors to the abandoned apartments were missing except one. That had to be where the hostages were being held.

She shoved it open and the sunshine cut through the doorway like a spotlight. Bags of nitrogen fertilizer were packed in the main room but she didn't see a detonator. She hurried across the room to an interior door and tried its knob. It was unlocked, and as soon as she opened it she was hit by the stench of urine, feces, human sweat, and rotting fish. Fighting the urge to vomit, she entered the stagnant blackness. As her eyes adjusted, she could see the outline of a window behind closed shutters, so she stumbled toward it and opened the shutter flaps. The five Marines and two State Department hostages were each tied in a four-point position on their backs to wooden bunk beds that rose to the ceiling. The scene was reminiscent of black-and-white photographs that Brooke had seen of Jewish concentration-camp survivors locked in Nazi barracks. Each hostage was blindfolded and his mouth was gagged. She ungagged McDaniels first.

"Water, water," he gasped.

Brooke spotted a plastic gallon jug of water on the floor next to several rotting bluefin tuna.

She grabbed the jug and a rusty paring knife next to maggot-infested fish that the terrorists had been feeding to the hostages. It took her several attempts to cut the thick twine with the dull knife. The rope had been so tightly wrapped around McDaniels's hands and feet that his flesh was raw and torn.

"When did they stop feeding you?"

"Yesterday, maybe two days ago. Who knows? In this darkness you lose track of time. No bathrooms. Nothing. Just left us here to suffocate and die. Lying here has been hell."

"There's a wounded man on the street. Gunshot to the chest," she explained.

"Is he one of us?" McDaniels asked. "I'm not helping any of them."

"Gunter Conner. CIA."

"Where's the rest of the cavalry?" he asked.

"It's just Conner and me."

He took a long swig of water and then forced himself to stand. She steadied him for a moment and he walked out the door.

Brooke moved to Sergeant Miles next. His face was badly bruised from a recent beating. She pulled off his gag and blindfold.

"Captain," he said through cracked lips. "Just happen to be in our neighborhood?"

"Looks like you lost a bar fight," she said, sawing through his restraints.

"I got a few licks in. What's the evac plan?"

"Still working on that."

"You don't have birds outside?"

"I'll need to make a phone call."

Having cut his bonds, she gave him the knife and water jug simultaneously. "You get everyone out. This place is rigged to blow. I'll check on Conner and call our ride."

Running outside to the street, Brooke scooped up her M9 pistol and checked the intersection in front of the apartment for onlookers. It was still empty.

"He's pretty bad," McDaniels said, as he worked to stop the bleeding coming from Conner's chest wound. "He's going into shock."

"How long can he last?"

"I can stop the bleeding, but shock is called the golden hour for a reason."

Brooke reached for the Samsung that was still in Mosi's left hand and called Commander Jackman aboard the USS *Hornet*.

"I'm with the hostages. We got a man down and need immediate evac."

"You're where?"

"With the hostages. All five Marines and both civilians. Plus there's me and Gunter Conner, who has a serious chest wound."

"What about the terrorists?"

"Both are dead."

"You were ordered to not engage. We haven't been authorized to enter Mogadishu."

"We can't wait. Conner is going into shock and hostiles will be coming."

"My orders are to *not* violate Somali air space without direct authorization from the president. I'll need to contact Washington for permission."

"Sir, we can't wait that long."

"You should have thought about this before you went cowboy."

McDaniels interrupted her. "Conner isn't going to last much longer. There's more internal bleeding than I thought."

"Sir," Brooke said, "we're going to lose a man if we don't get evaced now."

"I'm not going to start a war with Somalia over one man. Hang tough, Marine. We'll get there as quickly as we can."

Sergeant Miles emerged from the apartment courtyard helping a fellow Marine who had a busted leg. The final two Marines came next, helping the two diplomats.

"Where's our ride?" Miles asked, scanning the empty sky.

"Coming—maybe," Brooke replied.

Miles noticed the Somali sword impaled in Mosi's chest. "Your handiwork, Captain?"

She nodded.

"Here's some of mine." He showed her a cell phone with wires attached to it. "Found this attached to a detonator upstairs. Thought I'd hang on to it."

Glancing around, Miles said, "We'd better move to shelter. Word travels fast in these streets."

Brooke pointed at the shell of a house behind the lone *ghalab* tree where she had stopped earlier for shade. "Let's hide behind those walls. We can see in three different directions from there if we get into a firefight."

"What kind of firepower we got, Captain?"

"One AK-47 and two pistols—Conner's and mine."

"And a Somali sword," Miles said, putting his boot on Mosi's chest and pulling the blade free.

"You get everyone moved while I make another phone call."

She reached into the pocket of her dress and took out a business card that she'd transferred from her pants pocket out of habit when she'd changed clothes. She dialed the number written on its back. When a woman answered, Brooke said, "Ebio Kattan, this is Captain Brooke Grant. You gave me your number after you interviewed Ambassador Thomas for your Al Arabic network news segment."

"Captain Grant!" the reporter exclaimed. "Everyone thinks you're a hostage."

"I need an ambulance and safe passage to the airport," Brooke replied. She quickly explained the situation.

"I'm sorry," Kattan replied. "We're a news network, not combat soldiers."

"I'm offering you a world scoop. 'Al Arabic News Reporter Rescues American Hostages.' Think about it."

Kattan did think about how her Al Arabic viewers would react if she was responsible for helping free American hostages.

"I'll find an ambulance for your wounded man, but journalists don't rescue Marines. We're observers. The best I can do is call General Saeed and tell him where you are."

"He's the last person I want you to call, but I don't really have a choice, do I?" Brooke asked.

"No," Kattan said.

"Okay, but promise me that you and a film crew will come with the ambulance and you'll get here *before* General Saeed arrives."

"Why must I get there before the general?"

"Because I don't trust him," she replied. "I don't have time to explain, but please don't betray us!"

"Captain Grant, just because I am an Arab doesn't mean I am an Islamic terrorist. It only means I have a better understanding of why people hate America."

Brooke ended the call and hurried toward the shelter where the others had taken cover.

"You thumb us a ride, Captain?" Miles asked. "Conner looks pretty bad."

McDaniels had placed the wounded station chief on the floor of the half-destroyed house. Blood was soaking through an impromptu dressing. Conner was unconscious.

"I called a television reporter."

"The media?" Miles replied, clearly startled.

"She's sending an ambulance and bringing her news crew, along with General Saeed." Brooke pointed at the AK-47. "Bring the rifle, Sergeant. You and I are moving to higher ground."

They made their way south along the street to a vacant three-story building about forty yards away. The structure had Swiss cheese–like holes in its walls, yet somehow its roof was still intact. When they climbed onto it, they had a clear view of the streets in front of them and the W. 21ka Oktoobar/Warshahada highway farther south in the distance. It would be the main thoroughfare that the ambulance would use.

For five minutes, they baked under the gradually descending sun. Sergeant Miles, who was already dehydrated, rubbed his eyes and fought exhaustion but was the first to notice a figure lurking on the street.

"There's a Somali with a rifle at oh three hundred," he whispered to Brooke.

The approaching figure stepped catlike, stopping every few seconds to scan the area.

"You think he's Al-Shabaab?" Brooke asked.

"Anyone with an AK-47 who's not one of us," Miles replied, "is one of them, Captain."

Like a timid deer sniffing the air for hunters, the man stopped and ducked into a shell of a house. From their higher vantage point, Brooke and Miles could see over the roofless house's crumbling walls as the Somali rested his AK-47 against a pile of rubble and took out his cell phone. Rather than raising it to his ear, he sat down on a rock and stared at it.

"I'm guessing," Miles said, "he's Al-Shabaab's replacement for Mosi and the other jihadist. He's been sent to blow up the apartment after our rescuers arrive. He's got no clue I removed the detonator."

Miles took the cell phone that had been attached to the explosives in the apartment from his pocket and placed it next to them on the roof.

"Can you take him out from here?" Brooke asked.

"I'm guessing he's sixty yards away," Miles said. "An AK is accurate to about three hundred yards. Just tell me when."

Brooke looked south toward the highway and saw a convoy being led by two black Chevy Silverado pickups. General Saeed's vehicles were moving fast, followed by two military trucks filled with soldiers. What she didn't see was an ambulance and Kattan.

"Damn it," she cursed. "General Saeed is going to get here before the Al Arabic television crew and ambulance. If she's coming at all."

"Why's that a problem, Captain?"

"General Saeed is not one of the good guys. He'll just as soon kill us as save us, especially Gunter Conner. We can't trust him."

Picking up the Samsung, she said, "I've got to slow him down."

She dialed a number. The person who answered didn't say a word.

"General Saeed," Brooke said cheerfully. "It's Captain Grant. You offered to show me around Mogadishu, remember? You invited me to dinner and gave me your private number."

"It appears you have been sightseeing on your own," he replied.

"Where's Ebio Kattan?" Brooke asked. "She's supposed to be with you. With an ambulance and film crew."

"It appears she's been delayed. Tell me, how many are you? Are you armed? And is Gunter Conner with you?"

"Gunter Conner is wounded and needs emergency care. That's why I asked Kattan to bring an ambulance."

"I have my personal doctor with me. I will take good care of Mr. Conner and you."

Brooke didn't like his snide tone. "Are you aware a Predator drone is watching you right now?" she asked. "It can see your teeth at twenty thousand feet, so you might wish to smile."

Brooke looked at the highway. The general immediately stopped his convoy. Stepping from his vehicle, he stared upward at the sky with binoculars.

"That drone is armed," she continued.

"Are you threatening me, Captain Grant?"

"I just want you to know there are people in Washington right now watching you." She hesitated and then added, "And I told them that you murdered Charles "Cash" Kelley when you were supposed to be rescuing the ProTech hostages. That's why the drone is carrying Hellfire missiles. That's why they'll use them against you if they have to."

"Ah, so you are the eyewitness that your CIA director told me about?" he replied.

Brooke heard the sound of an ambulance's siren. The emergency vehicle and an Al Arabic van were on the highway about two miles behind Saeed's convoy. Brooke could see General Saeed stepping back into his Silverado. His convey pulled back on the highway and resumed coming in their direction.

"I am eager to see you," Saeed said, ending the call.

As she lowered the phone, Sergeant Miles asked, "Is there really a Predator watching us right now?"

"I have no idea. But neither does he."

"Remind me not to play poker with you, Captain. I didn't know preachers' kids were such good liars."

"You haven't known many preachers' kids, have you?"

Moments later, the general's two Silverados and troop trucks sped into the intersection and a dozen soldiers scrambled out to form a protective perimeter before Saeed appeared.

As Brooke and Miles watched from their rooftop perch, the Al-Shabaab gunman hiding near the hostages dialed a number into the phone that he was holding.

"He's trying to detonate the explosives," Miles said, raising the AK-47. The cell phone that Miles had taken from the apartment vibrated, and two wires attached to it sparked.

"Take him down," Brooke said.

Miles squeezed the AK-47's trigger, sending a shot into the man's torso.

The sound of rifle fire sent General Saeed scrambling for cover. Keeping her head down, Brooke called Saeed's cell phone.

"That was us shooting," she said. "Check the ruins of a house near where you're standing and you'll find an Al-Shabaab fighter who was trying to detonate explosives in the apartment building."

"Where are you?" General Saeed asked, scanning the nearby rooftops.

The ambulance and Al Arabic television crew arrived in the intersection and Kattan hurried out with a cameraman.

"Now you have the media, as well as that drone, watching you, General," Brooke said. "Make sure everyone gets to the airport alive. Especially Gunter Conner." She put down the phone.

From the rooftop, she and Miles watched two medical workers carry Conner on a stretcher to the ambulance while Kattan's cameraman filmed the scene. Private McDaniels climbed into the vehicle with him.

"I told McDaniels to keep an eye on Conner," Miles said. "He has Conner's pistol. He'll keep anyone from harming him."

Brooke used her phone to dial another number. "I'm calling a friend to get a ride out of here. You should get down there and go with the other Marines to the airport with General Saeed and the news crew."

"Why are you staying behind?"

"Al-Shabaab is still holding Ambassador Thomas and John Duggard as hostages somewhere in Mogadishu. I plan to stay here and help."

"If you're staying, I'm staying," Miles declared. "But there's a condition. Don't ask me to wear a burqa."

CHAPTER FIFTY-THREE

Shortly after nine a.m. (EDT)
The White House
Washington, D.C.

On the mammoth screen inside the White House Situation Room, Al Arabic reporter Ebio Kattan appeared larger than life as she told viewers that American hostages were being rescued from a Mogadishu apartment. Behind her, Gunter Conner could be seen on a stretcher being loaded into an ambulance.

Her report was being translated for Western audiences in a voice-over by a male interpreter whose summary narrative gave the newscast a stilted feel.

"General Saeed, where are you taking these Americans?"

"To the airport to be flown to a U.S. military vessel anchored a few miles off our coastline."

Muting the monitor, Mallory Harper addressed President Allworth, who was sitting to her left facing the large screen.

"I've scheduled a press conference later this morning so you can make an official statement."

"I'll make a brief statement, but I don't want to answer questions. As long as Al-Shabaab is holding Ambassador Thomas and John Duggard as hostages, we need to remain circumspect."

"Al Arabic is giving full credit for the rescue to General Saeed and his men," Harper noted. "There's been no mention of Captain Brooke Grant or Gunter Conner and how they were responsible for freeing the Marines and killing three Al-Shabaab fighters."

"Let's not complain. It's better their heroism remains a secret, at least for now," Allworth replied. "Let Al-Shabaab continue to believe General Saeed is responsible, not us. Otherwise, they might retaliate. It also leaves our diplomatic efforts to resolve this through General Grant's negotiations a viable option."

"We should get a nice boost in the polls because of this rescue," Harper said, "but our pollsters are saying we're still going to lose unless we end this crisis and get everyone out of Somalia before Tuesday's elections."

"And if I perform that miracle?"

"They're saying if the last two hostages are freed, the race will be too close to call on Tuesday. But at least we'll have a chance."

CIA director Grainger arrived and took a seat next to Harper.

"I'm sorry to be bringing bad news," he said, "especially after the rescue of the Marines, but Al-Shabaab has moved Ambassador Thomas and John Duggard out of Mogadishu. Our drone followed their vehicle for several miles outside the city but it was low on fuel and had to turn back. By the time we got a second drone there, we'd lost track of them."

"Do you have any idea where they've been taken?" Allworth asked.

"We're fairly certain they're now being held in Barawa, a former slave-trading port two hours south of Mogadishu that's currently an Al-Shabaab stronghold."

"A slave-trading port," Harper said. "Now a haven for terrorists. It must be a lovely place."

"We can't send SEAL teams knocking door-to-door in Barawa," Grainger continued. "I'm afraid our hands are tied militarily for the moment."

"General Grant will be arriving in Mogadishu Thursday with Cleric Abasi Mubarak," Harper said in a hopeful voice, "and the Egyptian cleric is still claiming that Ambassador Thomas and Duggard can be on a flight home by this weekend if we meet Al-Shabaab's twenty-five-million ransom demand."

"Do we really believe that can happen?" Allworth asked.

"I'm also suspicious," Harper replied, "but if we no longer know where the hostages are being held and you want to end this crisis before the election, the ransom payment appears to be our only option."

"My people will be working round the clock to locate Thomas and

Duggard," Grainger volunteered. "However, I'm afraid Mallory is correct. If you want them released before Tuesday's polls open, you'll have to green-light the ransom. I've arranged to work the payment through ProTech so it won't be obvious. We have everything in place, so all it will take is your approval."

President Allworth took a moment to consider what she'd been told. It was a decision that she'd been wrestling with ever since the idea of negotiating with Al-Shabaab had first been mentioned. But that hadn't made the back-and-forth in her mind any easier to resolve. Now, with the election in the balance and the chances of a military rescue becoming dimmer, her choices seemed obvious. "Contact General Grant and tell him to pay the bastards," she said in an angry voice. "I don't want to leave office with our ambassador and Mr. Duggard still being held hostage. I'd rather take the heat for negotiating with terrorists than having Al-Shabaab drag this on and Coldridge taking charge. But don't give up trying to find Ambassador Thomas and Duggard, just in case this ransom turns out to be a ruse."

"What's being done to safeguard General Grant when he arrives in Mogadishu tomorrow?" Harper asked. "He's not only a prime kidnapping target, he'll be carrying twenty-five million dollars in hundred-dollar bills into one of the most violent and corrupt cities in the world."

"The Somalis have agreed to allow Commander Jackman and his SEAL teams to enter the city in order to provide our delegation with security," Grainger answered. "They'll meet him and Cleric Mubarak when they land at the airport in Mogadishu and escort them to the USS *Hornet* for safekeeping."

"Why aren't they flying directly to the *Hornet*?" Harper asked.

"They're en route aboard a ProTech corporate jet. As I mentioned, my people decided paying the ransom through ProTech was the most appropriate way to handle this transaction in as quiet a manner as possible."

"A veil—thin, but still a veil," Harper said.

"There's another issue we need to discuss," Grainger said. "I'm assuming Al-Shabaab will want to make the prisoner exchange somewhere in Somalia, in which case we're going to need the cooperation of General Saeed."

"He's not someone we can rely on," Harper said, "especially around that much cash."

"He's not after our money," Grainger replied. "I've been on the phone with him, and he wants six Apache helicopters in return for his cooperation. I'm afraid we might have to give them to him, even if it leaves a sour taste in everyone's mouth."

"No," President Allworth said flatly. "I'll not reward that murderer. Find another way to get his cooperation. I'll call President Musab at the presidential palace if necessary. Am I clear on that?"

"Yes," Grainger said. "There's another matter that needs to be addressed. I've been summoned to the Hill by the Chairman. He's asking for a briefing."

A pained look appeared on the president's face. "I don't want him looking over my shoulder while we're trying to negotiate an exchange with Al-Shabaab."

"I'm afraid that I'm to blame," Harper said. "He wants a briefing, Madam President, because I specifically asked him to make a public statement supporting your decision to open the embassy. He's checking the facts, doing due diligence, before he decides whether or not he's going to make a favorable statement supporting you."

"If that's all he is after," the president said, "limit your briefing to the actual embassy attack. Nothing that has happened since Saturday night. Nothing about General Saeed murdering Cash Kelley during that failed rescue at that warehouse. Nothing about Captain Grant and Gunter Conner escaping capture and rescuing the Marines and two State Department diplomats. And certainly nothing about a ransom payment."

"Thank you, Madam President," Grainger said, standing. "I'll do my best to satisfy the Chairman in accordance with your guidelines."

As soon as Director Grainger was gone, Harper divided the television monitor into a half-dozen screens so she and the president could watch multiple morning news reports about the rescue in Somalia. A cavalcade of Middle East experts and members of Congress appeared. When Governor Coldridge surfaced on CNN, Harper switched the monitor back into one giant screen, catching him in mid-sentence.

"—delighted that our Marines and diplomats have been rescued. However, we cannot and should not forget that two Americans are still being held by these religious fanatics. Unfortunately, President Allworth's decision to expand our nation's role as the world's policeman by opening an embassy in an unstable, predominately Islamic country that historically has been hostile to the U.S. has accomplished only one thing: the death of twelve Americans."

The CNN reporter said, "The president has been accused in a recent *New York Times* editorial of opening the embassy in Somalia for purely political reasons—to get a leg up on you during the first presidential debate. How do you respond to that?"

"If there's even a smidgeon of truth to that accusation, and many people believe there is, then this president needs to be held accountable for putting our national security at risk for her own personal enrichment and gain."

"Are you implying impeachment?"

"I don't think impeachment is going to be necessary," Coldridge declared. "With the election only six days away, I would say impeachment by the ballot box is what is needed."

Muting the screen, Harper said, "Impeachment by ballot box? Who's writing his material?"

"Unfortunately, voters are responding to his rhetoric," President Allworth lamented. "We need to counter it by doing what Decker Lake suggested, by taking off the gloves."

"I've already told the campaign staff to do exactly that," Harper replied. "Have you heard anything privately from Decker Lake about that Somali American from Minneapolis who the Coldridge campaign is bringing in to attack you at a press conference?"

"No," the president replied. "I believe he's still looking for skeletons."

THURSDAY

Five days before the presidential election

CHAPTER FIFTY-FOUR

Eight a.m. (EDT)
Penthouse, Watergate apartments
Washington, D.C.

M r. Lake, you ever been to Minneapolis?" Lorraine Keys asked.
Her telephone call had caught Decker Lake during a pen-
sive moment, gazing through his apartment's window at two
Georgetown University rowing crews racing against each other on the
Potomac, young men slipping across the calm water impervious to the
chilly October morning air.

He was angry. Not at the caller. At life. Everyone dies. Death and
taxes. That was the joke. But the joke lost its humor the moment Lake's
doctor had uttered the C-word. The grim reaper had become a grim reality and Lake had begun spending more time remembering his past than
looking to his future. Lake had been married in his thirties but had been
a better Washington insider than husband, and he'd been a better husband than father. He'd not spoken to his firstborn namesake, Decker
Lake Jr., in several years. As a youngster, the boy had been an unwanted
diversion best left to his wife. After her unexpected death, "Deck Junior,"
as he was called, had been shipped off to private schools. He'd grown and
gone. Lake's grandchildren were merely bookshelf photos. He'd been too
busy for Deck Jr. and his family, and they'd made their peace with it
and moved on. The truth was, Lake had few regrets. When others were
collecting a gold watch at sixty-five—did anyone really get gold watches
anymore?—he was advising the Chinese on trade legislation. He'd
walked with giants, eaten private White House dinners with the last
nine presidents, and played poker with Tip O'Neill decades ago when
he ruled the House. He'd always been at the top of his game. And then
the C-word, and President Allworth had put him out to pasture in favor

of Mallory Harper. The moment he'd started chemo, the phone calls had slowed to a trickle. That's what made him angry. Being benched or whatever sports metaphor he chose. They all fit. Days that had never been long enough now were beginning to fill with idle hours. His clock was ticking. Ticktock. Ticktock. He'd met with his oncologist yesterday. A blunt man. No frills, no sugarcoating. That's how Lake liked it. The specialist said the cancer was spreading. It wasn't only colon cancer anymore. Lymph vessels. Part of the immune system. Ticktock. The window was closing.

President Allworth's weekend call—which had sent him scurrying from one network Sunday news show to the next after the Saturday-night embassy attack—had been better medicine than any of the costly vials of cancer-killing fluids being injected into his arms, more potent than any of the rainbow-colored pills that he swallowed to quiet the vomiting, and more satisfying than the half-finished autobiography sitting on his desk. He'd read somewhere that nearly 90 percent of Americans thought their lives were worth a book. It was a reminder of Americans' inherent need to believe their life mattered. His really did. Many in Washington had done interesting things during their careers. Fewer had done interesting things and also been interesting people. He was one of them. He would let someone else finish writing his story. He was still living out its final chapters and he had no interest in wasting his precious time hovering over a keyboard.

On his bad days, he indulged in self-pity. Did any of it matter? His personal assistant was a millennial who prided himself on being a metrosexual. Why would he be interested in the life of a political power broker who'd come of age when men didn't carry umbrellas and certainly never had a manicure? Did anyone really wish to plunk down thirty dollars to read his personal recollections about Martha Mitchell, Jack Kent Cooke, Edward Bennett Williams, and Washington when a young bespectacled John Dean was still a little-known White House lawyer? Would readers care about the dinners and private conversations that he'd shared with Jody Powell and Hamilton Jordan at the long-closed Class Reunion? His arguments with Pierre Salinger, Ron Ziegler, Jerald terHorst?

"Are you there, Mr. Decker?" Keys asked, snapping him back to the present.

"Sorry, yes. To answer your question, Ms. Keys, I have been to the Twin Cities on numerous occasions. I doubt there is a major city in our great nation where I've not been."

"Major or any?"

"Test me."

"Spearfish?"

"South Dakota, on the foot of the Black Hills," he replied. "There's a hatchery there I helped get additional funding before Senator McGovern ran for president. How do you know it?"

"I graduated from—"

He finished her sentence: "Black Hills State College."

"That's right, only now it's a university."

He tried to imagine what she looked like based only on their telephone conversations. "Did you get a private detective degree there?" he asked, knowing there was no such thing.

She missed his joke. "No, sir, I got my PI license later in Denver before moving to our firm's headquarters in Chicago. As you know, I specialize in background investigations, with an emphasis on political matters."

"You find the dirt everyone tries to hide," he said approvingly. "I've always used Jerry before at your firm."

"Oh, Jerry finally retired after forty years. Everyone wondered when he'd finally hang it up and get out of the way of us younger investigators."

Her Jerry reference irked him. Suddenly, he was bored with their banter. "Tell me what you found in Minneapolis," he said.

"I'm ready to fax you my full report but I can give you the verbal highlights now if you'd like about the subject of interest, Nuruddin Ayaanie Adeogo, better known as Rudy, and his wife, Dheeh."

"That would be lovely," he said, turning away from the window's picturesque view.

She spoke for ten minutes without interruption, and when Lake put down the receiver his mood had lifted. Walking to his liquor cabinet, he cracked the seal on a $400 bottle of Glenlivet XXV single malt that he'd been saving for the day his doctor would declare him cancer-free. No use letting it go unopened. He'd never drunk whisky before ten a.m. on a Thursday, but he'd never faced his own imminent death either. In the other room, he heard his fax line ring and the machine begin spewing out Lorraine Keys's detailed investigative report.

Hoisting the glass in a salute to himself, he said, "Time to win one for the Gipper."

Had his personal assistant been present, Lake wasn't sure the youth would know what he was talking about with a toast like that, but Lake didn't care. It was the final minutes in the final quarter and the president was calling him off the bench for one final time.

CHAPTER FIFTY-FIVE

9:30 a.m. (EDT)
Basement of Capitol Visitor Center
Washington, D.C.

Payton Grainger had one objective when he arrived at the House Permanent Select Committee on Intelligence's underground hearing room to brief the Chairman and Representative Ramon Garcia, the committee's ranking minority member, who'd been invited to join them.

The CIA director needed to conceal the facts about the events leading up to Al-Shabaab's attack on the U.S. Embassy, and like many others who choose deception over truth, Grainger reassured himself that his actions were necessary. Disclosing the unheeded NSA telephone intercept about the impending Saturday-night attack and Gunter Conner's plotting to use the embassy as bait would destroy him and the president. He could not let that happen. He would not let that happen.

As he took a seat in the committee's "torture" chair, Grainger briefly outlined Saturday-night's assault. He explained that protesters had gathered outside the U.S. compound shortly before midnight but General Saeed had assured ProTech and the Marines inside the embassy that there was no reason for alarm. What the general had failed to grasp was that Al-Shabaab fighters had infiltrated both the demonstration and his own police force. The embassy was overrun when Saeed's officers mutinied and joined Al-Shabaab's attack.

"While we are still investigating the incident," Grainger concluded, "our preliminary analysis shows that it was General Saeed's ineptness that resulted in our embassy being overrun."

In a voice edged with skepticism, the Chairman asked, "Given how dangerous Mogadishu was and is, why didn't General Saeed disband the demonstrators when they first gathered outside the compound? None of us live in a bubble, Director Grainger. Surely he was aware of the incident years ago at our embassy in Benghazi and also the Iranian hostage crisis."

"That would certainly be a fair question to ask the general," Grainger replied. "All I can tell you is that General Saeed assured our people that our embassy was being well protected."

"What about your station chief?" Stanton asked. "Where was he on Saturday night? Did he have any advance warning of a pending attack?"

Grainger chose his reply with a lawyer's care. "As you know, Mr. Chairman, our station chief, Gunter Conner, was severely wounded yesterday during a rescue operation in Mogadishu and is currently fighting for his life in a military hospital in Germany. We've not been able to debrief him. Therefore, I can't tell you what he might have known."

"Then tell me, Director Grainger, was anyone else inside your agency warned that an attack was pending?"

Grainger replied with polite obfuscation. "Mr. Chairman. As you just mentioned, everyone knew Mogadishu was dangerous, so I assume there were some in my agency who suspected the embassy might be attacked, but no one came to me with any verifiable intelligence before the attack that suggested our people were in peril."

This question-and-answer game was not a new dance for Chairman Stanton.

"Director Grainger," he said, continuing his probing, "did anyone at the CIA know from intelligence that you produced that our embassy was about to be attacked?"

His question required more fancy footwork. Grainger didn't wish to lie but he wasn't going to tell the truth, so he focused on the Chairman's phrase "intelligence that *you produced*." The telephone intercept warning of the attack had been overheard by the National Security Agency, not the CIA. It was information that had been obtained, not produced.

"I can assure you, Mr. Chairman, to the best of my knowledge, that the CIA did not have information that it produced that suggested an attack was imminent."

Despite Grainger's verbal dexterity, the Chairman continued to snoop.

"Director Grainger, are you telling me that this entire matter took everyone by surprise and couldn't have been prevented?"

Grainger decided to play dumb.

"I'm sorry, Mr. Chairman, but I'm not clear on what you are asking me. Am I surprised the embassy was attacked? As I've already mentioned, all of us were well aware of the dangers implicit in opening an embassy in Somalia, so I can't say that we were totally surprised. However, if you are asking me if the agency knew beforehand—based on evidence that it had produced—that an attack by Al-Shabaab was imminent, my answer would be no."

The effect of Grainger's wordplay was the opposite of what he'd intended. His answers appeared to make the Chairman even more suspicious.

"Since you say you didn't understand my question," Stanton replied, "let me rephrase and simplify it. To paraphrase the late Senator Howard Baker of the Watergate hearings' fame: What did your people know and when did they know it?"

This time, Grainger pulled out another trick used by experienced bureaucrats when being grilled by Congress. Frustration and guilt.

"Mr. Chairman," he said, "I have been sitting here patiently answering your questions. In fact, I have been answering the same question asked in a dozen different ways. If you and Representative Garcia would like for me to give you a minute-by-minute breakdown, complete with annotations, of who knew what and when, I'd be happy to do it. I want to be a hundred percent transparent. But I will need adequate time to conduct such a detailed probe. In fairness, you can't call me up to the Hill while we are still trying to resolve this crisis and expect me to know in minute detail everything that transpired. The fact that our embassy was overrun, hostages were taken, and twelve Americans murdered suggests that we need to do something better than what we've done. But I honestly can't tell you yet what those 'somethings' are."

He seemed both earnest and reasonable. And that led to a momentary quiet impasse that was finally broken when Stanton, staring intently at him, said, "Director Grainger, I believe you're being evasive."

"With all due respect, Mr. Chairman," Grainger replied, without flinching, "I can't provide you with information that I don't yet have. The attack happened Saturday night and today is Thursday."

Stanton leaned back in his chair but didn't end the fixed inquisitor's gaze that he was leveling at the director. He genuinely liked Grainger and felt he was one of the most capable CIA directors in recent years. Just as important, Grainger was well respected within the agency ranks, and that had not always been the case with previous directors. Several had been viewed internally as partisan directors who'd bent intelligence reports to support White House foreign policy. Grainger had not done that—until the White House announced it was restoring relations with Somalia.

During their initial private briefing after that announcement, Stanton had agreed to back off and not accuse President Allworth of playing partisan politics with foreign policy. But he'd known then that the CIA had tailored its reports from Somalia to buttress the president's campaign, and in retrospect he was angry at himself for not calling out the White House and putting a stop to this entire Mogadishu debacle before it started. His silence had made him culpable.

As he stared at Grainger, Stanton realized that any trust between them had been destroyed.

Taking advantage of the pause in the two men's give-and-take, ranking member Garcia asked, "Mr. Director, how long do you think it will take for you to prepare a thorough report for us?"

"I already have my people going over everything as we speak, so it shouldn't be long, but I must repeat that our current priority is getting the remaining hostages out of Somalia without them being harmed, and that is what we must focus on."

"Of course," Garcia stammered apologetically.

"It might be wise," Grainger said, "for us to wait until this crisis is resolved rather than rushing to an analysis that later could prove error prone due to a lack of credible information. I don't want to create another Benghazi misinformation fiasco."

The Chairman's gut was telling him that Director Grainger was hiding something.

"Director Grainger," he said, "we'll wait for your final report. We'll give you ample time to investigate exactly what happened. Meanwhile, I want you to deliver two items to the committee."

"What items?" Grainger asked, picking up a pen next to a writing tablet at the witness table.

"I want to read your station chief's original assessment of whether or not it was safe for the president to open an embassy in Mogadishu. The one your agency delivered to the White House."

"I can certainly make that available," Grainger replied.

"I also want an accounting of all communications about Mogadishu on the day of the embassy attack internally and externally by your agency. I want that to include any information that you received prior to the attack from other agencies."

Director Grainger flinched. It was only for a second, but it was long enough for Stanton to notice.

"Compiling that information will take some time," Grainger said.

"Sooner than later, Director Grainger, and please don't assume that our brief session here has satisfied my interest, the committee's interest, and the American people's interest in learning more about this embassy attack."

"That is not an assumption I would ever make, Mr. Chairman," Grainger replied. "I know you too well for that."

CHAPTER FIFTY-SIX

Late afternoon Somali time
Korfa's apartment
Mogadishu, Somalia

General Frank Grant was on the phone and he was furious.

"Brooke, why in the hell are you still in Mogadishu?" he demanded. "Why didn't you leave yesterday with the other Marines and the State Department employees?"

"Sergeant Miles and I believe we can be more useful here, in case Commander Jackman needs eyes and ears on the ground."

"No one needs *your* eyes or your ears in Mogadishu. Leave Miles if he wants to stay, but you're done. I'll be landing at twenty-one hundred hours in Mogadishu from Cairo and you will be waiting at the airport to fly with me to the *Hornet*."

Before she could challenge him, Grant added, "I was briefed by Commander Jackman about your antics yesterday, and you were specifically ordered to avoid all contact with Al-Shabaab, yet you engaged the enemy."

"Antics?" she replied, bristling at once again being cast in the role of an irresponsible teenager who'd disappointed him.

"Just because it turned out well," he said, "doesn't change the fact you disregarded his orders."

"I did not disregard his orders," she replied. "I was told to provide recon and that was what I was doing when Mosi, a member of Al-Shabaab, spotted me and confronted me. I had no choice but to defend myself and that is exactly what I did."

"Jackman's already briefed me," her uncle replied.

"Then I am confident, General," she said, intentionally referring to him by his title, "that you were told that I was confronted by two armed Al-Shabaab fighters and I not only resisted capture by them but they ended up dead. Eliminating them is what enabled the hostages to be freed."

"Don't speak to me in that tone," Grant replied. "You may be my niece but you will respect my rank. Is that clear, Marine?"

"Yes, sir," she replied. "Loud and clear."

"Now I am ordering you to report to the airport at twenty-one hundred hours."

"Will General Saeed be there?"

"He is supposed to greet us."

"I don't trust General Saeed, especially since I witnessed him murder Cash Kelley outside a Mogadishu warehouse. He knows I have accused him, and it would be easy for him to intercept us at the airport's front entrance before you landed and blame Al-Shabaab if Sergeant Miles and I disappeared."

"I'll send Commander Jackman to escort you to our plane."

"It would be simpler if you call me on this cell phone after you land. That way I can be on the phone line with you when we approach the airport's front gate. General Saeed isn't going to try anything if he knows you're talking to me."

"You do realize," he replied, "that only the president of the United States gives me orders."

He ended their call.

Brooke had been in the main room of Korfa's apartment when her uncle had telephoned, but she'd slipped into the bathroom to speak with him privately. She lingered there, gingerly lowering the top of her dress to her waist and removing a gauze dressing so she could examine the knife wounds on her chest and, in a mirror, on her back. The cut on her back was the most painful. Mosi's blade had sliced a six-inch-long gash that began at the top of her left shoulder and ran down to her spine, ending at the top of her bra strap. While the cut wasn't terribly deep, it was deep enough to leave a scar. She found fresh gauze and an antiseptic ointment but couldn't reach the wound by herself. Slipping her dress back onto her shoulders, she walked back into the main room, where Sergeant Miles and Caanood had been talking earlier.

"It's just the two of us," Miles said. "Caanood went to buy food. She wasn't expecting guests. Her brother is still at work."

Noticing the gauze, he said, "I'll help you with that."

"I'll wait for Caanood."

"Why?" he said, walking to the stove to heat water in a kettle. "You don't know where Mosi's knife has been. It's best to dress it again. If you're worried about me seeing anything that I shouldn't, I grew up with four sisters. I don't embarrass easily."

"I wasn't worried about embarrassing *you*."

He poured boiling water through the gauze to use as a sponge. She waited until he'd walked behind her before dropping her borrowed dress to her waist, exposing her back and bra.

"We've been ordered to reach Aden Adde airport by twenty-one hundred hours for evac to a command post on— OUCH!" she exclaimed.

The hot gauze had stung when he wiped it against her dried blood. She immediately felt foolish for crying out.

"So much for us being Commander Jackman's eyes and ears on the ground," he said, ignoring her outburst.

"You heard what I was saying to General Grant?"

"The walls in this apartment are thin."

"You shouldn't have listened."

"You should have talked softer," he replied. "So your uncle is coming to pay a ransom to Al-Shabaab. That's a mistake. The only thing these religious crackpots understand is a bullet to the head. Kill them now or fight them later."

Having cleaned her wound, he began dabbing antiseptic on her back, causing her to wince again.

"Scars," he said, "earned in battle were once a badge of honor among my people, the Crow."

"Well, a knife cut on a woman's back isn't going to be viewed as a badge of honor in Washington."

"I thought they left knives in people's backs there," he said, chuckling at his own joke.

He had a gentle touch for a soldier with callus-toughened hands. "No reason for you to hide your back, Captain," he said as he finished applying the ointment. "You got an impressive, well-toned one."

Brooke felt embarrassed. "I was a competitive swimmer in high school," she said. Hoping to change the subject, she asked, "Did you play any sports in high school?"

"There is only one sport on the Crow res. Basketball."

"You aren't that tall."

"I compliment you about your muscular back and you tell me I'm short. For the record, I'm five ten, but that doesn't matter in Montana. We played Indian ball. The rules are the same, but it's all run and gun. No defense. A hundred points per game is nothing in high school. We ran those white boys from outside the res into the ground. Best time in my life."

"Better than being here now?"

"When I was playing basketball, no one was trying to kill me in the name of Allah. We had this one kid—some said he was the best Crow player ever—on our team my senior year. Everyone thought he'd be the first American Indian to make it into the NBA."

"What happened?"

"What always happens? He came home."

"I don't understand," she said. "American Indians live in poverty under some of the worst conditions imaginable, but when they have a chance to leave, they don't?"

"That's because you don't understand Indians. Among the Crow there is no individual person. There's your family, your clan, and the tribe. You leave the res, you leave what defines you. It's sorta like a non-Indian going into the federal witness protection program."

"You left the reservation."

"Being a Marine is something my people respect. I had a few friends accuse me of selling out, but my people have always respected warriors. It's a noble calling."

"Think you'll ever go back?"

"Let's think about this," he said thoughtfully. "On the res there are no jobs, no businesses, and no real incentive to work because the federal government gives you an allotment that's barely enough to survive on but about the same as an Indian is going to get as a wage working off the res. You're stuck in perpetual poverty. There's no future. So, yes, I will definitely be going back." He chuckled again and added, "Besides, my mother would kill me if I didn't. I'm her favorite."

He'd finished tending to her wound, but rather than saying so, he put a hand on her shoulder affectionately, letting it linger for a moment. "I assume since the general is your uncle everyone expected you to enlist," he said.

"I never planned to until 9/11."

"All of us stationed at Mogadishu heard about your parents. How they were murdered in the Twin Towers."

"My uncle wanted me to go into the JAG Corps. When I refused, he pulled strings and I got stuck as an attaché." She pulled up her top and turned to face him.

He said, "If that's what you call getting stuck, then I wish someone would stick me."

"My uncle knew I wanted a combat assignment, or to be as close to combat as I could get. It may sound corny to some, but I genuinely believe freedom isn't free—you have to fight to defend it. And I don't apologize for feeling that way."

"I don't think any of us in the Corps believe that's corny. Otherwise, we wouldn't have signed up." Changing subjects, he said, "Everyone heard about you long before you arrived in Mogadishu."

"Oh yeah? What'd they say?"

"Are we just us talking as civilians, not as a sergeant and a captain?"

"You've been touching my back while my top has been down around my waist," she replied, "all the while telling me about the res and basketball."

"I'll take that as a yes. The black Marines called you an Oreo because you only date white men."

"That's not true."

"Just repeating what they said."

He'd offended her and her tone showed it. "I started dating white men in high school because all the black men were walking around posing as gangsters and rappers with their pants falling down. Who wants that?"

"That's nonsense, Captain," he said. "Your uncle is a general. You weren't attending some ghetto high school. I'm guessing you probably went to one of those fancy private schools with senators' and ambassadors' kids. You didn't find one black man—not even when you were in the U.S. Naval Academy—who measured up?"

"You knew I graduated from Annapolis?"

"When your uncle is a general, everyone in the Corps knows who you are."

"I'm not an Oreo," she said defiantly.

"I didn't think you were. I defended you."

"Thank you."

"I assumed you only dated white guys because you wanted to irritate your uncle." He chuckled.

"Now you're a shrink?" she said in a softer voice, her anger dissipating.

"Some things are obvious even to a jarhead Indian who grew up on the res."

She smiled at his self-deprecation. "If I'm being truthful, it probably is one of the reasons why I dated white men—because it does drive my uncle crazy." She paused and then added, "You didn't tell me what you thought of me?"

"You want me to be truthful?"

"Go ahead, Sergeant, I can handle the truth," she declared.

"I told everyone you were too hot to be a Marine."

"Are you flirting with me, Sergeant, or trying to be funny?"

"If I was doing either well, you wouldn't have to ask."

Caanood opened the apartment door, and Miles and Brooke went back to wearing their rank.

CHAPTER FIFTY-SEVEN

Late afternoon
Landstuhl Regional Medical Center
Landstuhl, Germany

E bio Kattan ducked into the commercial jet's tiny bathroom and changed into Western clothes before the international flight landed. She'd done her homework and approached the front security gate at the Army's largest overseas medical center at one of its busiest and most hectic times. After a cursory check, she was admitted, and ten minutes later she walked into Gunter Conner's hospital room.

Doctors aboard the USS *Hornet* had stabilized his collapsed left lung by inserting a chest tube between his ribs and lung tissue to release the air that had pocketed there. He'd been flown overnight to Landstuhl, where surgeons had repaired the bullet hole. He was sleeping and in stable condition.

Kattan took a seat on a metal stool on rollers and slid it next to Conner's bed. The monitor attached to his arm showed he had a slightly elevated blood pressure of 160 over 94 but all of his other vital signs were within acceptable ranges. There would be no reason for nurses to be coming and going every few moments. An IV morphine drip ran from an automated dispensing machine into his arm.

Kattan gently shook his leg under the bedcovers, waking him.

Through half-closed eyes, he asked, "Who are you?"

"We met in Somalia. You were shot."

"Oh." He dozed off, apparently groggy from the morphine.

She shook his leg again.

"What?" he asked, slightly irritated.

She decided to take advantage of his drugged condition. "You were explaining what happened the night the American embassy was attacked."

"Can I have some water?" The morphine drip was making his mouth dry.

She poured him a drink from a nearby plastic pitcher.

"I need more pain medication."

"I'll tell the nurses after we're finished. The quicker we're done, the quicker they can give you more."

He looked closely at her face. "I don't remember you being in Mogadishu."

"I need you to clarify a few things for my report. Then I'll tell the nurses you need more painkillers."

He winced in pain. She used that moment to slip her hand into her purse and remove a digital recorder, which she concealed inside her right hand, exposing only the built-in microphone at its tip. Leaning forward, she rested her hand next to his leg on the bed and aimed the recorder's directional microphone toward his head.

"You State or the company?" he asked her. "Sorry, but I don't remember what you said earlier."

"We've already been over this," she replied, acting slightly irritated. "I showed you my credentials. I only have a few more questions and then I can talk to the nurses about getting you more pain medication."

"Don't you want to record this?" he asked.

The question startled her. She raised her hand so he could see the digital recorder. "I've already turned on my recorder."

"Please, another drink of water."

Kattan laid the recorder on his bed and went to refill the water pitcher. When she returned, he was holding it. "I can answer your questions better without this." He kept it in his hand.

During the next half hour, Kattan listened to Conner talk, without having a chance to interrupt and ask a single question. After he finished, he said, "I'm too tired to continue. Maybe tomorrow." He handed her the recorder and said, "Tell the nurses on your way out I need more pain medication." He shut his eyes.

Kattan walked past several nurses in the hallway after leaving his room, but she didn't speak to any of them. As soon as she exited the base's front checkpoint, she began searching for a pay phone. She wasn't going to risk discussing what she'd just learned over a cell phone. The Americans might be listening. She called her producers in Dubai.

"I know the truth about the embassy attack in Mogadishu. I'll be on the next flight."

In the hospital, Conner waited for what seemed forever for a nurse to appear. When one finally did, he asked, "Why didn't you bring me medicine when that woman told you?"

"What woman?"

"The one who interviewed me."

"I don't know anything about any woman interviewing you. No one saw anyone in your room. You were hallucinating. It happens on morphine."

Conner asked her for a stronger dose, and when it kicked in, he began to feel better.

Gunter Conner had recognized Ebio Kattan from the moment she'd awakened him. He had not been confused, as he'd led her to believe. He'd known exactly what he was doing when they'd talked.

He closed his eyes. He needed rest. He thought about Sara and Benjamin. He thought of Jennifer. And he thought of the man who had taken so much from him.

CHAPTER FIFTY-EIGHT

Shortly before dusk
A walled residential compound
Barawa, Somalia

Déjà vu.

Ambassador Todd Thomas and John Duggard both stumbled as they were pushed down on their knees in front of two bright lights and a video camera. A concrete cinder block stained with what appeared to be human blood and with a large knife lying on top of it was positioned on the floor directly in front of them.

Abdul Hafeez strutted in with only his angry black eyes revealed under his ski-like mask.

The cameraman gave him a hand signal and Hafeez began.

"Enemies of Allah, we have seen you openly insulting the final Messenger of Allah. You should know that for every action there is a reaction."

He bent down, retrieved the large knife, and chanted, *"Allahumma munzilal-kitab, wa mujriyas-sahab, wa hazimal-Ahzab, ihzimhum wansurna alaihim,"* which translated meant "O Allah, Revealer of the Book, Disperser of the clouds, Defeater of the Confederates, put our enemies to rout and support us against them."

Hafeez walked behind the two hostages and grabbed Ambassador Thomas's forehead from behind, jerking his skull back so violently that the older man cried out in pain. With the knife pressed against Thomas's throat, Hafeez delivered a speech that he had memorized a few minutes earlier.

"We will never accept any system of government apart from the one stipulated by Islam, because it is the only way Muslims can be liberated. We do not believe in any system of government, be it traditional or orthodox, except the Islamic system, which is why we will keep on fighting against democracy, capitalism, socialism, and whatever. We will not allow adulterated conventional education to replace Islamic teachings."

He tightened his grip on the ambassador's forehead even more and lifted the knife high in the air as if he were preparing to bring it down and slash the American's neck.

"Allah has tasked all Muslims in the Holy Quran—chapter nine verse twenty-nine—to continue to attack Jews and Christians who refuse to believe in Him and His Messenger, the Prophet Muhammad. For those who we see on television saying that Islam counsels against jihad and war, I say, you know nothing about our Holy Prophet and his teachings. Those who say such things are witless. Islam says: 'Kill all the unbelievers just as they would kill you all! Kill them. Put them to the sword and scatter their armies.' "

Becoming excited by his own rant, Hafeez raised his voice to an even higher pitch and quickened his speech. "Islam tells us: Whatever good there is exists thanks to the sword and in the shadow of the sword! People cannot be made obedient except with the sword! The sword is the key to paradise, which can be opened only for the holy warriors! There are hundreds of other psalms and hadiths urging Muslims to value war and to fight. Does all that mean Islam is a religion that prevents men from waging war? I spit upon those foolish souls who make such a claim."

Glaring at the camera, he concluded: "If you wish to save these two men, every Christian and Jew in Somalia must convert by midnight on Friday. If all Christians and Jews do not renounce their false religions, both of these Americans will feel the vengeance of Allah and feel His sword."

The cameraman stopped filming.

Releasing his grip on Thomas, Hafeez said, "Not today, but soon I will enjoy removing both of your heads."

Thomas replied in a weak voice, "You're mad. How can you expect every Christian and every Jew in Somalia to renounce their religion by tomorrow at midnight?"

"This is a problem for your president now."

Hafeez exited into an adjoining room, where the lights had been dimmed and a lone robed figure wearing a hood to protect his face was waiting.

"You did well, Abdul," the figure said.

"Praise be to Allah for giving me the words."

"I have been thinking about the rescue of the Marine hostages in Mogadishu," the figure said. "Mosi called your phone before he died. He believed he was detonating the explosives. He was not a hypocrite. He was not a traitor."

"If he did not tell the Americans where we were hiding the hostages, then who did?" Hafeez asked.

"No one. I believe the Americans have been watching us with their drones and their satellites. I believe they have been intercepting our telephone calls. This is how they knew we were hiding the hostages in the warehouse and apartment building. They are spying on us with their electronics."

"We must tell everyone to stop communicating by cell phones," Hafeez said.

"My brother, Allah has revealed a great gift to us with this information. Do you have a cell phone with you?"

"Yes."

"Good. We will use it to give the Americans a message that we want them to hear."

CHAPTER FIFTY-NINE

Early afternoon (EDT)
CIA headquarters
Langley, Virginia

Charles Casterline hurried into Director Grainger's office carrying a transcript of a fresh telephone intercept.

"We've traced a call to a house in Barawa," he announced excitedly. "It's where they're holding Ambassador Thomas and John Duggard, but according to this phone call they're going to move them at daybreak."

Grainger studied the transcript while simultaneously checking his steel-banded Rolex Oyster. It was almost two p.m., which meant it was nearly nine o'clock at night in Somalia. Roughly nine hours before daybreak there. He called his executive assistant into his office and told her to contact the White House over the federal government's secure version of FaceTime. Within moments, Grainger was speaking to President Allworth and Mallory Harper on a monitor with a split screen. As he was telling them about the intercept, Casterline passed him a hastily scribbled note.

"Madam President," Grainger said after scanning it, "Al-Shabaab has just uploaded a video on social media that contains a new threat. I'm going to have my assistant show it on our screens."

Grainger's face was replaced by an Internet video of a masked, knife-wielding, hooded terrorist threatening Ambassador Thomas and demanding that all Christians and Jews in Somalia convert to Islam before midnight Friday.

"I've been told this video was just uploaded from the same house in Barawa as the intercepted phone call," Grainger explained, as soon as his face reappeared on the monitor. "This video is secondary confirmation that Ambassador Thomas and Mr. Duggard are being held in that house."

"Al-Shabaab's demand is absurd," President Allworth said. "We can't force every Christian and Jew in Somalia to convert to Islam by tomorrow night. Does this mean Al-Shabaab no longer wants to negotiate?"

"I think it's posturing," Grainger said. "They've lost two sets of hostages. They're reminding us they still have bargaining power."

"We can't be certain it is bluster," Harper warned. "These are the same fanatics who cut off Skip LeRue's hands."

"Have you been able to identify the hooded figure in these videos?" President Allworth asked.

"Yes," said Grainger. "I've conferred with General Saeed in Mogadishu and we're fairly confident the hooded man is named Abdul Hafeez. He's the one who murdered Robert Gumman and cut off Skip LeRue's hands before killing him."

Grainger added, "I'd like to show you another image now."

A black-and-white satellite photograph of Barawa appeared on their monitors. Although it was grainy, it showed a rectangular walled compound with a large house directly in its center.

"This is where the phone call and video upload originated. This is where it appears Ambassador Thomas and Duggard are being held."

"Appears? How confident are you they are in that house?" the president asked.

"Based on the intercepted phone conversation and the video that was uploaded, there's a high certainty they're there—at least until dawn, when they will be moved to a different location."

"Do you believe Commander Jackman and his SEAL teams could successfully rescue the hostages from that house?" Allworth asked.

"We'd be asking a lot, given such short notice," Grainger answered, "but this is what his SEAL teams are trained to do. The biggest threat that the hostages would face during a rescue would come from the terrorists who are guarding them. If they realize a rescue effort is under way, they will simply execute both men. We will need the element of surprise."

"Which means our men will have to go before daybreak in Somalia," Harper said.

"Yes. If the president authorizes a rescue, the SEAL teams would have to go tonight."

"Have you been in contact with General Grant?" President Allworth asked. "The reason why I gave him the green light to pay a ransom was because we didn't know where Al-Shabaab was holding the hostages. Now it seems we do."

"He and the Egyptian cleric are scheduled to land in Mogadishu any minute now, where they'll be met by a SEAL team and escorted to the USS *Hornet*," Grainger replied. "Because he's in transit, he's not yet been briefed on these new developments in Barawa or told about Al-Shabaab's video and newest threat."

"Madam President," Harper said, "sending a SEAL team into Barawa tonight is a huge, huge risk not only militarily but also diplomatically. President Musab has agreed to let us land at the airport to escort General Grant to the *Hornet*, but he has repeatedly warned us not to enter Somali airspace as part of any rescue attempt. We helped put Musab in power and he's been a good friend, but this crisis has forced him to take a step back. His ambassador has told us there's a strong anti-American feeling in Mogadishu being fanned by Al-Shabaab. Rumors of a U.S. invasion are rampant. If we send in a rescue team, there's a chance the Somali people will panic and see Musab as being an ineffective and weak president unable to stand up to the U.S. government. They could turn against him and his fragile democratic government."

"As long as we are discussing risks," Grainger said, "here's another one more worrisome than President Musab. This could be an Al-Shabaab trap. Having both a cell phone call and a video emanating from the same Barawa location seems reckless. Add in the caller's disclosure that the ambassador and Duggard are going to be moved at daybreak and the Friday midnight deadline—it all suggests that Al-Shabaab might be trying to make us act quickly, to lure us in."

"Was this intercept different from any earlier ones?" Allworth asked.

"No, not at all."

"That being the case, isn't it also possible that Al-Shabaab might not feel any need to safeguard the Barawa location because the entire city is under its control?"

"And that is exactly why it would be the perfect place to ambush us," Grainger replied.

He glanced at his Rolex. "Unfortunately, Madam President, you need to make a decision."

"I don't think we can chance that this new Internet video threat is simply bluster," President Allworth said. "I suspect notoriety and hubris are much more important to these religious zealots than the promise of a multimillion-dollar ransom."

She paused to collect her thoughts. "The American people will never forgive me if I let a gang of religious fanatics hack off the head of a U.S. ambassador on social media, especially if the public discovered that I knew the location of the hostages yet didn't take military action."

The president paused again. "I'm not going to micromanage this from Washington," she finally said. "I've got to trust our people to do their jobs and make the right calls. That goes for both Commander Jackman and General Grant. I want you to get this information to Commander Jackman aboard the *Hornet*. Tell him that I'm giving him the authority to decide. If he believes his SEAL teams can rescue Thomas and Duggard, he has my permission to go for it. If not, we'll stick with General Grant and the ransom plan."

CHAPTER SIXTY

Just before nine p.m. Somali time
Aden Adde International Airport
Mogadishu, Somalia

Twelve Navy SEALs emerged from the belly of the Bell Boeing V-22 Osprey aircraft seconds after it landed and formed a defensive ring around the tilt-rotor plane. The aircraft had come to transport General Frank Grant, Cleric Mubarak, and $25 million in cash to the USS *Hornet* amphibious assault ship off the Somali coast. The SEALs eyed two dozen Somali policemen waiting on the tarmac with General Saeed, who was casually smoking a cigarette inside his armored Chevy Silverado.

The landing lights of a ProTech corporate jet appeared in the evening darkness, and within minutes the Gulfstream landed and propelled itself close to the Osprey.

General Saeed stepped from his Silverado, smashed his cigarette on the tarmac under his boot, and watched as General Grant stepped down the jet's stairs while talking on his cell phone.

One of Saeed's officers hurried over to him. "Two American Marines are at the front gate," he announced.

"It's my niece," General Grant said as he neared Saeed. "I'm speaking to her right now on my phone. I'd appreciate it if you would have your men escort her to us."

General Saeed's facial expression didn't change, but Grant had spent much of his Army career sizing up other men and he could sense anger simmering behind the general's frozen smile. Saeed was being manipulated and he didn't like it. The general glanced at the SEALs, noting the gunner manning a .50-caliber M2 machine gun mounted inside the Osprey's open rear loading ramp.

"I've always enjoyed seeing your niece," Saeed said.

Speaking into his phone, Grant said, "The general is sending an escort to get you. Stay on the phone until you reach us." He handed his cell to one of the two Army security officers whom he'd brought with him from Washington to safeguard the ransom.

Now that he knew Brooke and Sergeant Miles were safe, Grant saluted Saeed.

"Thanks for giving us permission to land," he said. "We shouldn't be taking more than a few minutes of your time here. As soon as my niece joins us, we'll fly directly to our ship."

"You disappoint me, General," Saeed replied. "I was hoping you would be my guest for a late dinner where we could speak one general to another."

"Some other time, perhaps."

"And if I insist?"

"Normally, General, I'd love that opportunity, but I am under direct orders from the president to report immediately to our ship."

Saeed shrugged. "I've been informed by President Musab that you have been negotiating with Al-Shabaab for the release of the last two hostages and have arrived here to finalize that arrangement. Something about an insurance payment made by ProTech."

"That's correct. We'd like to resolve this crisis without further bloodshed," Grant said evasively. "So yes, we are in the midst of negotiations."

"I'm curious, General Grant. How do you intend to convince everyone in Somalia to convert to Islam by Friday?"

From the puzzled look on General Grant's face, Saeed realized his guest had been in flight when Al-Shabaab uploaded its most recent threat and demand on social media, so he explained it. After he finished, Saeed said, "General Grant, I have been dealing with these religious fanatics much longer than you Americans. They would rather be martyred than compromise."

"Our president believes otherwise."

"Do I look like a fool?"

"I certainly didn't imply that."

"But your president's actions do. You Americans are in Somalia for a moment. Once your hostages are either beheaded or freed, you will go back to ignoring my country and my people until it serves some purpose for you. I am here until I die. I know these terrorists better than you Americans ever will."

"Whether my country continues to remain in Somalia or leaves is a decision for our president and Congress," Grant said. "I'm just a soldier."

"You Americans believe democracy is the answer for every country," Saeed continued. "But the Somali people are not ready for democracy. We've been at war with each other for nearly thirty years. What Somalia needs is a strongman who can stop Al-Shabaab, stop Islamic radicals, and stop our different tribes and clans from killing each other. What happened in Iraq after you removed Saddam Hussein?"

"As I said, General, I'm just a soldier."

"You are not just a soldier," Saeed replied sharply. "You are a general, and generals understand men better than politicians and diplomats. We ask them to die and they go willingly. You cannot make peace with a scorpion. You cannot change it into a household pet. With a scorpion, you have only one choice. You kill it or it stings you. I need six Apache helicopters from your government. I need them to crush Al-Shabaab and unify Somalia. The African Union soldiers you have stationed here cannot do this. Somalia is not their home. The intellectuals cannot do this. They only know how to talk. Was it Jefferson who fought your revolution or was it a general who won your independence? Was it Lincoln who saved your republic or a general who defeated the South and freed people like you? Why do you ask Somalia to do what your own country could not do in a crisis? My people need a general to act on their behalf."

When General Grant didn't immediately respond, Saeed said, "Mussolini made the trains run on time."

"Mussolini also destroyed human freedom in Italy and murdered and tortured Italians whose only crime was that they opposed his fascist regime."

"When people are starving, they don't ask where their bread comes from. My people are starving."

The arrival of an armored personnel carrier on the tarmac diverted both men's attention. As Brooke and Sergeant Miles stepped from it, she pocketed her cell phone.

"Captain Grant," Saeed sneered. "Our paths continue to cross under the most unexpected circumstances. And now your uncle tells me you will be leaving Somalia before I can give you that tour I promised."

"I doubt this will be our final meeting. There's still some unfinished business between us."

General Saeed turned his attention back to General Grant. "President Musab instructed me to remind you that you are here only by invitation, and any military action on our soil by your government will be considered a violation of our sovereignty and an act of aggression and unjustified hostility. You must keep me informed of your negotiations with Al-Shabaab if you expect our continued cooperation."

He paused and then added, "I'm certain there is no need for me to remind you of what happened the last time your Black Hawk helicopters entered Mogadishu uninvited."

General Saeed saluted Grant and returned to his Silverado without waiting for a reply.

Cleric Mubarak and the ransom already had been moved onto the Osprey, and as soon as Brooke, Miles, and General Grant boarded, the Navy SEALs systematically withdrew from their positions. The aircraft's pilots took off vertically, in part because the Osprey had been outfitted with an Interim Defensive Weapon System—a belly-mounted, remote-controlled gun turret that could fire at targets while the plane's twin Rolls-Royce engines propelled it upward.

From a window, Brooke watched General Saeed and his soldiers exiting the airfield.

Now safely aboard a military aircraft, General Grant had access to a secure line and was immediately on the phone talking to Washington. By the time the Osprey landed, he'd been briefed, and he motioned to Brooke and Miles to follow him as they were escorted below the ship's deck. Meanwhile, a security officer chaperoned Cleric Mubarak to a berth.

Commander Jackman was waiting for them in a room the SEALs were using as a command post.

"I've just been told by Washington that my negotiations have been put on hold," Grant said.

"That's correct, sir," Jackman replied. "Washington has learned the location of the final two hostages and the White House has green-lighted a rescue operation for tonight, if I decide it's a go."

"Tonight?" Brooke exclaimed.

"You two haven't officially met, even though you sent her to do recon for you," General Grant said. "This is Captain Grant and Sergeant Miles."

After shaking hands, Jackman nodded toward a hologram image on an illuminated desk. "This computer image is being constructed from information we are receiving from the National Geospatial-Intelligence Agency outside Washington, where they're using maps, topography, satellite imagery, and live feeds from our drones hovering over Barawa to show us what we can expect."

A 3-D replica of the Barawa compound was being created before their eyes. New details were being added electronically, refining the spinning image.

"Can you share your rescue plan with us, Commander?" General Grant asked.

"If we go, we're reengineering Operation Neptune Spear," he replied, referring to the Navy SEAL mission that successfully killed Osama bin Laden in Abbottabad, Pakistan. "We don't have time to reinvent the wheel."

Two teams of eight Navy SEALs would board stealth versions of Black Hawk helicopters that had been customized to fly more quietly. A single Chinook helicopter would follow behind them, carrying additional SEALs and firepower for backup. Hovering above Barawa would be drones armed with Hellfire missiles. One SEAL team would fast-rope from a Black Hawk onto the roof of the Barawa house. The helicopter carrying the other team would land near the compound, and the SEALs would breach the exterior wall and enter the house from the ground floor, effectively trapping its occupants inside. The SEALs would move through the house killing on sight anyone who was not Ambassador Thomas or John Duggard, whose photographs already had been distributed to every team member. A specially trained working dog, a Belgian Malinois named Tennessee, would be part of the ground-based team and would be used to help locate the hostages, especially if they were being hidden in an underground bunker or secret room.

"It worked in Pakistan," Grant said, "but there's two differences between your mission and killing bin Laden. Your people haven't had weeks to practice an assault, and no one was trying to rescue anyone in Pakistan."

"That's true, General, but we've got some tricks up our sleeves that weren't available in Abbottabad. New electronics that arrived onboard only a few hours ago."

"What sort of electronics?" Brooke asked.

"Birds and dragonflies," he said.

CHAPTER SIXTY-ONE

Late evening
A walled residential compound
Barawa, Somalia

A slot on the belly of the boomerang-shaped RQ-170, the most sophisticated and advanced drone operated by the CIA, silently opened twenty thousand feet above the terrorists' suspected compound.

Ten minuscule objects and two larger ones dropped into the night sky. Almost immediately, the micro air vehicles, called MAVs, began flapping their ultralight metal wings as they glided downward. The two largest had been painstakingly painted to resemble Somali starlings, birds with a gray crown and dark body. Each of the fake birds' wings looked identical to an actual bird's—not only for appearance's sake but because flapping wings made the MAVs much more maneuverable. They allowed the operator to deal with shifting wind currents and direct the MAV into tight quarters. While flying, the two manufactured starlings were nearly impossible to distinguish from actual passerines. The only giveaway was that each had a clear plastic dome head with a 360-degree camera mounted inside it instead of a beak and eyes.

The ten tiny projectiles that were dropped were nano-MAVs that had been shaped like dragonflies with four tiny wings on each unit flapping furiously to keep them airborne. Because of their minute size, little had been done to disguise them. Their wings jutted from a rectangular box painted flat black.

One of the starlings swooped down and landed on a corner of the Barawa house's flat roof, where it perched. The other circled lazily above the compound's perimeter. Both were broadcasting live night-vision images to the RQ-170 drone, which in turn relayed them to the USS *Hornet* for Commander Jackman to study, as well as to the Pentagon, Langley, and U.S. intelligence agencies scattered around Washington. Through a communication headset, Commander Jackman spoke directly to the MAVs' operators and scores of analysts studying the Al-Shabaab hideout.

Pointing to a monitor, Jackman explained to General Grant, Brooke, and Sergeant Miles what was happening. "What you are seeing is a live feed that our two mechanic birds are transmitting outside the house. Those images are being fed into a software program that is building our hologram image here on the ship."

Every tree, rock, door, window, even cracks in the house's foundations began appearing on the hologram that was under construction near them.

"This is incredible," Brooke gushed.

"Actually, this is old-school technology compared to what you're about to witness," Jackman bragged. "Our dragonflies are about to land."

He explained that the controllers operating the ten nano-MAVs had directed their flying robots to separate windows in the Barawa house. Each nano-MAV affixed itself onto a windowpane and immediately began shining a minute laser beam on the smooth glass. The purpose of the dragonflies and their laser beams was not to look inside the house—a curtain covered each window. Rather, the laser beams were used to record vibrations that were caused by sounds coming from inside. The human ear could not detect these vibrations but the MAVs could, and they relayed the vibrations via the drone hovering above them to Langley, where state-of-the-art software converted the vibrations into audible sounds. These sounds were fed into another bank of computers, which refined them into recognizable speech. Within minutes after the dragonflies landed on the glass, interpreters in Langley were listening to conversations that were being spoken in the Barawa house.

"Langley just told me that our dragonflies are transmitting several useful conversations," Jackman said.

"You are actually listening to Al-Shabaab fighters who are talking in that house?" Brooke asked.

"Langley is not only listening, it's using voiceprint software to identify known Al-Shabaab fighters." He was interrupted by someone speaking to him in his headset. "I've just been told," Jackman said, "that the Al-Shabaab terrorist who has appeared on those Internet videos is one of the men having a conversation inside the house. Langley has confirmed that he is there."

Jackman listened to another message over his headset.

"Langley is telling me that Ambassador Thomas and Mr. Duggard are not in the house—based on conversations that our dragonflies have recorded. Both men were moved several hours ago."

While the nanos continued transmitting vibrations of private conversations from inside the house, Jackman directed the operators of the MAV starlings to change locations and switch on infrared FLIR thermal imaging cameras tucked in each of the two starlings' breasts.

Images began appearing on two overheard monitors.

"Hollywood likes to show thermal images as if they were X-rays capable of identifying humans hiding in the darkest shadows," Jackman explained. "In reality, it's not that simple. Infrared imaging identifies oddities in the amount of heat that all objects naturally emit. Humans register ninety-seven on emissivity scales, compared to sand at seventy-six. Hard rubber is ninety-four, which is why our Marine Corps snipers often hide themselves behind old tires that register near the human body's ninety-seven range. It prevents the outlines of their bodies from being detected."

As they watched, Jackman stepped closer to one of the monitors and with a pencil began pointing at different images. "These are definitely images of men, and there are a hell of a lot of them hiding in this compound."

"Then it's a trap," General Grant said.

"Yes, Al-Shabaab was trying to lure us in. By Langley's count, there are at least seventy-five Al-Shabaab fighters waiting for us to arrive. Lucky for us, they're waiting to hear the sound of approaching helicopters and aren't paying any attention to the flapping of bird and dragonfly wings."

"What happens now?"

"That depends on Washington, D.C.," Jackman said. Speaking to General Grant, he added, "I've just been told the president wants you on a secure conference call. I'll show you where you can speak in private, but first I need a moment."

He spoke into the microphone on his headset.

"I want you folks in Langley to know you saved the lives of some very good and grateful SEALs tonight," he said. "Thank you!"

Slipping off his headset, he said, "General Grant, if you'll follow me now, the president is waiting."

CHAPTER SIXTY-TWO

Early evening (EDT)

Frank," President Allworth said as soon as General Grant came on the secure satellite phone connection, "I'm here with Mallory at the White House and Director Grainger is on the line at Langley, where he's been overseeing the Barawa compound operation."

"Yes, Madam President," General Grant replied. "As I'm sure you are aware, I've been monitoring events with Commander Jackman here on the Hornet and I'd like to join him in thanking Langley for a job well done."

"Then you are aware Ambassador Thomas and Mr. Duggard have been moved from Barawa and are no longer being held in that Al-Shabaab residence."

"Commander Jackman told me that Langley had confirmed that both men had been moved away from Barawa."

"Langley has also confirmed," the president said, "that the Al-Shabaab leader named Abdul Hafeez, who has appeared in all of the Internet videos, threatening us and killing two Americans, is still in the Barawa house. We're assuming that he is personally in charge of the ambush."

"Yes, Madam President. Commander Jackman has told me that."

"Director Grainger has recommended that we destroy the Barawa compound before Abdul Hafeez leaves and his men disperse," President Allworth explained.

Before General Grant could react, Director Grainger joined the conversation. "Terminating Hafeez and eliminating dozens of Al-Shabaab fighters would deal a devastating blow to Al-Shabaab."

"No doubt," General Grant said, "but there's a risk Al-Shabaab will take revenge by killing Ambassador Thomas and John Duggard."

"Which might happen anyway," Grainger replied, "despite what our

Egyptian cleric negotiator has been telling us. Unfortunately, we really don't know how serious Al-Shabaab is about negotiating the hostages' release—despite what they've said—given their latest Internet demands."

"Let's review the facts," Mallory Harper volunteered. "Al-Shabaab has planted explosives in the apartment where the Marine hostages were being held. They have tried to lure us into an ambush. And they have posted a video, threatening to murder the hostages unless everyone in Somalia converts to Islam. Those are not signs of someone who wants to negotiate a peaceful resolution to this crisis."

"How will Americans react," General Grant asked, "if after we eliminated the Al-Shabaab stronghold, a new video surfaced, showing Ambassador Thomas and John Duggard being executed?"

"I believe the American people would still support the bombing," Harper replied. "Every American who has watched that radical Islamic madman on the Internet threatening to kill Americans wants him dead. If Al-Shabaab did retaliate, it would reinforce in the public's mind that these terrorists are savages and there is only one way to deal with them."

"We're assuming Al-Shabaab would harm the hostages," Grainger replied, "but what if that assumption is incorrect? If we kill Abdul Hafeez, the organization will lose its leader and up to seventy-five of its fighters. Rather than causing Al-Shabaab to break off negotiations, the bombing might have the reverse effect. It might force them to the bargaining table."

"It's pointless trying to predict what these Islamic radicals are going to do," Harper said. "Even if we don't bomb them, there's still Hafeez's threat that he's going to execute Ambassador Thomas and Mr. Duggard if everyone doesn't convert by Friday midnight. Madam President, a few hours ago you decided that threat was serious enough to risk sending in SEAL teams. How is the public going to react if Hafeez carries out his threat and the American people discover we could have killed him and decimated Al-Shabaab but didn't?"

More than an hour had passed by the time General Grant returned to where Brooke, Sergeant Miles, and Commander Jackman were waiting in the SEAL team command post.

"Can I assume all of your electronic birds and dragonflies returned to the drone?" Grant asked Jackman.

"All of the MAVs are back inside their nest," Jackman answered.

"Let's pay a visit to the bridge," General Grant said.

The *Hornet*'s commanding officer was waiting for them. "My orders just came through, General," he explained.

"Then you know that our president has decided to launch a surgical bombing of Barawa just before dawn," Grant replied. "Now we wait. Send someone to get us coffee because we're all going to need some."

At the appointed hour, two AV-8B Harrier jets lifted off the ship's flight deck.

Except for the ship's commander, who was giving orders, no one spoke as they waited patiently for the aircraft to reach Barawa. When the Harriers were within striking distance, the voice of the first pilot could be heard over a bridge speaker, confirming that the target was in range and that he was locking in the GPS coordinates for a JDAM (Joint Direct Attack Munition) 500-pound bomb, which would use a global satellite to virtually guarantee a direct hit on the compound's main house. Another anonymous voice gave the pilot permission to fire. A camera on the Harrier sent black-and-white images to a monitor on the bridge, showing what next happened. There was a flash and a volcanic eruption of debris on the screen.

A second pilot's voice could be heard confirming that he too had locked his JDAM bomb on the Barawa target. He was given permission to "re-attack," so he unleashed a second 500-pound smart bomb directed at the exact same GPS spot as the first. There was less smoke when it hit.

"I doubt anyone could have survived those blasts," Brooke said.

"It's unlikely," Jackman replied, "but I've seen some unlikely things happen in combat."

FRIDAY

Four days before the presidential election

CHAPTER SIXTY-THREE

The devastation was complete.

In less than a minute, the two-story house in Barawa, the out-buildings surrounding it, and the wall that had protected the compound for decades against intruders had been reduced to rubble.

Little recognizable remained except for the corpses of Al-Shabaab fighters. Although they had been burned and mangled, most of the bodies were still intact—a ghoulish tribute to the rag-doll elasticity of the human body. Newly arrived Al-Shabaab fighters who'd responded to the bombing attack carted their dead into a nearby field, where they were positioned side by side in long rows.

No one was thought to have survived until a fighter picking through debris on the edge of the blast hole heard a man's faint cry. A stone shed used as a goat shelter had been toppled—not by the actual blast but by waves generated by the two explosions. Walls of air had smashed into its rock walls at incredible speeds.

Hearing the man's call from beneath fallen stones, the fighter hollered for assistance. A half hour later the rescue workers had cleared a hole big enough for the trapped man to crawl through. Amid cries of "Praise be to Allah!" the workers shined their lights onto his grime-covered, sweaty face.

Abdul Hafeez raised his hand to shield his eyes as a Barawa doctor attended to his injuries.

The stone outbuilding that had entombed him had appeared to the MAV starlings to be nothing more than a refuge for livestock. Despite the high-tech gadgetry, the two fake birds had failed to spot a trapdoor in the shed's floor that led to a hand-dug cellar. It had contained a lamp, a wooden table, and a battery-powered computer that had not been connected to the Internet.

Hafeez's life had been spared entirely by happenstance. While waiting for the Americans to attack, he had decided to slip outside the house and retreat into the underground bunker. He had done this after the MAVs had been recalled at the same time the president and her advisors were conferring. Although the drone hovering above the compound had observed men arriving and leaving the house, no one watching the images had identified Hafeez, and his decision to leave the house had gone unnoticed.

Among his many responsibilities, Hafeez was in charge of keeping track of Al-Shabaab's finances, and he had gone into the bunker to balance the group's books. This was no small assignment. Al-Shabaab's spreadsheet, which he kept on a flash drive, would have shocked Western governments. Because the jihadists were affiliated with Al-Qaeda, they were awarded a monthly stipend from its "treasury." Some donations came from Islamic organizations based in the United States, including cash from mosques. But the biggest payments came from oil-producing Middle Eastern countries, many of whom were allies of the United States. These nations considered the payments tribute—part of the cost of keeping Al-Qaeda and other radicals from biting their hands. In addition to the treasury, Al-Shabaab drew income from piracy, stealing cars, kidnapping, and extorting local businesses.

His diligence in keeping an exact accounting of funds had saved his life.

As soon as a doctor finished treating his superficial wounds, Hafeez fell to his knees and began to pray: "Praise be to Allah, savior of the faithful, avenger for the faithful. Praise be to Allah, mighty and merciful. O Allah, You have blessed me today."

Allah had saved him to kill another day.

CHAPTER SIXTY-FOUR

Watergate apartments
Washington, D.C.

Decker Lake left his penthouse at three thirty a.m.

He was more of a night person than a morning one, but delicate meetings were often best held in the early hours when potentially prying eyes were closed. His personal assistant drove him east in his Jaguar XJ sedan along Constitution Avenue toward Capitol Hill. It was a route that reminded Lake of why he loved the city.

He was surrounded by history and grandeur. Romanesque façades, magnificent stone monuments. Washington, Jefferson, Lincoln, Roosevelt, Eisenhower, Kennedy, Nixon, Johnson, Reagan—all had traveled this avenue at some point in their careers. They had influenced world events. Although he'd chosen to work behind the curtains, Decker Lake had sipped the same aphrodisiac that had brought men before him to what some writers had called America's Rome and others had jokingly referenced as Hollywood for Ugly People. The allure of the Capital of the Free World that had drawn him five decades earlier had not dimmed. But the seductress whom he'd so faithfully wooed was fickle, insatiable, and now issuing her siren's cry to younger men and women.

Rudy Adeogo was answering the siren's sweet sound.

The remains of the twelve Americans murdered in Mogadishu were scheduled to arrive at the Dover Air Force Base later today. Lake had heard from his friends in the media that an afternoon press conference had been scheduled around their arrival. The featured speaker would be Rudy Adeogo, who was taking time away from his own congressional campaign to appear beside the grieving family members of the slain Americans.

Lake could visualize how the event would unfold. The distraught relatives would appear before television cameras carrying photographs of their loved ones. They would provide the emotional hook needed for a segment on the Friday nightly news. But it would be Adeogo who would be the star prosecutor pointing an accusatory finger at the White House and President Allworth.

He would tell viewers that she had opened an embassy in Mogadishu at a time when many Somali Americans had been too frightened to return home. He would tell viewers that Somali Americans had known how dangerous Al-Shabaab was—yet the president had not. He would accuse her of opening the embassy solely for her own political gain— American lives lost because she needed a bump in the polls. He would scare the public by asking if this crisis was the prelude of another Iraq, another Afghanistan. Was the ghost of Vietnam lingering now over Africa? Were we about to launch into another unwinnable conflict because of a desperate president's foolish campaign tactics?

Through Adeogo's moving lips, Mary Margaret Delaney would say everything that Governor Timothy Coldridge could not say in public for fear of looking as if he was using the deaths of the Americans for his political advantage. Adeogo would be Coldridge's shill—unless Decker Lake stopped him.

When Lake arrived, the entrance to the Hyatt Regency was deserted except for a lone, half-awake doorman. Lake strolled through the hotel's revolving doors into an atrium with polished travertine tile, shiny chrome, and burnished wood. An escalator took him down to its sunken lobby and the bank of elevators to the guest rooms.

Lake had instructed his personal assistant to give him three minutes before telephoning Adeogo in his suite and announcing that he was about to receive an early-morning visitor. Lake hadn't wanted to knock unannounced and possibly cause a disturbance that might result in hotel security being called.

The young Somali American was waiting in the hallway outside the suite's double doorway, wearing a Hyatt terry-cloth bathrobe. Lake was pleased. His reputation had preceded him.

"Why don't you invite me in?" Lake said softly.

"I'd prefer we not talk at all," Adeogo replied.

"And yet here you are in the hallway with an open door."

Begrudgingly, Adeogo stepped aside and Lake entered the suite's living room, taking a seat near the bar. The bedroom door was closed and Lake noticed dishes from two dinners delivered by room service were sitting on the walnut-and-glass-topped coffee table.

"At dawn in Somalia, our country bombed an Al-Shabaab stronghold," Lake announced. "That happened at eleven p.m. our time but the White House and Pentagon are waiting until later this morning to officially announce it. The bombing was in Barawa, and Al-Shabaab hasn't acknowledged it either. It's not a location that is widely covered. So far, there have only been a few scattered reports on social media."

"Why did you wake me to tell me this?" Adeogo asked.

"Because the bombing will be much bigger news than the little press event that you and Ms. Delaney have cooked up for this afternoon. It will overshadow it. Your big announcement will be a mere footnote. You do know Ms. Delaney, don't you?"

"What makes you assume that?"

"Because bringing you here for a press conference in Dover has her fingerprints all over it," Lake replied.

"Since you're so willing to share information, can I assume you're responsible for sending a private detective from a Chicago agency to Minneapolis to ask questions about me?" Adeogo asked.

"I am indeed," Lake replied. He was enjoying this.

"Can we get to the point of your visit? As you just mentioned, I have a busy day ahead."

"I've come to talk to you about choices. Good choices and bad choices. Let's start with some facts. I've found that it's always better to be armed with facts before you make a choice. Wouldn't you agree?"

"Will this take much longer?" Adeogo grumbled.

"A fact," Lake said sternly. "Governor Coldridge and Ms. Delaney have told you that Representative Clyde Buckner will withdraw this weekend and throw his support behind you in return for you attacking the president today at the Dover news conference, snippets of which I am certain will be used in last-minute Coldridge campaign ads. Is that right?"

"You're the man with all the answers," Adeogo said, but he was surprised at how much Lake appeared to know.

"Not answers, facts," Lake said. "Remember? Do you know why Representative Buckner is willing to help you? It's because Coldridge has him by his gonads. Or he believes he does. The governor has learned that the Justice Department has a thirty-count indictment pending against Representative Buckner for malfeasance in office and misuse of public funds. The man's a crook, a common thief. Putting his mother-in-law on the public payroll was just the tip."

From the surprised look on Adeogo's face, he could tell the Somali American didn't know about the pending indictment.

Continuing, Lake said, "Governor Coldridge has promised Buckner that he will either quash that indictment if he gets elected or see to it that Buckner gets a presidential pardon. That's why Buckner is willing to take a dive and drop out of the congressional race. A nice trade-off, I must say. They buy off Buckner and use him to buy off you."

"I'm not for sale."

Lake glanced around the suite. "If you weren't, Coldridge wouldn't have brought you here."

"I'd like you to leave now," Adeogo said.

"But we haven't gotten to the interesting fact," Lake said, feigning shock. "You haven't heard my offer." Lowering his voice, he whispered, "This is when I mention your brother."

Adeogo felt a sense of panic welling up inside him. "I have several brothers," he said, trying to keep his voice from cracking.

"Yes, but only one is an Al-Shabaab terrorist in Somalia who goes by the name Abdul Hafeez."

A look of fear swept across Adeogo's face.

"My private detective said your mother named him George. George Adeogo. That's his given name, an irony since she named him after George Washington, the father of our country—a country that he now wants to destroy. Given his radical Islamic beliefs, I can understand why he changed it."

"My brother is dead to me."

Lake withdrew an envelope from his jacket pocket and placed it on the coffee table. "Here's more facts. This envelope contains a plane ticket to Minneapolis. Go home, forget about today's press conference in Dover, forget about that silly PAC and the national ad campaign. Go home and endorse the president and I'll keep quiet about your brother's identity. I'll even talk to Representative Buckner for you. I'll make him an even better offer than the Coldridge camp and persuade him to resign on Saturday and support you—so you'll still win. The only difference between their offer and mine is that if you choose my way, your brother stays dead."

CHAPTER SIXTY-FIVE

Rudy Adeogo made certain that Decker Lake had walked down the hotel hallway and boarded an elevator before he stepped back into his hotel suite and closed its door.

Mary Margaret Delaney was waiting in the bedroom. She'd already gotten dressed. "What did Decker Lake tell you?" she asked.

"You didn't hear our conversation?"

"Only snippets. When I heard him mention a bombing in Somalia, I got on my iPad but there's not much there. I doubt Al-Shabaab has let anyone in. They're probably staging the scene. That's what they always do to make us look worse. You know, they'll claim we bombed a hospital or orphanage."

"You didn't hear anything else he told me?"

"No. Why did he come here to tell you about the bombing?"

"Forget the bombing. He told me that *he* controls Representative Buckner, not Governor Coldridge. If I get on an airplane and leave town without appearing at the Dover press conference, he said that he'll get Buckner to resign. He said I don't need your help to make that happen."

"Decker Lake wouldn't have come here unless he could beat our offer. What did he promise you? Or did he threaten you?"

"That's between us."

"No. It isn't. Listen," she said. "Decker Lake is panicked. He's running scared. You don't need to worry about him. We'll protect you."

She reached for her jacket. "I need to get going because the governor will need a statement about this bombing in Barawa. But I'll speak to the governor about Decker Lake and Representative Buckner. We'll get this all worked out before the press conference. Meanwhile, I left your speech on the nightstand for you to review."

She stepped forward to kiss him but he turned his cheek.

"Oh my God!" she said. "He's gotten to you. You need to pay attention to what I'm telling you. President Allworth is going to lose and Decker Lake is an old man dying of cancer. He's grasping at straws."

Adeogo lowered his eyes. "I'm not doing the press conference. I'm not going to be the face of your PAC. I'm going home to my wife and my family."

"No, you're not!" she snapped. "You need to grow a backbone. This is presidential politics. You don't get to just run home to your wife and hide. You can't just say, 'Sorry, I don't want to play anymore because Decker Lake scared me.' We're counting on you to be at that press conference and read the speech that we drafted. And you're going to be there."

"No," he said firmly. "I'm not going to be there."

She glared at him and in a menacing voice said, "I don't know what Decker Lake pulled out of his hat and quite frankly I don't care, because whatever it is, I can trump it."

"What are you talking about?"

"Two of us know what's been happening in this bedroom since you arrived. If you don't want a third to find out, you'll be at that press conference this afternoon giving our speech."

"You'd do that? You'd tell my wife?"

"In a heartbeat."

Delaney exited the suite, leaving him standing in the bedroom in his Hyatt robe.

Decker Lake and his assistant were sitting next to a window at an open-all-night café across the street from the Hyatt, having breakfast, when Delaney stormed out of the hotel entrance and signaled for a cab.

Lake was not surprised to see her. The two dinner plates from room service in Adeogo's room, the suite's closed bedroom door—both had been on Lake's radar. Seeing her leave the hotel immediately after his visit confirmed what he had suspected—that she had seduced Adeogo and been hiding in the bedroom. Lake had tangled with Delaney many times before. Although he was nearly twice her age, he too had found her Irish red hair, green eyes, and fiery demeanor arousing. But where Rudy Adeogo had seen only her feminine sexuality, Lake had recognized more. Except for her gender, she was like him. A political predator. Had she overheard their talk? Had she learned Adeogo's secret? He doubted it. He had whispered to Adeogo.

Lake stuck his fork into the mountain of freshly cooked biscuits smothered in white cream gravy that had been put before him.

"Your doctor says you're supposed to be eating healthier," his assistant said.

"My mother used to make these. They're a poor man's meal. It's filling, comforting. You should try them sometime."

"Too many carbs for me."

"I eat them sparingly as a reminder."

"Of your mom?"

"Of my past."

Lake took a big bite and as he did, he wished for a moment that he had time to linger at his perch inside the greasy spoon's window booth, where he could watch the Hyatt's entrance. He would enjoy waiting to see if Adeogo would take a cab to the airport or wait for a limo to take him to the afternoon press conference in Dover.

CHAPTER SIXTY-SIX

Four thirty p.m. Somali time
USS Hornet
Off the Somalia coast

Egyptian cleric Abasi Mubarak was near frantic.

All morning he had tried to contact Al-Shabaab by telephone, but after the bombing raid at Barawa his contact hadn't answered.

In front of General Grant and the other Americans, Mubarak claimed he was anxious because he was concerned about the safety of the last two hostages. But privately he was more worried about collecting his $2.5 million retainer. If Al-Shabaab broke off negotiations, he would lose it, and the cleric had two daughters enrolled in expensive U.S. universities. Their spring tuitions would soon be due.

A short, square-shaped man, Mubarak walked back and forth in his berth wearing a *taqiyah* skullcap, which was common among conservative clerics who believed the Prophet Muhammad had also kept his head covered. His scraggly Santa Claus–style salt-and-pepper beard made him appear much older than fifty-six. He had not been well known in Egypt until a BBC reporter interviewed him after the radical Muslim Brotherhood temporarily gained control of the government.

"If Christian women want to avoid being raped in Cairo," Mubarak had declared, "they must immediately begin wearing veils and respect the customs of our Islamic faith. Otherwise, they should expect to be raped, humiliated, and beaten in our streets."

With that single comment, Mubarak had been demonized in the West and exalted in fundamentalist Islamic circles. He'd become a regular commentator on Al Arabic and Egyptian stations, and he had both reveled in and profited from his newly gained fame.

It was nearly five o'clock Somali time when Mubarak's cell phone finally rang.

"It is me," Abdul Hafeez announced.

"Praise Allah, you're alive. I feared you were dead."

"Allah protects me. Tell the Americans that we are willing to withdraw our demand that everyone in Somalia convert to Islam by Friday midnight. Tell them we are prepared to accept their tribute and release the final two hostages but only if they comply with our instructions."

"I will do as you tell me," a clearly relieved Mubarak replied.

"Have you seen their tribute?"

"Yes, it is here on this ship. General Grant has brought twenty-five million U.S. dollars with him, just as you instructed."

"It must be in hundred-dollar bills and those bills must not be bundled or tied together in any way. Each bill must be separate."

"Yes, that is how it is. There are two hundred and fifty thousand one-hundred-dollar bills. I have done an accounting of the bills and I personally bought two large containers in Cairo that will be used for delivery of the cash. But I can't be blamed if the Americans have put some secret tracking devices in those cases."

"Do not concern yourself with their wickedness and trickery," Hafeez said.

"General Grant has been asking me when and where the exchange will take place."

"Tell him that he will need a helicopter to deliver the tribute to us."

"When will the delivery be made?"

"Saturday. A spot in the desert outside Mogadishu—a remote place where we will not be disturbed by General Saeed and his soldiers. Tell General Grant that I will expect him to personally deliver the tribute to us."

"My brother," Mubarak said, "the Americans are worried you are setting a trap. They have discussed this many times with me. They know the apartment building where the Marines were being held contained explosives. And now, after they have bombed your compound in Barawa, they are even more concerned about retaliation."

"I care nothing about their fears. Let them worry."

"They are not alone in being fearful. I have given them my word that you will release the hostages alive after you are paid the tribute."

"Be careful, Cleric. Do not question my honesty. I have told you that we will make the exchange. We will release the Americans as soon as the tribute is paid. I have promised this to you as one believer to another. What you have promised them is of no consequence to me. But tell me this: Why should the Americans cower? They have their drones. Will they not be watching us?"

Without waiting for an answer, Hafeez said, "The reason they cower is because of Allah. He is more powerful than their drones and bombs. He will destroy them."

"I will tell them to be ready on Saturday with the tribute," Mubarak replied.

"Tell them that I will call you Saturday morning and tell you the exact location," Hafeez said. "There is something more that I want you to tell them. Tell them that their bombs did not kill everyone at Barawa. Tell them that our Lord and master, the most blessed Allah, protected one of His most humble servants. Tell them that Abdul Hafeez is not so easy to kill."

CHAPTER SIXTY-SEVEN

Mid-morning
CIA headquarters
Langley, Virginia

Payton Grainger was reading news reports that were filtering out from East Africa about the dawn Barawa bombing when he received word that Abdul Hafeez was alive and Al-Shabaab was willing to release Ambassador Thomas and John Duggard on Saturday if paid a "tribute."

In that moment, the CIA director saw an opportunity.

General Saeed had threatened him during their last conversation. Unless the agency guaranteed delivery of six Apache helicopters by the weekend, the general would make public the damning recording that he had secretly made of Gunter Conner requesting the torture and disposal of a captured Al-Shabaab terrorist. Saeed would tell the world that Conner had ignored Langley's warnings that an attack was imminent and had used the embassy as bait.

Grainger knew Saeed would carry out his threat, but until this moment, the director had no idea how to appease the general. He needed the president's approval to deliver those helicopters. Now, the stars seemed to be aligning. He saw an out.

According to news reports, Somali president Musab had expressed outrage about the U.S. bombing of Barawa in a morning radio address. Even though the target was an Al-Shabaab compound, America had been warned not to violate Somalia's borders. Yet it had done exactly that without consulting or informing Musab and his government.

With President Musab's reprimand fresh in his mind, Grainger called General Saeed on a secure satellite line.

"Where are my six Apaches?" Saeed demanded the moment he came on the line.

Grainger had expected nothing less. "If we can reach an understanding on two matters, then you will get them."

"I'm listening."

"First, I need your promise that you will never disclose the fact that Gunter Conner warned you about the impending Al-Shabaab attack on our embassy."

"This is a matter of no significance to me," Saeed replied dismissively. "In return for my Apache helicopters, I will gladly keep your secret. Now what else must I do to get my helicopters?"

"Isn't it obvious? I need you to destroy the recording that you made when you tortured the terrorist who attempted to assassinate your president—the Saudi named Dilawar Bahar."

"I assume you are talking about the recording where Gunter Conner tells me to torture him and dispose of his body?"

"Don't be coy," Grainger replied.

"What you have asked is a reasonable trade for six Apaches, and we both are reasonable men, so I agree to your demands," Saeed answered. "Now, how do I get my Apaches?"

"Al-Shabaab has told us it will release our ambassador and John Duggard on Saturday, presumably outside of Mogadishu," Grainger explained. "I need you to send me an official cable from your government informing me that you and President Musab are so outraged about the dawn bombings in Barawa that you have decided not to allow General Frank Grant and the Egyptian cleric helping him to set foot on Somali soil."

"You're asking me to stop your negotiators from entering Somalia?" General Saeed asked, clearly surprised.

"Only temporarily. I'll need you to lift that ban after I use it to persuade President Allworth to authorize the delivery of six helicopters."

"Director Grainger, you have my congratulations," Saeed said. "You intend to deceive your own president." He paused, thinking for a moment, and then added, "Seven Apaches."

"Six Apaches," Grainger replied sternly. "But to sweeten the deal, I'll send you pilots to train your people. You can't fly Apaches without pilots."

"Agreed," Saeed said, "as long as you include Stingers."

"Sixteen to a crate, six crates. My final offer."

"Done. When can I expect the helicopters and Stingers?"

"After our election but before the end of the year."

"I will not destroy the recording of Gunter Conner until after I receive my helicopters."

"I would not expect you to, but understand this, General: Apaches break down; they need parts. If I hear about copies of the recording or that you have broken your promises to me and talked about any of this, you will never get any parts. You need me as a friend in Washington, not an enemy."

"I like you, Director Grainger. We trust each other just enough."

Grainger ended their call and an hour later his driver delivered him to the White House, where he informed President Allworth that General Saeed was banning General Grant and Cleric Mubarak from entering Somalia unless the United States supplied him with six Apaches.

As Grainger expected, President Allworth was outraged. "I can't believe that third-world snake is trying to blackmail us."

"Unfortunately, he has the upper hand," Grainger replied in a sympathetic voice.

"I'll call President Musab directly and reason with him," Allworth replied. "After all, we helped make him president."

"Madam President, we both know President Musab can't control General Saeed and his security forces. And even if he were able to, General Saeed could drag this out until after Tuesday's election or try some other trick to scuttle General Grant's rendezvous with Al-Shabaab."

Grainger gave her a moment to think about it and then added, "I can arrange for delivery of the Apaches through a third party. There's something else to consider. If we give twenty-five million in cash to Al-Shabaab, General Saeed is going to need those helicopters to counterbalance those funds. The Apaches will guarantee him an advantage over the terrorists. It will enable him to help destroy Al-Shabaab, which is what we both want."

"What's to keep him from using those helicopters against his own people or even President Musab?" President Allworth asked.

"We'll tell the general that he can only use the helicopters to attack Al-Shabaab."

"Please, Payton, that's an unenforceable threat."

"Not really. Apaches need parts. They need pilots. Leave it to me to control General Saeed."

"First I'm told I need to pay a ransom that I do not want to pay," Allworth said candidly, "and now I'm being pressured to supply this murderer with arms that I don't want him to have—all because of a decision to open an embassy in Mogadishu that was supposed to help me win reelection."

"A slippery slope, Madam President," Grainger said quietly, "but nothing is gained by looking back with regrets. Your best chance now at freeing Ambassador Thomas and John Duggard and getting them out of Somalia alive before Tuesday's election is to comply with General Saeed's request. Let's not allow six helicopters to destroy your presidency."

"Tell General Saeed we'll give him the helicopters in return for his cooperation," the president said.

"Madam President, you've made the right decision."

Grainger stood and started for the door, but before he could leave the Oval Office, Allworth called to him from behind her desk. "Payton, I want to thank you. You've become my administration's problem solver during this dreadful crisis. I appreciate you protecting my back."

"Always, Madam President. There's no need to thank me."

Grainger felt as if a huge burden had been lifted from his shoulders as he left the White House. He had successfully defused General Saeed's threats.

But he still needed to deal with two loose ends: Gunter Conner and Representative Thomas "the Chairman" Stanton.

Grainger had already dispatched a security team to Germany to watch over Conner and keep him under wraps until he was medically fit enough to return to Langley. Once Conner was stateside, Grainger would find a way to explain away Conner's screwups in Mogadishu—although he wasn't certain yet how he would achieve that.

The more immediate problem was the Chairman. Stanton had demanded an accounting of all internal and external communications about Mogadishu on the Saturday of the embassy attack, including contacts with other agencies. That accounting would disclose the initial NSA intercept warning that an attack appeared to be imminent. It would contain information that revealed Charles Casterline had called Conner in Mogadishu and informed him of the NSA warning.

By the time Grainger had returned to his CIA office, he'd decided on a plan. He would have Charles Casterline delete all agency records of the NSA sending it an intercept and his warning call to Gunter Conner. He would make it appear that neither had ever happened.

Grainger had just deceived and manipulated the president of the United States. Was hiding information from the Chairman any greater violation?

CHAPTER SIXTY-EIGHT

Noon (EDT)
Ronald Reagan Washington National Airport
Arlington, Virginia

Rudy Adeogo telephoned his wife while waiting at the boarding gate for the Delta flight to Minneapolis.

"I'm coming home," he announced.

"Thank goodness," Dheeh replied. "You haven't called. You haven't told me what is happening. I've had a bad feeling about this ever since those men invited you to Washington."

"Yes, you warned me not to come to Washington but I didn't listen."

"Husband, you sound troubled. What's wrong?"

"Just meet me at the airport." He told her the flight number and added, "Dheeh, I love you. You know that, don't you?"

"I know you do," she said, sensing a nervousness in his voice. "Tell me, do they know about your brother George?"

"I'll tell you everything when I see you," he replied, ending their call.

But would he?

He would certainly tell her about Decker Lake's threat to expose his brother and the deal that Lake had offered him. But what of his infidelity? Did he have a choice? Mary Margaret Delaney had warned him that she would tell Dheeh, and he believed her. Delaney would be vindictive.

"Imagine meeting you here."

Adeogo glanced up from his seat. He'd been so preoccupied with his thoughts that he hadn't noticed Delaney approach him. A stocky man was standing next to her.

"This is Jonathan," Delaney explained. "He's from the governor's security detail."

"Have you come to threaten me?" Adeogo asked.

"Heavens no!" she said, feigning shock. "I brought Jonathan to protect me from you."

"Me?"

Delaney removed two airline tickets from her satchel and said, "Jonathan and I are booked on the same flight as you. I sweet-talked the agent
and she agreed to put the three of us in the same row. Wasn't that kind?
I've asked Jonathan to tag along because I want him with me when I
meet your wife, Dheeh."

She bent forward and said in a low voice, "I warned you. I will tell her.
I will destroy your marriage. Now, why don't the three of us leave the
airport right now? We can still make it to the Dover press conference."
She patted her satchel. "I brought along your speech. Do what you promised us and your wife will never know. After you win your election, we
can pick up where we left off here in Washington. You know I genuinely
enjoy our times together."

Adeogo felt the anger rising up in him. He placed his hands on his
seat's chrome armrests to steady himself before pushing himself up from
the chair, forcing her to take a step back. Her bodyguard moved slightly
closer to Delaney in anticipation.

"In the hotel you told me I needed to grow a backbone," he said. "I'm
going home. Decker Lake is going to take care of Representative Buckner for me."

"Don't overestimate his abilities or your own," she replied.

"Don't overestimate yours. Lake will help me destroy you. We both
know candidates can't help create Super PACs. It's illegal. Do you want
that sort of damaging publicity four days before the election?"

"Your wife will leave you," Delaney hissed.

Moving closer to her face, he replied, "No, she won't. You said it yourself. No one knows what happened in that hotel room but the two of us.
I will deny anything happened. I will tell her that you're trying to pressure me, blackmail me, into supporting Coldridge. Go ahead and tell
her. Tell the media. Who will the public believe? A respected member of
the Somali American community or a political viper who's had dozens of
Washington lovers and is known for doing whatever it takes to get what
she wants?"

He hesitated and then added, "Decker Lake will bury you."

This was a side of Adeogo that she'd not seen.

Delaney slowly tucked the two tickets into her satchel. "I'll not forget this. Decker Lake is dying and we're going to win the White House. We'll see who will bury who once President Coldridge is in power."

He watched her walk away and wondered why he had ever found her attractive.

CHAPTER SIXTY-NINE

Five p.m. central European time
Landstuhl Regional Medical Center
Landstuhl, Germany

W e're here to protect you," a stoic-looking officer from the CIA's Security Protective Service explained when he entered Gunter Conner's hospital room.

"All the way from Langley?" Conner asked. "The agency couldn't assign someone from our German stations?"

"Director Grainger personally sent us."

"Were you told to protect me from harm or keep me under surveillance?"

Ignoring his question, the officer said, "A member of our team will be stationed outside your door twenty-four seven until you're well enough to fly back to the States."

After the officer left him alone in his room, Conner used the remote control by his bed to switch on the television in his hospital room. He searched the channels until he found the Al Arabic network. Within minutes, a promo appeared with a tabloid-like teaser: "Al Arabic international correspondent Ebio Kattan will expose secrets the U.S. does not want the world to hear. Don't miss *The Shocking Truth About Mogadishu* tonight, only on Al Arabic."

Conner checked the time. The documentary would begin in an hour. Director Grainger's security team had arrived too late to keep him under wraps.

Eager for a world scoop, Kattan's Al Arabic editor had been unconcerned when she'd arrived in Dubai from Germany without footage of Conner or digital recordings to back up her exclusive interview. Instead of proceeding cautiously, they had hurriedly prepared an hour-long exposé that the network had begun promoting.

By airtime, the show had attracted the largest worldwide audience ever for an Al Arabic documentary. Conner was one of the thirty million viewers.

"The U.S. Embassy in Mogadishu was ransacked last Saturday," Ebio Kattan explained during a voice-over at the start of the documentary, while footage of the burning embassy and Somali security forces exchanging gunfire with Al-Shabaab fighters appeared on the screen. "What really happened that night? You're about to hear the truth about the embassy attack and the real motives behind America's decision to return to Somalia. It will shock you!"

After a commercial break, Kattan appeared posed on a chrome stool positioned next to a television monitor inside Al Arabic's elaborate Dubai studios. The set design was intended to make viewers feel welcome, as if Kattan had invited them into her home to watch a family movie, and while her dress was modest, covering all of her body, it had been carefully tailored to show off her curves.

"We begin tonight with a dramatic human rescue story," she announced, as a photo of Brooke appeared on the monitor next to her. "This is a story of an American woman soldier and her personal vendetta against the Islamic group Al-Shabaab. Her name is Captain Brooke Grant and she was serving as the military attaché in Mogadishu when Al-Shabaab attacked the U.S. Embassy."

During the next several minutes, Kattan recounted how Brooke had been trapped inside the embassy when it was besieged by Al-Shabaab fighters but had ingeniously disguised herself in a burqa, a trick that enabled her to escape from the burning building undetected.

"After escaping on foot," Kattan continued, "Captain Grant made her way to Aden Adde International Airport, which was also under attack. She joined forces there with another American, Gunter Conner, who was fleeing from Al-Shabaab fighters attacking the main terminal."

Conner's photograph replaced Brooke's on the monitor next to Kattan. "These two Americans learned that Al-Shabaab was holding five

Marines and two American diplomats as hostages inside a Mogadishu apartment building rigged with explosives. Despite the danger and over-whelming odds, they attacked the Al-Shabaab guards at that apartment."

Kattan breathlessly disclosed that Conner had been critically wounded by Al-Shabaab fighters, leaving "Captain Grant to fight single-handedly, engaging at one point in hand-to-hand combat with a skilled Muslim fighter armed with a billaawe."

Kattan showed footage of Conner being carried on a stretcher into an ambulance outside the apartment building, but in this report there was only a slight reference to General Saeed being at the scene.

Al Arabic took another commercial break, and while images of a wealthy Dubai businessman shopping at a local Bugatti Veyron dealer-ship were being broadcast, Kattan's producer informed her that the number of viewers in the United States had tripled since the telecast had begun—a significant jump and one that pleased him, given the network's intense desire to compete with CNN and MSNBC in the States.

When the program returned, Kattan said, "More about Captain Brooke Grant later in our hour, but now we are going to discuss Gunter Conner and his role in Mogadishu."

Conner's photo reappeared on the monitor positioned next to Kat-tan. "Although he is listed as a senior State Department diplomat, I have learned from highly placed intelligence sources that Gunter Conner was actually the Central Intelligence Agency's station chief in Somalia." Sev-eral new photos flashed on the monitor. They showed Conner conferring with Somali president Musab and General Saeed.

"The reason Conner was sent by the CIA to Africa was to identify and capture this man," Kattan announced in a somber voice.

A video clip replaced Kattan on the television screen. It was of a masked Al-Shabaab fighter severing Skip LeRue's hands with a knife as the American screamed.

"For the first time tonight," Kattan said, when the studio camera showed her again on the set, "I will make public this Al-Shabaab fig-ure's name." She hesitated for a moment of drama and then declared, "The man in these Al-Shabaab videos is named Abdul Hafeez and he is a Somali American who left America to fight in Africa with his fellow jihadists."

Kattan explained that Conner first began tracking Abdul Hafeez after Hafeez led Taliban fighters in an assault on a Pakistani prison that resulted in hundreds of inmates being freed.

"The CIA station chief learned the prison break at Dera Ismail Khan was not an isolated incident but one of eleven prison breaks in the Middle East conducted to free radical Islamic fighters. Gunter Conner recognized these breaks were related."

Again, Kattan paused to add another bit of drama to her reporting. "The American CIA agent soon found that while Abdul Hafeez was the public face of Al-Shabaab, he was not the commander who actually was controlling the group."

She glanced down at a pad in her lap, as if she were checking her facts before speaking. "One of the U.S. secrets that I have discovered is that Gunter Conner's ultimate target was an Islamic leader who has been quietly forging alliances between separate Islamic groups across Africa and the Arab world, including Al-Shabaab, the Taliban, Al-Qaeda, and even ISIS. We cannot show you a photograph of this charismatic jihadist because no one has been able to identify him. Nothing is known about his past. He was known only to Conner by the nom de guerre the Falcon."

The camera did a close-up of Kattan's face and she lowered her voice as if she were sharing a secret. "Working in complete secrecy, the Falcon has a goal of achieving what no one before him has ever attempted: He is determined to create an OPEC of Islamic fighting groups."

The camera pulled back and a silhouette of Osama bin Laden appeared on the monitor next to her, but his face had been cut out. "The Falcon is being called the new Osama bin Laden," she explained. "Gunter Conner, the CIA's man in Mogadishu, came to Africa to hunt down and kill the Falcon, and he came for a very personal reason that I will reveal after a short break."

The network again cut to a commercial. When the program resumed, viewers saw a burning Land Rover on their TV screens. It was footage of the Conner family's SUV when he was stationed in Cairo.

The film startled Gunter Conner in his hospital bed, and he became emotional as he watched video of himself frantically pulling Jennifer from the burning wreckage, carrying her to the sidewalk, and then dashing back to the SUV, where Sara and Benjamin were stuck lifeless inside.

In a sympathetic voice, Kattan explained in a voice-over: "Gunter Conner believes his wife and son were murdered by the mysterious Falcon. He blames the Falcon for planting a bomb in the family's car in Cairo. Conner was able to rescue his daughter, Jennifer, but she was critically wounded."

The camera returned to the Al Arabic studio set, where Kattan was standing next to the monitor. A passport photo of Conner appeared on it. "Conner is now in a U.S. military hospital in Germany recovering from wounds that he received helping Captain Brooke Grant rescue hostages."

With her broadcast nearing an end, Kattan told viewers, "Gunter Conner is not the only American seeking revenge for the deaths of loved ones. I will now return to the story of Captain Brooke Grant."

Kattan quickly outlined Brooke's humble Oklahoma roots and then—with footage of the Twin Towers collapsing—she revealed that Brooke's parents had been killed during 9/11.

In the final minute of the show, the monitor next to Kattan split into three images: Brooke, Abdul Hafeez, and the hollowed-out portrait of bin Laden.

"Captain Brooke Grant will not rest until she completes her vendetta and either captures or kills Abdul Hafeez and the Falcon," Kattan declared with a dramatic flourish. "She has picked up where Gunter Conner has stopped. She has vowed to destroy both men."

Kattan looked at the monitor next to her as a bright red color—signifying blood—slowly flowed down the photos of Hafeez and the Falcon, leaving only Brooke's face unclouded as the newscast ended.

The final bloody photomontage was a bit overwrought, Conner felt, as he switched off the television in his hospital room. But Kattan had broadcast the message that he'd wanted the world to hear. He'd used her to achieve his goal.

The agency was sure to know that he was the source for Kattan's broadcast—a violation of the secrecy agreement that all employees were required to sign. Now that Al Arabic had revealed that he was a CIA operative, he would never be able to work outside the U.S. again—assuming he wasn't fired or worse when he returned to Virginia.

Conner didn't care about what penalties he faced at home.

Director Grainger, Charles Casterline, and all of the other skeptics who had belittled his theory about the Falcon would have no choice but to address Conner's theory. They had to either prove him wrong or admit that the Falcon was real.

Gunter Conner suddenly felt exhausted. Although he was in stable condition, his chest wound remained painful and he wanted more morphine. Using the remote, he buzzed for a nurse but none came. After several minutes, he yelled, "Hello! Help, please!"

The CIA guard outside his door stuck his head inside.

"What do you want?" he asked.

"I need more morphine."

"I'm not your nurse," he replied.

"Find one for me."

His guard closed the door.

Moments later, a nurse appeared.

"It's about time," Conner grumbled. "I need morphine."

"This will not be a problem," the woman replied in a thick German accent.

Conner had not seen her before but she was wearing the same uniform that all of the nurses wore, complete with an official nametag: GERTRUDE. RN. He didn't become alarmed until she jabbed a needle into his shoulder. Morphine was supposed to be added to his IV drip. He started to complain but no sound came from his mouth and he realized he could not move.

The nurse leaned down next to his ear.

"I bring a message to you, Gunter Conner," she whispered, "from the Falcon. The poison will stop your heart within seconds, but he wanted you to know that your daughter, Jennifer, will be the next."

Looking into his eyes, the nurse felt confident that Conner had heard and understood the threat. She put her fingers on his neck and left them there until there was no pulse. Slipping a cell phone from her smock, she snapped a photo of Conner and sent it to the leader of the Hezbollah cell that her Palestinian boyfriend belonged to in Landstuhl.

Using a nurse to murder a patient was a simple way to dispose of someone being closely watched, especially when the fatal Florence Nightingale was an actual hospital employee who had exchanged shifts with a friend to work on the floor where Conner was being housed.

In his last moments of life, Gunter Conner felt vindicated. He'd exposed the Falcon to a worldwide audience. The mastermind radical Islamist was no longer his private ghost, haunting only him. But the poison stopping Conner's heart was evidence that the Falcon's reach was far longer than Conner had ever imagined and with that awareness came a last-breath feeling of panic and regret.

Gunter Conner had put his beloved daughter in imminent danger.

SATURDAY

Three days before the presidential election

CHAPTER SEVENTY

Nine a.m. Somali time
USS *Hornet*
Off the Somalia coast

I've just spoken to Abdul Hafeez and there's a change of plans," the Egyptian cleric Abasi Mubarak declared.

"I thought he might pull something like this at the last moment," General Frank Grant grumbled. "What's he want?"

Grant was seated in the officers' mess, where he had been drinking coffee with Commander Jackman.

"The first instruction is where the payment of the tribute and the exchange will take place. It will no longer be in the desert outside Mogadishu. It will be in the city. Hafeez suspects you will use your drones to kill him and his men if they meet you in the desert."

"Did he give you an exact location for the exchange?" Jackman asked.

"At the Mosque of Islamic Solidarity. It is a famous one constructed in the 1980s with money donated by the king of Saudi Arabia. It is large enough to hold ten thousand worshippers, the biggest in eastern Africa."

"He wants me to carry twenty-five million in cash into a mosque filled with ten thousand people?" Grant replied in an incredulous voice.

"I am not certain you will actually enter the mosque or even if it will be the final location for an exchange. He has told me that you are to transport the money in a helicopter to the plaza outside the mosque and wait in the air until he gives you additional instructions. You are not to land."

"Is that all?" Grant asked.

"No. Al-Shabaab no longer trusts you, General Grant. The bombing at Barawa nearly killed him."

"Sorry we missed him," Jackman interjected.

"Hafeez will not turn over the hostages to you, General Grant."

"Then he won't get his money. I'm the only one authorized by my government to deliver the cash."

"You are to bring the money in the helicopter but Hafeez was very specific. He will not deal directly with you. It is a matter of honor with Abdul Hafeez."

"This is ridiculous. Who will he deal with—you?"

"No, I'm only an intermediary, although Hafeez has asked that I accompany you in the helicopter so there will be no miscommunication. This is a good thing. You will be safer if you are with me. He will not harm me."

"I wouldn't be so certain of that," Jackman said.

"He is my Muslim brother," Mubarak replied. "He has given me his word that there will be no bloodshed."

"If he won't deal directly with me, who does he want to deal with?"

"Your niece. Captain Brooke Grant. Hafeez saw her last night on Al Arabic. If you want the hostages freed, she must be the new go-between."

"Call him back and tell Hafeez that's unacceptable. I'm not going to put my niece in the middle of this."

"She already is. I was told if you refuse, the exchange is off and the hostages will be beheaded."

"He's bluffing. He wants the money. Call him back. Use some of your negotiating skills. Earn your commission."

"No, my friend. Hafeez was not bluffing. He will only speak and deal with your niece. She is to go to the steps of the mosque and wait for a phone call from him. You are to bring the money in a helicopter and wait above the plaza there for him to call your niece. He will tell her where the prisoners are located and where you are to deliver the money. If she is not on the steps to receive his phone call, he will execute Ambassador Thomas and Mr. Duggard and post a video of their beheadings on the Internet."

"I don't like these changes," Grant replied. "I don't like meeting in the city outside this mosque and I don't like him insisting that my niece be involved."

"You have no choice," Mubarak said. "He will make the exchange with your niece today at *salat al-zuhr*."

"What time is that exactly?"

"This is why it is fortunate that you hired me," the cleric replied. "Today, the prayer time is 11:55 a.m."

Rising from his seat, Grant said, "I need to notify Washington."

"I'll get everything ready," Jackman replied.

Grant turned to leave but stopped to address Mubarak. "Call Hafeez and tell him that I am not going to send my niece alone to that mosque regardless of what Washington says."

"This also was discussed between us this morning," Mubarak said. "Forgive me for failing to mention it. Hafeez said that the Marine sergeant who stayed with her in Mogadishu can accompany your niece. But no one else."

"Is there anything else that you have forgotten to tell us?" Jackman asked.

"No," Mubarak said. "I have told you everything."

CHAPTER SEVENTY-ONE

Eleven a.m. Somali time
USS Hornet
Mogadishu, Somalia

A fifteen-seat UH-1N Huey medical helicopter was waiting on the flight deck with its rotors spinning.

General Frank Grant, Cleric Abasi Mubarak, Sergeant Walks Many Miles, and Captain Brooke Grant boarded the aircraft along with Commander Seth Jackman and four SEALs. Two Navy medics, who were part of the regular four-member crew, were already inside. Jackman had opted to use a medical helicopter rather than a gunship because he believed that while flying over Mogadishu it would be less likely to draw fire from some trigger-happy Somali.

Grant had notified General Saeed about Al-Shabaab's newest demands and he'd agreed to permit the helicopter to land at the airport so Brooke and Sergeant Miles could disembark. Grant also had alerted CIA director Grainger, and Langley had positioned two armed drones above Mogadishu. Cameras on the drones were sending real-time images to Washington, where President Allworth and Mallory Harper were watching in the White House Situation Room. Grainger was in Langley overseeing the operation from a command post there. All of the key players aboard the helicopter were linked by headsets that enabled them to communicate instantly with one another, Langley, and the White House.

As the Huey lifted from the *Hornet*'s deck, Brooke checked her Beretta M9 handgun and tried to calm her nerves. She was wearing a red-and-blue *dirac* kaftan over black silk pants—an outfit that would help her blend in. Her face was exposed but her head was covered by a veil that fell down her back to her waist. Sergeant Miles was sitting on her right aboard the helicopter, wearing a Sudanese-style dishdasha, a white flowing robe with long sleeves. His head cover was a red-and-white King Abdullah–style Jordanian *smagh* with a black ring holding it in place. Because of his Crow Indian features, he could pass as an Arab.

"Nice dishdasha," Brooke quipped as the Huey flew toward the city. "Your first time in a dress?"

"It's a robe," he replied.

As they neared the airport, Brooke spotted General Saeed's now-familiar Chevy Silverado and armed entourage waiting on the tarmac.

"Think there might be another mutiny?" she asked Commander Jackman, who was seated across from her.

"Mutiny? No," he answered. "A robbery, possibly."

"General Saeed was very accommodating when I spoke to him on the phone," General Grant volunteered through his headset. "I believe he'll keep his men in check."

As soon as the Huey landed, Brooke and Miles stepped from it, followed by Commander Jackman and his SEALs with their weapons ready. General Grant and the others remained onboard. Brooke checked her watch. It was 1132 in Somalia, which meant it was 0432 in Washington. Brooke assumed that President Allworth and Director Grainger were watching her via the drone as she walked briskly from the helicopter toward General Saeed.

"First a Marine, then hiding under a burqa," General Saeed said when she reached him, "and now a Somali woman. You have many faces."

"Different disguises but only one face," she replied, "unlike you, General."

"And will you be this insulting when you speak to Abdul Hafeez?" he asked.

"Where's our car?" She loathed him and had no interest in chatting.

Saeed nodded toward a white Toyota Camry parked nearby. "The mosque is less than ten minutes away. My men will follow you to a large market adjacent to it, but your uncle has warned me to stay away for fear that Al-Shabaab will execute the hostages. There will be only one guard near the mosque, which is routine, and he will not be of concern to you. Once you reach the market, my men will fall back and you will be entirely on your own."

"That's what I want," Brooke said. "Dealing with Al-Shabaab is enough of a threat. I don't want to end up like Cash Kelley, being shot by you."

Brooke suddenly realized her comments were being overheard by her uncle and Jackman in the helicopter and the cohort in Washington, D.C., including President Allworth.

"Tread softly," General Saeed said, keeping his temper in check. "You are still a guest in my country."

"We need to go," Sergeant Miles said.

"You drive," Brooke told Miles as they walked to the Toyota.

The sergeant placed a modified M79 40-mm grenade launcher between them as he slipped behind the wheel. The weapon resembled an old pirate blunderbuss. "Just in case we run into trouble," he said. She rested her Beretta on her lap.

"Funny," she said, as he started the car. "If someone sees us holding weapons, they won't think anything about it, but if they saw a woman driving a man, they would be suspicious."

The Toyota exited the airport and they made their way to Makkah Almukarramah Avenue, the main thoroughfare that would lead them to the mosque. A pickup truck carrying General Saeed's men followed them until they neared the market, when it turned down a side street. As soon as they entered the market, their car was engulfed by Somali men, women, and children walking in the crowded street. None of them showed the slightest concern about being struck by the Toyota. They stepped aside as the car moved forward at a crawl. Only once did Miles sound the horn to warn an older man leading two camels to move clear. The man cursed and reluctantly did so. Brooke spotted several men reaching for their cell phones as they passed. She assumed they were Al-Shabaab.

Miles parked the Toyota at the edge of a vast public square in front of the mosque and looked at the hundreds of Somalis walking, standing, praying, and loitering on the concrete plaza now before them.

"Talk about hiding in plain sight," Miles said. "There's no way to tell the good guys from the bad guys."

"We'll need to look for inconsistencies," Brooke replied. "The slightest tells."

As they stepped from the Toyota, both of them glanced north at the façade of the Mosque of Islamic Solidarity. Painted white and with a bright-green tiled portico, the mosque's front contained three arches. Each was twenty feet high and led to three ornate wooden doors through which worshippers entered. To the right of the entrance was a minaret— a tower with a rounded top, edged by a narrow balcony—where a muezzin called the faithful to prayer.

Miles nodded toward an elderly Somali policeman stationed near the mosque's front steps. The guard was holding a World War One vintage rifle.

"Which is older, him or his gun?" he asked.

"General Saeed wasn't joking when he promised to keep his men away. Either that or he's hidden them well," Brooke responded as she surveyed the crowd.

A breeze brushed her cheek from the nearby Indian Ocean and she thought about how idyllic this city had once been. Most of the Somalis in the plaza were men, but there were enough women to keep Brooke from being noticed as she and Miles stepped from the street into the plaza. They kept within eyesight of each other but walked toward the entrance about two dozen feet apart. No one appeared to be paying any attention to them.

Cleric Mubarak had given his cell phone to Brooke and had instructed her to climb the mosque's steps, which led to the triple arches. Because only men would be entering the mosque for Saturday's prayers, she would be easy for Abdul Hafeez to spot. In the growing crowd, he would not be.

Both Brooke and Miles had watched the Internet videos that Hafeez had uploaded, to familiarize themselves with his appearance. But in those videos, only Hafeez's eyes had been visible. Still, they'd memorized his height, weight, and how he'd moved.

"See anyone like him?" Brooke asked through the headset.

"Dozens," Miles replied.

They reached the mosque and Brooke started up its front steps. "Where are you going to position yourself?" she asked.

"If you're near the minaret tower, I'll move to the opposite side, but I'm not climbing the steps. I'll stay moving through the crowd."

When Brooke reached the top of the steps, she turned to face the square and the throngs gathered there. She was now standing about four and a half feet higher than the plaza, giving her an elevated view.

"How many people are outside the mosque?" her uncle asked over the headset.

"About a thousand," Brooke replied. "I don't know how many are already inside."

"More are coming from the market to say their noon prayers," Sergeant Miles volunteered.

"Do you see anyone who looks suspicious?" General Grant asked.

"No one—and everyone," she replied.

"I'm looking for someone who is watching you," Sergeant Miles said. "That's what Hafeez would be doing. Do you see anyone staring at you?"

Brooke scanned the swath of humanity before her. Most of the men approaching the mosque didn't appear to notice her, but she did lock eyes with one. He glared at her as he approached the steps, but he turned his head when he walked past her into the building.

From above her left shoulder she heard the mosque's muezzin begin the *adhan*, a call for prayer, and the crowd entering the mosque became larger as men congregated near the steps, waiting their turn to climb them.

The cell phone that Mubarak had given her rang.

Before she answered it, she said into the headpiece, "Sergeant, look for someone talking on his phone." She waited for it to ring a second time and then lifted it to her left ear with her left hand because the headset earpiece was in her right one. All the while, she scanned the plaza. She spotted a half-dozen men talking on their cell phones. Glancing to her right, she looked for Sergeant Miles but couldn't see him in the approaching horde of men.

"I'm here," she said into the cell phone.

"Captain Grant," a male replied. She recognized Abdul Hafeez's voice from his Internet rants. Her eyes darted from one man to the next in the crowd. *If he could see her, then she could see him.*

"I understand from the Al Arabic network you are hunting me," he said. "I understand you want to kill me."

"Everyone who is sane wants to kill you."

Where was Sergeant Miles? she wondered. *Had he spotted Hafeez?* With the prayer service about to start, the men hurrying toward the steps were like a giant wave.

Hafeez said, "The Prophet Muhammad says: 'I have been ordered to fight with the people till they say none has the right to be worshipped but Allah.'"

"Let's skip your twisted scriptural rhetoric. Where are the hostages?"

"The television news reporter said your father claimed to be a religious leader, yet you mock the scriptures. In *Surah* nine, twenty-nine, it is written: 'Fight the people of the book'—which means your Holy Bible—'who do not accept the religion of truth, until they pay tribute by hand, being inferior.'"

"Is that what the twenty-five-million-dollar ransom is—a tribute from inferior people?"

"Yes, just as your parents' death was a tribute. They were inferior and their deaths were well deserved."

His reference to the murder of her parents—along with the tension of the moment—caused the anger inside Brooke to surface.

"Don't you dare mention my parents," she snapped. "My father was nothing like you. You preach hate and bigotry. You have hijacked Islam. You don't care about Allah or Islam. You care only about yourself. You're a narcissistic psychopath, an insignificant insect. No, you are less than that. You are a flea feeding on a camel turd."

"And you are an ignorant woman," he replied. "I will not waste my time trying to explain what you are incapable of understanding. Tell your uncle to bring the tribute here in the helicopter."

"There's no place for him to land. There are too many people."

"I did not tell you to have him land, only to fly here. Now do it or I will kill the hostages."

Lowering the phone so that Hafeez could not hear her, she spoke into the headset mouthpiece. "You are to bring the cash to the plaza but don't land. He wants you to hover above the square and wait for my next instruction." A thought came to her. Hafeez knew she was in communication with her uncle in the helicopter. Had he simply assumed she was wearing a headset or had he actually come so close to her during the past several minutes that he had spotted it?

Most of the worshippers had entered the mosque but there were still about three hundred Somalis lingering in the square. Some were women and teens. Some men dropped to their knees facing Mecca. Even though the crowd was now smaller, she couldn't locate Sergeant Miles.

As she was about to return the phone to her left ear, Miles spoke to her through the headset.

"I think I've spotted him," he whispered. "To your right. He's wearing a bright yellow shirt."

It took her a moment, but she saw the man in the yellow shirt talking on his cell phone at about the same time the whooshing sound of an approaching helicopter could be heard above the plaza. The white medical Huey appeared and hovered sixty feet above the square's center. Its arrival caused the people beneath it to look upward, but no one seemed alarmed.

Keeping her eye on the suspect, she returned the phone to her left ear. "The money is here," she told Hafeez. "Now what?"

She saw Sergeant Miles. He was slowly edging closer to the man in the yellow shirt.

"Begin throwing handfuls of bills down to the people."

"Wait!" she said. "What did you say?"

The man in the yellow shirt glanced up at the helicopter. He was still speaking on his phone.

"Begin throwing money from the helicopter," Hafeez repeated.

"But why? That doesn't make any sense."

"These people and those inside the mosque are hypocrites, just as your Egyptian cleric is a hypocrite," Hafeez answered. "They claim to be believers, but they value money more than Allah. They are not willing to defend Allah. They are not willing to join our fight."

Brooke was only half-listening to Hafeez's rant. Sergeant Miles was less than six feet from the man in the yellow shirt.

Hafeez continued, "The Imam of this mosque has sold his soul to the

Western puppet government now in charge of Somalia. He instructs the people to live in peace with infidels."

Brooke saw Miles reach into a slit in the side of his robe. He was going for his handgun. Just then, the man in the yellow shirt lowered the phone and put it in his pocket.

But Hafeez was still talking.

"Like you Americans, money is these people's idol, and now you will deliver it to them! Begin throwing money from the helicopter. Do it now!"

Brooke quickly lowered the phone so Hafeez could not hear her speak into the headset.

"Back off, Sergeant!" she exclaimed. "The man in the yellow shirt is not Hafeez."

Miles pulled his empty hand from inside his robe and stepped by the unsuspecting man in the yellow shirt.

Returning the cell phone to her ear, Brooke said, "Hafeez, I'm not going to tell them to begin dropping money until you tell me where the hostages are."

"Begin throwing out the first case of money," he ordered, "and I will tell you where the Americans are."

Speaking into her headset, Brooke said, "Hafeez wants the first case of money dumped from the helicopter into the crowd."

She immediately heard Director Grainger's voice through her ear-piece. "That's twelve-and-a-half million dollars."

"If we start dropping cash," General Grant interrupted, "there's going to be a riot beneath us."

"Which is exactly what he wants," Brooke said.

"Why would he want that?" a woman's voice asked. Brooke realized it was President Allworth.

"I don't know," Brooke replied. "He just described the people here as a bunch of infidels and said the Imam at the mosque was a traitor to Allah. Hafeez said he would tell me where the hostages are after we empty the first case."

"He's insane," the president said.

The side door of the Huey opened and two SEALs began tossing out handfuls of hundred-dollar bills. The Somalis below had no idea what was fluttering down until the first wave of currency reached them. Men who had been kneeling in prayer jumped to their feet to snatch the falling cash as soon as it came within arm's reach. Women and children scrambled to retrieve bills that made it to the concrete. Gusts of air from the helicopter's rotors sent the cascading currency off course into the adjacent market. Within moments, merchants and shoppers were bolting into the square, eager to claim their share of the falling booty. Word reached the men praying in the mosque, and they too began rushing outside. Brooke was forced to step clear of the doorways to keep from being trampled.

From her perch, she watched humankind at its greedy worst as the swelling tide of pushing, shoving, kicking, and screaming Somalis grabbed at the bills raining down on them.

When the last handfuls from the first case had been released, the Somalis turned on one another. A man punched an elderly woman to the ground and snatched the hundreds in her hand away from her. Several scuffles broke out.

"We've done what you've demanded," Brooke told Hafeez through the cell phone. "You've shown these people for what they are. Now where are the hostages?"

"Look to your left," Hafeez replied. "Look for a familiar sight."

Brooke turned to her left but didn't see anything and then, as she gradually looked beyond the square, she saw it. Parked near a palm tree across from the plaza about fifty yards away was Mosi's old Mercedes-Benz—the patched-together sedan he had driven while chauffeuring her around Mogadishu before she'd discovered he was a traitor and killed him with his own dagger.

"They're in the car," Hafeez said. "The trunk. Now throw out the second case."

Speaking into her headset, Brooke exclaimed, "He says the hostages are in a car parked across the street."

"Can you see them?" General Grant asked. "Is he with them?"

"No. He said they are locked in the trunk."

"I'm not throwing out the rest of this money until we know the hostages are actually in that car," Grant replied.

Brooke lifted the phone back to her left ear. "They're not going to toss out the second case without proof Ambassador Thomas and John Duggard are in the trunk."

"Then go look, Captain Grant. I left the key in the lock for you. I'll wait for you to open it."

Brooke lowered the phone and started for the stairs, but stopped when she reached the first step down. Speaking into the headset, she said, "You need to throw out the money. Do it now!"

"I'm not going to drop any more," her uncle replied, "until we know if they're in that car trunk and are alive."

"No!" Brooke exclaimed, her voice rising in desperation. "Don't you understand? This has never been about the money. You've got to begin throwing out those bills. It's the only way for us to spot Hafeez."

"What are you talking—" Grant said, but she interrupted him.

"The ransom is not the tribute. He's after human lives, not cash. Throw out the money now before it's too late."

"Do what she says," Director Grainger ordered.

Brooke didn't look upward. She kept her eyes glued on the crowd and, as she watched, she saw hundreds of faces stare up at the helicopter. She heard yelling and saw hands rising to collect the new shower of bills falling down.

"Sergeant Miles, are you there?" she asked in her headset.

"Yes, to your right."

"Hafeez is on his cell phone. Look for a man on his cell phone."

"That's what I have been doing," he replied. "I thought the man in the yellow shirt was him and he wasn't."

"Yes, but now look for the man in the crowd who is on his cell phone and is *not* looking up at the helicopter. The one who doesn't care about money. That will be Hafeez."

Brooke reached behind her back and drew her pistol with her right hand.

"I've got to keep him talking," she said into the headset, raising the phone to her left ear.

"Hafeez, you don't care about the money, do you?"

"So you understand then, don't you?"

In her right ear, she heard Sergeant Miles's voice.

"I see him!" Miles said. "He's thirty feet to your right near the edge of the mosque. He's on the cell phone and watching you, not the money."

With her left hand still holding the cell phone and her right one grasping her pistol, Brooke slowly turned to her right and looked down the steps near the entrance. A man was standing there looking—not at the helicopter but at her.

Their eyes met and she knew it was Abdul Hafeez.

"Hello, Captain Grant. I'm happy you see me," he said, "before we both die."

She did not have a clear shot at him. There were still men exiting the mosque who were in her way. But she could see him clearly enough to realize that he was raising his left hand as if he were about to wave at her. Only she knew that he was not waving. He was about to detonate the suicide vest that she assumed he was wearing, as well as the explosives packed into Mosi's Mercedes. The millions being dropped into the square were intended to draw as many people as possible into range of the explosives.

"I'm going to paradise, Captain Grant," Hafeez said. "And now I am sending you to join your parents in hell."

Despite the noise of the hovering helicopter and the mob, Brooke heard a single gunshot. She spotted Sergeant Miles less than ten feet behind Abdul Hafeez. She saw the Somali American terrorist collapse.

Brooke lowered the phone as she made her way across the portico and down the steps. Hafeez was on the ground, not moving. Miles was standing over him.

"His hand," she screamed as she approached them. "A detonator."

Miles fell to his knees and removed the switch from Hafeez's fingers. Brooke checked for a pulse. Hafeez was dead. She felt his chest. Lumps under his shirt. Proof that he was wearing a suicide vest. A black wire led from the switch in Hafeez's left hand into his sleeve. "Just like the vest in London," she told Miles. She disconnected the wire, rendering the trigger harmless.

Speaking into her headset, she said, "You can stop throwing the money now."

"What the hell is going on?" her uncle demanded.

"Hafeez is dead. We stopped him just as he was about to detonate a bomb. He was using the cash to attract more people to the square."

"The hostages?" Director Grainger asked over the headset.

"We'll check on them now," she explained, but first she retrieved Hafeez's cell phone from his other hand. It would contain telephone numbers that would prove useful in hunting down other Al-Shabaab terrorists.

Abandoning Hafeez in his own blood, Brooke and Miles began threading their way through the still-frantic mob en route to the Mercedes. None of the individuals near Hafeez paid any attention to his body. They were too busy fighting for cash.

"Do you see the Mercedes by the palm tree?" Brooke asked Commander Jackman aboard the helicopter.

"Yes," he replied. "We can see you. I'll maneuver over it, but we can't risk landing. The crowd may think we have more cash and rush us. You'll have to wait for us to fast-rope down."

"The car could be booby-trapped," General Grant warned. "I'll radio the ship and get a bomb disposal team out here."

By this point, Brooke and Miles had reached the Mercedes.

"There's no one inside the car," Miles confirmed, glancing through its windows. "Just boxes of what probably are explosives and nails."

"There's a key in the trunk," Brooke noted, stepping toward it.

"Don't open it!" her uncle said.

"We don't know how long they've been locked in there," she replied. "They could be dying. We can't wait."

"But it could be a trap," her uncle warned.

"There's no booby trap," Brooke said, reaching for the key. "Hafeez wanted to control when he would kill himself and detonate the car. He wasn't going to chance some curious Somali noticing the key and setting off the bomb."

She turned the key. And the trunk popped open.

Ambassador Thomas and John Duggard, both bound and gagged, were crowded inside it. They were unconscious and had weak pulses.

Ropes dropped from the helicopter now hovering above them and four SEALs slipped down, followed by two bright-orange basket stretchers and Commander Jackman. Three of the SEALs set up a perimeter with their weapons ready to keep the mob away while Jackman and the other SEAL loaded Thomas and Duggard onto the stretchers so they could be hoisted up.

"You're damn lucky that trunk wasn't booby-trapped," Jackman said.

"Hafeez wanted us to die at his hand."

"Why did he wait?" Jackman asked. "He could have exploded the bombs after we threw out that first bundle of cash."

"Yes, and he might have—if you hadn't started throwing out the second case of bills," Brooke explained. "That's why I told you to do it. Once you started tossing out the second case, I knew he would wait."

"But why?"

"Because Hafeez wanted to make certain that every last hundred-dollar bill of tribute was paid. He wanted to take all of our money as well as kill us."

Brooke heard the sound of another helicopter and looked across the plaza just as General Saeed's Agusta A129 came into sight. The gunship dropped low, sending Somalis running for cover.

At the end of the square opposite them, General Saeed's Chevy Silverado came bolting onto the plaza, followed by the truck of soldiers that had escorted Brooke and Miles to the nearby market earlier. Through a loudspeaker in the Chevy's grille, General Saeed ordered the crowd to disperse or be fired on by the gunship, which made another menacing pass.

Saeed's motorcade reached the Mercedes just as the SEALs were ready to lift Brooke and Miles up to the Huey.

"Abdul Hafeez is dead," Brooke announced. "His body is near the mosque steps. He's wearing a suicide vest and there are explosives in this car."

"Allah favored you today, Captain Grant."

"No, I think Allah was just tired of Abdul Hafeez," she replied as the rope she was grasping pulled her to safety.

CHAPTER SEVENTY-TWO

Fifteen minutes later
Aboard a helicopter
Flying over Mogadishu, Somalia

Brooke felt a vibration in her pocket. It took her a moment to realize it was the cell phone that she'd removed from Abdul Hafeez's body.

"Captain Grant," a male voice said when she answered.

"You seem to know who I am, so who are you?"

"We can use the name that Gunter Conner gave me before I arranged his death."

"The Falcon," she replied, angry at the mention of Conner. "We just put a bullet into Abdul Hafeez's head. That was before he could detonate the explosives in the plaza. I assume it was your plan to murder hundreds of innocent men, women, and children by having us dump cash there."

For a moment, Brooke thought he might have hung up, but he said, "There will be other opportunities." He was quiet a moment and then continued. "If you believe Hafeez's death troubles me, it does not."

"Why did you send him? Wasn't he one of your most faithful? Or don't you care about anyone but yourself?"

"His failure in Barawa made him expendable. No one follows a leader who is responsible for the deaths of everyone around him."

"Hafeez was a failure so he deserved to die," she repeated. "Aren't you a failure after today? Why don't you tell me what rock you're hiding under so we can come put a bullet in your head?"

"Allah has awarded me an advantage. I have seen you and I know where I can find you. No matter where you go. You will never know the time or place when I will come, only that I will."

"You don't frighten me."

424 NEWT GINGRICH and PETE EARLEY

"Gunter Conner thought he was safe in an Army hospital. He wasn't, and neither is his daughter."

"Conner's daughter? She's no threat to you."

"When you attack a Messenger of Allah, you condemn yourself and everyone you love. I tried to teach that lesson to Gunter Conner in Cairo. Perhaps you are smarter. I know you have brothers. You have an uncle and aunt. One by one. They and the daughter of Gunter Conner and finally you—after you have witnessed their deaths."

"My government will track you down and kill you before you can hurt anyone else," she replied. "Gunter Conner might have pictured you as a Falcon circling high above everyone else, but at the end of the day you're just another sociopath who will end up like Abdul Hafeez with a bullet in his brain."

"Next time, I will send more than one bomber."

The phone line went dead.

CHAPTER SEVENTY-THREE

8:00 a.m. (EDT)
East Room
The White House
Washington, D.C.

President Sally Allworth interrupted the Saturday morning television schedule with a White House news conference.

"At roughly five thirty this morning, eastern daylight time, our military, with assistance from Somali security forces, rescued Ambassador Todd Thomas and Mr. John Duggard from Al-Shabaab terrorists in Mogadishu, Somalia, ending what has been a weeklong nightmare," she announced. "I am happy to report that both Ambassador Thomas and Mr. Duggard are alive. The rescue was successfully completed at twelve thirty in the afternoon in Somalia, which is seven hours ahead of us. Both Ambassador Thomas and Mr. Duggard have been taken to one of our ships, the USS *Hornet* anchored off the eastern coast of Africa, where they are receiving emergency medical treatment for dehydration and trauma before being airlifted to our Army medical facility in Landstuhl, Germany, for further observation and recuperation.

"No American soldiers or any of the local Somali security forces that assisted in this rescue operation were injured or killed. Abdul Hafeez, a Somali American who has been identified in the media as a leader of the Al-Shabaab terrorist organization, was killed.

"In a remarkable act of courage, Marine military attaché Captain Brooke Grant and Marine Sergeant Walks Many Miles together identified and neutralized the terrorist Hafeez before he could detonate a suicide vest that he was wearing and a car bomb that—had it exploded—would have resulted in their deaths and the wounding of hundreds of innocent Somalis outside a popular mosque in Mogadishu.

"Hafeez has been positively identified as the Al-Shabaab terrorist who brutally murdered two Americans—Robert Gumman, a State Department regional security officer, and another diplomat, Skip LeRue, after mutilating Mr. LeRue. Our intelligence sources believe Hafeez was responsible for other murders, including the execution of a young Canadian man who was inspecting a prison in Pakistan for possible human rights violations. He also is believed to have planned the attack on our U.S. Embassy in Mogadishu.

"Our nation's ongoing diligence and determination in identifying, tracking, and ultimately eliminating Abdul Hafeez is a reminder to the world of our nation's relentless resolve to wage war against radical Islamic extremists who threaten us, our friends, and the security of the United States.

"I will now turn the microphone over to Payton Grainger, the director of the Central Intelligence Agency, who oversaw this operation, for a brief statement."

Allworth stepped to the side, allowing Grainger behind the podium as photographers snapped pictures.

"During our investigation and today's rescue, we became aware of a radical Islamic leader who was overseeing Abdul Hafeez and has been responsible for numerous bombings and murders via Al-Shabaab and other terrorist organizations," Grainger announced. "While we are confident we eventually will be able to identify this leader by name and nationality, at this point we are referring to him by the moniker the Falcon. I have been authorized by the president to offer a thirty-million-dollar reward to anyone who can assist us in bringing this known terrorist to justice."

As soon as Grainger stepped away from the microphones, the White House press corps began shouting questions, but neither Grainger nor the president responded. Instead, White House press secretary David Sheese announced, "We will be releasing details of today's military action later today."

His statement didn't deter reporters from rushing forward as the president and Grainger were leaving the podium.

"Reports on social media in Somalia are claiming a U.S. medical helicopter from the USS *Hornet* was seen dropping hundred-dollar bills over a square in Mogadishu," a reporter called out. "Was that part of the hostage rescue plan?"

Grainger looked at the president, who nodded approval, so he replied, "The investigative techniques used to identify and eliminate Abdul Hafeez must out of necessity be kept confidential, but I can assure you that no ransom was paid directly or indirectly to Al-Shabaab by our government. The U.S. government does not negotiate with terrorists."

"Then why was a helicopter seen dumping cash out over a mob?" a reporter called out.

"I'd be curious to know if those reports on social media were posted by Somalis high on khat," Grainger replied, laughing as he left the room with the president.

Mallory Harper was waiting in the Oval Office when the president and Grainger arrived.

"You both did a great job," Harper said.

Allworth thanked her and then turned pensive. She had sent Americans to Somalia for the wrong reason and, in doing so, had set off a chain of events that she now deeply regretted. Gunter Conner and twelve additional Americans were dead. Regardless of what Grainger had said, she had been forced to negotiate with terrorists and had agreed to pay them a ransom even though the money had ended up being taken by a mob. Plus, she'd approved the surreptitious delivery of six Apache helicopters to a general who had murdered a U.S. citizen.

Glancing first at Harper and then Grainger, the president said, "Is this nightmare really over?"

"Yes," Harper said. "Within a few weeks, the public's attention will be focused on something new—your inauguration. People will eventually forget the embassy attack."

Allworth looked to Grainger.

But the CIA director stayed uncharacteristically silent.

CHAPTER SEVENTY-FOUR

Representative Clyde Buckner appeared before reporters at the Saturday press conference only long enough to announce that he was withdrawing from the race for the Fifth Congressional District seat. He cited unspecified personal reasons, asked his supporters to vote for Rudy Adeogo, and ducked out a back door after refusing to answer questions.

The chairman of the Minnesota Democratic-Farmer-Labor Party immediately stepped forward with Rudy Adeogo and Dheeh beside him. He announced that the DFL was enthusiastically backing Adeogo now that the incumbent had withdrawn. Grasping the candidate's hand in his own, the chairman raised both up and declared, "We're going to work hard to ensure that Rudy will be elected our new congressman from Minnesota on Tuesday!"

When they unclasped their hands, Adeogo thanked the DFL chairman and then took a moment to congratulate President Sally Allworth for resolving the Mogadishu crisis and winning the safe release of Ambassador Thomas and John Duggard.

"As a Somali American I greatly admire President Allworth and her resolution of this horrific ordeal," he declared, "and I will be casting my vote for her on Tuesday. There is another candidate whom I will be voting for too." He paused before delivering his punch line: "A man who knows how to sweep!"

At that moment, Dheeh retrieved a wooden broom from a friend standing near her and raised it up for everyone to see. "It's time to send an honest man to Washington who can clean house and fight for all Minnesotans!" she declared, handing the broom to her husband.

Adeogo began swinging it briskly in front of him on the stage as if he were cleaning the floor where Representative Buckner had been standing only moments earlier.

The photographers loved it.

Washington, D.C.

Inside his Watergate penthouse, Decker Lake watched the DFL press conference over an Internet connection on his computer with much satisfaction. Adeogo had boycotted the Dover press conference that the Coldridge campaign had engineered, and as Lake had predicted, the national media had paid only scant attention to the arrival of the twelve dead from Somalia.

Lake had kept his promise to Adeogo after the Somali American had returned home that Friday. The Washington fixer had met privately that same day with Congressman Buckner and offered him a better deal than Governor Coldridge, setting the stage for his Saturday withdrawal.

Lake had not suggested the broom-sweeping gimmick that Adeogo had used during the press conference. But he'd seen it before. Unlike the reporters and photographers clamoring around Adeogo, Lake knew an Oklahoma candidate for governor had used that same stunt in the mid-1970s after the Watergate scandal, forming a "Broom Brigade" of supporters who were determined to "sweep out the Old Guard."

The fact that Lake recognized the trick was a reminder to him of just how many years he had been in the trenches.

Lake decided to call the White House. He wanted to congratulate the president on ending the Somali crisis and also brag about what he had done to help her campaign. But as he was reaching for the phone on his desk, he changed his mind. Instead, he took a tattered address book from a drawer and dialed a different phone number. Raising the phone to his ear, he waited until a man answered. Lake's voice caught in his throat.

Decker Lake was a man who'd talked to presidents and heads of state, but at this moment he was speechless. He'd handled dozens of tricky negotiations between warring sides that despised and distrusted each other, but Lake recognized that none of those hostile negotiations was going to be as difficult as this call.

"Is anyone there?" the man asked.

"Yes," Lake said, mustering his courage. "Deck Junior, it's your father calling. I know it's been years since we've spoken, but I thought it was time we talked about you and me—and my grandchildren. I'd like to come see you, if you'll allow it."

MONDAY

One day before the presidential election

CHAPTER SEVENTY-FIVE

Representative Thomas Stanton's office
Basement of Capitol Visitor Center
Washington, D.C.

On most days, the Chairman arrived at the House Permanent Select Committee on Intelligence offices shortly after five a.m. to prepare for his workday. He had never been a coffee drinker, so he depended upon a can of Diet Coke to give him a caffeine jolt while he read the morning papers. Unlike many of his colleagues, who got their news from websites or from summaries prepared daily by their staffs, Stanton enjoyed the feel of newsprint. He always began with the *New York Times*, followed by the *Washington Post*, and finally the *Wall Street Journal*, often finding himself amused at how differently each covered identical events.

On this Monday morning, all three newspapers led with stories about the presidential campaign and all three agreed that tomorrow's election between President Allworth and Governor Coldridge had become too close to call. The release of Ambassador Thomas and John Duggard had given the White House a last-minute surge in spot polls. The death of Abdul Hafeez and the bombing of the Barawa compound that had killed scores of Al-Shabaab fighters had helped solidify the president's image as a forceful commander in chief who could defeat radical Islamic terrorists.

On those same front pages, Stanton read that Captain Brooke Grant, chairman of the Joint Chiefs of Staff General Frank Grant, and Sergeant Walks Many Miles were scheduled to return to the U.S. late Monday night. Their military flight would land at Joint Base Andrews, located on the edge of Washington, D.C., where President Allworth would welcome them home personally. The papers also noted that the president would host a breakfast to honor them on Tuesday morning. It was unusual for the White House to schedule an event on Election Day. Even so, most of official Washington was expected to attend. Governor Coldridge had not been invited. One of his campaign advisors, identified by reporters as Mary Margaret Delaney, was quoted grumbling about how the White House was trying to unfairly influence Tuesday's election by fêting the two heroes.

Stanton had finished reading the newspapers and turned his attention to other matters when he looked up from his desk and realized it was ten minutes after nine o'clock. The committee's executive director, Nancy Szabo, was late, and that was uncharacteristic of the serious-minded thirtysomething lawyer and mother of twin five-year-olds who lived in the Maryland suburbs with her accountant husband.

A light dusting of snow had fallen overnight, and the first snow in Washington always caused traffic delays regardless of how little actually fell, so Stanton assumed Szabo had been delayed by the weather. But when she had not arrived by ten o'clock, he became concerned enough to call her cell phone.

Her voice recording picked up on the first ring, a sign that her phone was turned off. An hour later, Stanton telephoned Szabo's husband, who told him that she'd left their house early on "committee business," which was a warning in their marriage that he was not to probe any deeper, given the confidentiality of her work.

Stanton was about to telephone the Capitol Police when Szabo finally burst into the underground office suite at 11:45 a.m. and hurried directly to Stanton's office without removing her coat.

"I'm sorry I'm so late," she said, "but I have something important to share with you."

"I was worried. I tried calling your cell and it went right to voice mail. I even called your husband."

"That's sweet," she said affectionately. She greatly admired Stanton and appreciated his fatherly concern. "I must have forgotten to turn my phone back on after I left the NSA. I had to leave my phone in the car while I was there, you know."

"Why in the world were you at the NSA this morning?"

Everyone else who worked in the underground offices had gone to lunch, but Szabo closed the door to Stanton's office to ensure the two of them couldn't be overheard.

She placed her briefcase on the floor and, while removing her coat, explained: "When Director Grainger briefed you and the ranking minority member last week about the attack on our embassy in Mogadishu, you asked him to follow up by sending the committee two items."

"Yes," Stanton said. "I asked for a copy of the CIA station chief's assessment that assured the White House it was safe to open an embassy in Mogadishu, and an accounting of all agency communications regarding Mogadishu, including communications with other agencies. Has he done that?"

"No, the agency has not sent us any of those items. Director Grainger's liaison officer says it is still compiling the information, and then the agency will need to have its lawyers go over it—a process that could take several weeks. Clearly, they're stalling."

She opened her briefcase and removed a manila envelope. "After you met with Grainger, you asked me to make similar requests to other key agencies, including the NSA. You wanted to learn what role, if any, the other agencies played during the Saturday of the attack."

"That's correct. I have no interest in having another debacle like the one over the events at Benghazi years ago."

He glanced at the envelope in her hands.

"The NSA was the first to respond," Szabo continued. "It sent a flash drive over late Friday night. I knew this was important, so I came in Saturday morning to upload it into our system."

"I wasn't aware you were working here on Saturday."

"Saturday and Sunday," she said. "The NSA thumb drive had hundreds of pages of telephone calls, e-mails, and other communications it had exchanged with the CIA about Mogadishu. As I was working my way through the material, I discovered that Gunter Conner, the CIA station chief in Mogadishu, had asked the NSA shortly after he'd arrived in Somalia to begin intercepting telephone calls between suspected Al-Shabaab terrorists. He explained that he needed the intercepts because he was writing an assessment for the White House, but he clearly was after something more."

She opened the envelope and removed a single sheet of paper. "The NSA didn't bother translating the telephone intercepts. It figured it was the CIA's duty to actually decipher the messages since they dealt with Somalia and Al-Shabaab. The NSA did, however, carefully note the times of each overheard phone call, where the call was intercepted, and the individuals who were believed to be speaking. One of those messages caught my eye. It took me all of Sunday and a visit to the NSA this morning to hunt that message down."

She handed him the sheet. "I persuaded the NSA to translate it for me. I told them that you had personally asked them to transcribe it and it was a high priority."

"You used my name and the committee's authority without asking?"

"I'm sorry, sir, but please, just read the intercept."

Stanton did, not once but twice, before looking up at Szabo.

"Are you absolutely certain," he asked, "that this intercepted phone call was delivered by the NSA to the CIA before the attack?"

"Yes, it was sent to Charles Casterline, the chief of the OA at the CTC. I verified that. I also verified that it was delivered to Casterline four hours before the embassy was attacked. Sir, that message suggests that Casterline knew Al-Shabaab was planning to attack on October twenty-fourth—at least four hours before it happened."

Stanton didn't immediately respond. He was recalling his exchange with Grainger when the CIA director had come to brief him about Mogadishu. He was recalling how Grainger had insisted that the agency did not know beforehand about a pending attack.

Stanton returned the sheet to Szabo. "For now, I want this information kept between us. I want to wait for the CIA to send over its materials. I want to see if Director Grainger will include this NSA-intercepted phone call on his list or if he'll try to hide it from us."

"I hope Director Grainger has some plausible explanation," Szabo said. "I've always thought he was a good person."

"Good people who do bad things are not actually good people, are they?" the Chairman replied.

CHAPTER SEVENTY-SIX

Early afternoon
Soft Wind Meadows
Fairfax County, Virginia

An envelope marked URGENT and addressed to Miriam Okpara was hand-delivered to Daphne Oliver, the Soft Wind Meadows residential facility's director.

Oliver carried the envelope through the locked door into the "town square," where Okpara was watching Jennifer Conner play yet another round of Dance Dance Revolution.

"This is from a Washington, D.C., law firm," Oliver said, handing the private caregiver the envelope.

Okpara tucked it into a large pocket on the front of her red work apron without opening it.

"Don't you want to read what it is?" Oliver asked.

"I expect it will be my severance notice," Okpara whispered, "now that Mr. Conner is gone."

Okpara fought back tears as she glanced at Jennifer, who was fixated on the game console, seemingly unaware of the two women's conversation. "I've not told her yet about her father."

"It should be you who does tell her."

"The doctors say she doesn't know who he is anyway but I don't believe them."

"She's lucky she doesn't have much cognitive ability. Having a car explode while you're inside it and seeing your mother and brother die is tragic enough. And now her father. How much can one person take?"

"Oh, this young girl, she is much smarter than anyone knows," Okpara replied. "I've been watching her play this game every day for months. I'm telling you, I wouldn't be surprised if one day she just started speaking and told everyone that she was ready to leave here."

"The brain has been known to rewire itself."

"Then that's what is happening," Okpara declared. "This girl isn't going to spend her life living here. I can feel it in my bones."

"I'll probably be getting a letter from that law firm too, once Mr. Conner's estate is settled," Oliver replied. "I hope he left her enough money so she can continue living here with us and not end up being declared a ward of Virginia and moved somewhere..." Her voice trailed off. She'd noticed that Okpara had started to cry.

"How long have you been Jennifer's caregiver?" Oliver asked.

"From the moment Mr. Conner returned from Cairo after the attack there. I was at this child's bedside with her until doctors said she could move here for rehabilitation."

"It's hard not to become attached, isn't it? Oh well, life moves on. I know of some other families who could use a private caregiver. You stop in my office on your way out tonight and I'll give you their names. You're a good worker and a fine woman."

Oliver left them, and when the Dance Dance Revolution game ended, it was time for Jennifer to have lunch. But Okpara knew Jennifer would not want to stop playing. It was a daily battle between them. Okpara readied herself for a stamping-feet tantrum. The only way she could force Jennifer to leave the machine was to unplug it.

The beat of a new song blared from the arcade speakers as Okpara walked toward the plug.

Jennifer didn't begin dancing.

Okpara stopped. This had never happened before.

Jennifer moved in front of Okpara and removed the plug from the wall, silencing the game on her own.

"Did I just see you do that?" Okpara asked. "You know it's time for lunch, don't you? See, I knew you were getting better."

Jennifer walked toward her, stopping when they were face-to-face. She reached into Okpara's apron and removed the letter from the law firm, which she placed in Okpara's hand.

"Oh, honey," Okpara said softly, "I don't want to read that right now."

Jennifer thrust the letter at her as if it were a knife, until Okpara took it, reluctantly sliding her fingernail under its lip, breaking the seal. She removed the letter. As she expected, it contained a letter and a check.

"I am writing on behalf of my client," the letter began. "From this point forward, the cost of your daily services as a caretaker for Miss Jennifer Conner will be paid through my office. Note that you have received a five-percent raise. My firm also will be in touch to arrange the transfer of Miss Conner to a more secure and more modern therapeutic facility where she will begin a rigorous treatment regime aimed at helping her better adjust to her brain injury and receive the latest treatment for her post-traumatic stress so that she can live independently. Of course, you will be part of this process."

Okpara let out a whoop and shook both the letter and check in the air. She grabbed Jennifer and hugged her.

"This is an answer to my prayers!" she exclaimed. "How did you know it was good news, girl? I thought I was being fired."

Jennifer had never reciprocated a hug, but this time she reached around Okpara and pulled her close.

Running her fingers through the child's hair, which was still moist from Jennifer's exercising, Okpara said, "I love you, little girl, and your daddy loved you too!"

In a soft voice, Jennifer whispered, "I know."

CHAPTER SEVENTY-SEVEN

A U.S. military flight
Somewhere over the Atlantic Ocean

Captain Brooke Grant woke when the military aircraft hit an air pocket, causing it to drop momentarily. She had dosed off. She checked her watch. It was a few minutes after 0100 German time, Tuesday. She moved the hands to 1900 (EST), Monday, and chuckled. She'd just gone back in time six hours. Something about turning back her watch always amused her. If only she had the ability to turn back time permanently. How many events in her past would she revisit and change?

The flight would be landing at Joint Base Andrews in another three hours. She was weary of being on airplanes and was mentally exhausted as well. Along with Sergeant Miles and her uncle, she had flown on Sunday from the USS *Hornet* to Germany, where they'd teamed up with the four Marines and two State Department diplomats whom she'd rescued at the apartment building and sent to Landstuhl for medical care. Before everyone had boarded their current transatlantic flight to Washington, she'd checked her cell phone messages. She wasn't certain how they'd gotten her private number, but at least a dozen news organizations had called to request interviews. She'd skipped over their pleas but had stopped when she reached a recording of Jean-Paul Dufour's voice.

"You're a hero," he gushed. "Not just in the U.S.—worldwide. Apparently, stopping a suicide bomber in London wasn't grand enough for you. Even in France, the newspapers are publishing your photograph and talking about how you helped kill this terrorist Abdul Hafeez and now are chasing after this mysterious Falcon fellow.

"I need to hear from you, my love," he'd continued. "Since you've been in Somalia, I've moved forward with my promises. I've arranged a transfer to our embassy in Washington so we can begin our new life together. The diplomat I'm replacing is willing to sublet his apartment in Georgetown. We can jog along the canal and drink coffee at your beloved Starbucks. Yes, I'm divorcing my wife. Yes, it's true. The paperwork will be completed shortly and then I'm a free man. Please call me. You can't keep ignoring your future husband, now can you? We can be married and you can put away your Beretta and live the comfortable life of a French diplomat's wife in Georgetown."

She had not called him back before leaving Germany.

Sergeant Miles appeared in the airplane's aisle holding two cups of coffee.

"Just made these," he said, slipping into the vacant seat next to her.

"You scrambling eggs for me next, Sergeant?"

"Might be the last time you'll have coffee with a jarhead like me, now that you're a national hero."

"Once a jarhead, always a jarhead," she replied, taking the cup from him. "Besides, you're the one who actually spotted Hafeez and shot him. That makes us both heroes." She raised the coffee in salute to him, took a sip, and gagged.

"Too hot?"

"Too strong."

"Wakes you up."

"From now on, I'll make my own coffee." She put down her cup.

"You got your speech ready?" he asked.

"I'm not giving any speeches. I'll leave that to you."

"You got to say something when we meet the president at twenty-two hundred at Andrews and attend the White House reception tomorrow morning."

Brooke glanced around. "Seen any parachutes?"

He laughed. After everything that they'd been through, there was a natural ease between them.

"I know what I'm going to ask for when we meet the president," he said.

"Whoa, what makes you think we get to ask for something? We were just doing our jobs."

"I want a transfer," he said, ignoring her comment.

"I thought you liked being in the embassy guard force."

"I do, but I think I would like being a military attaché even more."
He'd been looking at her, but that ease between them now vanished as
he shifted his eyes to his coffee. She sensed his embarrassment.

"I certainly will recommend that you get a transfer and a promotion,"
she volunteered. "Why do you want to be an attaché?"

Still avoiding her eyes, he said, "I thought it would be a way for us to
keep working together. We make a good team."

That explained his embarrassment. "I would like that," she replied
softly, "but I may have to take some time off to deal with a personal
matter."

"The man who sent you flowers in Mogadishu?"

"He asked me to marry him but I have no intention of ever seeing
him again. He was a mistake. Being in Mogadishu reminded me of how
important it is to be with someone you can trust. Someone like you. But
this personal matter has nothing to do with that mistake."

"So what's it about then?" he asked, finally making eye contact.

"Gunter Conner's daughter. The Falcon has threatened her. My uncle
called the agency from the USS *Hornet* and got a law firm involved. It's
ironic. There was a time when I literally thought about killing Gunter
Conner because of things that he did in Mogadishu. But I promised him
that I would take care of his daughter and I plan to do that. I know what
it's like to lose my parents to terrorists, and she's lost hers too. We'll see
what happens, but if the two of us get along, I might end up becoming
the guardian of a teenage girl. Imagine that."

"You would be a good guardian."

"Anyone who is interested in being with me needs to know that Jennifer might be part of my life."

"Any man worth your time shouldn't have a problem with that."

"That's kind of you to say, but there's more to it. The Falcon has
threatened to kill her and my family before he kills me. He's threatened
to kill anyone I care about or who cares about me."

"Any man who is worth your time shouldn't have a problem with that
either," he said.

Neither spoke for a moment. They simply enjoyed sitting next to each other. Finally, Miles said, "Captain, there's something I've always wanted to ask you, and now seems like a good time. You remember when I was giving you a back massage at Korfa's apartment last week?"

"Are you referring to when you were putting a new dressing on my wound?" she said, smiling. "That was hardly a back massage."

"You asked me what everyone thought about you when they heard you were coming to Mogadishu."

"Yes, and you told me that the other Marines thought I was an Oreo, which I am not."

"You never told me what you thought the first time you saw me," he replied. "So what did you think when you saw me at the airport?"

"I thought you were too hot to be a Marine," she replied, repeating exactly what he'd said when she'd asked him that same question.

"C'mon, Captain, everyone's asleep but us. Your uncle is up in the front snoring like a bear. It's safe, you can tell me. No one else is going to hear."

"The first time I met you," she said. "Well, let's see. You were standing on the tarmac in Mogadishu waiting for me wearing nonregulation mirror sunglasses and snakeskin cowboy boots, and looking very handsome. Sorry, I don't remember a thing about you. You didn't make much of an impression."

"I can live with that," he said.

He'd finished his coffee so he reached over and took a sip of the coffee that he'd brought her. "No use letting this go to waste." He slid her nearly full plastic cup of coffee into his empty one so he could take it with him and stood to leave. "I'll go look for a parachute for you."

Brooke shut her eyes after he left, but she couldn't sleep. She was preoccupied. She wasn't concerned about writing a speech. Whatever she said would be brief. She didn't need publicity. Her thoughts were about the Falcon.

Suddenly, she felt a burst of pride. She was going home. When she'd been in high school, she'd been assigned to read a presidential speech and report to her class about its meanings and origins. Her uncle had suggested a speech by Abraham Lincoln or Thomas Jefferson, but she'd chosen President Ronald Reagan's 1989 farewell address where he'd described America as the "shining city upon a hill."

> ...in my mind, it was a tall, proud city built on rocks stronger than oceans, windswept, God-blessed, and teeming with people of all kinds living in harmony and peace, a city with free ports that hummed with commerce and creativity, and if there had to be city walls, the walls had doors and the doors were open to anyone with the will and the heart to get here.

When she'd researched it, she discovered that Reagan's imagery had come from a 1630 sermon by Puritan pioneer John Winthrop, who'd predicted when he arrived on the American shore that this new nation would become a "city upon a hill"—a beacon watched by the entire world. Further digging showed Winthrop had drawn his inspiration from the Sermon on the Mount, where Jesus told his listeners: "You are the light of the world. A city on a hill cannot be hidden...Let your light shine before men, that they may see your good deeds."

Her experiences in Mogadishu had shown her what it was like to live in darkness. She'd seen the suffering there, the squalor, the killing. Somalia. Russia. Iraq. Afghanistan. Pakistan. North Korea. China. There was too much darkness in the world. Too much unnecessary suffering. Too much pain caused by tyranny, cruelty, greed, and intolerance.

Her thoughts returned to the Falcon, a faceless voice still audible in her ear who preached hate against anyone who didn't believe as he believed, didn't obey what he decreed, didn't worship as he worshipped.

He was still out there. And he'd sworn he would murder everyone she loved before killing her. Someone needed to protect the city on the hill. Someone needed to protect the light. She was proud to be one of those someones. That would be a life worth living.

EPILOGUE

President Sally Allworth was reelected to a second term by a narrow margin on Election Day. On January 20, she was administered the oath of office during a private swearing-in ceremony in the Blue Room of the White House before a select group of her supporters, including her longtime friend Decker Lake, who was accompanied by his son, Decker Jr., and his grandchildren.

A public ceremony marking the occasion took place the next day at the U.S. Capitol Building.

Congress already had convened, as prescribed by the Constitution, which mandated it begin a new session at noon on January 3, but out of respect for the incoming president, Representative Thomas Stanton waited until the day after the president's public ceremony to announce that the House Permanent Select Committee on Intelligence would hold a public hearing to investigate the attack on the U.S. Embassy in Mogadishu.

The *New York Times*, *Washington Post*, and *Wall Street Journal* each quoted an unnamed Capitol Hill source who said that the Chairman was investigating whether the CIA had known an attack at the embassy was imminent but had failed to take steps necessary to avoid the taking of American hostages and the deaths of Gunter Conner and twelve other Americans. The source speculated that the director of the CIA, Payton Grainger, was a prime target of the probe, along with Charles Casterline, another CIA official.

ACKNOWLEDGMENTS

The authors wish to thank Joe DeSantis for his contributions to the development, writing, and editing of this book. His political experience and insights were invaluable.

We also are grateful to our agents, Kathy G. Lubbers (Newt's daughter) and David Vigliano, as well as Kate Hartson, our editor at Center Street, an imprint of Hachette Book Group, and our copy editor Rick Ball.

In addition, Newt Gingrich wishes to acknowledge: Steve Hanser, who for forty years taught him to think historically; General Chuck Boyd, who tutored him about national security (and more important, about life); Joan Dempsey, whose long career in intelligence has been dedicated to protecting America; Congressman Bob Livingston, who was in many ways the model for "the Chairman"; Barry Casselman and Annette Meeks, who introduced us to the vibrant and exciting Somali community in Minneapolis; daughters Kathy Lubbers and Jackie Cushman, and their husbands Paul Lubbers and Jimmy Cushman, who have encouraged all of his adventures; grandchildren Maggie and Robert Cushman, whose future safety keeps him focused on national security and politics; and above all, his wife Callista Gingrich, whose companionship and love make it all worthwhile.

Pete Earley wishes to thank: Dan and Karen Amato, David Bosley, William Donnell, Walter and Keran Harrington, Marie Heffelfinger, Michelle Holland, Don and Susan Infeld, Kelly McGraw, Dan Morton, Richard and Joan Miles, Bassey Nyambi, Nyambi Nyambi, Jessica Phung, Mike Sager, Lynn and LouAnn Smith, and Kendall and Carolyn Starkweather. He also is grateful for the love and support of his wife, Patti Michele Luzi, and his children Stephen, Kevin, Tony, Kathy, Kyle, Evan, and Traci, and granddaughter, Maribella.

THE STORY CONTINUES WITH
TREASON
On sale October 11, 2016

Captain Brooke Grant, Sergeant Walks Many Miles, and Representative Thomas "the Chairman" Stanton are marked for death when the Falcon brings his radical Islamic war on terror to American soil. After an attempted assassination on the president, and other horrific acts of terror, it becomes clear that there is a traitor inside the highest corridors of power. The Falcon must be stopped at all costs...

ABOUT THE AUTHORS

NEWT GINGRICH is a former Speaker of the House and 2012 presidential candidate. *Gettysburg, Pearl Harbor,* and *To Save America: Stopping Obama's Secular-Socialist Machine* are three of his 14 *New York Times* bestsellers. Learn more: GingrichProductions.com

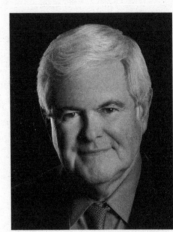

MICHAEL COLLOPY

LLOYD WOLF

PETE EARLEY is a former *Washington Post* reporter and author of 13 books, including four *New York Times* bestsellers. He was a finalist for the 2007 Pulitzer Prize and has written extensively about Congress, the White House, the FBI, and the CIA.